CW01497988

BRAGGLE

c. p. chambers

book design and illustrations
Philip Risdill

fp

foliot publications

I

For Willem and Betty
who make it all worthwhile

'The question is not what you look at, but what you see.'

Henry David Thoreau

BRAGGLE

fp

foliot **p**ublications

prologue

The town was like all other towns. Its population was fixed give or take a few percentage points. Ten thousand one hundred and fifty was its ideal weight, and so a little on the smaller side – some towns could boast more than twenty thousand. Its numbers would fluctuate slightly depending on deaths and retirements, but it wouldn't be long before they were replaced, an A_3 replacing an A_3 in the case of a death, and fresh young blood reinvigorating the town once a retiree had been removed.

It was flavoured with all that was necessary to keep it sweet; an organism that was able to trim itself when necessary and to accept its limited limitations. It preened itself relentlessly and felt comfortable in the warming rays of its reflection.

It may well have been a town in body but it also had the spirit of a thriving village, and gossip was on maximal drive. And the consensus was that Daniel Marks, this quiet, gentle man who had turned inexplicably violent, had also turned a little mad.

ONE

Daniel Marks lay in his bath staring at the clock. The water was tepid and the regulation twenty centimetres deep, enough to cover his thighs and leave the leg hairs floating gently back and forth on the surface of the water. He hadn't tubbed for a month and was irritated that the rules had changed - it no longer mattered whether you'd saved up your water ration – a bath was twenty centimetres deep and no more. At all times. What he wanted, what he really needed, was a bath he could plunge into, create waves, hold his head under the water until his lungs were fit to burst; something to envelop him like a blanket, warm, comforting and indulgent. What he got was a layer so thin it felt like he'd been lying in a puddle. Admittedly, the water had been piping hot a half hour before, and as he'd lifted himself gently in, he'd gasped at the force of the heat, but it had now cooled inexorably and if it wasn't for the clock he'd have got out long before. It was one of those really old ones – Pre-Change with no numbers around the edge, just a thick hour hand and a sliver of a second hand which clicked and clicked as it moved round and round. It might have been 8.35 or 8.45. But it didn't matter. Time was determined by the sun and the stars and an inner ticking that kept one grounded and connected, albeit a minute out of kilter here or there.

An hour earlier Dan had taken the clock out of its tin, which was hidden at the back of the cupboard in the bedroom where most of the non-negotiable stuff lay. Just this once, he wanted to stare time directly in the face. He'd tried it earlier in the day, watching the sun collapse behind the wood, but it was so smooth and uneventful that he wanted to snatch it from its orbit and squeeze it into nothingness. So he took the clock from the tin, and looking over his shoulder (which was always the case when he did something illicit), turned the key at the back until it was tight. The second hand jerked into motion. He guessed it must be 7.40 or thereabouts and adjusted the hour hand accordingly.

And here he now was, lying in his not very warm bath, his fingers as shrivelled as walnuts, transfixed. The clicks had become hammer blows, tangible and excruciating. Like prodding an infected tooth. And it was exactly what he'd wanted; something solid to push him towards the morning and the tribunal that would determine his fate.

He knew the elders could make a considerable fuss, but he hadn't meant to kill Price. There was nothing pre-meditated and it was nowhere near as bad as what Maia had done, and all she received was a slight reduction in her A_3 status. It meant fewer books and the indignity of degradation, which admittedly to some was worse than the deed itself, but life continued without much of a backward glance.

He'd seen Maia earlier that day at the distribution. She had her ration of carrots poking out of her bag and was leaving just as he entered. They met at the main gate, stood silently and awkwardly side by side, just for a few seconds, before she nodded briefly and walked briskly away. It had taken all his courage to step out of the house in the first place and so being publicly ignored, by her of all people, was a humiliation *and* a kick in the face. He leant against the gate to compose himself and thought about going straight back home. Tuesday, however, was carrot day. It wasn't universally appreciated, as with many distribution edicts, but Dan loved carrots and looked forward to Tuesdays. He could mix them with parsley, mash them with cream, and in the summer, bake them with lemon and honey. It was incentive enough for him to absorb the slight and go into the heart of the distribution to collect his rations. And it was only as he placed each carrot delicately into his tote bag that he realised that if carrots did not exist, then perhaps, just perhaps, Price might still be alive. It made him hesitate. He looked into the bag, thought briefly about placing them back on the trestle table, then shrugged and walked directly home where he diced them with a little more force than normal as though to exorcise the demons of a week before.

He cooked them plain with a few mashed potatoes and onions, placed the mix gently on to his plate and sprinkled it with butter and some chives he'd picked from the herb patch. He took it to the table with a glass of his homemade elderflower cordial and stared down at a concoction that now looked more like a plate of razor blades than a dish he'd eaten with relish a thousand times. He picked at it with his fork, made a trench through the middle with a few dimples and waves, and then placed it on the floor for the dog before walking into the garden where he pulled haphazardly at some bindweed.

It was a few hours later that Dan finally pressed the button in the tub and felt the water being sucked away from under him. A few minutes before, the clock had suddenly stopped, forcing him back into himself. He rose gently and gave a slight groan as though he was twice his actual age, but it felt good to deliver a sound, any sound. He dried himself carefully, taking his time, enjoying the abrasive glide of the towel on his skin, and combed his wad of dark hair. He didn't look at all bad considering the stress of the past week, and he rather liked the few silver hairs that had appeared around the temples, giving them a little flick with his hand as though attempting to strike them into life.

He weighed himself. Seventy-one point four. Not bad. A little weight loss was a bit of a bonus. His penis though was so irreconcilably flaccid that it reminded him of the catkins that lay in their thousands in the wood behind the house. Admittedly his penis had a more robust colouring but it served little purpose, it hadn't felt the touch of another's hand since the time a C_2 was doing some repairs to the house the year before and even then it was Price's initiative. It was an experience he'd never forget and not just because it flagrantly ignored the edict that they should stick to A_s and B_s.

He gave the tip a rub with his forefinger. Nothing. And as he closed his eyes and thought of the C_2, an image of Price lying in the communal pit wrapped in a simple cotton sheet pushed itself to the surface. It was better than the one with all that blood, the one that he could never forget, ever, even in sleep, but nonetheless, it was enough to smother any hope of a quick release.

He turned the key in the clock once more, sat on the edge of the tub with his head bowed and listened to the click, click, click. It reached 9.20 or thereabouts before he slowly stood, put on his bath robe and went downstairs. Braggle lay asleep on the sofa and he pushed his head gently into her fur. She gave out a puff of recognition and slid back into oblivion.

Dan made a lavender tea and sat next to her with his palm flat against her side, feeling the gentle rhythm of her breathing. He felt his eyelids dropping and the first signs of a rest which had alluded him for so long. His head began to tilt.

A gentle knock on the front door jolted him upright. Braggle jumped off the sofa as though she'd just heard a starting gun and swept through the house to the hallway, barking uncontrollably.

'I'm so sorry,' Maia said as Dan opened it, 'I know it's late but I felt I had to see you,' and turned ninety degrees to thwart Braggle's welcoming spring.

A subdued 'hello Maia' was all Dan could say and he pulled his belt tighter around his bathrobe.

A few minutes later the two of them were sitting on the sofa with a small glass of home-made plum brandy in their hands.

'Is it from this year?'

'No, it's from last year. Price made it. He was better at that sort of thing, as you know.'

They both took a second tentative sip and discussed the merits of different fruits for making alcohol. Even though it was on the Red List, everyone made their own and exchanged bottles. The elders accepted it, not least because the majority were firm believers in the uplifting power of forty-degree proof.

'It's very good.'

4

'Yes, it is.'

Another sip.

Maia sat upright with perfect posture. She'd never been taught deportment, but had read plenty about how to keep the body in shape and the lower back muscles supple. It gave her the appearance of an overwrought piano teacher, not helped by her unusual height which meant most of the time, as in this case, she looked down on the person she was talking to. Everything about her was pure A_3, or rather A_4 since her reduction in status, although some in the village came to question it after the death of her partner – and for a few months, to avoid the sharper end of the town's rumour mill, Maia was rarely seen around town. She had no choice but to go to the Saturday meat market to collect her rations and barter, and she'd occasionally show her face at a daily distribution, but she mostly stayed within the confines of her home on the edge of the town, using up her provisions until she was forced to resort to normal activity. By then the speculation had calmed and she felt she could ride her bike or her horse without feeling she was on parade. But a town of ten thousand individuals has a deep capacity for remembrance and so Maia remained oblique and cautious. Dan had been feeling something similar this past week although it hadn't stopped him stepping completely away from the visual embrace of the town; acting any differently would only exacerbate rumours of his excessive violence.

'You know why I'm here of course,' Maia finally said. 'We haven't had a chance to chat since…..' She paused, not knowing how to put it into words. Even thinking about it brought a lump to her throat. She settled on … 'the incident'. 'I know it's the tribunal tomorrow,' she continued, 'and seeing you at the distribution, well, it felt like a sign, that I should come to see you.'

She looked directly into Dan's eyes giving him little chance of escape. But it was a statement more of encouragement than altercation. At least, that's how Dan saw it. The past week he'd said nothing about what had happened, those were the rules – he had to wait until after the tribunal – and had felt the accumulating silence weighing him down a little more each day.

'You know I have to wait until tomorrow's over.'

His reply lacked both vitality and conviction and was said staring down at his dog who lay quietly on the kilim. Maia then pushed off her shoes with each heel and brought her legs cross-legged onto the sofa, moving her body sideways with her back resting against the arm rest.

'This is just like old times,' she said.

Dan didn't respond. He didn't want to say that it wasn't like old times at all. It was far from the old times. And anyway, she'd sit like that next to Price, not him. Dan was always in the chair opposite feeling like an intruder, knowing their light and easy chatter would flow with even more zeal if he wasn't there. Sometimes he would get up from his chair and leave the room and neither of them would notice. He would sit in his study waiting for the sound of voices in the hallway and the front door to open and close. Maia never once poked her head around his door to say goodbye. He knew their friendship wasn't sexual, Price's birth genome was pure A_3 homotype, the same as him, and the idea of stroking a breast that wasn't covered, at least in part, by some hair, was improbable if not unimaginable, but when the door closed he felt a little lighter, a little looser, freed from something he wasn't quite sure of.

Maia tried another tack. 'How are you feeling?' she said, still staring directly at him. The question sounded genuine, and if journalists existed, she would have made a good one.

'I've been better.' He took another sip of his drink. 'I'm sure everyone's talking about it and that there's all sorts of nonsense swirling around.'

'Oh, I don't take any notice of that,' Maia swiftly replied. 'I don't care what people say or think, the truth is ours and ours alone.'

She shuffled slightly, flicking away an imaginary fly from the side of her nose. 'But Dan,' she said softly, 'what you tell the elders tomorrow doesn't have to be the exact truth. You might be better just saying as little as possible.'

'But I have nothing to hide.'

'We all have something to hide.'

'I don't.'

'Really?'

'Yes, really.'

'So you're going to tell them about the C_2?'

Dan's eyes tightened. So Price *did* tell her everything. He thought about the clock ticking loudly upstairs and felt sure she knew about that too. But so many red lists and non-negotiables create a communal atmosphere of indifference (with the occasional looking behind one's back), and Dan lifted his shoulders gently and smirked, partly at the thought of the C_2 and more so at Maia's resolve.

'So you're saying that I should be economical with the truth.'

'I'm saying you should be very clear how you're going to present the truth to them all tomorrow.'

'But why?'

'Tell me first what happened.'

Dan slowly stood, knelt down next to Braggle and gave her a gentle kiss on her head. The dog stirred briefly, stretching her legs and letting out a contented puff of air before flopping her head back onto the kilim and closing her eyes. Dan kissed her again and sat in the swivel chair next to her. He preferred it there, a little distance from Maia, just like old times.

And all he told her was what he felt he could. Price was being as cantankerous as ever, probably drunk. It was a Tuesday. Carrot day. Price sat at the dinner table, looked derisively at the carrots (with honey and lemon) and just threw the plate at the wall. It was too much for Dan. After months of unbearable tension, he went to the kitchen, took the heavy antique copper pan that had cooked the carrots and which had come with the house (and was considered a luxury, even for A_{3s}), walked back to the dining table and before Price had a chance to react, whacked it against the side of his head. He said nothing to Maia about the blow being so hard that the left side of his skull seemed to disintegrate on impact and his ear disappeared into a mass of hair and gunge.

'And that's it really.'

7

Maia made no effort to wipe away the tears that were falling on to the back of her hands. She did not immediately respond and allowed the silence to deepen. She pictured Price's final, violent goodbye and felt sick, as though her own skull had been brutally torn apart, but at least it must have been quick and so broadside that he only had time for a half breath before the pan smashed into his skull. She could feel her chest pounding and she clasped her hands together so Dan couldn't see them shaking. And not for all the world could she say anything to take the edge off her revulsion.

'But why carrots,' she asked? 'You know he hates carrots.'

'I just wanted him to try them. Just once.'

'But he loathes carrots,' she repeated.

'Yes I know. Of course I know that. I just wanted him to try them. Just once. It was a failure. Obviously. So can we just leave it at that?'

Maia looked at him quizzically as a child looks at a puzzle missing a couple of pieces.

'So is that all you're going to tell them tomorrow?' she asked.

'That's about it,' came the reply.

'I know he hadn't been at his best for a few months, but do you know why he was so out of sorts?'

'You know what he was like Maia. He wasn't easy from the beginning. It just got worse and worse.'

'Do you know why?'

'Why are you asking me all this Maia? Do *you* know why?'

'No,' she said bluntly, 'I do not. You're the one who lived with him.'

'And you're the one he confided in,' Dan replied.

Now it was Dan's turn to stare. He looked directly at Maia willing her to reveal something new, unwrap something about Price that made sense, that could unravel why he'd become impossible to live with in those last few months. He knew she knew something. She'd told him the week before, when he saw her in the market square, that she'd taken a bit of distance from him. There must have been a reason.

'You told me last week that you'd not seen him for a while.'

'Yes, I did. I know I did. And I wish I could change things, but I can't. I wish I could turn around the whole year, but I can't.'

There was more silence and sipping of plum brandy. Dan bent down and touched Braggle's head with his hand. It was getting late and he wanted Maia to go, but politeness, which had been drummed into him since childhood, stopped him from telling her to go. Instead he said: 'I still don't know why I shouldn't just be straight with them tomorrow? Price's behaviour was hardly a secret after all.'

Maia nodded. 'I understand that you need to give them the background Dan, and as you say, they all knew him anyway and are fully aware of his reputation, but it's more the details. I'm saying you don't need to go into any detail.'

Dan really did want her to go. He said he probably wouldn't give the full details, he'd probably keep it to the bare facts - that his living arrangements had become impossible. It wasn't an unusual occurrence after all; and surely some fault lay at the hands of those who put them together in the first place - compatibility between ninety and ninety-five per cent they said. A sexual attraction yes, they'd got that right, and they both enjoyed the classics, that was true, and they were both good musicians (they were A_{3s} after all), but he was far more serious and edgy, whilst Price was, well, unpredictable.

And as Dan sat back in the swivel chair, turning it slightly from side to side, he felt himself moving effortlessly into himself and his past. He spoke as though talking to no-one except the ghosts of the house, and Maia, lying on the sofa with her bare feet nestled tight together, listened without saying a word.

~

The day he met Price was one of those rare and scattered moments in life that etch themselves onto the brain as though meticulously scraped onto it with a knife. He had arrived first and was busy for at least an hour looking around the house, thinking how much smaller it looked than the virtual display he'd been given a month earlier. The bed, however, was spacious, and the mattress admirable; the bathroom tiles a pleasing apple green; the tub and shower white and ceramic; the two studies (A_{3s} always had one each) equal in size and filled with all the right books. The kilims were perhaps a little threadbare, but they added to the antique grandeur of the living room together with the leather swivel chair which, Dan had been told, was a famous design from way back. The kitchen was equipped with all that was necessary, including, to his surprise, a row of copper pans laid out on a shelf about the oven. He took the largest one down, almost dropping it from the sheer weight of the thing, and put it carefully back using both hands.

He was most pleased with the garden. The edible section was enough to bring delight to even the most demanding of barterers. The strawberries and redcurrants clamoured for attention; the vegetable leaves vied for space with glistening courgette flowers and every kind of herb, from lovage and marjoram to four different sorts of mint. The rest of the garden was a blaze of blues and purples attracting enough bees and butterflies to make any collector giddy with excitement (although wildlife collecting sat at the highest table of non-negotiables). Dan saw buff-tails and carders and marbled whites and admirals. Every virtual insect garden he'd experienced (and it was many) fell limply short of the real thing, and he shuddered at how amateurish his own efforts had been on his plot at the Academy. It was clear the couple who lived here before and who'd both reached seventy-five, had gone beyond the bounds of duty, and Dan thought how sad they must have been to leave.

Price arrived at his new home at 1.25pm or thereabouts, an hour later than arranged. Dan heard his arrival from the first floor where he was looking out over the garden from the small balcony. He heard Price call out his name from the kitchen and he liked the sound, a bass timbre, a good start. He took a deep breath, shoved his fingers through the hair above his ears and walked down the stairs. He called out 'here I am', and for the first time became conscious of the sound of his own voice; a higher, more penetrating pitch which he found conspicuous and inappropriate.

Price came towards him with the broadest of smiles

wearing a heavily creased shirt and coarse linen trousers the colour and texture of a potato sack. He took off his tatty, light blue denim cap and thrust his not inconsiderable frame towards his new life partner. He looked like his virtual image, but his bulk was a surprise. Price was large, much larger than Dan had expected and so when the embrace arrived, it felt more like a frontal attack than a welcome. But it was meant with a warmth and an energy that was almost impossible to dislike. Dan felt the tight grip of Price's arms as he lifted him up from the bottom stair and brought him to the same level, and enjoyed the way he pushed their groins together in a manner he had never experienced before. It wasn't the gentle encounter Dan had been rehearsing or contemplating, and it had the disorienting effect of diminishing his ability to think or talk with any semblance of educated casualness, forming the pattern for years to come as he became almost subsumed under the power of his partner's personality. But at that moment, as their bodies touched, Dan felt the inexplicable beauty of togetherness.

The first weeks slid past effortlessly, with Dan reacting to, rather than instigating, conversation. Their interests were keenly shared and felt, and even though they went to different Academies, they recognised, with the slightest whiff of disappointment, that their upbringings were almost identical. They recounted stories of avuncular and sturdy institutions which was all they both had known, helping to cement their beliefs and confirm the inevitability of their alliance. The bedroom was enjoyed both night and day with an intensity that befits the new and with a refreshing lack of roll play or timidity. They shared the same culinary palate (carrots apart), both experimented with flavours and ingredients, both liked to barter for the more unusual spectrum of vegetables, both loved working in the garden all year round, and even though the words were never said, from that first day, their love was plain and unambiguous. Until, somehow, over the steady course of a period unbeknown to either but felt achingly and equally by both, the relationship became sharp and brittle. Perhaps it was five years, perhaps ten, and perhaps there were times

11

of pleasure threaded through the decline, but after twenty years the climate in the house was so febrile that the smallest details exploded into the widest of provocations.

~

'I've never talked about that to anyone.'

Dan said it as though to himself. He was kneeling next to Braggle with one hand on her tummy and had no recollection of getting off the chair or of once looking up at Maia. Even as he sat back down and pushed himself gently around, he kept his eyes to the floor with his sight on his memories and not on what was directly before him.

Maia, although not the best of listeners, had remained implacably quiet and still. She allowed Dan a little more time before making a little cough to break the silence.

'Are you ok?' she asked.

Dan looked up. It took him a while to re-adjust, lifting his head slowly and looking around the room before quietly replying. 'I'm fine Maia. I'm fine.'

Maia was now sitting upright on the sofa, her hands in her lap. She waited a few more seconds.

'Just to go back to what we were talking about before Dan, about the tribunal, about what you're going to say, it really is best if you keep it simple. I can almost guarantee they'll be lenient.'

'How could you possibly know that Maia?' Dan replied wearily.

She clasped her hands even tighter.

'It's just a hunch.'

'Because you were let off so lightly?'

'Perhaps,' Maia calmly replied. 'What I do know is that the elders hate scandal and will do anything to avoid further investigation. This is a town devoid of imagination Dan. It lacks the collective will to deal with anything but the mundane. Don't give them the ammunition to begin something they'd rather just forget.'

'You've never told me directly what happened with Theo,'

Dan said, 'I heard a bit from Price, but not much, he kept it to himself, like a lot of things.' He finished off his plum brandy and without the inflection of genuine interest, it was very late after all, asked her to fill in the gaps.

Maia told it quickly, as though she was used to giving a synopsis of her motives, and it diverged from the official course of events. She didn't tell the tribunal, for example, that there had been enough dried henbane hidden in Theo's spring roll to kill them all. The tribunal didn't need to know *that.*

'Maths was never my strong point,' she said.

They also didn't need to know the minutiae of their tempestuous relationship: just enough to understand that her situation had become intolerable and the henbane a disastrous miscalculation; she hadn't meant to kill him - it was more of a warning, and she gave hints to the tribunal that she got there first and that if she hadn't, perhaps she wouldn't be here to tell the tale.

Dan gave out a slight puff of air. It didn't sound like the Theo he knew. A tempestuous relationship?

'Did Price know about all this?'

'Yes.'

'So you're saying that if you'd told them all of that then they might not have been so lenient?'

Maia's head clicked towards her left shoulder. 'Dan, all I'm saying is that I was economical in my dealings with the elders. I just said what was needed, knowing that they wouldn't do much anyway. And that's what's going to happen tomorrow. They won't do much, I can almost guarantee it. And so why bother to go into details when the outcome will be the same.'

'You sound very sure of yourself Maia.'

'Perhaps. But Dan, I just want to help you. I really do. Don't you want to be let off lightly? There are other scenarios of course.'

Dan stood up. It wasn't a rushed movement; he didn't want to show his irritation or emotion. Maia stood too, rising to her full, impressive height, and walked across to him, putting her arms tight around his shoulders. It felt to

Dan like a stranglehold and lasted what felt like an age as he put his arms loosely around her lower waist and waited awkwardly for her affection to conclude, making sure his bathrobe remained in place.

'I loved Price,' Maia said before hastily putting on her shoes and walking out of the room and out of the house, closing the front door gently and not looking back as Dan watched her disappear into the darkness.

For a while, he stood silently in the hallway, Braggle at his side nudging his shins with her nose. He felt numb. He thought he knew exactly what he'd say at the tribunal and now Maia had come and blown it all into the water. And why? Why would she want them to be lenient anyway? He walked back into the living room, picked up a frame that was lying face down on the sideboard and brought the photo so close to his face that wisps of his breath condensed onto the glass. Price smiled back at him wearing the denim cap he'd worn on the day they met.

Dan began to cry so unashamedly that Braggle brushed her head against his leg and whined gently in tandem with her master.

TWO

T he church – which was no longer officially called the church, but everyone still did – was where the G9 always met, once a week, to discuss all that was necessary, and no more. It was the highest-ranking forum in the town, but its members deemed that all was well and therefore interference in the flow of life should be kept to a minimum. The Townhouse, to give it its correct name, still looked like a church: the brickwork was weather beaten to perfection, the wooden ceiling was a striking aqua green, it was still possible to see a few burnished inscriptions of the dead on the cold stone floor and the wooden pews were still as uncomfortable as ever, but the G9, which consisted of nine hand-chosen elders, sat in cushioned seats in the chancel where, every Saturday, just before the meat distribution, they would gather and be seen.

The Saturday gathering was a congested affair, considered almost compulsory for those with an ear for gossip. The pulpit, decorated with a wooden latticework that weaved its delicate leaves and flowers around the speaker's head, was available to anyone who wanted to vent their concerns or share their thoughts. In practice, it was seldom used. Townsfolk of every grade mingled and chatted, making little use of the pews. They brought their animals, mostly dogs, a few cats too, and one cockatoo that perched, as though glued, to the shoulder of its owner. The church-cum-townhouse showed no sign of its religious past, but every Saturday, for as long as anyone could remember, it gave off a deep and continuous reverberation with echoes of its previous existence.

But today it was deadly still. And as Dan walked across the stone floor, he realised with increasing unease that he should not have worn his best shoes with those hard, uncompromising soles, each step a sharp clap signalling his arrival. He'd never been in The Townhouse when it had been so quiet, and certainly never on his own, and he'd never, even for a moment, contemplated saying anything from the pulpit. A couple of times in the past year he'd had to refrain Price from doing so and each time felt relief that his partner had not drawn attention to himself. This morning, before entering, he'd looked up at the clock tower which was always stuck at midday, or midnight, and wished it was the latter so he could hide in the darkness and avoid eye contact with everyone except the stars above. Instead, he just felt sick. And he'd slept badly. Braggle lay on the bed all night, outstretched and tight along the length of Dan's legs, leaving the blanket taught and hot, her gentle snoring the only thing that gave him comfort.

After peeling himself from the bed, Dan wound up the clock once more and took it downstairs so he could listen to its beat as he ate fresh berries from the garden, occasionally tapping his spoon on the table to the rhythm of the ticking as though counting the seconds to his departure. He methodically washed and dried his breakfast things and then walked into the garden, meandering through the plants, pushing away with his foot some of the heaps of earth formed by the moles, and watched the bees and the butterflies flit effortlessly from one flower to another. But this morning the collective buzz of the insects seemed loud and accusatory and the bird song a chorus of jarring notes. Two swallows that had nested in the eaves of the house for the past few years seemed to fly lower than normal, swooping above Dan's head and forcing him to hunch his shoulders.

Inside, he washed his hair in the shower using his homemade lavender shampoo and waited for the cold water to kick in. Normally, he'd be finished within the regulatory three minutes, pushing the button just before it went instantly cold, but this morning he braced himself for the sudden change and when it came, he clenched his shoulders, puffing and panting under its icy embrace. He'd never liked the sharp cold against his skin and had always resisted Price's attempts to convince him of its invigorating power, but as he dried himself, a tingling enveloped his body and he thought he should perhaps do it more often.

In the closet, he laid out a few shirts and trousers, opting for a smarter than normal look and his best shoes that he'd bartered five years ago for an old, rusting bicycle he never used.

The G9 had asked Dan to arrive at around 11. There was still one hour to kill, so after giving Braggle the shortest of walks and leaving her clawing at the door, he walked to The Townhouse via the long route. He went along the path through the fields in their summer coats and took a deep, cleansing breath, thrusting his chest out and briefly closing his eyes. He picked an ageing valerian flower head, putting it to his nose, smelling a hint of morning vanilla. Some larks flew into the air. The clouds were thick, but the rain that had been so incessant in the previous weeks had stopped. The path he took threaded along the edge of the town. He passed fields of potatoes in bloom and a furry mass of barley which he brushed with his palm. He walked slowly, avoiding the puddles so as not to soil his shoes and picked the leaf of a great mullein so he could polish them at the end of the walk. The spire of The Townhouse poked above the skyline and he stared at it so intently that it seemed to grow and fill the space around it.

The Townhouse door was solid oak and when Dan pulled it open, it gave a low groan as though a living thing. He had just polished his shoes with the soft mullein leaf and re-arranged his clothes, making sure they sat well on his frame. Another deep breath. He was ready. Clap, clap, clap across the stone floor. He turned a corner and saw three members of the G9 sitting in the chancel. Just three? They stood up as he approached, not smiling, not frowning. Almost indifferent. In the middle was Otto Cladders. He wore an ox-eye daisy in his lapel sandwiched by two strands of wheat, the symbol of The Reformation. As Dan got closer, Otto walked down the three steps and thrust out his hand in greeting. Dan was ushered to his seat.

'Just the three of you,' he muttered.

'Yes, just the three of us,' Otto replied. You know Gilda and Petra of course.

Dan nodded. Everyone knew everyone, at least by sight, although the nine elders were a little more restrained in their socialising than most, restricting their contact mostly to the Saturday gatherings. It was a rarity to see them bartering at the markets or participating in the non-negotiable collectives.

'The others can't make it today I'm afraid, but we'll keep them fully informed of the proceedings in the normal way.' Otto's voice penetrated the surroundings, and he spoke without looking directly at Dan as though there was something of more interest and consequence on the wall behind. He sat down, brushed his trousers with his hands, and began.

'Now then. Daniel, 'Every Death is a Tragedy'. You know those words well of course.'

It was so unexpected that Dan could only say, after a few seconds, that of course, everyone knew it. It goes without saying. We all grew up with it ringing in our heads.

'So you had it every morning too, at the Academy assembly?' Otto continued.

'Yes, of course. Every morning.'

The image of his Academy Principle thrust itself into Dan's mind. He also wore the symbol of The Reformation. He also had a booming, authoritative voice. Each morning, two thousand boys stood in the great hall. They'd all showered and slept well. Now they had to listen, religiously, to the Five Great Dictums, or, as some of the A homotypes would call it, the Five Big Dicks. But Dan wasn't one of them. He took the Dictums seriously and would berate his friends when he heard the FGDs being mocked. Yes, he was a stick-in-the-mud but he didn't care, nor that they taunted him for his prudishness.

As far as Dan was concerned 'Every Death is a Tragedy'

referred to the natural world. The Academy principal made that perfectly clear every morning, with stories of the extinction of animals and plants that had once been common place. He would sometimes place on the table in front of him a dead bird or rodent he had found the previous day and ask for a minute's silence to contemplate the death of beauty. One of the biggest scandals of Dan's time at the Academy was the systematic murder of at least a hundred song birds over the course of a week. Each one had been shot with a homemade pellet shooter and then decapitated. Robins, sparrows, warblers, tits, bramblings, finches. None was immune to the massacre. For that week, it was as though the foundation of life itself had been torn apart. The assembly silences were prolonged and the natural world embraced like never before. Then one boy admitted to the killings and implicated two others. From one day to the next the three disappeared never to be spoken of again.

The death of a hundred birds contrasted heavily with that of a boy or a member of staff. Fatal diseases were not uncommon. The person would be quarantined and then buried in the communal pit if unable to overcome the symptoms. There was a short, no-nonsense burial service. Everyone was treated equally. The names of the dead were engraved on a large piece of granite on the edge of the pit which anyone could visit if they wanted. Few did.

'But doesn't it refer mainly to the animal kingdom?' Dan said. 'Isn't that what it's meant to mean?' Dan's voice became quieter, as though he now wasn't quite sure himself of the bearing of a dictum that had accompanied him for most of his life, and to which he held dear.

The two women remained silent. Otto Cladders continued to look over Dan's shoulder. 'Are we not part of the animal kingdom?' he replied, and then allowed the silence to continue.

Dan could feel his head warming and wanted to touch the top of his forehead to smooth away the moisture. He kept his hands clenched tight in his lap.

'You were both A_{3s} weren't you?' Otto continued.

'Yes.'

'It's quite unusual for such excessive violence between A_s, isn't it?'

'Yes, as far as I know, that is the case.'

'So tell me Dan, in your own good time, what happened?'

Dan waited a while to answer, collecting his thoughts, not certain of what he would say. He disliked the way Otto wouldn't look directly at him and the way the two women just sat there, mouths closed. He knew Otto's ways. He knew the most important person in the town would rarely look directly at anyone, and that people made fun of it in order to make sense of it. Price had especially mocked Otto, and with a vehemence that Dan often found distasteful, but now, sitting in front of him, he realised there was some depth to his dead partner's contempt. Until now, Dan had always seen him at a distance at the Saturday gatherings, sitting erect on his chair on the podium speaking occasionally to those either side and observing the mass in the nave below. His lapel always bore the symbol of the Reformation when the flowers themselves would permit, and when not, the official Reformation badge with the same motif. Otto was the only person Dan knew who always wore it, everyone else sticking to the protocol of the Solstice and Harvest celebrations when it was considered bad taste not to show one's appreciation of the Reformation's greatness, although just a few weeks before, at the last Solstice festivities, Price had worn a cardboard ox-eye daisy that he'd fixed to his head with some twine twisted around his ears and a board hung around his neck on which he'd written 'Time for Pruning'. Dan found it distasteful and provocative and told him so, but Price had shrugged it off with an irritation that had become commonplace between the two.

Dan said nothing about that to the G9 minus six. He didn't need to. Price's behaviour had been so disruptive that even the most hard-nosed of stay-at-homes had heard of his shenanigans by dusk. Instead, looking directly at Otto and occasionally at Gilda and Petra, and with Maia's words the night before in his head, he stayed focused and opaque.

'You all know Price,' he began. 'You all know how difficult he was. The demons he had. I put up with it for twenty

20

years. It had been building up. Our relationship was on tenterhooks. Something in me just snapped. I'd had enough. You know I'm not violent, I haven't hurt anyone in my life, but I just got hold of the first thing I could grab, and hit him with it. I didn't mean to really hurt him. But it was unfortunate it was the copper pan. It's heavy.'

He said more, but it was all half-truths and the barest of facts. He didn't care what the G9 minus six thought or what would happen to him anymore. He just wanted it to end. And quickly. It was none of their business, especially Otto's. Sweat was sliding down the side of his face and landing on his shoulder, turning his yellow shirt a darker hue. He touched it with the tips of his fingers and wiped it onto his trousers creating streaks along the length of his right thigh.

Gilda and Petra remained quiet, nodding their heads in tandem, whilst Otto remained inscrutable, staring up at the vaulted ceiling of The Townhouse as though he was assessing imaginary repairs.

'I have nothing more to say,' Dan said with a clarity his testimony had resisted.

Otto brought his head slowly down and smiled. He thanked Dan for his honesty, and for the first time Petra spoke. It must have been hard, she said. Dan nodded and looked down at his streaked trousers. He looked up once more and Otto was staring directly at him. He felt a jolt sweep through his body. They said nothing, their eyes fixed on each other as though each knew something intimate and revealing about the other.

'The Truth Will Out', Dan said to himself – one of the Five Dictums to which he had never given much thought.

Dan walked out of the main door in a daze. It made its customary sound as he pulled it open but he didn't notice, nor each crack of his shoes on the stone floor as he walked away from the chancel. He had no sense of time or place; no sense of how long he had been sitting in front of them, or how long he had been talking. He had never been so disoriented. Otto, Gilda and Petra had retired to the old vestry at the back of the building; Petra had given him a glass of water and had placed her hand gently on his shoulder before walking away. Dan remembered nothing of the intervening period other than a feeling of such intense emptiness that the walls of The Townhouse seemed to close in around him. He felt hollow, as though he could snap into a million pieces. The clattering sound of the three returning, jolted him upright in his chair. They sat back down and Otto made his declaration.

'Daniel, we have listened carefully to your answers and what happened that day. The death of any A grade is a great misfortune and fortunately a rare occurrence. But is has happened and life must go on. We all know each other Daniel, and the three of us have been discussing your character and what we know about you and how unlike you it is to act so violently against another human being, indeed against any living creature. For you to have done what you did, you must have been provoked to the utmost. The three of us are also well aware of Price's reputation and behaviour. This past year especially he has been, shall we say, less than amenable. In public, he has often been rude, unappreciative and offensive, and one must not forget his bizarre behaviour at the Solstice ceremony. So we can only guess what it must have been like for you, living with him day in, day out. We can understand how you could have snapped; how you could have finally just had enough. Yes, it was violent, but perhaps also inevitable. So, with considerable thought and deliberation, the three of us have decided that no further action should be taken, and that you are free to go and enjoy life as it should be lived. We see no purpose in any punishment. We hope that you can recover quickly from this sad episode and move on, with a new partner being found for you before the year is out.'

Otto spoke slowly and clearly as though to a greater audience. At its end, he walked towards Dan with his arms outstretched and a broad smile on his face. Gilda and Petra followed a few paces behind, both looking slightly awkward as though by-standers relieved the whole affair could be forgotten without delay. Dan muttered a thank you, unable to process what had just transpired. He probably shook their hands and smiled too, but he could not remember. He had no recollection of saying goodbye, nor of saying thank you. He just wanted to get out and breath the open air.

But it was not a feeling of relief. As he looked up at the sun poking through the clouds, he felt the aching pain of guilt and that he didn't deserve to be walking away unblemished. Of all Otto's words, he remembered most those he used to describe Price: rude, unappreciative and offensive. They were words that described aspects of Price yes, but nothing like the whole story, and they stung Dan as though they were said about himself. And how could Otto use such words? They hardly knew each other. Rude? Yes, sometimes. Unappreciative? What did that even mean? Dan's testimony had been curt and untrustworthy, and yet their condemnation of Price was complete. It now seemed to Dan that it wasn't him who sat before them this morning, but his dead partner.

He walked quickly away from the building, taking long strides. His back was soggy and his shirt clung uncomfortably to his shoulders. He took the short route through the centre of the town, past the communal bakery and the sports centre, through the park with its stone memorials and the arboretum with its cache of rare trees, and on to the vast main square which dominated the centre of the town. He walked past the mass of bicycles, through the main entrance, and took out his pass tablet from his pocket to show it to Oswald, the janitor in charge of distribution. Oswald said hello and scanned the tablet. 'There are extra zucchinis today,' he said, 'it's been a good year for zucchinis.'

Dan borrowed a small hemp bag from the central table and collected his ration. His tablet had already been altered to reflect the change in his situation - just the one zucchini, despite the glut, and one onion. He would cut some thyme from the garden and make a soup. He added the lettuce leaves to the bag, a couple of greenish tomatoes and some pellets for Braggle made by the local collective from the town's waste. He nodded at people as he went by and they nodded politely back. No-one mentioned the tribunal, just as no-one had said anything about Price in the week gone by. And as he walked along the square's periphery under the line of linden trees and watched others chatting, bartering, smiling, a searing loneliness hit him with such force that he rushed to the nearest bench to steady himself. He sat with a heavy thud, his head bowed and his eyes closed, taking long slow breaths, in through the nose, out through the mouth, smelling dust and heat. He'd done it many times before, and it had always helped, slowing his breathing, calming his anxieties, pushing Price from his thoughts, but this time, with each inhale, it was Price he was thinking of and the last thing he wanted was to force him away.

When he lifted his head and opened his eyes, the light seemed brighter and the noises louder. He watched two women bartering over a brass candlestick, and a man, holding what looked like a wicker bread basket, walk from one stall to the next, picking up cups and cutlery and glasses, holding them to the light and moving on, and as Dan followed the man's progress along the left flank of the square, he saw Maia sitting on another bench looking directly at him. She gave a cautious little wave, her head tilted, and he nodded in return, feeling his insides turn as she got up, walked towards him and sat down on the same bench.

'You're free then,' she said quietly without emotion. And without waiting for an answer, 'any change in your status?'

'No,' he replied.

'No,' Maia said matter-of-factly. 'And does that surprise you?'

'I don't know. I don't know what to think. I'm just ....' Dan paused for a moment. He didn't know exactly how he felt. Relieved? Possibly. 'I'm just exhausted actually,' he decided to say. 'I feel utterly exhausted.'

Maia put her hand on his shoulder and started stroking it gently as she would a cat. 'I followed you from the Townhouse,' she said, 'I was waiting for you. I was worried about you.'

'No need Maia, I'm fine.'

'You know that's not true.' Maia took hold of both his hands. 'You're welcome to come to my house whenever you want you know. We've been through the same thing remember.'

Dan slowly took his hands away.

'Maia, why didn't you see much of Price in those final weeks?'

He could see he'd taken her by surprise. 'A silly little tiff,' she replied after a moment's thought. 'He wasn't easy in those last months. I had to take a little distance.'

'I thought he was staying some nights with you, to comfort you. But he wasn't.'

'No.'

'Do you know where he was staying?'

'I'm afraid not Dan. I'm sorry.'

'Well I guess it doesn't matter anymore does it.'

'Not much Dan, no, it doesn't.'

And as though to draw a line under it, Maia abruptly stood up and took a small glass bottle out of her jacket pocket. 'This is the other reason I wanted to see you,' she said. She shook the bottle gently and handed it to him. 'I'd like to exchange this with you.'

'What is it?'

'It's poison.'

'That's not very funny Maia.'

'I'm deadly serious,' she replied deadpan, 'but it's not for you, at least I wouldn't advise drinking it.'

Dan stood up slowly and pushed the bottle back into Maia's hand. 'Maia, please, I'm tired, I'm really tired,' he said wearily. 'I know you must hate me for what I did, but please don't play games, I don't have the energy for it.'

'I don't hate you Dan, but it's time to open your eyes. Please, take this and when you get home put a few drops on one of your plants in the garden.'

'No.'

'Please.'

'No.'

'Do it for Price.'

'What the hell has Price got to do with it?'

Maia didn't respond, but Dan could see from the look on her face that it was a dumb question, that Price had *everything* to do with it.

He looked around him. No-one was looking. 'I have to give you something, you know that. Someone might see.'

25

'I can almost guarantee it,' Maia replied.

'But I have nothing to give you.'

'What about your shirt?'

Dan laughed. And then realised she wasn't joking. Maia stood perfectly still, perfectly composed. 'It's a good deal,' she said, 'this bottle is worth a lot more than that shirt.' She touched his arm, squeezed it gently, and smiled. 'Dan, it's time to wake up. I'm serious. Price didn't tell you much because he thought you wouldn't be able to cope, but he's dead Dan. You killed him. Now take off your shirt and I'll give you this bottle and you can take it home and pour it on a few flowers.'

Dan stood under the shade of the linden tree not knowing what to do. He looked around him once more, saw people he knew walking slowly around the square, stopping to chat quietly to others. He saw Oswald looking into someone's bag, and a small dog who had once bitten Braggle, peeing against one of the railings. He looked up at the sky, then at Maia, and then started unbuttoning his shirt. 'I never liked it anyway,' he said, and felt the air caress his shoulders as he took it off and handed it to her.

She placed the bottle in his hand and clasped her own hands around it. 'Look after it Dan, it's not your normal poison.'

'With my life,' he said. He put it casually in his pocket and walked away.

There was nothing unusual in being half naked. On warm summer days men and women of all shapes and sizes walked topless through the town and the square, and there was a small communal lake with its artificial beach where nudity was encouraged if not expected. Dan had always worn a t-shirt and covered himself with a towel, and only swam when it was just him and Price alone. Price would make fun of him, trying to whip the towel away whilst others watched, but Dan wanted none of it. And now, as he walked through the square semi-naked, he felt embarrassed and uneasy. He walked swiftly to the exit trying not to make eye contact, walked past Oswald, saying a brief goodbye, not noticing there was no response in return, and walked along the main street. The communal scything had not yet begun and the verge was filled with purples and yellows and gave off a sweet, comforting smell. Dan touched them with his left hand as he walked quickly by and a mass of cabbage whites darted into the air. A soft warm breeze cradled his torso and he could feel it touch the few hairs on his chest and those under his arms.

He reached the house and saw Braggle poking her head above the window in his study. He walked in and knew someone had been there, he could just feel it, as though the chemical composition of the air around him had been altered. He opened the door to the study and Braggle bounded out, running around the house, sniffing uncontrollably. Dan looked into each room; as far as he could see nothing had been disturbed. He opened all the doors and windows making the curtains swirl into the rooms, the warm through draft hitting his chest. In the kitchen, he poured himself a small glass of plum brandy and drank it in one gulp. He thought about who might have come into his house but no-one came to mind, and as he leaned against the larder door and looked down at where Price's body had lain, he realised he didn't care, he really didn't care at all.

He took the small glass bottle from his pocket, walked into the garden and poured a couple of drops into the soil around a clasp of loosestrife. With his arms outstretched, he turned slowly, taking in the mass of colour and the incessant movement of insects, took off his shoes and socks, then his trousers, and finally his underpants. He walked along a thin path that led to a small patch of mossy grass, lay down with his arms and legs splayed, looking up towards the sun that by now had taken a full hold of the sky, closed his eyes and fell asleep.

He awoke with Braggle by his side. It took him a while to penetrate the time of day. He saw the sun skirting the tops of the trees and guessed he'd been there for at least a couple of hours. He lay there a little longer with his head turned to one side, staring from ground level up at the wild flowers that caressed the edge of the grass. They seemed so grand to him now, towering above him with such natural elegance, hiding the scurry of spiders and insects that crawled through the tangle of undergrowth. The petals absorbed the light from above giving them an opaque intensity which magnified their colours. He could see the veins etched into the leaves. A valerian shimmied upwards with its skeletal bare flower-head silhouetted against the sky, a few wisps of seed still clinging to its delicate edges. Dan closed his eyes, trying to capture the images. He must remember this. This feeling.

And he knew what he had to do. He gathered up his clothes, went inside to change, and walked directly to Maia's house taking Braggle with him. He'd been kept in the dark long enough.

THREE

It was Price's turn to cook but he had about as much desire to prepare the evening meal as he had to sit across the table from Dan and chat about the day gone by. He just wanted to eat quickly and cycle straight to Maia's. He had a lot to tell her. He looked at the faded leek, the onion and the anaemic-looking cheese and thought if he just chopped them all up and threw them into a pan with some butter and fresh thyme, and left it all simmering for half an hour, then surely that must taste ok, no? It might look a bit messy, but it's the taste that's important, right? 'Wholesome mush, wholesome mush,' he said aloud as he tapped his fingers on the table. Then he laughed. He did that a lot and never quite knew where it came from. It was just always there, inside him, waiting to burst out. Maybe he was just good at making the most of the situation and letting events, or people, especially Dan, slide over him as though they weren't real or happening. And maybe he was difficult sometimes, but then so was Dan, and at least he was able to laugh and not just sulk and be miserable and go to bed early. That brooding silence always left him drained. He just felt lucky, and relieved, that last year's batch of plums had been almost inexhaustible and the corresponding batch of his excessively good 'pick me up' was equally abundant.

He wanted to tell Maia, but not Dan, not yet anyway, about the puppy he'd seen that day in the market square. It was cupped in the hands of a man he barely knew. 'Twelve-weeks', he'd said. Price took it in his own arms and brought it up to his face, their eyes fixed on each other in what he was convinced was love at first sight.

It was rare to see a live animal being bartered in the square and Price was surprised Oswald had even let it through; maybe the man had concealed it in his shirt or bag or something. And he was now at the far end of the square under the shade of a linden tree stroking the puppy gently as it slept in his arms, no bigger than one of the Bramley apples Price picked every autumn from the garden. He liked the man, even thought there was some sort of *click* going on, and he adored the puppy. It had been more than six months since their spaniel had died. They'd had her for seventeen glorious years and was probably the link that kept him and Dan from strangling each other. Each time Dan irritated him, and that was often, he'd look straight at Aphrodite and she'd look straight at him, and a sort of warming, electric wave coursed through his body. She'd died suddenly, dead on the bed, cuddled up between them when they woke in the morning. They were both shot through with grief and buried her at the end of the garden even though it was non-negotiable - all animals had to be buried in the communal pit for animals, next to the human one. They couldn't bear that, so they told everyone that she'd disappeared one night, must have gone off somewhere to die; she hadn't been well for a while, they said.

Price told the man to come back the following week and please, please, not to barter the dog with anyone else as he was almost certain that he'd be able to take it and love it. He'd also barter it with something he knew the man would love, and it involved plums. The man had agreed with alacrity. He left the square with Price, parting at the entrance with a touch on his arm which Price was sure was more than a touch on his arm.

The dog was black and white, the man said it was probably somewhere between a springer and a collie but impossible to really tell. Price didn't care. He just knew that he wanted the dog.

He raced home, saw Dan in the garden, and clammed up. The right words just didn't come, and then, with the moment gone, they disappeared. He spent the rest of the day thinking about it. Maybe he should just surprise Dan. But maybe he shouldn't. He walked to Maia's. She wasn't there. Walked back to the square. Empty. He just had to be patient. Not his strong point.

Price put all the ingredients in a pan with some butter, put the lid on and left it for half an hour on a slow heat. It was served unseen, coming as much of a surprise for him as for Dan when he lifted the lid with an exaggerated fanfare. Then the usual silence as Dan contemplated what lay before him. This time it was unadulterated mush. Dan guffawed. Price laughed. Dan was the one with a culinary flare not him, and anyhow, how was it possible to create wonders from such simple ingredients?

Dan scooped up some of the mush and put it on his plate, saying nothing. The signs weren't good. Price had to lighten the mood.

'We're getting a puppy.' It just came out.

Dan dropped his fork. What ensued wasn't a row exactly, and not really much about the pros and cons of getting a puppy. Instead, it consisted of accusations and recriminations that had been voiced a thousand times before and would continue, on and off, until the day of Price's death. Clichés filled the space around them, nothing resolved. Dan vented his frustration over unilateral decision-making, then agreed it was a good time for a new dog in the house. He ate his food, and yes, it was actually quite tasty.

'You can't really go wrong with cheese, leek and thyme,' he said.

The intervening few days were difficult for Price. He wasn't good at waiting. The rain came down hard, hitting the ground with such force that the soil, already soggy from an incessantly wet winter, splattered into the air, coating the paths and roads with a thin layer of sludge. But Price had to get out of the house. On the Sunday, he put on his old yellow waterproofs, got on his rusting bicycle and headed for the edge of town. The front tyre threw the sludge onto his clothes and face. He stopped every few minutes and looked to the skies, the rain quickly washing him clean. He bobbed

31

along the old railway track and took the easterly country lane out into the fields sending the spire, the one feature of the town which seemed impossible to shake off, blurring into the mist. Price placed the bike against a tree and continued walking. The field path became narrower and indistinguishable from the mud all around him. The rain thudded against his canvas waterproof and he could feel the water seeping inside and heavying his shirt. Then he heard a different sound. A sharp crack. Then another. He lifted his hood away and heard it again. It was still a long way off, probably on the other side of the wood about half a kilometre away. Another crack. He left the path and trudged across the field. Mud squelched. His feet disappeared. Twice he stumbled and his hands penetrated the slosh. He reached the wood, breathing heavily, standing in the rain to cleanse himself. It was a small coppice wood, the trees showing gentle signs of coming to life. Another crack. Closer. He walked through the wood and stopped at its outer edge, hiding behind a tree. He could see three men. One was pointing something up in the air and moving it sharply from side to side in rapid movements. Two cages rested on the ground. A large brown dog stood next to them, its tail and neck rigid. Then bang. Price's body shuddered in response. 'That's a gun', he said out loud. 'That's a shotgun'. Then he saw three geese flapping their wings, somehow fixed to the ground, unable to fly away. The dog had run off and returned with a limp bird in its mouth. A pile of them lay next to the cages. Price rested against the tree making sure he was out of sight. The men were about fifty metres away but the rain made it seem further. He saw them pack everything onto a trailer, cover it with tarpaulin and leave. He clawed his way back to his bicycle, not caring how often he collapsed into the mud, his clothes and face and hands covered in a layer of sludge that the rain could hardly budge.

He arrived home dishevelled. Dan laughed and took a photo with his tablet.

'What on earth have you been doing?' he asked, helping Price take off his waterproofs.

'I fell.'

'Are you hurt?'

'I'm fine.'

Dan wetted a towel and started gently cleaning Price's face. 'You're totally covered in mud. Have you been in the fields?'

'Maybe.'

'But why?'

'Too many questions Dan'

'So you're not going to tell me?'

'Nope.

Dan picked up the waterproofs from the floor, folded them loosely and took them outside. 'I can probably guess,' he said, 'and what do I care if you go around looking like you've been braggled.'

Price walked after him. 'Braggled?'

'You don't know what braggled is?'

'Why should I.'

'I'm sure I've said it to you before. We used it at the Academy. Braggle's what we called the mud that covered us when we played in the sports field.'

'Never heard of it.'

'We were always making up words. Braggle was one of those that stuck – a bit like it is on you now.'

'Very droll,' Price said with a smile. He grabbed the towel and hit Dan playfully across the buttocks. 'I tell you what,' he said, 'let's name the puppy Braggle, in honour of the occasion.'

The next time it rained, a few days after collecting the puppy from the market, and with a slight disappointment that the man had declined his offer to come and see his garden, Price went back to the wood but saw nothing. He went again a dozen times in the course of the following month, still nothing. He spent longer than usual at the town archives researching guns and hunting. It was of little help. He knew that guns were in the first rung of non-negotiables, up there with hunting, and he assumed the live geese were used as bait to attract other geese, and that the men were probably shooting in the rain to drown the sounds. He hoped it was a one off and he could place it in a compartment in

33

his brain marked sealed, but every time he looked at Braggle, who accompanied him everywhere, including sitting on his lap in the town archives, the geese re-appeared in his mind, flapping their wings in a desperate attempt to escape before being picked up roughly by their legs and thrown forcefully into the cage the way he would throw the rubbish into the communal waster.

Price confided in Maia and no-one else. They'd meet a couple of times a week in the Waterhouse next to the square listening to each other's concerns. She spoke of life with Theo, how he showed no interest in her, that he was always in the garden, even in the rain, tending his plants, whilst Price spoke of Braggle, geese and Dan, in that order. They agreed that no-one else should be told, aware that there must be others who knew, that you can't go around shooting geese and keep it a secret. They'd keep their eyes and ears open.

Price and Maia had both been to Academies where the sanctity of all life was drummed into them; they knew little of what happened at the lower Academies apart from hearsay and perfunctory conversations at the distributions and the Townhouse. They knew that C_s and certainly D_s were less inclined to adhere to the norms, and witnessed their crude behaviour during the communal harvest, but also saw how they reacted with the utmost care when they stumbled across late nests in the fields or an injured animal. And it was common knowledge that some of the larger water birds were sometimes poached using a simple net. Rabbits too. There were so many that the odd one disappearing was of no consequence. It was all non-negotiable of course, although they'd never known anyone to be punished, and yet the threat of punishment still hung in the air like an old tree waiting to fall in a storm.

Price became increasingly distracted. His meals with Dan were embarrassingly quiet, the stillness punctuated only by the wind creaks of the trees and the first mutterings of the songbirds. It irritated Price that his partner asked no questions. It irritated Dan that Price wasn't confiding in him. Both eat their meals with the rigidity of the wronged in a silent stalemate neither felt inclined to break.

And so begins the collapse of a relationship. Over the course of the year the silence grew louder, both men recognising their frailties and both disinclined to counteract them. Price felt guilty that he couldn't share his thoughts with Dan. Dan felt aggrieved and ashamed that such an ebullient man had become so muffled in his company. Their public faces remained intact with few people witnessing the decline. The two men still interacted when on display, laughing together, even touching. It was only when alone, facing each other across a table, lying next to each other in bed, that the fragility of their relationship re-surfaced. Braggle was always by their side, oblivious to their plight. Her presence helping assuage the tension and lighten the extravagance of the silences.

It was exhausting for both men, each finding solace in their solitude, each searching for a stimulus that would lighten their mood, spending hours in the town archives or on their tablet increasing their understanding of the living and the long dead. But this newly acquired knowledge wasn't shared as it was. They no longer returned with ideas for virtual journeys where they could marvel in the rich catalogue of the extinct and lament the hubris of mankind. Instead, the knowledge was absorbed, finding no outlet for wonder and reflection. It saddened them both and cracked their enjoyment of existence. But there was nothing either could do.

Price had Maia. Dan had no-one. Eighteen years in the town had brought no single person, apart from Price, with whom he had a unique and reciprocating bond. He was never able to counteract his shyness with a fabricated public face, and relied on Price's abilities to get by. That had now all but dissolved.

The spring days quickly vanished in a haze of silence and sadness. It had been very wet and mild, although the sun had managed, at times, to poke through the blanket greyness and create swathes of colour which made life so rich and worthwhile. The cowslips and dead nettles had thrived, the stitchwort and digitalis covered the hedgerows, and the insects were abundant. The birds too. And now the summer days had begun. It was early May and excessively warm. The grains had been sown and Price had watched the C_s and D_s in the fields, hands full with seeds, throwing them with a grand sweep on to the ground, followed by others scraping them into the soil. Some wore their shirts tied loosely around their waists, all wore wide brimmed straw hats. Price saw them chatting and laughing, making him yearn for the same, wishing he could strip to the waist and join in. But he had to keep his distance and walk around the fields, smelling the sweat of others and yearning for the harvest when he would be able to take part. Each morning he rose early and took Braggle for a long, winding walk through the edge of the town, chatting briefly and inconsequentially with other dog walkers, watching the dogs sniff and play. Price had a natural gaiety and people seemed to enjoy his company and the way he would laugh unexpectedly with a deep heave of his shoulders. It gave Price a lift too, but it was swiftly erased when he reached home and felt the weight of the sadness around him.

Price hadn't forgotten the geese, but had seen nothing more. He told himself the three men were from out of town, probably hunting so far from their own homes that, if seen, they wouldn't be recognized. He remembered how they walked, their silhouettes. One was noticeably taller than the other two, with an exaggerated stoop, but maybe he was just protecting himself from the rain. It all swirled in Price's head and refused to budge: Guns, violence, dead birds. He had grown up with the rough and tumble of the Academy with its hierarchies and petty quarrels, using his size and humour to deflect attention and unwanted aggravation, finding a gentle middle ground which allowed him to negotiate aggression and avoid the harder end of life there. He had never witnessed the use of weapons or violence against animals, it just wasn't done. Price loved, as did everyone, the weekly wildlife hologram where they'd sit on the floor in the main hall, transfixed by the colours and movement swirling around them. Each week was a different species;

most had long disappeared into a murky past, tangible and yet mere ghosts of an unfathomable age. An hour glided by, and when the images faded away and the lights turned on, an overwhelming silence filled the hall, broken only by the principal announcing it was time to leave. The boys would rise slowly, their thoughts filled with wonder and a profound sadness, and a disbelief that their ancestors allowed the natural world to collapse around them.

So instead of it all fading into a protective corner of Price's brain, the geese and the hunt grew larger, refusing to disperse, exhausting his delicate equilibrium. And Braggle was always close-by to remind him.

FOUR

Neither Dan nor Price was looking forward to the day. Festivities tended to set off gratuitous bickering between the two, leading to more silence and a period in which each ignored the existence of the other. The previous year, a discussion over which dish they would take to the communal buffet led to a week of frayed nerves. And this year seemed to be leading in the same direction. They eat breakfast communicating via the dog, who sat on the floor between the two men, looking up and hearing soft, high pitched voices, as though they were speaking to a six-month old baby.

'I don't think Price can be feeling too good this morning Braggle do you, considering how much he drank last night'.

'It's not surprising Price drank so much last night, is it Braggle, it's the only way to make any sense of the world'.

'It's difficult to make any sense of the world, isn't it Braggle, when one's had so much to drink'.

'I may drink Braggle, but at least I know how to have some fun'.

And even though he wouldn't admit it, Price wasn't feeling his best. It had been a long, boozy night (the Solstice Eve always had that effect on him) and the supply of plum brandy had been depleted to alarming proportions. He'd taken a bottle out into the main square with the intention of keeping some back for the rest of the week. He'd never meant to drink it all, but with all the noise and laughing and dancing and music, it just seemed the right thing to do. It was the tradition to stay up until the sun tipped above the horizon, people joining hands to watch the spectacle so long as the clouds didn't spoil the party. Some went home after sunset to get some sleep, waking in time to walk to the edge of the town to re-join those who hadn't wilted through the darkness hours.

Dan had gone home with Braggle around midnight, taking the empty bottle of plum brandy with him, his shirt still tucked neatly into his trousers, leaving Price behind with his shirt wrapped carelessly around his waist. Dan found it hard to find him amongst the crowds, eventually noticing him (and hearing him) as he danced and sang in the centre of a group, his arms raised in unison with the others as they swayed to the music and bawled the words to the song. Dan clawed his way through, shouted something in his ear, took the empty bottle and walked home. He fell asleep on the sofa and awoke to the sound of the front door banging shut and Price chuckling as he clanged against the door frames still half naked and clutching another empty bottle which he methodically placed on the side table. He then got on his knees and shuffled towards Dan, smiling broadly. 'My darling, beauteousness', he said, and scooped him up in his arms, aiming kisses wherever he could. Dan didn't resist, succumbing to his partner's fumbling and enjoying the feel of chest hair scraping against his face. Clothes were haphazardly removed and thrown across the room. They kissed with the intensity of a brief encounter and tangled their bodies into one.

An hour or so later Dan left Price in a deep sleep, picked up all the clothes and went to the bedroom, lying on the bed with the curtains open, watching the light intensify and touching his chest lightly with the tips of his fingers. He waited a few more hours before going back downstairs, opened the door as quietly as he could, tip-toeing over to Price who still lay naked and comatose on the sofa, and nudged him gently. No response. He nudged him a little harder. Still no response. He put his mouth to his ear and whispered 'good morning'. It came out harder than he'd wanted. Price's body jolted upright. He gazed at Dan with the look of someone who didn't know where he was, squinted, and said harshly 'why can't you just leave me alone,' before walking out of the room and upstairs.

So it was a late breakfast. Dan prepared the table with slices of freshly baked bread, some blackcurrant jam from last year's bumper crop, and on Price's side added a glass of fresh orange juice with ginger. Price appeared wearing yesterday's crumpled clothes and smelling of tired alcohol. He sat down on his chair with the weariness of an elderly man and said nothing, apart from a small grunt as he sipped a little of the juice. Dan waited for any sign of what had happened between them and when nothing came sank further into himself with a resignation that bordered on despair. He was unable to respond to Price's silence with any natural sympathy, instead drinking the juice himself with an exaggerated gesture and saying something facetious to Braggle.

Price remembered everything. He remembered arriving home and pouncing on Dan. He remembered watching the sun move softly into dawn and the collective purring of the onlookers as they stood together hand in hand. And how the young man standing next to him squeezed his own hand a little too long and a little too hard, and how it sent a continuous gasp of excitement charging through his body. They stood there, side by side, not looking at each other, absorbing the closeness. Price didn't know how long it lasted, maybe five minutes, maybe fifteen. It lasted until the young man released his grip, whispered 'goodbye' in his ear and walked away. Price watched him as he disappeared amongst the diminishing crowd. He saw the curly blond hair, the bright red shorts and the leg hair glistening in the young light. 'I have everything to give but myself,' he murmured and then wondered why he'd chosen those specific words. 'I can give everything, everything,' he said. 'I can give myself, utterly.' He picked up an empty bottle from the ground, walked home feeling elated and in need of sexual release.

And now here he was, sitting opposite his partner of God knows how many years, unable to utter a single reassuring word. He knew he was being unfair and that he must have wounded Dan with his harshness, but he just couldn't help

40

himself. Dan was an attractive man with his fine, delicate features, and a good man; gentle, quiet, thoughtful. How could he be so mean to him? It just all seemed too late for niceties and worthless conversation. There is more. Surely there has to be more.

They were late. The celebrations had started half an hour ago and they still weren't ready. They squeezed together in front of the mirror, fixing their Academy Reformation decorations to their shirts. Each had the obligatory ox-eye daisy and wheat motif but each showed a little originality to distinguish it from the rest. If anyone didn't know of their A status then a simple glance at their decoration was enough. It was the one time in the year when appearance mattered. Everyone was encouraged (but not obliged) to wear the Reformation's symbol of 'The Natural Order of Nature' that conveyed the very essence of the Change and its essential ingredient of recovery and preservation. Price's had a bee in the centre of the flower surrounded by an extravagant swirl of grain heads; Dan's was more constrained with a simple silhouette. He felt it had an elegant, refined quality that highlighted his Academy's purity of style; Price saw it as a distinct lack of imagination. Both had worn the same badge every year without questioning its legitimacy, without considering its meaning. It just was. It gave an order to things; a continuity and a structure. The Summer Solstice was grand and immobile, as solid as the ground they were standing on.

Price touched Dan's shoulder, a gesture of contrition and recognition of the traditions that bound them together, and felt a crick of dejection as Dan ignored it and left the room. Price remained in front of the mirror, looking at his sturdy frame and again at the decoration pinned to his shirt, and wondered why he was wearing it. He had no recollection, ever, of not wearing it for the Solstice. One of his first memories was being given the badge and told to cherish it as he would his own life (or maybe 'as he would the lives of others'). He was in a line with other young boys, maybe there were girls there too, and someone very tall stooped over him, pinned the badge on his blazer and brushed his face lightly with the palm of his hand. It was that touch he remembered above anything else; the badge was secondary, of no consequence.

He ran the tips of his fingers lightly across and down the left side of his face, the place that was touched so many years before and where, last night, a young man placed his mouth so close that he could feel his warm breath. He moved closer to the mirror, his fingers now touching his skin so lightly that it felt like a feather being brushed delicately across his facial hairs. He ran his fingers slowly down from his hairline, drawing small curves down to the tip of his nose and across his mouth. He closed his eyes, tracing his ears and jaw and chin until he heard Dan's voice from below. They had to leave. Price took off the badge, put it back in its pouch and into the drawer.

There are non-negotiables and then there are conventions that act as such. The Solstice was so wrapped in tradition that altering its shape was like a punch to the face. There was nothing stopping someone from staying at home, from not bringing two dishes to the communal lunch, from not wearing bright summer colours, and from not getting into the spirit of the occasion, but as a general rule of sensibility one played along. The town buffet was astounding in its predictability, but a testament to its occupants' ingenuity and taste buds. Yellow, in all its shades, predominated, making the crowd, from a distance, look like a giant swarm of carder bees. The centre of the town was decked with ox-eye daisies, either growing along the verge of the road or tied in pretty bundles to doors and gates of the small terraced houses that predominated. The overall cheerfulness was contagious and for some intoxicating.

Dan and Price arrived just before the Solstice anthem (Braggle was wearing a yellow collar studded with false gems that Dan had made for Aphrodite) and placed their dishes on the buffet table which ran the length of the square. They had missed a couple of long speeches and a pompous welcome from Otto Cladders as he asked everyone to give thanks to the sun's precious gift and to man's continuing ingenuity, causing a few in the crowd to raise their eyebrows, after all, wasn't the day about celebrating the endowment of nature and not man's dubious historical contribution?

At 3pm or thereabouts a bell was struck and a silence fell upon the square. A trumpet filled the void with a simple smooth note followed by the famous opening chords of the Solstice anthem. Dan drew his arm across his chest and touched his decoration with the palm of his hand.

Oh rising sun, fill me thus with lightness and with splendour.

Price kept his hands down, mumbling the alternative version he'd known since childhood and which, as an A_3 homotype, felt far more appropriate. Dan nudged him in the side. Price huffed and scanned the crowd searching for red shorts and curly blond hair. He saw plenty, just not on the right body.

The anthem ended with a collective cheer and a wave of arms swaying in the air. Dan and Price strolled through the crowd, nodding and chatting briefly to those they knew and those they didn't. It was one of the few occasions each year when the orders mingled so unobtrusively that one would have been forgiven for believing the divisions had been abandoned altogether. Price especially appreciated its sentiment and the rawness of the celebrating, eating the same food, drinking the same beer. There seemed to be an ease to the revelry of others, a freeness to their chatter, an uncomplicated love for the moment. He could talk to a C with his guard down and his voice raised, the cloak of pretention dissolving into a straight-forward joy of living, and it wasn't long before his reluctance to leave the house had been forgotten in the blaze of smiling, genuine faces.

Dan wasn't so keen and tugged at Price's shirt to pull him away. 'It's too much for Braggle,' he said, 'the noise is unbearable. I can hardly hear myself think.' They moved towards the far corner and saw Maia and Theo sitting on a haystack under one of the lindens.

'Where's your decoration?' Maia said curtly to Price,

ignoring the hellos, her own decoration almost hidden in the flounce of bright yellow frills circling her shoulders and swooping down over her chest.

'It fell off,' Price answered, suppressing the urge to say she looked like one of those old-fashioned flowers which were so over-cultivated they'd lost all their charm and sophistication.

It was clear Maia was not happy, her facial expression so unyielding that Theo looked at the other two with uncertainty and embarrassment, attempting to lighten the atmosphere by being jollier than he was accustomed to, and making them feel a little sorry for him in his obvious discomfort.

Maia and Theo arrived in the town the same year as Price and Dan and it seemed appropriate they'd become friends. But neither Dan nor Theo required anything too suffocating and so Price and Maia formed a separate, stronger bond in which their desire for gossip and fun was satisfied. Price was more outspoken, whilst Maia was more discerning, choosing her moments and topics, guiding the conversation to her whim. Her occasional grandiose gestures appealed to Price, and his ability to laugh at himself and situations lifted Maia from her depressions, a melancholy which Price was never able to fully decipher or predict. And it seemed like today was one of them. Her responses were monosyllabic, her interest in others non-existent, and her posture even straighter, as though Theo had forcibly glued a metal pole to her back.

Theo told Dan how Maia had been out of sorts for a few weeks, almost frozen with a dislike for anything and everyone. She had eaten little, refused to go to any of the daily distributions, and rarely rode her horse, leaving it to him to feed and brush her. 'Something has happened,' he said, 'but I have no idea what it might be.'

Maia and Price walked to the buffet table together. 'There are times,' Maia said, 'when I just can't bear to be near him. It sends me into a spiral that I can't shake off. And the worst thing is, the more he tries, the worse it becomes.'

Price took a large plate and filled it with meats and salads and breads. Maia took a small plate and added a green salad.

They walked back to the haystack.

'I met someone last night,' he told her as they sat down, 'and I think I might be a little bit smitten.'

'How many times have I heard that before,' Maia replied.

'Yes, but this one is different. Nothing happened. We just touched and it felt magical. It felt special.'

Maia hardly acknowledged it, looking down at her plate, pushing the food with her fork. Price put a slice of marinated beef into his mouth avoiding the temptation to say something he shouldn't; he'd met a man who had altered his perception and Maia was so absorbed in her own torment that she was unwilling to appreciate the significance of his disclosure. They sat in silence, Price giving Braggle pieces of smoked pork that sent her spiralling on the spot with excitement. Then Maia started to cry. At first, Price ignored it, unable to sympathise with her mood swings, but as her sobs intensified and her shoulders began to shudder, he put his empty plate onto the floor and put his arms around her.

'What's wrong Maia,' he asked.

'Everything,' she said.

'It can't be that bad surely.'

'I just feel helpless, so utterly helpless.'

'Is it so bad with Theo?'

'Oh, no, not really. He's such a sweet man. I know I'm hurting him and I know he'd do anything for me. But I just can't help myself.' Maia blew her nose with the bright yellow handkerchief she'd made especially for the celebrations. 'The fact is ....' and before she could finish her sentence Theo and Dan returned from the buffet table.

'We'll talk about it another time,' Price whispered in her ear and giving Theo his seat, walked back to the buffet to re-fill his plate taking Braggle with him. The meats, which had been so elegantly arranged, had by now been picked at roughly, with the left-overs draped over the edge of their platters and covered in flies. Price plucked at the lightly cooked beef and added some chargrilled chicken, his thoughts on the young man and Maia's sobs and not on the queue of people patiently waiting their turn. He just needed some cured pork, Braggle loved that; he just needed to stretch across the table to grab a couple of slices. Just a bit further.

A tall man holding an empty plate pushed him roughly back, then stood in front of him, deliberately blocking his view of the table. Price took a step back, slightly bemused, gave a half-hearted apology and began walking away, feeding Braggle titbits as he went. He turned to watch the man move slowly along the buffet, towering above those around him, a slight curvature to his spine, bending inelegantly over the table to fill his plate. Price stared with his mouth open. Was it him? The goose man?

He walked back to the buffet, more convinced the closer he got that this was the man he'd been looking for, and when they were side by side said: 'Nice meat, really tasty, shame there's no goose, I'm very partial to goose. What about you?'

The man continued to look down at his plate, picking at the chicken and the beef. He then tilted his head to look directly at Price and with the faintest of smiles put a slice of pork in his mouth. Price could see he'd pushed a button. He started walking backwards, still looking at the man, not aware Braggle was directly behind him, tripped over her and fell to the floor, the contents of the plate collapsing on to his head and chest. The tall man laughed; it was a mean-spirited, sadistic laugh. And Price knew for sure it was the man he'd been looking for.

'What on earth happened to you,' Dan said when Price returned to the haystack.

'So you didn't see me deliberately fall over Braggle and cover myself in meat?'

Dan took a handkerchief from his pocket, wiped Price's face and shirt and said, 'you need to go home and change,' squeezing his arm with a gesture of such gentleness that Price felt a surge of self-hatred shooting through his body. 'Thank you,' he muttered, and stroked Dan's arm with as much tenderness as he could manage. 'And I'm sorry.' He pulled Dan towards him and kissed the side of his face and then the lobe of his ear. Dan glided his hand along Price's chin and caressed the long, unkempt, greying hairs at his right temple, gently pulling them through his fingertips. 'I won't be long,' he said, and went home to change.

He pulled at a few ox-eye daisies on the way, finding them crushed and bruised in his hand by the time he opened the door to the house. He put on a clean, crumpled shirt, drank a glass of water and sat for a while in the black leather chair. He tried to concentrate on the man with the red shorts but quickly felt it blurring into Dan's soft, forgiving touch. They wrestled and then merged with the menace of the third man at the buffet table who wedged himself in and refused to budge. He'd never been good with anything intimidating. He remembered sitting in a class, he must have been about five, listening to a teacher with a gentle, lyrical voice. He wanted to touch her hair and feel the warmth of her own touch. Another woman entered the room whose voice was harsher, more abrasive. He started to cry, making no sound, his head down, his tears darkening the small oak desk. He then felt the touch of the first teacher's hand on his shoulder. It lasted just a few seconds, then drifted away into the buzz of the classroom and the severity of the other woman's sounds. He searched for those gentle, reassuring echoes in the years to come but nothing came. And so he learned to control and internalize his fears, building a cheerful façade to deflect the uncharitable behaviour of others and a sensitivity he knew he had to contain.

How long had he been in the chair? Half an hour? An hour? He'd told Dan he'd not be long and he knew he'd see it as yet another broken promise. He left quickly, slamming the door behind him and rushed along the path that led from the house to the street. He got half way and stopped suddenly. At the end of the path the tall man from the buffet came into view and started walking slowly towards him. Price was unable to move. The man came closer and closer and stopped a metre in front of him.

'Paul,' he said, holding out his hand.

His voice was softer than Price had imagined.

'Price,' he said, keeping his hands in his pockets.

'I'm sorry I bumped into you like that,' the man said.

'You were a little rough.'

'Yes, I was. Sorry again. It's just that I'd been waiting a while in the queue and you just pushed right in front of everyone.

It was a bit irritating. And I'm partial to a bit of pork.' He smiled.

'How do you know where I live?' Price asked abruptly.

'Oh, come on Price, everyone knows where everyone lives.'

'I don't know where you live.'

'Ah, that's a bit different, I don't live in this town.'

'Is that possible?'

'For some people, yes. I'm a land official. I have permission to travel. It's part of the job.'

Price had never heard of a land official and decided not to push it. Instead he asked, 'so why are you here for the celebrations? Why not your own town?'

'I have friends here. Acquaintances. It's a nice place.'

'And these friends told you where I live.'

'Something like that.'

'So why are you here?'

'I just wanted to say hello.'

Price gave out a little snort. 'You just wanted to say hello? Are you serious?' Inside he was shaking, his stomach tight, his lungs swelling.

The man smiled again. 'Well, of course there is the small matter of you mentioning something about a goose. It did take me a little by surprise.' He took a step back. 'I'm not sure how or what you know but it's of no great importance and don't worry, I haven't come to warn you.' He paused, looking down at the ground, playing with his fingers. 'Well, I suppose it is a sort of warning.' Another smile. 'But only in the sense that you know we know you know, but you know that anyway.'

It was said with such gentleness, his voice calm, his face relaxed, that the words seemed to dissolve into irrelevance. Price looked at the man's hair, the way it curled over his ears, the freckles scattered across his nose and cheeks, the moisture on his lips.

The man took another step back and scratched at his nose nervously as though scraping away an imaginary scab.

'And I want to apologise for laughing at you when you fell. That wasn't nice of me.'

'No it wasn't,' Price replied.

'Well, I'm here to say sorry.' He took a step forward. 'I like you,' he said.

'You like me? That's a strange thing to say.'

'I'd like to touch you.'

'Is that a joke?'

But he was true to his word. He moved forwards and brought his hand across Price's chest and slowly down his midriff.

When Price returned to the main square Dan was still sitting on the same haystack. Maia and Theo had gone.

'Thank you so much,' Dan said sarcastically, 'you've only been gone for two hours, it's been so much fun waiting for you to come back.'

'I'm so sorry,' Price replied. 'I fell asleep. I didn't get much sleep last night if you remember. Why didn't you come and get me?'

'You've been drinking.'

Price didn't reply. He'd shared a small glass of plum brandy with Paul once they'd finished in the bedroom. He was still in a bit of a daze, not because of the sex, it's just that it was the *last* thing he'd expected. This was the man who went around killing geese and treating them with a sickening malevolence, the man who had kept him awake at night with thoughts of guns and bullets and violence. There was a moment, on the bed, when Paul had both hands close to his neck, his fingers pulling at his skin, when Price felt vulnerable, that the whole thing was a ploy to get him to the house, but Paul's hands moved up around his face, roughly caressing his chin and cheeks until he brought his mouth to Price's right ear and stuck his tongue tenderly into the cavity, licking around its edge and then nibbling gently at the earlobe.

Drinking the brandy afterwards, Price asked why he'd really come to the house. 'I was just feeling horny', Paul had answered, 'and sometimes you just have to go with your instincts'. He'd been living with a woman for twenty years he said and always had a bit of a thing for men even though his genotype suggested otherwise, had to go for it when the opportunity arose; 'and it certainly rose'. They both laughed.

Geese were not mentioned. Nor shotguns. Paul drank his brandy quickly, left via the back door, his stoop less pronounced, saying only 'I enjoyed that'. Price waited a few minutes and left the same way, leaving the door unlocked, and as he walked to the main square his pace waned in direct proportion to how much logic he added to his thoughts. He stopped next to one of the communal sun dials which lined the walkways, leaned against the stone base, and placing one hand on the dial, read the inscription *sic labitur ætas* (thus passes a lifetime). A bumble bee flew onto the tip of the metal dial. Price pushed it delicately onto the palm of his hand and felt it lightly graze his skin as it matter-of-factly ambled towards his fingertips. He brought it closer to his face so he could see its delicate features and the wisps of ginger hair on its thorax. He knew it was a carder bee, which species he wasn't sure; a female on its unassuming quest to gather pollen. She reached the soft palate of his index finger and stopped, antennae twittering and enormous eyes pondering her surroundings. Price stretched his arm to its full length, his index finger pushed out further still. The bee waited a few seconds before taking flight, making a sweeping curve around Price's head and flying swiftly out of sight. Price had done it many times before, mostly late in the season when the bees were exhausted and sun bleached and waiting for death, accepting of their fate, but this bee was at the height of its powers, vibrant, strong and sure of its purpose.

He leant further against the sun dial and felt horribly sick.

FIVE

Dan sat at Maia's kitchen table listening intently and with disbelief to what she was saying. He'd turned up on her doorstep a few hours before, Braggle in tow, with an urgency to his questions, first telling her of the break-in and that he'd poured the liquid around some loosestrife in his garden, and then asking her to fill in all the gaps. Maia had been expecting him, had been planning what to say, telling Price's story piece by piece, chronologically.

Dan remembered how Price had kept him waiting at the Summer Solstice, his half-hearted excuse on his return, and shortly after, how he had rushed over to the nearest tree, bent over double, and wretched three times. Dan had put it down to the alcohol and had, once again, deliberately ignored it, pulling Braggle back as she tried to console him. Price had looked frail, his hand resting against the tree, head down, breathing heavily. Dan felt it as yet another betrayal, that Price had torn up any affection left from their very different encounter a few hours before. A reconciliation had felt palpable. Now it had vanished. And it was all Price's fault. As usual.

He remembered how Price had hugged Braggle with an exaggerated force, apologising to her for his behaviour, and how he avoided his stare, simulating an over affection for their dog rather than go through yet another act of contrition.

'I knew nothing about those men,' Dan said to Maia. 'Price mentioned nothing, not about those two anyway.'

'I know he was very secretive about it all,' Maia replied,

'but I thought perhaps he might have said something. I'm surprised he didn't say anything at all.'

~

Dan had taken Braggle home directly after the toast to the Ox-Eye daisy, the one event of the day that was non-negotiable. It took place at five o'clock across the Territories, or as close to it as the locals could manage. A group of five, chosen carefully according to their time keeping skills, would ring a bell to signal *the grand gesture to the ox-eye daisy*, or in effect, to the ultimate wisdom of the Reformation. A flag would be raised by the newest addition to the town and a short speech given by the oldest. It was always the same, give or take a few words.

Folly is the wisdom of the past in which deeds expressed as courage found their expression in destruction and hate. Generations have now passed. Many moons have waxed and waned. But the purity of The Change remains, seen all around you in the flora and fauna that flourishes and in the restoration of the delicate balance that nature so desperately required. We, as a species, remain at the fulcrum of that balance, ensuring its stability, enabling its continued success. There is no-one left who can tell us first hand of that momentous period in our history, their bodies now gracing the earth from whence they came, but we must remember that peace is not an ever fixéd mark and we must cherish and nourish the freedom we have, never taking it for granted, always alert. We are the sum of all things. Never a master. Always a friend.

An ox-eye daisy would then be raised into the air. And the final words spoken:

This is so. Let Be.

The speech was inviolate. Everyone standing and still, mouthing the words in tandem, those at home doing the same. It had an air of expectation and the stiffness of tradition, its staging overly theatrical and its brevity an anti-climax, but it was something tangible that gave everyone goose-bumps, and a sense of togetherness and pride which sealed the words into the very fabric of the town.

Dan stood at one end of the square, Price the other, both standing stock still, for different reasons. Dan once more brought his right hand to the left side of his chest, Price had his hands in his pockets, staring at the man who had raised the flag. He was wearing a pale, yellow suit with an ox-eye daisy motif and stood with his head raised high. Price was fifty metres away, a dense throng of people between him and the stage, yet he felt they were side by side and alone, his body melting in the intensity of the moment, droplets of sweat on his forehead glistening in the overhead sun. It was the man of whispers and an electric touch.

~

'Was that the beginning of something then?' Dan asked Maia.

'Not really,' she replied. 'They saw each other a couple of times but it very quickly fizzled out. It exhausted Price. You must have noticed it. He built it up in his head and then it just, sort of, collapsed in on

itself. I think this man was toying with him really. He'd only just come to the town and he was looking for experiences, new friends.'

'Did you ever meet him?'

'No, it didn't get that far, although Price talked about it incessantly.'

'Not to me.'

'No, not to you.' Maia looked away as she said it.

'Why are you telling me all this Maia? I mean, you say it didn't go anywhere, so why do I need to know this? What's it got to do with anything really? We all have our little infatuations.'

'I just thought you'd want to know. You said you wanted to know everything, and perhaps after this Price sort of gave up a little bit, felt that nothing good could happen to him anymore.'

'Did he tell you that?'

'Not in so many words, but you must have noticed a change in him, seen how … distant he'd become.'

Dan didn't answer. Of course he'd seen a change. He just hadn't given it too much weight. He'd seen it as the inevitable consequence of twenty years together, not a free fall due to some unrequited love.

'I'm sorry Dan,' Maia continued. 'I know it must hurt, trying to make sense of everything, but it's time to know the truth, to try and give you some sort of closure. Let's have some soup shall we. I'll heat up it up and then we can talk some more.'

She went to the kitchen whilst Dan stroked Braggle who'd been unusually quiet. He looked around the room. It seemed different, brighter. Had it been freshly painted? A vast antique cabinet filled one wall, the grain of the wood shimmering with a newly restored glow. And was that a new painting? It was large, abstract, old. The red strokes that glided freely across the canvas were cracked and the white background had lost its lustre. But it had quality.

'I got it a couple of months ago at the ArtBart,' Maia said later. 'I exchanged it for two rather ugly landscapes I had in my study.'

Dan couldn't remember them. 'I should go to the ArtBart more often,' he replied.

The soup was filled with vegetables that were a little too soft and some meatballs. Maia put some in a bowl for Braggle who ate the meat and left the vegetables.

'Don't be so ungrateful,' Dan said jokingly, but she walked slowly to the other side of the room and lay against the wall under a framed Delft ceramic tile, her head laid out flat on the carpet and her eyes fixed on Dan.

The two ate the soup at the table, conscious of trying to lighten the mood. They spoke of the forthcoming communal harvest, both dreading the prospect, and of the glut of tomatoes, although it hadn't been a good year for aubergines. The chat was polite and a little forced, both knowing it was a faintly disguised diversion before they returned to the main discourse.

Dan placed his spoon into the empty bowl and rubbed his

eyes with the palm of one hand. 'Thanks,' he said, 'I needed that.'

'It was a bit simple, I know. Next time I'll make something special.' Maia began to fidget slightly in her chair. She played with the ring on her index finger and brushed her tongue against her lower lip. 'I guess we should continue,' she finally said.

'Yes,' Dan replied. 'The bottle.'

'Yes, the bottle.'

'I guess the loosestrife will be dead by tomorrow?'

'Yes, it will.'

'But where did you get it?'

'It's complicated,' Maia said, 'and I'm afraid I can't tell you everything, not at the moment anyway.'

'But why did you give it to me at the market? Why didn't you just bring it to the house?'

'That's also complicated.'

'Maia, you can't just give me some sort of poison in the square, make me take off my shirt, and then leave me in the dark. It was you who told me to open my eyes remember. So please, tell me. What's it all about?'

He watched her drag her spoon around the edge of her bowl and suddenly drop it, making it clink against the porcelain as though she was ringing a bell.

'I have a confession to make,' she said. 'It's to do with Otto, and actually, it's all to do with Otto.'

~

Maia sat next to Price on the haystack under the linden feeling wretched. All Price could do was talk about himself and this new man he'd just met who'd whispered something in his ear. It was all of no consequence, just another of Price's little infatuations. Couldn't he see that *she* needed comforting? She needed someone to ask some questions, simple ones like 'what's the matter', and yet Price was impervious to her needs. He'd already irritated her by not wearing his decoration – another of his childish attention-seeking exploits. Theo had been no better, not saying a word as they walked to the Solstice festivities. He was looking drab to say the least, no effort made to get into the mood, his decoration about the only thing with any shine or colour. She'd spent weeks designing her outfit and it had received about as much praise as if she'd thrown on a potato sack. He had said something quite nice as they left the house, but it was too little, too late. She wanted enthusiasm. She wanted a bit of life. And to make matters worse, much, much worse, Otto had ignored her. Their paths had crossed just before his welcome speech; she hadn't expected anything profound, just a small recognition of their recent intimacy. Instead, she received a blank stare. She later confronted him, biding her time, finding the right moment and the right place, away from prying eyes. He'd disarmed her by grabbing her waist and pulling her roughly towards him, kissing her with such passion that her indignation gave way instantly.

She'd known Otto since she came to the town. His natural indifference had repelled her, so she had kept her distance, their paths occasionally crossing at communal functions. Otto wasn't one for gentle camaraderie and feigned merriment, his behaviour instead moulded by his exclusivity; his family had been landowners in the town for generations and had clung onto its long shadow despite the upheavals of the Reformation and the loss of its complete entitlement. He heard stories from his father and his father's father and they had become his own. Privilege in its old form had dissolved into the mud, but its heritage remained deeply embedded in the land around him. Unlike everyone else in the town, Otto had grown up there, had known his parents, his past. He was given no birth category although it was naturally assumed he was an alpha of the highest order. He lived in the house of his childhood, had seen the oak in their garden become proud and generous, and just like his father and his father's father, had become the town's de facto primus inter pares. He was afforded genuine respect for being a rare example of continuity, as fixed as the bricks and mortar and as steadfast as the constitution itself. His very presence in the town with his fixed, impermeable memories, gave others a solidity and purpose. The town's archives gave them perspective and Otto gave them depth.

But Maia had remained unimpressed. She hated the way he didn't look at her when they spoke, uninterested in what she had to say. She would find herself becoming haughty and disdainful in his presence, an attempt to put shine to her status. And yet she had always liked the shape of his face, the way his mouth tilted to one side when he was amused, never smiling directly or showing his teeth. She liked the sheer weight of him. He wasn't fat or indulgent and yet he seemed bulky. He had appalled and appealed for almost twenty years. Then things changed.

A couple of months before, she'd been riding her horse in the beech wood a couple of kilometres outside the town. It was late April and the light still penetrated the bridal path, shining on the bluebells and swathes of sweet-scented wild garlic. She had left early, leaving Theo to his breakfast and morning read. She trotted through the centre of the town, nodding to a few people as they headed for the distribution, and passed the demolished shebeen on the town's edge. A couple were walking a dog. A hare screamed away from her. She gave the reigns a jolt and the horse tightened its pace.

She could smell the ramsons before she entered the wood and felt the temperature fall as she passed the first trees. She relaxed the reigns and kept her head tilted to the skies, watching the light dictate the shapes above her, and the silhouettes of birds darting between the branches, their sounds competing with the gentle creaking of the trees. It took fifteen minutes to ride through the wood, the other side was wild pasture, and sitting on the base of a gnarled beech root was Otto, staring at the land before him. He must have heard the rhythmic thud of hooves on the soft path but chose to ignore it, giving the impression of someone deep in thought, oblivious to his surroundings. Maia didn't see him until she was almost beside him, her horse nervously shaking its head and scraping its right hoof on the ground. She showed no sign of surprise or nervousness, a product of her Academy and the importance it assigned to the art of composure. She politely asked him how he was. His reply was bland and non-committal. He asked her nothing. Maia got off her horse, prompting Otto to stand and look directly at her.

As she rode home, the exact sequence of events had squeezed themselves into an overriding sense of release. She took deep, long breaths, pulling the crisp spring air through her nostrils, feeling light and remarkable. Had she placed her hand flat against his shoulder first, or was it a response to a fleeting touch from him? She remembered their tongues meeting spontaneously and an exploration of each other's bodies that felt so natural, and an acquiescence from both so complete, that it felt like an episode in both their lives that would shape destinies.

Otto had dressed without a word and walked away, leaving Maia, still naked, under the beech tree. But his behaviour had seemed appropriate. And she wanted more. Much more. She took her horse to the same spot every day, at the same time, hoping to see Otto again. She would sit on the root of the beech, exactly where Otto had sat, and wait. He did not return. She went to every distribution. He was never present. Then at The Townhouse the following Saturday, when she knew he would be there, seated on the chancel, her desire for any form of contact threw aside her sharp sense of etiquette. After biding her time, she strode to the podium where the elders sat and spoke to Gilda Rosen who was perched on the far-right chair with her legs crossed so tightly it was a wonder any blood flowed beyond her knees. Their conversation was polite and irrelevant, as both had said barely a word to each other in the years they'd had the chance. Gilda was too plain for Maia and Maia was too clever for Gilda which, as a member of the elite (a word never used), she felt was too humiliating for comfort. And Maia had a natural grace which contrasted so sharply with Gilda's more robust frame that the two together was as incongruous as a beetroot sharing a plate with an asparagus. They talked without warmth for a few minutes, both waiting for it to end, until Maia made her excuses and moved gradually towards the G9 epicentre. She spoke to three others, including Petra, and then came to her catch. Otto had seen it coming and had tilted his head in the other direction.

'Hello Otto.'

No response.

'Otto.' A little louder.

'Oh, Maia. How are you?'

'Gilda was just telling me how good you are with horses.'

'Horses?'

'Yes, she said that you ride them with abandon.'

'It depends where I am.'

'Maybe that was you I saw the other day then – out beyond Forum wood. I saw someone there riding with *great* abandon.'

'That might well have been me yes. I often go along that way for a morning ride. Probably going tomorrow.'

'Well I hope you enjoy yourself,' Maia replied before moving on and nodding to his neighbour, another member of the G9 she barely spoke to, but now feeling an obligation to continue along the row.

Otto was there the next morning. Not with his horse. But he rode nonetheless with the abandon Maia was hoping for. The same the following week and every Sunday morning thereafter just as the sun poked through the wood and lit the wood anemones surrounding the beech tree. Their meetings had become a habit for both, perhaps even a necessity, for Maia especially, and her irritability towards Theo increased exponentially. He cooked, cleaned, gardened, bartered, in an attempt to improve her mood, but by the time the Solstice celebration arrived he had all but given up. He offered Maia a compliment on her Solstice outfit saying how the yellow flounces around her shoulder made her look like a charming Welsh poppy. Maia turned so abruptly away that the flounces, if they had been real petals, would have escaped their anchor and twirled with a flourish to the ground.

~

'I was a bitch,' Maia said to Dan at the dinner table as she clanked the soup spoon once more against the bowl. 'I just couldn't help myself. I was so wrapped up with Otto that I just couldn't bare being around Theo. I just couldn't even be civil to him.' She again dropped the spoon, as though it was too hot to handle, and poured a finger of apple brandy into her glass, offering Dan nothing. 'That's the day he found out about us. He saw us kissing. He didn't tell me that he knew until much, much later, kept it all hidden beneath that gentlemanly veneer. And stupidly, I allowed myself to believe that he knew nothing. Otto and I started seeing each other a lot after that and I'd say to Theo I was going off to do this and that, without really giving a thought to how flimsy my excuses were to leave the house. But he knew all along.' Maia took a slow sip of her brandy, licking the residue from her lower lip. 'He knew all along,' she repeated.

A silence followed. Maia stared down into the soup bowl, oblivious to Dan's presence. Dan stared at her, thinking how Price and Theo were lying in the communal pit, maybe next to each other, heads side by side, both being gradually broken down by the same fattened worms, uniting the two like they had never been in life.

'So Theo tried to poison you?' he said quietly.

Without looking up, Maia nodded her head.

'With the henbane?'

Another nod.

'But you found out and got there first?'

'Yes.'

'And is it henbane in the bottle you gave me?'

This time Maia looked up, and after a pause in which Dan wondered whether she was ever going to answer, she said no, it wasn't henbane.

'Then what is it?'

'It wasn't made by Theo.'

'That's not really an answer Maia.'

'I found it somewhere.'

'You just happened to stumble across some poison?'

'Sort of, yes.'

Dan began to tap his fingers on the table. 'Maia, why don't you just tell me?'

'I'm sorry Dan, I know it must seem strange, but it's hard. And I wish I hadn't given it to you.'

'But you did, and you gave it to me in the square where other people could see, so I think I have a right to know where

60

it's come from, don't you?'
'Yes Dan, you do.'
'So?'

Dan took the longer route home so that Braggle could pee and poop without being hurried. His torch lit the way, and he could see sharp beams of light in the distance as others walked their dogs or took advantage of the warm nights. The moon had not yet risen and he could hear the rustling of the trees and a robin sing, and Braggle's relentless sniffing along the hedgerow. The dog had been overly subdued in Maia's house and Dan purged his guilt by allowing her a free reign. So she went where she wanted, following scents, with Dan lighting her way.

And the walk was helping calm him down. He'd made his own way out of the house, leaving Maia in her chair seemingly weighed down by her own thoughts. She had still not told him everything and he kicked the side of the pavement in frustration. Price had always been so positive about her, talked about her as though she was something special. Dan couldn't see it. Over the years he'd tried to enjoy her moments of vivacity and charm, but somehow always came away feeling he'd been supplementary to requirements. She'd offered up some things which were good to know and gave a sharper edge to past events, and so why did he feel she was playing out a role in which she'd learned her lines to perfection. He couldn't quite allow himself to say that actually, when all things were stripped bare, he didn't like her much, for Price's sake, and yet it was moving closer to being spoken aloud and being made real.

Braggle sniffed her way to the outskirts of the town where the C_s and the D_s lived. Dan rarely came here at night. The darkness unnerved him. He shone his torch on the houses. They were smaller, more tightly packed, fewer trees and hedges. It gave him a feeling of not belonging, as though he was trespassing, even though he would often walk here during the day on his way to the sports fields to watch the games and the camaraderie and the laughter, anything to lighten his mood. And yet now, the silence felt harsh and threatening and he just wanted to turn back, to be on his side of town and in the comforting embrace of what he knew.

Braggle stopped by a garden filled with bright purple salvias that had turned a leaden red in the darkness. She rushed through the open gate, barked once and lay down on the edge of the garden on top of some withered ox-eye daisies. 'Shush,' Dan said and tried to drag her away by her collar. She barked again; a high-pitched tone which he'd rarely heard. 'No,' he said sharply and shone his torch on the house to make sure he wasn't disturbing anyone. It had freshly painted shutters and a panelled main door, possibly pre-Change, in remarkably good condition. Probably C_s Dan thought, they were always good with their hands. There were no lights on inside the house and Dan assumed they must be asleep, although, just fleetingly he thought he saw something move in the top window. 'Braggle, let's go,' he said quietly and firmly, 'that's enough, you're waking people up,' and when she refused to budge, he again grabbed her collar and tried to pull her back onto the path. She yielded, eventually, and Dan allowed her to dictate the way back, the sharp calls of a few song birds following them home.

It was gone midnight and as they reached the house, the torch guiding their way, Dan saw Maia sitting on the stoop. His heart sank.

'I'm so sorry,' she said standing quickly, 'I couldn't leave things as they were. Can I come in?'

Dan said nothing. He opened the door and walked in. Maia followed. She went straight to the sofa and sat with her legs together and her hands resting in her lap. Dan sat on the other side of the room with Braggle lying by his feet.

'I'd love a glass of something,' Maia said.

'Sorry Maia,' Dan replied, 'but that's not going to happen.'

It forced her into another apology which would probably have come anyway, only less punctured with uncertainty. She brushed her hands along the top of her thighs as though she was wiping away some crumbs, and cleared her throat. 'I was rude earlier,' she said, 'and you have every right to be annoyed.' She reached down and started taking off her shoes. 'It's just that it's difficult for me. And I hope you'll understand once you've heard what I have to say.'

'Try me,' Dan said.

~

With a plate of smoked pork and apple sauce in his hand, Theo left Price and Dan alone. Price had returned from the buffet with his shirt splashed with meat sauce and the two were being so tender with each other that he felt a little embarrassed being party to such intimacy, so he went to look for Maia despite the fact she'd probably continue to treat him like a spare part. He was never good in crowds and preferred to stand in her shadow where he could blend into the background. His deafness in one ear made it hard to orientate noise and he'd often have to crick his neck to listen to someone, sending a sharp pain down his side and arm relieved only by a stronger dose of the St. John's wort he grew in his garden. He called it his physic garden, basing his knowledge and content on centuries old archive material rather than the Reformation's standard texts. It took up far more space than was permitted, filling the bottom half of the garden with every *officinalis* and *vulgaris* he could get his hands on. Where others spent their energy refining their brandies, Theo distilled his natural remedies.

He lost his hearing at the Academy when a fellow pupil thought it would be fun to poke his ear drum with a sharp pencil. He should have known better than to try and break free from those pinning him to the floor, and should not have jerked at just the wrong moment. The pain was soothed using opiates from the Academy garden and started Theo's fascination, sometimes out of necessity, for medicinal plants. His expertise grew, and his reputation in the Academy spread. Teachers came to him for advice on their aches and pains and nervous disorders. He gave them prunella for their headaches and verbena to calm them down, rosemary for muscle pain and agrimony for diarrhea. By the time he was delegated, the Academy had requested a special dispensation for him to be given a garden large enough to accommodate his needs, and now, twenty years later, even though he would never say it, no-one knew more than he about what he called 'his cornucopia of pleasures'.

Theo put an ear plug in his good ear to dull the sound of the band as he passed the main podium. He searched the food stalls and the beer tent, but couldn't find Maia anywhere. He asked a few people if they'd seen her, but no-one had. He walked to the shade of the lindens. Nothing. And then he saw a glint of yellow, half hidden between the hedge and the stone wall that divided the outer perimeter of the square. Maia's dress had caught briefly in the sun. At first, he thought she was alone and then an arm released itself from her waist and a body peeled itself from hers. The two parted quickly in opposite directions.

~

'So he found out near the beginning,' Maia said, 'and said nothing about it. I had no idea he knew. Really. Not a hint. He continued as though nothing had happened. He knew it was serious because I kept it from him, all the others I'd been honest about and he'd sort of liked it, said it enhanced his fantasies, and wanted all the details. But this one remained secret and so he knew it was a threat.'

Dan kept silent, leaving her to continue her story uninterrupted.

~

Theo kept his counsel. He remained outwardly calm whilst his insides burned with a feeling he'd never had before. His body thudded from within each time Maia announced she was going for yet another ride on her horse, and the thuds jumped up in waves into his chest and throat. Maia's excuses to leave the house accelerated to the point of careless disregard and she quickly lost any compassion for Theo, becoming so consumed in her passion for Otto that he became a bystander in her life. When they sat each evening for dinner Theo avoided any mention of her wanderings and she approached their meals together with the nonchalance of someone with more important matters on their mind. She became more animated when they had guests, so she invited more, and entertained more, the superficial conversations lightening the mood, the excess of people a simple and necessary diversion from everything that remained unsaid, and Theo, as ever, watched from the sidelines.

And by the time of the autumn equinox, Maia declared she wanted a party. 'We shall call it our harvest aperitif,' she said to Theo, giving him little chance to refuse.

The communal harvest had taken place with its usual fanfare and the harvest festival was still a couple of weeks away. The aperitif would be its prelude, Maia said. She wrote fifty invitations, delivered them personally, leaving half of the guests to rush to the archives to find out what an aperitif was. It included Gilda Rosen who accepted her invitation with a studied refinement, as was expected from a town elder. Her contact with Maia had been minimal and strained, but in the past months Maia had made an effort to get to know her and the relationship had developed into something resembling a fragile friendship. Gilda adored gossip which endeared her to the majority of the town's population and Maia made the most of her indiscretions to discover more about her lover.

'Shall I invite Otto and Els?' Maia asked Gilda as she gave her the invitation. 'I know he never goes to these things, but it might be nice for her, I hardly ever see her around town.'

'You can always try,' Gilda replied, 'but I wouldn't hold your breath,' and she gave the sort of smile which Maia took as more of a challenge than the calculated inference it was meant to be. Half an hour later she was at Otto's door ringing the bell. Through the frosted glass, she could see the static figure of a woman at the end of the hallway. She rang again. The woman remained where she was.

'Does she know?' Maia asked Otto the next day as they rode side by side on their horses through the wood.

'Of course not,' Otto replied brusquely, 'but don't ever come to my house again.' His tone was firm, his body language cold, and Maia knew she'd crossed a line.

'I'm sorry,' she said, 'it's just that I thought it might be nice for the two of you to be there.'

'We're not coming,' Otto replied. 'And that's final.'

Theo helped in the preparations as much as he could. He went every day to the distribution and returned with wine, beer and brandy. It meant using up most of his bartering goods and putting himself into situations he'd rather avoid, but if it meant pleasing Maia, then so be it. He researched recipes he'd never cooked before, using ingredients he'd hardly ever used, spending days in the kitchen so the buffet would surpass all expectations and leave the town's culinary aficionados gasping with admiration, and with luck bring Maia back into his willing embrace.

The party started around three in the afternoon. Price and Dan were the first to arrive, Maia asking them to come a little earlier. Braggle came too and lay in the shade under the trestle table. The food had been laid out, petals from the last of the season's ox-eye daisies scattered between the bowls, a wheat sheaf was given centre stage, the drinks, mostly alcoholic, were on another trestle table under the pergola, and the rose-hip cordial was in a bowl in the kitchen for the few who abstained from anything with a proof, in public at least. That did not include Gilda Rosen who, despite being in the G9, considered alcohol a priority, without which the world and its people would be diminished, so she made no secret, at any opportunity, of showing her admiration for its life-giving properties. She arrived on the half hour, Maia clasping her hands and taking her to the pergola where she introduced her to the selection of drinks. Gilda began with a beer that looked more like treacle.

'Oh no, no, no,' she said screwing up her face, 'this is far too sweet,' and took another sip, then another. 'It tastes too much of raisins and figs. Mine is much better.' Theo came to join them and told them of ancient flavourings for beer. 'Henbane is meant to be the best,' he said, 'although I've never tried it myself.' He touched Gilda gently on her arm. 'Come with me,' he said in a hushed tone, and took the two of them to the bottom of the garden. He pointed to a creamy, ink veined flower. 'It's past its best, but that's the henbane. It has a very unpleasant smell.' He trod carefully between the other plants, tore off a section of the flower's toothed leaf and pretended to put it into his mouth. 'Every part of this plant is poisonous,' he said smiling, and putting a finger to his lips jokingly whispered, 'not a word to anyone.'

'My lips are sealed,' Gilda replied, 'but if you ever make some beer out of it, let me know, I'd love to try some,' and she returned to the pergola where she sniffed at a few of the bottles and poured a generous helping of tonic wine into her glass.

Maia kept to the rose-hip cordial and moved from guest to guest with all the aplomb of a host at the height of their fraternising powers. She smiled and laughed and joked, absorbed the praise with an 'oh, it was nothing' approach, and didn't think of Otto once.

At three o'clock or thereabouts, she rang a small brass bell, and putting one hand onto her chest, asked the guests to come closer. Theo stood next to her and clasped her other hand in his. She did not pull it away.

'Thank you all so much for coming,' she said, 'and I do hope you've been enjoying yourselves. We've been blessed with glorious weather and I'd be delighted if this little harvest aperitif of mine becomes as fixed in the calendar as the harvest festival itself.' She looked at Theo and clasped his hand tighter. She said something about enjoying the fruits of one's labours and appreciating the abundance of nature. It was little removed from the real harvest festival speech made every year and caused some in the crowd to move uneasily from foot to foot, including Gilda Rosen who had a niggling sense of being upstaged, as it was her turn to make the actual harvest speech, and on hearing sentences that could have been torn from the same page, she felt she had to say something and to smother any presumptuous behaviour before it got out of control. And although she considered herself to have that common touch, she was not averse, when necessary, in using her status to downgrade anyone she felt had upgraded theirs. So, when Maia had finished, Gilda stopped the gentle applause by waving her arm and making a gurgling noise with her throat. She stood next to Maia and Theo and said:

A lovely little speech Maia, but one can't help thinking it's come a couple of weeks too early. You've made us all very welcome here with your food and drink, and very fine it is too, but one can't help thinking it has a whiff of overindulgence to it, a little like gilding the lily before the lily has even flowered. We all know our FGD's of course. And maybe some have more potency than others, but the one I can't help thinking of at this moment is 'everything in moderation unless otherwise stipulated', and although I like good food, one can't help thinking that there are times when the flavours stick in the throat, as though we are being force fed a little too much of a good thing. And so, I salute your intentions, but suggest those intentions are not all good ones, so it gives me little pleasure, as a senior member of this community to declare that it is the harvest festival that must take precedence and not an aperitif that declares itself as something above its station.

The silence thereafter was only broken by a sharp howl from Braggle as someone stood on her tail as they moved backwards as though to protect themselves from the fallout. Maia, looking shell-shocked, released her hand from Theo's and was about to make an unreserved apology for overstepping the mark when Theo intervened. He clapped slowly three times and in a voice unused to sarcasm, said 'thank you so much Gilda, what a sweet, generous response that was. We welcome you into our home with open arms, feed you, offer all sorts of drinks, which quite clearly you have enjoyed more than most, and you pay us back with your own pathetic and petty little inflated ego.'

He was about to say more when Maia, pulling on his shirt, said sharply, 'no, do not embarrass me.'

'I'm embarrassing you?' he replied. 'Are you serious?' He moved closer to Gilda and poked her in the chest. 'Did you hear that,' he said with his face almost touching hers, 'I'm the embarrassment. You act like a complete and utter bitch, which comes as no surprise to me of course, and yet I'm the embarrassment.'

Maia grabbed his arm and pulled at him roughly. 'No,' she said again, her voice louder, 'stop it. Stop it right now.'

Theo flicked her arm away and caught her face. Maia slapped him. He slapped her back. Gilda shrieked and whacked the back of Theo's head with her fist. He turned, grabbed the lapels of her jacket and pushed her against the trestle table. Gilda grasped the nearest bowl, which contained the remnants of a salad niçoise, and hit him over the head. Her partner ran from the drinks table where she'd been enjoying the apple brandy, and threw herself into Theo's chest. The two grappled awkwardly like a couple of adolescents before Theo pushed her so hard she fell across the buffet and onto the grass. Bowls scattered. Gilda grabbed him around the waist. He shrugged her off and struck her lightly on the cheek. She collapsed to the ground as though she'd been whacked with a crowbar. Maia, screaming for him to stop, pulled so forcefully on his shirt that the seam under the armpit ripped and she fell clumsily to the floor. Theo then grabbed the table cloth with both hands and pulled it sharply. The rest of the contents of the *harvest aperitif* buffet spilled on to the three prostrate figures lying in various states of distress on the grass. Theo twisted the table cloth around them, pushed others away who tried to intervene, and walked out of the garden and away from the party.

~

Dan got up from his chair, went to the cabinet in the kitchen and poured two small brandies. He passed a glass to Maia who was still sitting in the same position on the sofa. 'So that's why he did it,' he said, 'it was bizarre, so out of character, but it was building-up over the months.'

'Not completely,' Maia replied. 'He'd shown bursts of temper before. I was just good at covering it up.'

'Really,' Dan said incredulously, 'Theo?'

'And do you remember what happened afterwards?' Maia asked.

'I remember everyone leaving really quickly and me and

Price staying behind to help clear up the mess.'

'Anything else?'

Dan also remembered Gilda's melodramatic exit as she was helped to her feet by a posse of men and left without saying a word, covered in the leftover juice of the carrot, honey, lemon and cumin salad, with the seeds of the cumin clinging to her greying hair as though she'd been dipped into a heap of mouse droppings.

'No,' he replied, 'nothing else, well, apart from Braggle eating the food on the grass and throwing up on the kilim when we got home.'

'You must remember what Gilda said as she left?'

Dan didn't.

'She was screaming at me that Theo was a maniac and that there would be repercussions.'

'Oh,' said Dan, 'I don't remember that at all.'

Maia began to relax. She pulled her hands from between her knees and rested one elbow on the arm rest.

'Don't you remember her throwing her arms in the air like a mad woman and being calmed down by her partner who had blood running down one side of her face? And then she became hysterical that her blood was staining her jacket even though it was already covered in honey and lemon juice.'

Dan searched for the same images but couldn't find them. 'I really can't remember,' he repeated.

'And of course, you know nothing of the tribunal?'

'What do you mean?'

'There was a tribunal a week later. No-one knows about it because Theo wanted it kept quiet, he was so embarrassed and upset by the whole thing.'

'What happened?'

'Oh, not much really. He just had to apologise, but he was deeply affected by the whole experience and just wasn't the same after that.'

'Carry on,' Dan said as he sat back down in the chair.

~

Theo left the tribunal humiliated. He apologised to Gilda

in front of the other eight members and she had made the most of it. Against Otto's advice she had forced Theo to kiss the left hand of those present and repeat each time 'violence is the territory of the weak and the realm of the ignorant'. Gilda liked the FGD's, using them at will to make her point. And despite her lax attitude in applying them to herself, she made sure to apply them to others when necessary, which in practice meant adding lustre to her status and diminishing that of her adversaries.

Theo stayed calm throughout, returning home quickly, making eye contact with no-one. Over the coming weeks he spent most of his time in the garden and the archives, not caring or perhaps even noticing Maia's comings and goings. He hardly spoke and rarely went to the distribution, leaving Maia to cook, which she did with reluctance and peevishness bordering on spite. The food was basic, the conversation almost non-existent and the tension unbearable, for Maia at least. Theo spoke when he was spoken to, as though the events of the previous few months had drained him so completely that he was incapable of interaction, and the occasions Maia refused to cook, he would shrug his shoulders and retire to another room. He became thinner and paler.

'That I do remember. We assumed he was ill,' Dan said.

Dan remembered how Theo had fallen into himself, and yet he'd done nothing to help lift him from his misery. He asked no penetrating questions, and allowed him to wilt without the comfort or support of friends. Maybe Price had been more sympathetic, but if he had, Dan knew nothing of it.

'I think Theo began to really despise me after that,' Maia said. 'He spent all his time in the garden, down at the end where all those poisonous plants are, and I think he just mulled over and over in his mind what had happened and started to blame me for his predicament.'

'And then one day he said he wanted to start cooking again.' Maia took off her shoes and brought her legs on Dan's sofa. 'And if you don't mind, I could really do with another drink.'

'Do you remember how sick I was?' she said as Dan handed

her the glass. She took a sip, felt the heat flow down her throat and made a short clacking noise with her tongue. 'For weeks.'

Dan did have some vague recollection of Maia being ill. Price had mentioned it a few times, saying how she'd been vomiting, but he thought it was just for a few days, a stomach bug or something similar. It wasn't unusual. There had been a severe outbreak the year before and an edict was announced curtailing all activities in the town for as long as was necessary.

'For weeks,' Maia repeated. 'I thought it was some sort of stomach bug, but every time I thought I was getting better, it would hit me again. Pains, oh the pains.' Maia clasped her stomach and groaned. A little too theatrically Dan thought.

'So Theo was poisoning you gradually with the henbane?' he said with quiet precision and little inflection.

Maia looked towards the window into the pure blackness of the night and slowly nodded her head still clutching her stomach. 'After a couple of weeks I started to suspect,' she said. 'I hadn't eaten for a few days and Theo suggested he make a soup, but when we were at the table I just couldn't face it and I said he could have mine. It was the way he refused it that suddenly made me wonder. He looked sheepish and tried to insist I eat it up, to regain my strength. It was like wiping the window clear.'

'So you returned the favour,' Dan said.

'I didn't mean to kill him. Honestly. I didn't.' She sounded defensive. 'I found all this dried stuff in a draw in the shed, all wrapped in paper and each one labelled, but not written in anything I could understand. He'd made up some sort of coding system. I just shook out a bit of each and put it in my pocket.'

'So it wasn't just henbane then?'

Maia looked away again, taking her time before replying. 'Well, probably most of it was henbane. It was probably a mix of all sorts of horrible things. So I gave it all to him, in a spring roll, with rice and a spicy tomato sauce.'

'And you didn't think it would kill him?'

'No, honestly. No,' Maia said adamantly. 'I just wanted him

to taste a bit of his own medicine.' She paused.

'That came out wrong,' she added hastily. 'I just wanted him to experience what I'd been through. I realised pretty quickly I'd gone too far.'

'So what happened?'

~

On the evening of his death, Theo's conversation was surprising and elaborate. He willingly accepted Maia's offer to cook and offered to pour an aperitif, though he apologised for using the word. They drank it together in the garden, watching the trees rattle in the breeze and losing the last of their leaves in giggling bursts. He said how good he felt and how much he was looking forward to Maia's food. He spoke almost without pause, going back and forth through his life as though picking blindly from a pack of cards splayed on the floor. He spoke of the boys in the Academy who pinned him to the ground every lunch time for a month just for fun and just because they could. He told her how, at the age of seven, he'd held the hand of the girl standing next to him as they queued to go into dinner. It was his first memory of touch. He caressed his own hand as he said it, gently rubbing his right thumb into the ball of his left palm. He told her of the wild flowers he picked every day in the spring, and how he'd put them in a vase on a table by the entrance of the dormitory. They were for everyone he said. No-one ever mentioned it, but he knew everyone liked it. He did it every spring day for more than a decade, relishing the chance to brighten up the room with the yellows of corn marigolds and the striking reds of the poppies whose petals would be scattered on the floor the next morning, and which he'd gather and place on the communal breakfast table, a red line snaking between the jam jars and the butter dishes.

He also told Maia something he said he'd never told anyone before.

Every pupil at the Academy had to get involved with the communal sowing of the crops in the fields around the estate. They were all A_s and as such were not obliged to take part, but the principal, a woman of stout beliefs and a vehement upholder of the core principles of the Reformation (a prerequisite for all Academy heads), insisted that, in one form or another, everyone should, for a few days a year, mingle with the lower orders and see up-close the essentials of modern agriculture. The tilling of the soil was done by machine, the green manure squelched into the ground as they moved almost silently across the fields releasing sweet smells that softened the air. Sowing took place in the first few months of the year depending on the crop and the weather. Theo always asked to be assigned to the fields, scattering the seeds, wearing a soft leather harness with large pouches that settled against each hip, returning to the storage barn for a refill once the pouches were empty.

In his final year, he was asked to help out in the barn. He hid his disappointment and arrived with the others at the allotted time to see C_s and D_s already at work pouring seeds from linen sacks into huge communal containers. The sacks were piled up in a pyramid on one side of the barn, with a person at each level handing one down at a time and then along a line of people to the containers where someone cut it open along its upper seam, making sure not to rip the cloth. This was Theo's task. He was given a curved, long knife with a wooden handle and was shown by the co-ordinator how to make a clean cut, 'it's like cutting into the belly of a deer,' she said, 'a vertical thrust, though not as forceful of course, and then a smooth sawing motion across the seam, like this. You can see the thread's quite tough, not as tough as sinew, but you still have to give it some elbow.' She touched Theo on the shoulder and laughed, 'of course, I'm talking hypothetically, I've never actually cut into a belly.' She gripped the knife firmly in one hand and gave him another demonstration with the sack upright so as not to spill any seed. 'That's it,' she said, and then told him to get on with it.

After a few attempts, he found his rhythm and after opening each sack pushed his hand, wrist deep, into the seeds to see whether he could guess which crop it was. He listened to the chatter and laughter of the others and settled into a routine, counting the sacks he'd completed and guessing correctly every time.

He opened number ten, and shoved his hand into the seeds. They felt different. He grabbed some and held them in his palm. They were much larger than the others, and black. 'Corncockle' he said under his breath. And then a little louder as though he couldn't quite believe it. He didn't know what to do. Should he carry on or should he alert someone? Surely it must be a mistake. A corncockle between the wheat and the barley and the oats? It had no function as far as he knew. It would add a touch of colour to the fields, but it would make the harvesting so much more difficult. He had to inform the co-ordinator. He found her outside sitting on a hay bale, looking out over the fields.

'It's not corncockle,' she said abruptly without hesitation.

'But it is, come and see,' Theo replied.

The woman stood up from the hay bale slowly. 'It is not corncockle,' she repeated with more emphasis. 'So just go back to your work and do what you're meant to do, and don't come harassing me again,' and she walked away.

Theo did what he was told. Went back to the line, apologised for holding them up, and continued dipping his hand into the seeds. Every tenth sack was corncockle. He knew it was corncockle. But he said nothing.

In the following weeks, Theo returned to the fields and saw them poking through the ground in the proportions he had expected. He'd come to the conclusion it was an experiment, perhaps for attracting insects or maybe for the pure beauty of a purple haze across the fields once they'd come into flower. And perhaps it wouldn't be so difficult for the C_s and D_s to pluck them, one by one, before the harvest. He would even be able to cut some and place them in his vase.

Then suddenly they were gone. He returned in the first week of June when they'd be coming into flower but all he saw was a mass of brown and shrivelled leftovers, merging into the soil.

'I've never told anyone about it,' Theo said to Maia. 'And actually, I'd sort of forgotten about it till these last few months.' He stared intently at her. 'What happened was so unfathomable that I almost started to believe that I was wrong, that I somehow imagined the whole thing. But these past few months have made everything totally clear. Now I know Maia. Now I know.'

And he said nothing more about it.

They ate inside. The table was laid simply with two white plates and two glasses. Theo had become more subdued and waited in silence for Maia to serve the food. 'It looks great,' he said, 'I can't wait to try it,' and before he put the food to his lips stared directly at her and said 'thank you.'

Within a few minutes he was clutching his stomach, after ten he'd started to vomit. The sheer violence of it took Maia by surprise, and each time she touched him he thrashed out, trembling uncontrollably. He looked at her one last time and his eyes were almost black. He walked through the house with an unsteady gait, bumping into walls, banging his head, and hitting out at something imaginary. 'There are animals,' he said. He found the toilet, locked himself in, and Maia heard groaning, vomiting, groaning, vomiting. Then a thump and nothing more.

~

Maia's legs were stretched out on the sofa, one foot tapping against the arm rest, and as she described Theo's final moments, Dan thought he could see a vulnerability so complete that if he poked her gently she would collapse on to the floor and cry till she was raw. There was a heaviness to her that changed the shape of her face. She closed her eyes and drew in the air through her nostrils, visibly raising her chest and shoulders.

'So that's it,' she said.

Dan knelt on the floor and stroked Braggle gently across her back. The dog opened her reddened eyes, stretched her legs, emitted a long, audible sigh and went straight back to sleep.

'You still haven't told me what was in the vial?' Dan said without looking up at Maia. 'I'm guessing it's not henbane then.'

'No,' Maia replied, 'but it's just as poisonous. I told you the story Theo told me because it's important, and he knew it was too. You see, he found out it's still happening. They're still using poison on the fields.'

'Did he tell you that himself?'

'No, Price told me.'

'Price?'

'Yes, Price knew about it too.'

Dan shook his head in disbelief as though he'd just been told the world really was flat. He remembered Maia telling him in the market place that Price was involved, but he'd pushed it aside as one does a bad dream.

'It shouldn't surprise you Dan,' Maia continued, 'I did mention it yesterday.'

'Actually Maia, you said very little yesterday,' Dan replied irritatedly, 'and yes, it does surprise me considering Price said nothing, absolutely nothing to me. Ever.'

'I told you that he didn't want to worry you.'

'I'm not made of cotton wool Maia.'

'He felt that you'd be more intimidated by it than he was.'

'Well he was wrong,' Dan said firmly. 'And you still haven't told me where you got the poison from.'

'Where do you think?' Maia snapped. 'Isn't it obvious?' She gave him a withering look and then covered her face with the palms of both hands, bringing them slowly down towards her neck, and with the ends of her fingers, pinched the loose skin under her chin. 'Surely, it's obvious.'

D an had a bad night. He went to bed around three but couldn't sleep. Maia had told him so much that it was difficult to untangle the mess. And it was a mess. And what he couldn't fathom was how he'd been kept completely in the dark, and why. It gnawed at him more than anything else. Was he not to be trusted, or was it staring at him the whole time and he was just incapable, or too self-absorbed, to notice any signs? He could now have a go at unravelling it piece by piece to create a vague picture of the past year, but as he lay on his back looking up at the bedroom ceiling, the overriding sensation was one of betrayal, and that if Price had confided in him, at any moment, then perhaps he'd still be alive.

He did sleep, eventually, with the help of Theo's sleeping potion, a Solstice present a few years before that had remained untouched, by him at least, in the bathroom drawer. There was no label, and as he brought the small brown bottle to the light he could see it was half empty. Theo had said something about the root of valerian and probably something about how much to take, but it was so long ago and Dan was so tired and he so wanted to fall into the deepest of sleeps that he took a generous swig.

When he awoke, he felt he'd been dipped in alcohol and left to dry in the sun. His head throbbed mercilessly which endless glasses of water refused to budge. He opened the back door to let Braggle out and she ran immediately to the end of the garden and pooped under one of the elders. He was disoriented and stiff and unable, even staring up at the greying sky, to decipher the time of day. He walked in a daze around the garden, his eyes half closed from the sharpness of the light, and stumbled slightly as he trod on a mole hill, feeling a twinge in his back. He did a few simple stretches against the plum tree and walked back into the house leaving the door open so Braggle could make her own way in.

In the bathroom, he slowly undressed and stepped into the shower. He pressed the on button and the warm water hit his head and shoulders with such a welcoming embrace that he made a noise of exquisite relief. He held his face towards the shower head and clasped his arms across his chest, and could have stayed in the same position for hours. But after exactly three minutes the high-pitched beeper went off and the water went instantly cold, taking Dan so much by surprise that his arms jerked sideways and knocked the ceramic soap dish onto the floor of the shower, breaking the dish in two. He bent down to pick it up and a piercing sharp pain tore across his lower back causing him to crumple on to the floor, half in the shower, half out, and each time he tried to move, a searing spasm ripped through his back. It took him half an hour to crawl on to the bathroom floor, but he could go no further.

His back was his weak point which had rendered him helpless for many weeks on numerous occasions, the only positive being how Price became kinder, doing everything in the house until he was able to move more freely. He cooked and cleaned, spoke in softer tones, stroked Dan's head as though he were a cat, became his crutch and nurse. And despite the excruciating pain each time he tried to move in those first few days, it felt almost worth it to see his partner's other side. Now he was alone and becoming uncomfortably cold. A draft was sliding up from the open back door and biting into his wet skin. His clothes and towel were a few metres behind him, so he slid in tiny increments towards them uttering squeals of pain along the way. He just needed to grab something to wipe away the cold and cover himself until he could, somehow, go further.

And then came a knock on the front door. It sent Braggle

tearing down the stairs in pursuit of the noise. 'Please, please, don't let it be Maia,' Dan said to himself. He heard Braggle's outlandish barking become more distant and finally stop. She's gone outside he thought.

Necessity may well be the mother of invention, but in this case, it was also a very welcome anaesthetic. Without knowing how, Dan seized the towel and placed it, like a shroud, over his nakedness. Braggle came bounding back up the stairs and into the bathroom, stared at Dan for a couple of seconds, wagging her tail with an extra zeal, and then ran back down the stairs, huffing out puffs of excitement. Dan then heard a man's voice. Did he just say 'Braggle'? Then at least it's someone he knows. Yes, there it is again, 'Braggle', louder this time.

The man walked into the bathroom and stood by the door, arm resting against the frame, staring at Dan prostrate on the floor with a bright red towel covering him from ankles to chin. He said nothing. Dan tensed his muscles in embarrassment and yelped as another spasm sent a violent surge of pain coursing through his body. He muttered a breathless apology and closed his eyes for a few seconds to compose himself.

'Could you help me,' he asked nervously, 'I can't move.'

The man took a few paces and stood over him, still impassive, still staring at him as though he was a stuffed animal in The Museum of Extinction which all Academy children were obliged to visit once a year.

'You're in pain?'

'Yes. A lot.'

'What can I do?'

'I need a painkiller. There's a bottle in the cabinet in the hallway. Second shelf.'

'I know where the painkillers are,' the man said with a deadpan expression, and left the room. Braggle went with him, springing up against his legs as though a ball was about to be thrown. 'Not now Braggle,' he said gently, and shuffled the hair on her head.

He returned to the bathroom with the bottle, put a few drops into a glass with some water, knelt down next to Dan and carefully guided the liquid into his mouth.

'Thank you,' Dan said as he took the final sip, 'I'm not quite sure what I would have done without you.'

The man didn't reply.

Dan gripped the edge of the towel with both hands and pulled it further towards his chin. 'It's Tom isn't it.'

The man sat slowly down on to the edge of the bath. 'You remember,' he said almost in a whisper.

'Of course.'

'I wasn't sure you would.'

'I'm hardly going to forget *you* am I,' and as Dan said it, another spasm shot through his body making him shout out in pain. He closed his eyes and between deep breaths said 'I'm hoping that stuff should kick in quickly. I always have it in the house, for my back.'

'And for Price's migraines,' the man said impassively.

Dan let the remark go. This man, whom he'd only ever met once before, was saying the oddest things and making him uneasy, but he was also his only hope of getting into the bedroom and onto the bed.

'Can you help me up?'

Half an hour later he was lying on the bed, a sheet covering his nakedness in place of the towel which had been discarded in the bathroom leaving Dan feeling more vulnerable than ever. Every movement, one small step at a time, was like being stabbed anew, not helped by his helper who offered no word of encouragement as they made their way across the hallway, arm in arm, and whom Dan couldn't help thinking was enjoying his discomfort. When he finally reached the bed, with one gruelling heave he fell exhausted onto the mattress, uttered a barely audible thank you, closed his eyes and fell asleep.

When he awoke, maybe an hour later, Tom was sitting on a chair in the corner of the room with Braggle between his legs on the floor. Dan shuffled slightly and groaned as it set off another spasm. Tom sat on the edge of the bed and offered him some water he'd set on the side table.

'I can't thank you enough,' Dan said after drinking the whole glass in fitful gulps.

Tom said nothing.

Dan repeated his thank you, and seeing that Tom's eyes were filling with tears, touched his hand.

'Tom, why are you here?' He said it gently, no hint of accusation.

It took a few seconds for Tom to respond. A few jumbled words came out of his mouth which Dan couldn't understand and the tears began to drip down his cheeks as he twisted part of the top blanket between his fingers, his shoulders twitching up and down as he tried to control himself. He took out a red kerchief from his pocket and blew his nose. 'I will not apologize for it,' Tom said, rubbing his eyes. 'I will not apologize for crying.'

'I didn't ask you too,' Dan replied, squeezing his hand, and asked him to put another pillow under his head so he could look at him without straining his neck.

'Tom, what's going on? I can hazard a few quick guesses, jump to a few conclusions, but please, what's this all about?'

'I didn't want to come, but seeing you and Braggle last night.'

'What do you mean you saw us last night?'

'You were in my garden.'

'That was your place?'

'So you weren't there deliberately?'

'No, Braggle practically dragged me there. I didn't see *you* though.'

Tom walked over to Braggle, knelt on the floor by her side and hugged her. 'Price didn't tell you then?'

'I'm guessing the two of you were seeing each other.'

'Yes.'

'Ever since what happened between us last year?'

Tom guffawed. 'You really don't know anything do you.'

~

Price's hand was wayward. He couldn't help himself. He just needed to glimpse at Tom and he'd want to touch him, stroke his hair, pat a buttock, caress a thigh, squeeze his fingers, fondle just about any part of him; no, every part of him. Tom liked it, called it Price's ache, but not this morning. They were in Price's house and Dan would be coming back from the distribution any minute, so any 'aching' would be highly inappropriate. Tom had heard a lot about Dan, how quiet and unassuming he was (Price had never said the word boring, but he guessed that's what he meant), and he wanted to meet him, curiosity and impulse had dictated it would happen, and so Price had suggested the following day, a Thursday, knowing it was Dan's favourite distribution day (eight varieties of potatoes) and he'd be out until at least midday. Price had wanted to show Tom the house first, but Tom had arrived late and there was just enough time to show him under the bathroom sink in case some justification was needed for Tom's presence in the house. Price had told him to wear something workmanlike and to bring along a few tools, a spanner certainly, that's useful for anything, and a screwdriver, every C_2 has a screwdriver in their pocket don't they? 'Not this one', Tom had replied, 'although I'll see what I can come up with'. They both giggled. They did that a lot.

Dan arrived just after midday and Tom rushed to the bathroom. Price was sitting at the kitchen table pretending to read a new book he'd downloaded from the Archives called *The First Hundred Years*. In reality, since meeting Tom at the Solstice celebrations, he had been nowhere near a book, couldn't concentrate, could never get past the first few paragraphs without his thoughts moving back to his lover.

Dan plonked two canvas bags on to the table with a thud, and took out one large potato. 'It's an agria,' he said, 'they're saying it's been one of the best crops for years. I'm going to make a dauphinoise with it, it'll just need a bit of rosemary, *et voila*'. Dan was bordering on sprightly, the Thursday distribution tended to have that effect on him. He sat down and picked up the blue jacket on the back of the chair. 'This isn't yours is it?' he said.

'There was a leak,' Price said, 'there was water everywhere, so I called the emergency line.'

If Price had called the emergency line, he would have picked up the connector and pressed the go button. It was used predominantly by the A_s, as their technical skills were

83

hopeless at worse, hapless at the very least. In fairness, Dan tried to do as much as he could (within limits) and once took a carpentry course which helped over the years with repairing shelves and tables, but it all seemed a little frivolous when compared to C_s or D_s who were practically weaned on grease and wood shavings. Leaks however, no matter how small, were definitely a matter for emergency technicians.

'He's upstairs, and I must say, very sexy.'

Dan took little notice. He was used to Price's simplistic musings over other men, and knew his 'type' well enough.

'Is he blond, tall and younger than you,' he asked.

'Might be,' came the rather deflated reply.

Tom came into the room a few minutes later. He was holding a spanner in one hand and a wet towel in the other, and told them, with a smile, that all was fixed.

'What was the problem?' Dan asked. It stymied Tom, who could only say something vague about u-bends; he felt infinitely more comfortable with dove-tail joints and fine-scale planing.

'Would you like something to drink?' Price asked, 'you must be exhausted after all that heavy toiling under the sink.'

'Well, I wouldn't exactly call it that,' Tom replied cautiously, 'but yes, a drink would be very welcome, thank you.'

Price didn't ask him *what* he wanted to drink and tapped some mint water from the glass vat. 'Something tells me you might like this,' he said teasingly. It made Tom nervous.

' And this is Dan, my very lovely partner, and the maker of your very delicious minted water with a hint of elderflower.'

'It's not elderflower,' Dan interjected, 'it's infused with a little lemon grass. And you know that, you know I grow it in the greenhouse.'

'Elderflower. Lemon grass. All much of a muchness,' Price replied smiling.

'They're about as much the same thing as a cow is to an owl.'

'You're quite right. My sincerest apologies. I stand before

you humbly corrected and bow before your infinitely superior knowledge of culinary matters.'

Tom and Dan looked disconcertedly at each other and then laughed simultaneously.

'Don't worry,' Dan said, now looking at Price, 'we're laughing *with* you, not *at* you.'

But the ice was broken and the three of them sat at the table and chatted freely. Dan liked him and asked questions he would normally only save for A_s. He heard how Tom had only recently arrived in the town, that he was still waiting for his new life partner to appear because the first one had had the misfortune to die the week before the home-coming, and that it was proving very difficult to find a replacement. Tom asked him if he'd seen him lift the flag at the Solstice ceremony, or at least noticed the suit he was wearing with the ox-eye daisy motif; it was made especially to his specifications, a gift given each year to the person chosen to raise the flag. Dan said he had no memory of it, but most likely because he was distracted by Price's abysmal behaviour that day. 'He'd just vomited under a tree,' he said.

Price remained quiet, locking his memory into that Solstice Eve and the young man in his red shorts standing so close that the hairs on his arm stood on end.

'Do *you* remember him?' Dan asked Price.

'Alas not,' he said, 'but I can't imagine why. Tell me Tom, are you a homotype one hundred per cent?'

Tom blushed. He could see the mischief on Price's face who then stood up, walked behind him, and started massaging his shoulders. Dan watched, saying nothing. Price pushed his hand down Tom's T-shirt and started stroking his chest with his palm. Dan was unable to speak, watching Tom tense up and heave his chest upwards as he tilted his head back and closed his eyes. The two men kissed and Price's hand moved gradually towards his stomach. Dan stood up, walked over to them, pulled up Tom's t-shirt and began to gently slide his fingers along his mid-riff. He knelt down and licked his nipples and chest hair, listening to Tom's heavy breathing and Price's words of encouragement.

~

'So you already knew each other,' Dan said as he lay rigid on the bed, unable to move.

'Yes,' Tom replied. 'We met on Solstice Eve and then again the next day, which is when it really took off.'

'So you'd already been seeing each other for a few months when you came to the house?'

'Yes.'

'I guess you just wanted to meet his silent partner.'

'Something like that, yes.'

'And you've been his lover for more than a year?'

'Yes.'

'And all that stuff that happened in the kitchen, that was all prearranged?'

'No, not at all. I had no idea Price was going to do that.'

'Oh,' Dan said. 'Good. I guess that makes it a bit better.'

Tom was sitting on the edge of the bed looking at Braggle who lay on the floor next to him. He turned slowly to Dan and said: 'He was not my lover, he was my life.' He lowered his head, his tears dropping onto the sheet. 'I wasn't going to come here. I just couldn't face it. Didn't know what I'd do when I saw you, or what I'd say. I thought you'd killed him because you found out about us, but that's not true is it. You knew nothing, amazingly, you knew nothing.' Tom's voice became louder and higher. 'Did you not even suspect? How can you live with someone and not see that anything was wrong, different, changed. Completely changed? Are you blind?'

Dan lay on the bed with two pillows holding up his head. He wanted to spring up and run out of the room, avoid these accusations. How could he possibly not have suspected? Of course he knew Price's behaviour had changed, but it hadn't entered his head that he'd met someone who made him feel vital and alive.

Tom pulled some of the sheet up to his nose and blew hard. 'Don't worry, I'll clean it. You're in no fit state to do anything are you? Not even clean yourself.' He sniffled and unblocked

86

his throat with a gruff cough. And still not looking at Dan said, 'why, why did you do it?'

Dan told him what he told Maia; how he'd just snapped, couldn't take any more of Price's indifference, his intolerance of everything he said, his disinterest even in the food he dished up. It was nothing pre-meditated, it was just a moment of madness, of inexplicable violence, an action so tight in its construction, that perhaps it was also inevitable, not the absoluteness of it, but the motions towards it, and an atmosphere so febrile that everything had aligned and combined to disturb the rational thoughts of a rational man.

'It's still no excuse,' Dan said, 'but it's the only explanation I can give.'

Tom had heard various stories, all nipping at the truth, but now that he knew the precise details, making it solid, it all somehow dissolved, pushing the events into another realm, dragging them into a terrible past instead of an acute and interminable present that refused to give way. He remained quiet, unable to bring words to his thoughts, and when Dan's fingers touched his hand lightly, he brought his other hand across and gently laid it on top.

'Do you know Maia?' Dan eventually said.

Tom's reaction made him jolt, sending another tortuous spasm swirling through his body, and an expletive, that Dan rarely used, to come out of his mouth. Tom had spontaneously jerked his hand away and made a sound so contemptuous that Dan was left with no illusions about how he felt about her.

'Oh yes, I know Maia. Of course I know Maia.'

'It's just that, well, she told me you were just a fleeting presence in his life.'

Tom laughed. 'I bet she did. Has she been here?'

'Yes, we've had a long chat.'

'Oh, she must have been terrified.'

'Terrified?'

'She would have been trying to find out how much you know; about me, about Price, about Theo, about Paul and Otto, about the experiments and the field trials.' Tom paused, and tilting his head, looked quizzically at Dan as he would a frog with two heads. 'What *do* you know?'

Tom could see on Dan's face that he really didn't know anything. Price had told him so, but he couldn't believe that it was possible to live in the same house, share the same dinner table, the same bed, and still have it all fall under the radar.

'You know nothing about any of it? Seriously?'

Dan bobbed his head methodically against the pillows, desperate to burst out of the bed and away from these questions. He felt ridiculous. Foolish.

'Tom, I wish I could say yes, but I don't. I really don't. All I know is what Maia has told me, and that's only in the last few days.'

'What *has* she told you then?'

'I could see she was nervous,' Dan replied, 'little things she did which weren't like her at all.'

'Did she tell you that she and Price had fallen out?'

'Not exactly no, but I knew something wasn't quite right.'

Tom laughed disdainfully. 'That's an understatement,' he said. 'He hated her.'

'Hated her? I can't believe that Tom. They were best friends.'

Tom stood up and walked to the window. He looked down onto the garden and watched some red admirals darting playfully above a clutch of verbena. Without turning, he said again 'what has she told you?'

Dan's story took a while, there were pauses when Tom helped him pee into a glass jar and took Braggle out for a short walk, and as the light began to fade, he disappeared to the kitchen and returned with a simple dinner of potatoes and beans on a tray which he placed gently on Dan's chest and tied a towel around his neck to absorb any splashes.

The two sat in silence as the bedroom darkened, the clink of cutlery the only sound. It was a welcome break from the intensity of their conversation and a distraction from the revelations which had left them both exhausted. Dan stretched across the bed to turn on the side light and groaned as the pain once again tore into his lower back.

'Let me do that,' Tom said, and as he flicked it on he saw the light glimmer in Dan's watering eyes.

'Thank you so much,' Dan said. 'I can't believe how nice you're being.'

'No, neither can I,' Tom replied.

'You're very welcome to stay the night,' Dan said, 'the sofa downstairs can be made into a bed and
Braggle would clearly love it.'

'No,' Tom answered without hesitation, 'too many memories. But I'll come and check up on you.'

'Thank you,' Dan said again.

SEVEN

T om's Homecoming was on the first of May and he'd arrived in the town unaware his life partner had died from the pox the previous week. They told him once he'd entered his new home, and to sweeten the blow offered him the coveted position of flag raiser which he had no hesitation in accepting.

He was a little relieved that Stephen, his life-partner to be, was dead. The holograms he'd seen had been disappointing to say the least. He expected at least a frisson of excitement when he pressed play for the first time, instead, it was more of a soggy limpness that engulfed him, as though he'd been served a dish with little spice or flavour. He knew his own specifications, which he'd so meticulously detailed in the wish form and interviews, were just guidelines and that, ultimately, the decision was out of his hands, and that stating his preferred age was 'mature' was just wishful thinking, but it still came as a disappointment that few of his suggestions had been considered, and the most important criterion - the hairy bit, had been overlooked altogether - his dead partner had about as much chest hair as a spotty adolescent and his white legs seemed to glow with a shiny smoothness. When he'd queried the match, he'd been told these were superficial requirements and they'd been joined because of their uncompromising gene match.

He was given the flag raising honour, he was told, to sweeten the bitter pill of disappointment and sorrow, an assumption he was more than willing to propagate. His

acting skills (he was always the lead in his Institutions theatre productions) came into good use for what he considered to be a suitable mourning period, the ending of which coincided with the Solstice celebrations. So by Solstice Eve he was released (and relieved)
to mingle without hesitation or guilt, and he was determined to make the most of it. He stayed to watch the sun rise, chatting and dancing and drinking freely, enjoying his new life away from the Institution and experiencing life in the raw, where, for the first time, he was able to do whatever he liked without time constraints or timetables holding him back.

He was surprised by how many men he found attractive, helped by the alcohol glossing over imperfections and the twilight dimming the blemishes. Tom glided happily between people, introducing himself and feeling at ease in the company of others, and by the time the sun began to rise he found himself standing next to an older, hairy man whom he fully intended to flirt with, in a controlled and respectful fashion. The man had clearly over-indulged, his shirt was around his waist, revealing a welcome surplus of greying chest hair, and the zip in his trousers was undone, probably more by accident than design.

Custom dictated everyone held hands as they waited for the first glimpse of the new sun, and as the darkness gently ebbed away, Tom held the man's hand lightly at first, allowing his middle finger to wander across the man's palm, tightening his grip as a slither of sun finally appeared on the horizon. They didn't speak or look at each other, and as people started to leave Tom felt an irrepressible urge to whisper in his ear. He didn't know what he would say and in the end just a simple 'goodbye' came out. Then he walked away, giddy with tiredness and excitement.

He had one of those enviable complexions that exhibit no signs of over-exertion or fatigue, even after a night of considerable excess, and after just three fitful hours of sleep his skin was still taut and alive. He told everyone who commented on it that he never used lotions or creams. The reality was a little different. After a slow late breakfast, he spent the next hour covered in thinly sliced cucumber, followed by a self-made mud facial.

After showering, he tried on his new Solstice outfit one more time which had been designed especially for the occasion as a gift for the flag raiser. It hugged his outline to perfection making him, even if he did think so himself, something of an Adonis. Tom adored the subtle ox-eye daisy motif, marvelling at its creation and how each flower rose delicately from the weave of the cloth intertwined every now and then with a delicate outline of pansies and columbines. He'd been very specific about the cut and the motif which mustn't be too garish or overstated, and the yellow had to be a gentle, late summer yellow. He brushed his hands over it, savouring the texture and the quality, then took the suit off and laid it out carefully on his bed, as he would a precious heirloom. He put it back on two hours before the ceremony, made sure his hair was fixed in place with a particularly viscous aloe vera gel, and before heading off took one last look in the full-length mirror in the hallway which, more often than not, made him feel better about himself. It gave him the incentive to forge an impression of someone far removed from a C status, a ranking which had always rankled, and which, even as a child, he felt was a terrible mis-judgment on the part of the authorities, and he wondered whether Stephen's mishap was, in fact, a saving face acknowledgment that pairing him with another C_2 had been a mistake all along and his next partner just might be a few ranks higher.

For now, he was free to do what he liked without the constraints of a life partner. He had a home all to himself for the very first time, and didn't have to worry about waking others or preparing food for others or being told what to do by others. There were no curfews, no eviscerating responsibilities and no rules (at least not ones that felt so tangibly directed at him). Tom had been testing the waters the past few weeks, getting to know people, orientating himself to his new surroundings, working on his home and garden, and just gently taking his time, waiting for his moment to be presented to the town at the Solstice festival celebrations; it was then he would truly belong.

When he stood on the podium in the middle of the square in his fabulous ox-eye daisy suit, feeling once more like the lead actor in a school play, and after having raised the flag with such prowess that it didn't stutter up the pole like an inexperienced boy climbing a tree but glided effortlessly skywards as though defying gravity, he smiled in a way he thought both enticing and enigmatic, waiting for admirers to surround him and adorn him with praise. Otto said a couple of encouraging words with some of the other G9 elders, although few mentioned his suit and none went beyond the artifice of an official occasion, playing their roles according to Solstice protocol which involved being seen and politely detached. So when they quickly disappeared and left him alone on the podium, his smile evaporated and he did his best to look occupied by pretending to tighten the halyard around the cleat, words he learned in preparation for his flag raising duties. He looked up at the limp flag showing no signs of life on such a still, sunny day, and in a hushed voice said, 'I know how you feel'. A tap on the shoulder brought him back to ground level.

'I've been looking for a beautiful man in red shorts, not one in a suit covered in ox-eye daisies,' the man said, 'you look breath-taking.'

Tom's smile returned. 'That's very kind of you,' he replied. 'It's a lovely suit isn't it. It was made especially.'

'I can see. You certainly stole the show.'

'Oh, I don't know about that.' Tom giggled, trying to remember if he'd met this man before.

'I'm Price by the way. We met last night.'

Tom's nonplussed expression sent a shiver of disappointment through Price as though he'd been doused in cold water. 'Last night,' he repeated, 'as the sun came up.... we stood next to each other.... we held hands.... you whispered in my ear.' Each sentence was uttered with slightly more desperation, forming a question in his mouth rather than a statement of fact, but by the time he'd finished, Tom knew exactly who he was, not by sight, but from information, and he could see well enough that this man, with dark rings under his eyes which resembled bruised apples, had seriously over-indulged the night before.

'Oh .... you.... of course, I remember you ... we watched the sun come up ... yes, yes, we held hands ... hi ... I'm Tom,' and he held out his hand in recognition. Price grabbed it with both his, engulfing it, crushing it with heartfelt enthusiasm, shaking it until Tom was forced to pull his hand away in fear of permanent damage. 'You have a sharp eye for detail,' he said, 'you're the only one who's mentioned anything at all about the ox-eye daisies.'

'They're exquisite,' Price replied, and brushed his hand along one sleeve just as Tom had done earlier in the day. 'Extraordinary craftsmanship. And what are those other flowers?'

'Wow, you really do notice everything. They're pansies and columbines.'

'Must have taken an age. Did you have a hand in it?'

Tom laughed, and then realised he wasn't joking. And before he could reply, Price pulled two chairs close together, dragging them loudly along the podium floor with such purpose that Tom sat immediately in one as though he'd been given a direct order.

Price sat down in the other chair, clasping his hands together with his fingers bobbing restlessly up and down, and leaned forward so his head was almost touching Tom's. He gushed with hyperbole using words Tom had never heard before and which he promised to himself he would look up when he got home. He found it endearing and a little embarrassing, and after a few minutes leaned forward himself and squeezed Price's thigh as if to say 'that's enough'.

Price understood the gesture. 'I'm talking too much aren't I,' he said, 'I'll shut up.' He pulled his chair even closer and looked directly into Tom's eyes. 'So tell me a bit about yourself. How long have you been here? Who are you with?'

Tom felt as though he was auditioning for a part in a play, but Price's questioning felt real and warm, and without realising it, he pulled his own chair closer until their knees were touching. He told him a little of his arrival in the town, and how he was still adjusting to post Institutional life despite the year of preparation with countless lectures and the three months in the Half-way Town where he'd learned how to barter and get used to the outside world. The two shared experiences and how, over the course of twenty years, little had changed, Price remembering his own time in his Academy's adjustment camp, as it was then known, and laughing when he recognized Tom's stories as his own, although his status, as an A_3, was far higher. As he laughed, he placed his hand on Tom's thigh and gently stroked his middle finger against the cloth of his suit as Tom had done the night before in the palm of his hand, and as though it was the most natural thing in all the world.

'Would you like to see my house?' Tom suggested.

Perhaps all humans are creatures of habit and need patterns and permanence to define their existence, and perhaps the shapes formed can be ragged and inappropriate, but Tom and Price signed up enthusiastically to its import and over the following months became rapidly accustomed to the habitual thrust of being wanted and appreciated and loved. Price had taken possession of Braggle's morning walks, telling Dan how, after years of procrastination, he'd decided to do something about his fitness, and the best way would be breathing the morning air in large doses. Dan saw how Price enjoyed it; he seemed chirpier after his walks, although by the afternoon had often reverted to type, so he suggested he take Braggle out for his evening walk too. It hurt him to see how Price accepted the invitation with alacrity and how obvious it was that his partner's humour was directly related to how little he saw of him.

Price told Maia about Tom, offering up all the details. She seemed disinterested at first and declined to meet him, listening to Price's full accounts of his new, secret and utterly delightful life, whilst asking very little about it. It felt sordid to her and too closely mirrored her relationship with Otto for comfort, reflecting all its squalid deception. She gave nothing of her own affair and felt no need to divulge anything, not even to Price. She revelled in the fact of its being, more than re-living it by sharing the facts. But after a couple of months, and with Otto's encouragement, she agreed to meet Tom and took the morning walk with Price and Braggle to his house. Tom had made oatmeal biscuits and on Price's insistence, brewed some bergamot tea, Maia's favourite.

Price, Maia and Braggle arrived together, the latter running to the kitchen for her daily treat and effulgent welcome, her tail wagging at double speed as Tom got down on his knees and embraced her like no-one else. She licked his face, as always, and fell on to her back with her legs in the air as Tom rubbed her belly and pushed his face into hers.

'Sorry,' he said to a waiting Maia, 'that's our little ritual.'

Maia ignored it and held out her hand to introduce herself. 'What a cosy little house you have,' she said. 'I rarely come to this part of town but I must say it's actually rather nice.'

Tom didn't react, not knowing whether it was a provocation or a simple statement of fact, gave Price a kiss, took Maia's coat, and made the bergamot tea. They sat at the small oak table that hugged the side of the kitchen (Maia said something about how snug it all was), and offered his guests a biscuit. Price was unusually quiet, taking chunks out of his biscuit whilst Maia nibbled gently at hers.

The conversation was guarded, a little awkward, and with elongated silences which grew longer and more embarrassing as time went on. Maia had tucked her esprit neatly away to the point where Tom wondered whether it had ever actually existed, and his own youthful air had begun to age with every passing minute. Price seemed so desperate for the two to get on that his attempts to inject some revelry felt so misplaced that it would have been better if he wasn't there at all. What Tom remembered most, apart from Maia's bright red shawl which she'd draped meticulously over one shoulder, was how she ignored Braggle completely. And there was nothing that annoyed him more. So at regular intervals, he snapped a biscuit in two and threw it in the air for Braggle to catch.

'She loves a hazelnut crunch,' he said. 'And you Maia, do you like them?'

'They're very nice,' she replied.

'I'll write out the recipe for you if you like. It's very simple.'

'Oh, that won't be necessary, I'm sure I know how to make a simple biscuit.'

'Do you make many biscuits then?'

'Now and then.'

'I can't imagine a house without a larder full of biscuits,' Tom said, and pausing for effect, 'or dogs.'

He broke another biscuit, gave half to Price who was looking at him with a half-smile, half-grimace, and threw it so high it almost hit the ceiling. 'A house without a dog is like a pond without water,' he added, 'there's no life, no energy.'

'Each to their own,' Maia answered a little flatly, 'I'm more of a cat person.'

'She has a beautiful cat,' Price interjected, 'the colour of autumn leaves.'

'Orange, yellow, or brown?' Tom asked.

'A fiery brown,' Price answered.

'I'd say more of a gentle orange,' Maia said. 'She's called Hathor.'

'Hathor?' Tom exclaimed.

'Yes, after the Egyptian goddess of beauty.'

'Oh yes, of course,' he replied unconvincingly as Maia dusted a few crumbs from her lap.

And so the conversation went. With so much said from so little. And after another silence which seemed to shake the very walls, Maia took a final sip of her tea and placed it back on its saucer with a faint clank which was a clear signal of her intentions.

'Well, I must be going,' she said, 'I promised Theo I'd cook a broccoli and spinach terrine and you know how long that takes to prepare.'

Tom didn't. He'd never even heard of a terrine. He stood before she'd finished the sentence and didn't care if she saw the look of relief on his face. Maia thanked him for his hospitality and it sounded genuine enough, although everyone in the room knew it would not be repeated and no-one saw fit to say, even out of politeness, 'we must do it again'.

When Tom shut the front door and watched them disappear down the street, he sat lumpenly onto the sofa, pushed his hand into his hair and started twisting a few strands around his index finger. He was a C_2, he thought, and would always be so; others would make quite sure of that.

Price apologized when he returned late afternoon, almost suffocating Tom with his embrace.

'I shouldn't have put you through that, it wasn't fair of me,' he said, 'I should have realised it wouldn't work.'

Tom peeled himself free, took Price's hand and walked him to the bedroom. They sat on the edge of the bed.

'This is all a bit silly isn't it,' Tom said, 'everything's against us.'

'But that's no reason to stop,' Price replied, squeezing Tom's hand tightly with his own.

'Let's just see what happens, shall we,' Tom said quietly, 'but I don't want to go through something like that again.' He took his hand away and traced a finger down Price's cheek and across his lips. Price closed his eyes and tilted his head backwards.

'I was always taught we were all equal,' Tom continued, 'but it's ridiculous isn't it. And the likes of Maia will always be there to make sure the likes of me know it.'

'She said some nice things about you on the way back,' Price said unconvincingly.

'Oh, like what?' Tom replied sarcastically.

'She really *did* like the biscuits.' Price laughed and pulled Tom back on to the bed. He kissed his forehead, then the tip of his nose. 'We *are* equal,' he said, and began to unbutton his shirt.

But that day was a marker which defined the rest of their time together. Their relationship was to become a closed one, unsullied by the interference of others until events ensured otherwise. Tom and Maia did meet a few more times, with a mutual distrust swirling around them, until the moment when that distrust became equipped with enough evidence to give it substance, and nothing was ever the same again.

EIGHT

Tom sat in a chair next to Dan's bed. He'd made Dan some toast and had brought along a jar of quince jam he'd been given at the distribution. He placed it on a tray on Dan's chest and once again carefully tied a towel around his neck. He'd already taken Braggle for a walk, helped Dan pee into a glass jar which he'd then emptied and cleaned, and spent an hour on the electro-bike, refreshing the energy levels in the house which had flicked into the red zone. And when he'd brought the breakfast, he brushed aside Dan's relentless thank yous and apologies by telling him to shut up or he'd smother him with a pillow. He laughed as he said it.

Tom had been feeling surprisingly upbeat since he jumped out of his bed that morning with an energy which had eluded him since reading about Price's death in the town's weekly round-up a couple of weeks before. For days, he'd curled himself under the sheets, eating little and ignoring the calls summoning him to work, and when he did peel himself from the bed, he walked around the house in a daze, unable to shake the image of Price's broken corpse from his mind. He went to the main square, piecing together the facts from the fragments of gossip he heard at the stalls, returning with a burning hatred for the man who had killed him. And when he saw Dan in his garden, it was only watching Braggle lying on her back, wiggling from side to side, which stopped him from racing out and grabbing him by the throat.

He spent that night staring at the ceiling, building fantasies and scenarios, wondering why Dan had come to his house. Was it a warning? Had he killed Price after finding out about them? And yet it seemed preposterous. Price may have been dismissive of Dan, but he had always described him as kind and placid, and sometimes irritatingly so. And the one time Tom had met him, he had been tender and gentle, and made him feel, for a while at least, a little guilty. Tom needed answers; a release from his torment, and knew the only way was to confront it head on. He walked to the house not knowing whether he'd have the confidence or the will to knock on the door, but when Braggle came bounding out of the house, his anxiety faded and he followed her in.

The rest of that day had been so far removed from anything he could have imagined that when he woke early the next morning, the dawn just beginning to throw some light into his bedroom, it took him a few seconds to adjust to the new reality – that he was looking after the man who, the day before, he could have happily poisoned or strangled or hit on the head with a crowbar – and as his eyes adjusted to the gathering light, he smiled as it all sank in. They had chatted until late, sharing Price and piecing him back together with their own private stories. But there was so much more to tell and only he could fill in all the gaps, so after untying the towel from Dan's neck, he placed the tray on the floor, and wasted no more time. He no longer cared if he was being too forward.

'When Maia opened up to you a few days ago I guess she must have told you about Theo, about how he died,' Tom said, sitting back on the chair which he'd dragged closer to the bed.

'Yes,' Dan replied, 'she told me all about what happened.'

'And did she tell you how she killed him?'

'Yes, with Theo's poison.'

'Did she tell you that he'd tried to kill her first?'

'Yes. Sort of.'

'And you believed that?'

Dan hesitated, recognizing the truth in the question. He thought about what Maia had told him; how sick she'd been from Theo's attempts to slowly poison her, and how she'd accidentally killed him by using too much of his own dried plants. Why shouldn't he believe it? It seemed plausible a couple of nights before, didn't it?

'I never met Theo,' Tom said. 'I wish I had. Price told me a lot about him, especially in the last month of his life. They'd become very close you see, saw a lot of each other before he died. Did you know that?'

'No,' Dan replied, 'I had no idea.'

'Theo was nervous, very nervous actually, and needed someone to confide in. It started during the communal harvest. Do you remember it?'

~

Most A_s dreaded the communal harvest. Everyone was expected, although not forced, to take part – the C_s and D_s in the fields with their scythes, the B_s supplying the food and drink, the A_s asked to offer moral support which, in practice, involved not doing very much. This year, Price had volunteered to be at the cutting edge. Tom, who had fine-tuned his scything skills from an early age, gave him lessons on the grass at the bottom of his modest garden, keeping resolutely calm as he showed him the action to use; the blade horizontal and the gentle swishing arc across the base of the grass.

But enthusiasm built on an overriding passion for the instructor rather than a passionate desire to learn the skill itself, has a habit of falling exasperatingly flat, and when Price arrived for the harvest, showing the town's harvest guardian his scything motion, she politely guided him away from the main fields and pointed to the beginners' class as far from the harvest as possible. So instead of a few glorious days shoulder-to-shoulder with his lover, he attended a series of jarring lectures on 'everything you ever wanted to know about the harvest and more' followed by some practice on a field which had been kept apart especially for the purpose.

On the second day, Dan, Maia and Theo came to watch, bringing mint and blackberry cordial and some spicy root vegetable pasties. Maia soon left, her disinterest apparent to

101

all. Dan stayed a while longer, but Braggle began tapping his thighs with her paws, making it clear that she was as bored as Maia. Theo, however, signed up for the next day's training and found himself scything side by side with Price, the two synchronizing their actions and singing communal songs from Academy life.

The harvesting and the training normally lasted a week, depending on the weather, and the two men started early and left late, with numerous breaks whenever the fancy took them. They could see the main harvest from a discreet distance and heard the whistle which determined the harvesters' meagre interludes with a waning stab of guilt afforded only the most spoilt of citizens. The two kept themselves to themselves, wrapped up in each other's company and stories of Academy and town life. It was a relief to both men, their conversation neither sullied by expectation nor restricted by the presence of others.

By the fifth day they'd each brought the other's lunch; Price made Theo a roasted pumpkin and garlic sandwich, and Theo prepared a salad of pomegranate, nuts and couscous. They sat under an oak tree looking over the beginner's fields on an old rug that Theo had found in his shed. The sky had begun to shed its purest azure and they could see the line of dense cloud threatening from the west. They heard the whistle in the distance and assumed the workers had been called back early to try to complete the harvest before the rains. The uncut wheat had begun to swagger in the strengthening wind and the oak tree began to groan. On the far side of their field they saw two men walking close together, checking the crop. Price recognized them immediately and watched Paul, with his long, inelegant stoop, tear an ear from the wheat, rub it in his hands and place it under Otto's nose. They walked a few paces further and did the same, repeating the procedure every few metres.

'I know him,' Price said, almost to himself.

Theo said nothing.

'I know that man,' Price repeated, 'the tall one with Otto, he's called Paul, and I don't like him, I don't like him at all.' He told Theo about the geese and the encounter at the Solstice celebrations, leaving out the sex as shame sometimes outweighs principles.

Replaying the details made them sharper. Firmer. Price had been pre-occupied with Tom, sending Paul's semi-concealed threats and the geese out of his immediate vision, but now his contempt resurfaced and it was enough not to storm over and confront him. Then the rain came and flourished, thudding against the trees and driving the crops flat. The two remained under the oak, protected under its canopy, and watched nervously as Paul and Otto ran over to join them, their coats folded over their heads. No-one spoke, overpowered by the sound of the rain, Paul giving Price a slight nod of recognition. Otto ignored them entirely.

And as the rain faded and a fresh, earthy smell lingered over the fields, the four men remained under the oak, two on one side of its trunk and two on the other, no-one uttering a word. It was a silence filled with the roar of discord and when Otto and Paul finally stood, Price couldn't help himself.

'Hi Paul. Hi Otto,' he said loudly. 'It's been a while hasn't it. Back in town I see. Up to anything in particular?'

'Just here for the day,' Paul replied, his voice calm and monotone. 'Checking it's a good crop.'

'No gun needed for that I guess.'

Neither Paul nor Otto responded.

'But luckily there are lots of other things you can use it on. Who needs a field of wheat when there's a whole flock of geese you can shoot down.'

Otto touched Paul's arm as if to say 'let me deal with this' and walked to Price's side of the tree. He nodded first to Theo and then said: 'Price isn't it. I heard you'd been nosing around a few months ago, outside the perimeters of the town where you had no permission to be. I could do something about that you know.'

'What's that meant to mean?'

'Exactly what it's meant to mean.'

'I can go where I like.'

Otto sniggered. 'You know that's not true,' he said. 'Just like you can't go around cavorting with the lower orders, but let's put that back into its little box too, shall we. Or would you prefer that I prise it open?'

Price said nothing.

'And what you saw was all perfectly above board and according to the wishes of the authorities. Have you seen how the geese eat the seeds and destroy the crops? Someone has to take responsibility for feeding the population. For feeding you, Price. So I'd appreciate it if you didn't go around smearing this good man's name. He has broken no edicts. He has done no wrong. And if you don't mind, we're busy men.' He turned around without waiting for a reply, touched Paul on the arm again, and they walked off.

It took a while for Price and Theo to say anything, both feeling as though they'd been reprimanded by the Academy principal and forced into submission. Theo was the first to speak. 'Awful,' he said, 'that man is worse than I thought.'

Price remained silent.

'Are you ok?'

Price leant against the trunk of the oak. 'Not really,' he replied quietly.

'Shall we call it a day then?'

'Good idea.'

They took their scythes back to the communal depot in silence, cleaning and sharpening them before handing them in.

'You're being very quiet,' Theo said as they left the depot. 'That really shook you didn't it.'

'He was threatening me Theo.'

'They're empty threats Price. Ignore them. All that crap about feeding the population. There's always been enough to go around, for everyone, geese included. If you ask me, what happened there was a sign of weakness.'

'Maybe, but he was still trying to scare me off.'

'Exactly, which means he's nervous.'

'Yes, I agree, but it's just the *way* he tried to scare me.'

'I guess you're talking about that lower orders bit.'

'How did he know?'

'So have you?'

'A bit.'

'A bit, or a lot?'

'Ok, more than a bit. There's a C_2 I've been seeing, and I really like him.'

Theo touched his arm. 'It's nothing unusual Price. Don't worry about it.'

'But it's more that he knows about it. How does he know about it?'

'Forget about it Price. Everyone's up to something, Otto included.'

'Really?'

'Yes, Really. If Otto goes any further with this, then there are some things I know about him that will stop him in his tracks.'

'Like what?'

'I'll let you know if and when. But enough of that, I want to show you something. Come with me.'

Theo took Price to a neighbouring field where the harvested wheat was heaped in neat parallel rows and the uncut crop misshapen by the rain and wind. 'Do you notice anything unusual about that field?' Theo asked.

'Not really, no. Why?'

'Can you see any wild flowers?'

Price walked closer. He could see the occasional shot of yellow, probably dandelions or sow thistles, and a gentle rising mist as the rain began to evaporate on the warm soil.

'Wouldn't you expect far more,' Theo said, 'even at this time of the year? Where are the corncockles? The fleabane? I noticed it right away. Compare it to some of the other fields, they're full of flowers.'

'But the D_s pull out a lot of them no? Pull three, leave one, isn't that the rule?"

'Well the D_s have gone beyond the call of duty here,' Theo replied.

Theo told him what he'd seen many years before at the Academy, and what he'd suspected even then. 'There must be field experiments going on,' he said. 'And it's been going on for years, but it's the first time I've seen it here, and I've been checking, I've checked every year and seen nothing. I wasn't going to tell you, but now I know about the geese, well, it's all part of the same pattern isn't it. Controlling nature.'

Theo paused to take in what he was saying. It had been there, within him all his adult life, tucked securely away for his own protection, hidden from view, as though saying it aloud would make it too real and undeniable, and once spoken, he must confront it, react on it, and he didn't know whether he could, whether he was strong enough. And what *could* he do anyway? But hearing Otto's imperious defence of his actions had stirred him to form the words in his mouth. 'They are controlling nature' he said again. 'And there's something else I want to show you.'

Instead of walking home, they went in the opposite direction, to the western edge of the town where the houses thinned out and the gardens grew larger. They stopped at the last property along a driveway lined with plane trees. A huge oak tree obscured the main house. Price knew it belonged to Otto, he'd walked there a few times with his previous dog and had found it rather pompous. He'd always stopped at the main entrance and retreated, but now they walked on, under the oak tree, past a pergola covered in climbing roses and a large pond filled with water lilies and lotus, until they came out onto a massive lawn. It was a striking lime green with alternating light and dark parallel strips running along its length. It reminded Price of the striped green wallpaper he so disliked in the archive reading room.

'It's hideous,' he said. 'What's the point of it?'

'It's a green desert,' Theo replied. 'Not one single flower, not one. He's either got someone who spends every waking hour picking them out by hand, or he's using something to kill them, which of course is against everything the Reformation stands for. And what would he use? Where does he get it from? This is about as non-negotiable as you can get. And no mole-hills. Nothing. There's no way this is allowed. No way.'

'How did you know about this?' Price asked.

Theo hadn't told him about Maia and Otto, and didn't want to, and certainly not that he'd followed her here.

'I just like walking around, exploring,' he said, 'after all, we're allowed to go wherever we like no?'

They both laughed.

'If only,' Price replied.

They walked along the length of the lawn looking for any disfigurement, anything other than blades of grass trimmed to a tight perfection. Price then took giant strides into the middle of the lawn, avoiding stepping on each line as though it was a child's game, knelt down on one knee and brushed the tips of his fingers across the turf. It was absurdly smooth. 'This is grotesque,' he called out to Theo, 'it feels artificial, like it's been made from brushed cotton.' He took out a pocket knife he always carried and gouged out a piece of lawn the size of a table mat. 'A little souvenir,' he said and walked back to where Theo was standing, ostentatiously treading over each line with the turf held aloft and drooping over the side of his palm. They turned to leave and from the window of the house saw Otto looking directly at them. Price waved theatrically. Otto kept his arms to his side and walked away.

The two men left the grounds quickly, giggling like two Academy boys stealing apples from the communal orchard. They came to the oak tree and started to run, reaching the main street out of breath and leaned against the town's sun dial panting heavily and unable to speak, the square of turf held limply between Price's fingers. He took out his knife once more and cut the piece into two. 'One for you and one for me,' he said, 'let's plant them in our gardens somewhere they're easy to see, so they're always staring us in the face, and that we don't forget.'

The next day they met again at the field and walked directly to the archives, spending the whole day there and much of the following week. But knowledge is only as expansive as its availability and it wasn't long before they knew the archives would reveal only so much, which wasn't much at all.

Price explained everything to Tom, and told Dan nothing. Theo alternated between the archives and helping Maia with her 'harvest aperitif' which she'd announced the day before. He'd agreed to it reluctantly, knowing her motives, but thinking it might also do them good.

They found nothing relating to any experiments or field trials, and nothing suggesting, even obliquely, the authorities had relaxed the unwavering environmental policies. They spent hours reading through back issues of the weekly Reformation news, and read periodicals with titles like 'Manage Your Natural Space' and 'Living with the World Around You'. The most rewarding was 'The World as it Was', with its titbits of pre-Change policies written from a post-Change vantage point, detailing policies which stripped the land and seas of life, covering anything deemed in the wrong place, which was just about everything, with a toxic combination of liquids. The information was more detailed than they'd learned in the Academy (which concentrated wholly on demonizing the old and venerating the new) yet vague enough to frustrate them both. They found no names of the compounds or what they contained, just the knowledge that they existed and an account of the devastation they inflicted.

Price and Theo still enjoyed it, meeting at the archives as the doors opened, together for much of the day, sharing any new information, however small, and knowing that in unity was strength. From now on they would encourage each other to go further and not allow simple distractions to alter their course. They didn't know what they would do or how, they just knew they'd found their reason to exist and that a doubling in numbers had infinitely increased their collective tenacity.

For Theo in particular, it was a catharsis. He was conscious of his social faults, feeling ill at ease in groups, more comfortable watching from a safe vantage point; more of a voyeur than a viveur. He'd accepted it from an early age, but still felt it as a defect, a blight on his personality which stopped him from really living. And now, he'd found a true purpose which he could share. It scared him too; he knew the power of others outweighed his meagre status, but to his surprise and relief, it didn't matter anymore. He had a calling, and he was going to see it through.

It put him in good spirits for the harvest aperitif. He enjoyed bartering for goods he'd never been interested in before, and preparing dishes he'd never cooked. A fresh energy churned through his body which made him feel younger and chirpier. Even Maia noticed a difference, and was slightly unnerved by the change, wondering whether he was enjoying a bit too much her being away from the house so often.

Price and Dan arrived at the party early, on Maia's wishes, and it helped put Theo at ease. And for the first time since the two couples had met many years before, Price gravitated more to him than to Maia. 'You two seem quite the adoring couple,' she said with a whiff of sarcasm, and took Dan's arm to show him the buffet table and the drinks. Theo and Price walked down to the physic garden which he'd told him so much about over the previous week. Otto's grass was perched on a mound at its centre like a sentinel purveying its surroundings. 'It inspires me,' Theo said, 'and I know exactly what I'm going to do.'

He tore a leaf from a dried and shrivelled foxglove and ground it between his fingers. 'I'm going to do my own experiments,' he said excitedly. 'I'm going to find out how easy it is to make a poison that could wipe out some flowers and not others. It must be possible. I have a good basic knowledge, so I reckon I can give it a shot.'

'Isn't it too late in the season,' Price replied, 'I mean, you need flowers to experiment on, no? And most of them have already flowered, haven't they?'

'To an extent yes, but there are still a few around I can use, and lots of other flowers in the garden. I can give it a start and get into full swing by next spring. I might even start my own little crop plot here, I have the space. The more I think about it, the more excited I get.'

'But what's the point of it Theo? Why would you want to make something that kills plants? Isn't the whole point trying to stop that happening?'

'Of course. And if I can show that it's possible, we can prove that it's happening.'

'Prove to whom?'

Theo laughed. 'Good question,' he replied. 'But I don't believe what Otto said about it being officially sanctioned. I think it's a few people with power who think they can do what they want.'

'Just because they can?'

'Exactly. So let's be a thorn in Otto's side. Let's make him even more nervous than he already is.'

The two shook hands as though making a secret pact and went to the drinks table where Maia was chatting uncomfortably with Dan.

A little later, when all the guests had arrived, Gilda Rosen came to Theo with a strong beer in her hand and asked to see his garden 'filled with the most exquisite plants known to nature', as she put it. Theo was inwardly peeved. Maia must have told her about it when he'd expressly said to tell no-one. He smiled and walked her to the end of the garden.

'Which one is the henbane,' she asked.

'Henbane? Why henbane?'

'It gives great flavour to beer,' she replied, 'as well as being profoundly poisonous of course,' and she gave out a shrill laugh as though her wit had overwhelmed her. 'Oh, and what a lovely piece of grass. It's just perfect there. Where did you get it?'

'I think you know perfectly well,' Theo replied. He picked a leaf from the henbane and handed it to her. 'Give this to Otto,' he said, 'it might do him some good.'

Gilda dropped the leaf as though she'd been handed a burning bush. 'I'd be very careful if I were you,' she replied, in a voice she usually kept for more official occasions.

'What is it with you lot? Theo replied, 'not an ounce of humour between you.'

'It didn't sound like a joke to me.'

'No, you're right there. It really isn't a joke.' He plucked another henbane leaf and held it out to her. 'They say henbane also brings people down a peg or two. Might be worth nibbling some yourself,' and he walked away. Gilda stood a little while longer where she was, to compose herself, before returning to the buffet and determined to get her revenge.

Maia gave her welcoming speech. It was followed by Gilda's retort and the buffet brawl, with Theo, who had never succumbed to violence before, at its epicentre. He pushed and kicked and pulled the table cloth from the trestle table sending its contents hurling onto a trio of prostrate figures. He left without looking back, Price hurrying after him.

Gilda Rosen was helped by a posse of fellow party goers. She remained calm, wiping the blood from her face and ignoring the stains to her outfit. She left the party without a word, ignoring Maia's apologies.

Price caught up with Theo and clasped him tightly to absorb his friend's uncontrollable shaking. Theo's head collapsed onto his shoulder. 'What have I done,' he said almost unintelligibly. 'I'm an idiot. This changes everything. And we hadn't even started.' He embraced Price and told him to go back to the party to look after Maia. He walked to a copse on the outskirts of the town and leaned against a silver birch. 'I'm a fool,' he said once more to himself.

NINE

T here were stories of pre-Change life in which closets and cupboards and so-called walk-in wardrobes were so cluttered with clothing that it was a wonder any decisions could be made at all. The archives were full of information on oddities in materials that defied either logic or comfort, available in such overabundance that its very existence now seemed an embarrassment to the sober wardrobe of the modern age whose citizens relished the soft touch of quality against their skin, but accepted the limited choice as a fact of life. Some people, like Otto Cladders, had inherited clothes; a rather musty smell encircling him when he wore his favoured tweeds, rumoured to have been his great-great-grandfather's. Others, like Tom, were fortunate enough to choose something which, due to its symbolic importance, no expense was spared, and which showed that, even though the Reformation had a temperate quality sewn into its very fabric, it was also conscious of the need to indulge its citizens on days of collective significance, sprinkling largesse and satisfaction with it.

Occasionally the choice of clothes, however limited, becomes a deliberate act of defiance and when Theo looked into his wardrobe to choose what he'd wear to his tribunal, he ignored the shelf with his best shirt, and the railing with his best trousers and jacket, and pulled out his gardening clothes which although freshly washed, were still stained with the dark green and brown residue of garden maintenance. The trousers, which had lost all

112

form, especially at the knees, and his shoes, which had weathered remarkably well considering their provenance, joined together in a statement of intent.

Truth be told, Theo was more nervous than he'd ever been, not helped by Maia's uncompromising behaviour since the harvest aperitif. She had ignored him with such intensity that the walls of the house seemed to groan with embarrassment. When their paths crossed, Theo looked at her with the hope of reconciliation, but none came. Maia neither cooked nor cleaned, preferring to go hungry rather than sit at the same table as her partner. Theo didn't know where she was eating, presuming her many hours out of the house included food with Otto, or possibly other friends. He knew she'd been to Price's a few times and how contorted with fury she still was more than a week after the buffet brawl; Price had told him so. They still met daily at the archives, but the intensity of their research had softened due to the worries of the tribunal, and they spent many hours discussing what Theo should say. Price was kind, supportive and encouraging, which Theo needed more than ever and received from no-one else. He escorted him to the Townhouse on the morning of the tribunal where he hugged him with the intensity of a lover, pushing his hand through his hair and laughing once more at the shoddiness of his clothing.

'Are you sure you don't want me to come in with you?' he asked.

'No,' Theo replied firmly. 'This is my mess.'

Price watched Theo go through the large oak door which creaked of oldness, giving him a farewell thumbs-up as he looked back, repeating that he'd be waiting when he came out, however long it took.

Theo's soft shoes made no sound on the stone floor as he shuffled to his seat at the base of the podium. The G9 was complete, sitting in a line above him, with Otto in the middle and a stony-faced Gilda Rosen at his side. Theo nodded politely. A few formalities of tribunal etiquette were observed as Otto introduced each member of the G9 followed by a description of the complaint against him. Otto then asked Gilda to give her account of what had taken place. She described in detail what had happened, including her use of the salad niçoise as a defensive action, and how it took hours to remove sticky cumin seeds from her hair. It was a performance of theatrical quality encased in a deep dislike for the man who had committed the unforgiveable offence of making her look ridiculous. It was nothing Theo hadn't expected, although he winced once or twice when she punctuated her account with comments designed to inflict as much remorse as possible. She stood the whole time, flaying her arms when needed, adding drama to her story, and sitting with a heavy flourish when finished. Otto stood immediately and without looking directly at Theo began to speak. It took Theo by surprise. He'd read the protocol for a tribunal over and over and this was the moment for him to give his version of events. Instead, Otto seemed to have fast forwarded. Theo rose abruptly from his chair, pushing it back with force so it spilled over and clanked to the floor.

'No,' he shouted, 'this is not correct. It's my turn to speak.'

'You are misguided,' Otto replied. 'I can do what I see fit.'

'You cannot silence me Otto Cladders,' Theo interjected, his words echoing violently around the Townhouse giving them more force than intended, and when Otto shouted in response, the two voices created a swirl of noise in which individual words evaporated. Neither man gave way and the cacophony continued and expanded as other members of the G9 joined in.

Price, who had been sitting on a bench just outside, heard the rising, echoing vibration. He rushed to the entrance and put his ear first against the main door, and then ran inside, rushing to Theo, grabbing him by the waist and pulling him away. Each G9 member stopped abruptly. Only Theo's voice could be heard.

'You are a liar and a cheat and you will not get away with it. You can be sure of that. You will NOT get away with it.'

'You're pathetic Theo Fanter,' Otto replied, 'even Maia thinks so. Weak, deluded and pathetic.' The rest of his reply faded away as Theo was pulled out of the Townhouse and down the pathway to the main street.

The next day a letter arrived on Theo's doorstep. He opened it slowly, unnerved by the official seal on the envelope.

Theo Fanter,

Your conduct at the tribunal has been discussed by the full quota of G9 members and reported to the main authorities. There is a unanimous consensus that your behaviour has been reprehensible, both at the tribunal and the preceding event for which you were originally summoned. The two combined are considered a serious breach of the trust and support every citizen is given. As you are aware, the stability of society is based on mutual respect in which everyone is expected to adhere, the erosion of which places considerable pressure on the balance of everything the Reformation stands for. Violence is unacceptable in every form. We have been in contact with your partner Maia Gertler who has informed us of your frequent violent behaviour towards her and she is in full agreement with the subsequent decision which has not been taken lightly or without considerable discussion.

It is as follows:

As from the beginning of the new year, three months from now, your A_3 status will be revoked and downgraded to B_3. All privileges relating to your status will be stopped and you will be required to leave your current premises. A new premises in keeping with your new status will be offered you. You can choose whether to stay in the town or move elsewhere, the latter is highly recommended, as it seems unlikely your presence in a community you have resolutely undermined will be tolerated. Your partner has already been informed of this decision and is in full agreement. The termination of your relationship will be enacted in due course and you will each be assigned new partners according to status. This may take some time as interviews need to be conducted and new tests performed.

You will be kept informed of developments.

It is with deep regret that these steps are being taken.

Yours,

The Highest Authority of The Reformation.

Theo read it through to the end, then folded the letter into two, then again, and again, until it was no larger than a bottle top. He put it in his pocket and walked silently to the bottom of his garden, sitting on the bench overlooking his physic garden and staring at the veined coarseness of the henbane leaves and the petals which had darkened and wilted. He felt utterly alone. Every fragment of his body ached with disbelief. Maia had betrayed him in the most abhorrent way, and it left him broken. He had seen her briefly yesterday before the tribunal, but she had left whilst he was showering without saying goodbye or offering any word of support or encouragement. The same this morning. And now it was clear why. How could she look him in the face knowing what she had done and the horrible and blatant lies she had told? Their relationship was now dissolved in the coldest of fashions and all Theo could do was wait. His resolve collapsed in on itself. He would do nothing more. No archive, no collaboration. It was over.

He said nothing more about it. Nothing to Maia. Nothing to Price. He had taken the G9 decision and hid it within himself, accepting its inevitability and its consequences, but wanting to experience it alone, without interference or sympathy, as though sharing it would only heighten its power. He deflected Price's concerns, saying there was nothing to worry about and everything would be OK, he just needed some time to himself. Price reluctantly accepted his friend's reasoning, believing their collaboration would resume in due course. He knew nothing of Theo's fate or Maia's involvement, or of her affair with Otto. Twice a week he would call on Theo and each time he was given the same gentle brush-off. He noticed Theo becoming paler and thinner and less communicative as the weeks wore on, with any attempt to draw him out of his detachment met with an increasing wilfulness. Theo rarely ventured out, going occasionally to the distributions to collect the bare minimum of provisions which he would cook with little enthusiasm and eat across the table from

Maia in a deathly silence.

He said very little in the final months of his life, preferring to write down his thoughts and feelings in a notebook he'd found at the back of a draw in his study. It had been handcrafted with unbleached, heavy paper and a mottled green cover which reminded him of a leaf under a magnifying glass. He had bartered for it a couple of years before and kept it for something special, placing it in the draw and promptly forgetting all about it. When he found it again, at the climax of his unhappiness, he knew immediately what he would do. On the cover in large bold writing he wrote *De Profundis*. He then turned to the first page and wrote:

To Price, my dearest and brightest friend, here lies the truth of my final months in this town. I'm sorry I was too much of a coward not to share it with you face to face. I hope you can understand why. Please be careful. And please don't give up.

The notebook gave Theo a boost and the strength to endure those final months. He wrote in it every day, detailing all the events leading up to his departure, leaving nothing out. His eating and sleeping pattern was there, Maia's comings and goings, the communication between them, or lack of them, and the detailed work on his physic garden and how he'd painstakingly taken each plant, using both leaves and remaining flowers, drying each, creating tinctures, experimenting on himself to see how it affected him and writing his conclusions with scientific clarity using a code he'd developed and which he'd written out at the end of the notebook, so that Price, if he felt so inclined, could decipher them. Theo ate tiny doses of each dried plant, knowing little how it would affect him, and not really caring. He documented dizziness, headaches, stomach pains, ear pains, urinary problems, gentle hallucinations, blurriness, lack of co-ordination, dis-orientation, and one time when he'd had trouble breathing. There was nothing that caused great distress; he ingested the tiniest of doses, increasing it incrementally until he experienced a noticeable symptom.

Each plant was kept in a paper envelope in his shed at the side of the garden, a place where Maia rarely visited as the garden was, and had always been, his domain. On each, he had written, in code, the conclusions of his experiments which he duplicated in the notebook, together with their location – a side drawer next to the tool box.

His symptoms may have been slight, but the accumulation of side-effects over a two-month period left him weaker and paler and with a meagre appetite, which was just as well, as he had little desire to cook or to eat with Maia. And the feeling was mutual. Their communication was embarrassingly light, kept to a brusque politeness that managed, just, to avoid any open hostility.

Maia became ill in the final month. Theo assumed it was probably due to stress, but couldn't be sure. For a week, he put enmity aside, cooked simple food for her, and eat together when she felt up to it. It seemed to diffuse the tension. Then suddenly Maia became better and once again was more out of the house than home. Theo continued his basic experiments, using his tinctures on the autumn flowers in his garden to see how they fared, but it was of little use. He knew he needed the following year to make a real go of it, time he didn't have.

A week before his departure, when he'd been informed of his new address in a different town, and had immersed himself in a hologram of his new garden and house, which as he'd expected was more basic and compact, he noticed his pile of dried plants had been tampered with. It was clear someone had taken some from each envelope as he'd kept meticulous notes of their weight. A day later, out of the blue, and for the first time in many weeks, Maia declared she wanted to cook the next day, describing it as a farewell dinner and a chance for them to part company as friends. That night, he lay naked on top of the bed with the curtains open, his body lit by a waning moon, thinking over his life. He hardly slept, but when he rose that morning, he felt more alive than at any time over the previous weeks. He went straight to his study, took his notebook from the drawer, and started writing.

Maia is cooking for me this evening. As I've already written, it's probably she who took the dried plants from the shed and I await with interest what she will cook. I had a wonderful night, lying naked on my bed, looking out of the window at the constellations, thinking over my life. I told you a lot about it already Price, and I've probably repeated it in this notebook, but when I think over it, I smile. I've been lucky. And perhaps a new chapter awaits me that will help me rediscover myself and that self-reflective contentment I have been fortunate to possess. But perhaps not. This will be the last time I write in this notebook as I've decided to give it to you today. I had planned to give it to you next week, the day before I leave, but there's no time like the present and I want to make sure it's in your safe hands and that you know exactly what has happened to me over these past months. I'm sorry I haven't had the strength or the courage to tell you personally, that's just who I am. I can't help being who I am, even though it seems the rest of my life I'll be forced to live otherwise, so perhaps it's not so bad if Maia cooks for me tonight, and you never know, perhaps sleeping angels will send me to my rest.

It has been a great pleasure to have had you in my life Price, I only wish we'd connected a little earlier instead of waiting so long, but I guess that's the power of Maia, she has tended to overshadow me, of which I have no regrets. I have been a man of the side stream, observing more than participating, reacting instead of pushing, and it has served me well. Of course, it has meant I have been of little use these past months, which is exactly what I said I wouldn't be. I said that we would work tirelessly together, that we would achieve something. We haven't, or at least, I haven't. I have had no energy. For that I apologise and can only hope that you have enough energy for the two of us, as there is much to do. This notebook might help, it might not. Please keep it safe. It has been my life-line.

He walked to Price's just before midday knowing that Dan would probably be at the distribution. Price bounded out of the house to embrace him, with Braggle close behind. He held him tightly, feeling the delicate lightness of his body.

'You look terrible,' he said half-jokingly, slapping him on the side of the arm, 'but I am so pleased to see you.' He hugged him once more and invited him in. Theo smiled and politely refused, holding out his hand and gently placing the notebook into Price's.

'Price, this might all sound a bit melodramatic, and actually, it sort of is, but I want to give you this. I've been writing in it the past few months, since the tribunal actually. I know I've kept you in the dark, but it's all in there, everything is explained. I'm sorry I haven't been open or honest with you, I just haven't had the will you see.'

He placed his hand on Price's arm to stop him from interrupting, and continued.

'I'll be leaving in a week, all being well, because the authorities have downgraded me. It's clear that Otto wants rid of me, and he's been successful, so please, watch yourself, he'll be after you too.'

He squeezed Price's arm again to prevent him from talking.

'Price, I want you to promise me that you won't read any of this until I'm gone. Look at me in the eyes, and promise. Please. No hesitation. Just promise.'

Price was dumbstruck. He leaned against the side of the door to steady himself, saying nothing.

'Please Price, you must promise.'

'I promise.'

'Thank you.'

Theo knelt down and buried his head into Braggle's side. 'Bye-bye Braggle,' he whispered, and then abruptly stood up and walked away.

~

Tom was perched on the bed next to Dan, who was now able to sit up with the help of a few expertly placed pillows. In short bursts over the previous couple of days, Tom had told him everything he knew about Theo; Price had been so thorough in recounting it that he felt he'd almost experienced it himself. Occasionally, he would stop mid-sentence and ask incredulously whether Dan really knew nothing. And between these stories, whilst he was cooking or walking Braggle, he would suddenly halt, rigid, and ask himself why he was helping the man who killed his lover. There were moments when he fantasized about grabbing one of the pillows and smothering Dan until he faded brutally away under the bedsheets, and one time, when he was helping him to the bathroom and past the top stairs, when he thought how simple it would be to push him and watch him fall and smash his head against the bottom stair. But these moments dissolved, replaced by an almost avuncular sense of togetherness as he saw in Dan the essential goodness that Price had so often spoken of. A bond developed between them with Price at its centre, a necessity for both as they dealt with the coruscating grief and an increasing realization that they were going to need each other in the months to come.

Dan remembered Price telling him that Theo had been to visit, and had looked far from well, but said nothing about a notebook, and when they heard about his death a few days later, how he had gone straight to his study, locked the door and stayed there for the rest of the day, possibly even the day after too, refusing any food, coming to the kitchen just to fetch a glass of water and returning immediately to his room.

Dan was upset by Theo's death; Price was devastated.

'I didn't know they'd become so close,' Dan said to Tom, 'so when he reacted so hysterically, I just thought he was being, well, theatrical.'

'Have you thought how strange that sounds Dan? I mean, a friend of yours dies, and you think Price is being hysterical by showing some strong emotion. Isn't that just a natural response when you find out a friend has died? Isn't it called being human?'

'I guess so. But doesn't it all have to be put into proportion? I mean, people die all the time, every day, we could be struck down tomorrow, no?'

'With a copper pan you mean.'

'That was below the belt Tom.'

'No Dan, it was very much a blow to the head.'

The two fell silent. Tom sidled over to Braggle who was splayed out on the other side of the bed, and rubbed his face against her fur. Dan closed his eyes and tried to push away the sight of Price's crushed head, something he'd been quite good at since it happened, but there was something about the simplicity of what Tom had said that distressed him, as though he was hearing what he'd actually done for the first time. He clenched his teeth to prevent himself from crying, trying not to show the effect of Tom's words.

Tom slowly released his head from Braggle's chest, and laid one hand on her neck, feeling the beat of her heart and the gentle coarseness of her breathing. He then turned quickly to Dan and said bluntly:

'I'm only half way through Dan. Theo is dead, but there are another six months before Price followed. And if you think it can't get any crazier, then you'd better hold on to the mattress.'

Price was drowsy with grief and glad he had a lock on his study door. He couldn't bear to speak to anyone. Not even Tom, and certainly not Dan, although they didn't talk much anyway so it wouldn't make much difference. Dan had knocked a couple of times and asked how he was and Price had answered politely, even though he wanted the whole damn world to cave in on itself. He'd been in the room for half the day with the notebook lying expectantly on the table, but the thought of delving into the very core of Theo's mind when he no longer existed, well, it was just too much, too raw. No, the words of a dead man would have to wait. For now, all Price wanted to do was to think about the living person, his form, his nature, his humour.

He sat in his chair with a view of the climbing rose, which in the summer gave him a cascade of joy, but was now rigid with the mortification of winter. He could hear the melancholic song of a robin which every now and then perched on the highest point of the rose, and watched it squabble with another robin as they darted across his line of vision. He knew they'd be lucky to survive the winter and everything the natural world threw at them, and marvelled at their ability to live at all, these little specks of life entrancing and dying in the blink of an eye. Were these the same robins of summer – the ones who almost rubbed against his ankles as he turned the soil in the garden, who gave him comfort in proximity; the ones who worried him when they didn't appear? He once held a dead robin in the palm of his hand, so light that he could hardly feel its weight. It had smacked against his study window, breaking its neck and dying instantly, just a trickle of blood on one side of its mouth to indicate the violence of its end. It wasn't the first time of course, many birds had succumbed to the perils of the window pane, but robins felt like companions and its death felt like the loss of a friend.

He'd been to many burials before. But what would he do now, at Theo's burial? Should he say something? He'd already been to Maia's, banged on her door, to console her, to find out what had happened, to ask what he should do. No answer. He returned once more. Still no answer. He pushed a note through her letterbox, desperate for more information. All he had was the news that Theo was dead, a short notice in the daily round-up that Dan had read at the distribution, and that the burial would be the following day, as was the custom. He would certainly pluck some of the daisies and yarrow which were still flowering in the garden and place it on Theo's shroud, just like he'd done the previous year when their neighbour had died after pricking himself on a rose thorn, his jaw locking within the day and the stiffness in his muscles spreading rapidly until his lungs gave up altogether. But surely he should do more this time, even if it was to read a short poem, say something that would bring his friend back to life. He stared blankly at the climbing rose, at the thorns which seemed threatening and lifeless, trying to piece together what could possibly have ended Theo's life so suddenly. He knew the answer must lay in the notebook and that he must somehow will himself to read it before the burial, even if it took him the whole night. He picked it up from the table and stroked the front cover, leading his fingers along the veins of the printed leaves as though he was touching his dead friend's hand. He opened it to the final entry: *Maia is cooking for me this evening ….*

The next morning Dan knocked on his door to say the burial was in an hour, and as the pit was at least half an hour's walk, they'd have to leave soon. Price opened the door immediately and apologised for his behaviour. He showered, brushed his teeth, ran his fingers through his hair, put on his best clothes (although for a moment considered wearing his gardening clothes as Theo had done to the tribunal) and was ready in ten minutes. They walked slowly and silently to the communal pit on the edge of town, meeting a few others along the way, so by the time they reached the site, about twenty others had joined them. Dan nodded to those he knew; Price kept his eyes focused on the ground. He had picked some heather by the side of the path to go with the other flowers and held them gently in his hand as his did the dead robin a few years before. He heard the crunching of the wooden wheels as the small wagon approached with Theo's body, Maia walking behind. He felt utterly numb. He had decided, as he lay on his sofa in the small hours of the morning, after finishing the notebook, that he would act normally. He mustn't let anyone know, least of all Maia, of what he knew. So, as she walked past him, he nodded with everyone else at the recognition of her sorrow and her loss, somehow finding the strength not to strike her down. He must play the comforting friend, as she was now playing the stricken partner. He let out an audible grunt when Otto came into view, but nothing that rippled offensively through the crowd. A space had already been dug and as Theo's body, naked beneath the tight cotton shroud, was lowered into the ground, he walked to the edge of the pit and threw in the flowers. 'Sweet dreams,' he whispered, followed with a louder, 'I won't forget. I promise.' As he turned, he looked at Maia who was staring at her feet and sobbing, unable to watch the proceedings, and uttered faintly: 'The weeping wounds of a widow wallowing in her wintery depths.' And as Otto, who as head of the G9 always conducted the service, began to read the common burial eulogy, he walked away, resisting the temptation to push him into the pit.

He heard later from Dan that after the service, which lasted no more than ten minutes, Maia thanked everyone for coming, and as she hugged Dan, asked him why Price had gone off so abruptly.

'He's distraught,' he replied. 'I've never seen him like this before. I'm sorry, I'm sure he would have wanted to say something to you. He'll probably come over later today.'

'I hope so,' Maia replied, 'I really need to see him.'

And so began the play. It lasted for many months, and had a number of acts in which Price played the concerned and loyal confidant who supported his grieving friend. He did it with great skill, as Maia had no idea that he knew everything, and that each time she cried in his arms, he would hug her, not in a comforting embrace as she thought, but with an agonising desire to squeeze the life out of her.

He went to see her the evening of the burial. He'd already heard the rumours, via Dan, that Maia had accidentally killed Theo with his own poisons, that it was self-defence, that she was the victim, that life had been hell with him, and the harvest aperitif had been the perfect platform to let such rumours escape and fly. He felt desperate for his friend, and was determined, slowly, and when the time was right, to put the record straight. How, he wasn't quite sure, but he would, even if it killed him.

Maia opened the door and embraced him, flinging her arms around his shoulders with such emotional force that he had to steady himself against the wall. Her crying sounded real and heart-wrenching and lasted longer than Price had expected or felt comfortable with. He guided her to the sofa, gave her a glass of water, sat beside her, and listened to her full story. She said she was terrified about the forthcoming tribunal. What if she was downgraded? Forced to leave the town? Price knew nothing would happen.

He offered to stay the night, and to his relief she refused. When he finally left the house, with no food inside him, he reached the end of the lane and retched three times, before returning to Theo's shed and taking everything from the drawer containing the dried plants that he'd read all about. He then walked directly to Tom's where he collapsed on to the bed and cried his heart out. And for the very first time, they slept the whole night together, entwined around each other like the stems of the honeysuckle which graced the front of the house and curled around the bedroom window.

The next morning, he walked home to tell Dan he'd stayed with Maia and that he'd be spending considerable time with her over the next few days. He then walked back to Tom's, taking the notebook with him.

The best intentions need resourcefulness and wit to give them weight; patience and luck to get results. Price knew that the anger that coursed through his body was not enough to push him forward. He'd seen how the previous months, which started so promisingly, had fallen so acutely flat, and how he'd allowed circumstance to dictate his behaviour. He needed a structured, well-conceived plan with specific goals. And one that had a chance of success.

Tom calmed him, gave him direction, prevented any rash moves. He listened, gave useful suggestions, and instilled in Price a sense of right which would furnish him with the strength to continue when all felt lost.

A plan was conceived. Yes, full of holes and uncertainties, but a plan all the same.

Dan was kept in the dark. It was helped by his inability to ask the right questions or see much further than his own image. Price treated him as a bystander, unfairly and disdainfully, so although they were living together, the distance between them was boundless. The atmosphere was civil bordering on contempt. Dan felt abused and unloved, which was palpably true, whilst Price just didn't care, and if anyone observed them together, one couldn't help but be swayed by Dan's hopelessness in the face of so much insensitivity. Price was often abrupt and curt. His lack of appreciation in the qualities he once found so appealing in Dan was embarrassingly unambiguous. Dan continued to cook despite no word of thanks, and continued to accept Price's absences despite no explanation of his whereabouts. The tension rose incrementally, waiting for the inevitable burst of uncontrolled anger. It took a little over half a year for the relationship to collapse in the most violent of manners.

ELEVEN

Otto Cladders was a creature of habit. It hadn't taken Price long to work that one out. He'd been following him, on and off, for almost a month and his mornings seemed rigidly precise in their routine. The lights in his bedroom would go on at 7am, followed swiftly by the one in the bathroom. The kitchen light went on ten minutes later and Otto, wearing a dark blue bed-suit, would pour himself a glass of milk, gulp it down in one motion, then prepare his breakfast, which, from Price's vantage point, looked like bread and cheese. He would eat it alone reading a book, occasionally stopping to stroke the cat that would jump onto the table and sit uncomfortably close to his plate. His partner Els, a curious woman of indeterminable age and a mass of black hair, would arrive a little later. Conversation seemed negligible. At 8am Otto left the kitchen, not to be seen again for an hour, then, no matter the weather, would walk around his garden, inspecting the lawn for blemishes, always walking purposefully to the middle where the square had been dug and which was now replaced by a piece of turf which, no doubt to his extreme irritation (and Price's delight), was a lighter shade of green.

Mondays to Thursdays Otto walked for an hour to the bio-factory on the edge of town, stay for a couple of hours before walking back to his house, always avoiding the distributions and the market. On Fridays, he drove out of town. He was one of the few to have a car, and whether it was his or just a loan was a matter for conjecture, but it was replaced every year with a new one and was always a dark blue with a silver top. Price had seen it close up in the side garage, had smelled its metallic newness, and resisted the temptation to draw his penknife across its edge. Tom was right to advise against any rash behaviour, he knew that, but sometimes his anger welled and his rage was hard to control. He had only been in a vehicle once before, when he was driven to the town to start his new life, and had found the experience disappointing and uncomfortable, sharing a van with twenty others and a guide who didn't seem to stop talking for the two days of the journey. The road was narrow and so straight it was a wonder the two drivers who shared the driving didn't fall asleep at the wheel. And the views were mostly obscured by hedges and trees, causing the sun's rays to strobe onto his face. The toilet breaks were minimal, the food miserable, and the seats so hard and small that any attempt at sleep was doomed to failure. Thank God he was given a day at one of the welcoming centres to freshen up and look his best for his homecoming. The travelling experience, even for an A_3, had been a miserable one, although Tom's story had far eclipsed his, so perhaps he should be thankful, but peering through the window of Otto's car and seeing the comfort within made him hate the man even more.

Four times a week, in the afternoons, Otto visited Maia. And at least twice a week, Price waited half an hour before knocking on her door, acting the caring and concerned friend, making sure he outstayed his welcome, with Otto hiding somewhere in the house. Saturday mornings were spent at the Townhouse, and Sundays seemed the only day Otto remained at home. From what Price could see, although binoculars from a fifty-metre distance can never be considered a truly accurate chronical of life, Otto never once cooked.

He built a picture of Otto's daily life; whom he met and where he went, discovering no hunt connection and no secret meetings (excluding those with Maia), and he had no idea where he went each Friday. But it did put the spotlight on one place – the bio-factory, where Otto spent much of his time. Somehow, Price was going to have to get inside.

The bio-factory, which every town had, and which was always a couple of kilometres from the periphery, provided enough meat to serve the sober meat-eating habits of the local population. It was the largest structure in the town with three buildings, one each for the pigs and chickens, and a slaughterhouse. The walls and the roofs were green, the latter perforated with sky lights, and it seemed to melt into its surroundings, engulfed by so many trees and shrubs that it gave the impression it wasn't there at all. It was far enough away from the town not to smother the houses in a noxious smell although a northerly wind brought its residue closer and those living nearest had to close their windows and take in their washing. Few people bothered getting any closer except on the annual open day every summer when it opened its doors and the stench had been tempered following a week-long effort to suppress it. Price had been a number of times and marvelled at the cleanliness and size of the animal quarters and how well the animals were cared for. It put his mind at rest and allowed him to consume meat without the gnawing discomfort that an animal had to suffer for his personal gratification. Admittedly, he avoided the tour around the slaughterhouse but abuse of animals was unthinkable and against the very founding principles of the Reformation, so there was no need to overly exercise his conscience.

But now he knew differently, especially if Otto Cladders was involved. He spent a few days observing the massive complex, walking around its perimeter to find the best point of entry. The buildings were connected via gangways, all with skylights, and each had a separate gangway which led out to a pathway lined with hedgerows which went directly to the fields a further half a kilometre from the factory. As far as he could tell, there were no guards after sunset or patrols to stop him, and no locks or cameras, complying with the general policy of openness and clarity. It was late February and cold, and no animals wandered into the fields. All activity was hidden apart from the occasional comings and goings of the D_s who worked there, and all Price could hear was a faint rumble of animal noise.

He decided he would enter via the same door as Otto, probably the main entrance or office, and from there to each building. And he would do it in the early hours, taking Tom with him.

The two of them walked quickly along the dirt path, taking them past the last houses and into the open countryside where the delicate late-night rumbling of the town gave way to a sharper, cleaner tone, and the trees and hedgerows glistened with a pearly light from the full moon. Their breaths formed tight wisps in the cool stillness.

'I'm nervous,' Tom said as he caught his first glimpse of the bio-factory.

Price took his hand and kissed him on the forehead. 'Me too,' he replied, 'but don't worry, it'll be fine. We won't be long and then we'll be back in bed and I'll give you the biggest hug you've ever had.' He pulled Tom towards him and clasped his arms around his shoulders. 'I'm serious Tom, you don't need to worry.'

Tom gave him a half smile in return. Price had said it numerous times the past few days and it had begun to wear thin and lose its meaning, so that each time he heard *don't worry* what bounced around in his head was *of course we should worry, what we're doing is crazy.*

'You don't look convinced?' Price said.

'I'm not, but I know we have to do it, so let's get it over and done with.'

They walked silently to the main door which Price opened slowly and as gently as possible. There was no-one, as he'd expected. Their torches guided them passed a small office and along the first of the gangways which led directly to the chickens. They half opened the huge sliding door into the first complex and an acrid stench pushed its way into their lungs making them both cough, forcing them back into the gangway.

'That's much worse than I thought it would be,' Price said, 'we'll have to wrap our scarves around our faces.'

'Is this wise,' Tom said, 'we have no idea what we're going

131

to find.'

'That's the whole point isn't it?'

'But it's hard to breath.'

'We won't be in there long.'

Tom said nothing. He untied his scarf from around his neck and brought it around his nose and mouth, tying it at the back of his head. He then helped Price do the same.

'Let's go in,' Price said assertively, 'and don't worry, I'll be right beside you.'

They opened the sliding door once more and stepped inside. The door closed slowly behind them. At first, they noticed a slow, rhythmic undulation lit unevenly from the small openings in the roof, and as the torchlight scanned across the floor, they could make out individual forms, thousands of them, scurrying away from the light, forming a wave which seemed to hit the walls and bounce back. Chicklets no bigger than a baby's fist filled the tiny spaces between the older chickens. Some were streaked with blood, squeaking as others pecked at their heads.

Price shone the light on Tom's face. Tears streaked his face and disappeared into the fabric of the scarf.

'Be careful where you tread. And don't slip. The floor's covered in shit.' He took hold of Tom's hand and they walked haltingly through the middle of the building's vastness, Tom lighting up their path whilst Price lit up the surroundings, moving his torch slowly from side to side across the mass of frightened birds. They saw chickens with their bald chests ragged with dried blood, others limping so badly their sides slid across the concrete floor. Above them were more chickens, sprawled along a slatted metal decking that spread itself along the edges of the walls.

Tom tugged at Price's sleeve, and shouting so he could be heard above the constant shrill din of the chickens, he called out 'my eyes are stinging. I want to get out of here.'

'Mine too. It's the ammonia,' Price replied.

It took them another minute to reach the next sliding door. They wrenched it open, thrust it shut behind them and pulled off their scarves, gasping as though they 'd been holding their breath the entire time. Price dropped his torch and fell against the wall, letting out a single, exasperated yell. Tom sat beside him, and with a shaking hand, stroked Price's head.

'That's impossible, how is that possible,' Price said, 'there must have been ten thousand chickens in there. At least. Ten thousand chickens. That's impossible. How is that possible.' He repeated himself over and over, banging the palm of one hand against the floor. Tom remained silent with his head down, his arm wrapped around Price's shoulder.

'But the open days,' Price said. 'I've been here for the open days and it's been fine. Just a thousand chickens or so. This is insane.'

'When was the last time you came to one?' Tom asked quietly.

'A few years ago. But that doesn't matter. It's held every year. Hundreds of people go to see it.'

'They must thin the chickens out gradually as it gets closer to the summer,' Tom said. 'Or maybe this is all new. Maybe this is a new experiment.'

'It has to be new,' Price replied. 'There's just no way he could get away with this for long. There are too many people working here. There's no way it could be kept quiet.'

'You forget they're D_s,' Tom said.

'What the hell's that got to do with it?'

'D_s do what they're told Price.'

'No-one would accept this or keep it quiet.'

'If they're told to, then they will,' Tom replied.

'Nonsense.'

'It's not nonsense,' Tom said calmly. 'It's how it is.'

'Even with something as terrible as this? I just don't believe it,' Price said indignantly.

'You're an A Price, since when did you know anything at all about D_s?'

And before Price could reply, Tom stood up quickly and pulled him to his feet. 'We have to go on,' he said. 'We can't turn back. We have to go on,' and pulling his scarf back over his face, he took Price's hand and they walked tentatively along the gangway, sliding open the next door and shining their torches into the vast space that confronted them.

It was much bigger than the previous one, and split into two sections. The machines on the left were so unexpected that, for a moment, they overshadowed the pigs on the opposite side. They were giant machines with wheels as tall as a man and with long metal arms which folded in on themselves. Stacked against the wall next to them were plastic containers the size of baths each containing a clear liquid.

'Have you ever seen anything like that?' Tom asked.

'No,' Price replied curtly, 'I haven't. Nor that.' He shone his torch to the other side of the warehouse where the sound of squealing, frightened pigs beckoned them. 'I'm not looking forward to this,' he said.

In front of them were at least five hundred pigs crammed into a third of the entire space. Metal barriers divided them into groups of about fifty, with little room for them to move, and as Price shone his torch into each partition, they squealed, pushing frantically against each other and the barrier. Some had blisters to their nose and side with open sores which glistened a deep red under the torch light. Some had their tails missing, chewed away by other pigs. And some were chewing the metal bars that caged them. Price moved closer, ready to open the gates to free them, but Tom stopped him. 'Later,' he said. 'We'll do it later.'

They walked along the rows and rows until they reached two thirds along. And once more Price gave out a sharp, desperate cry. The partitions had become tiny metal cells, and in each one lay a single female surrounded by her weaning piglets. The space was so small there was no room for the adult pig to turn, and as the two men went from one cell to the next, they saw piglets with the life squeezed out of them by the weight of their mother. Some of the females had been strapped into place, unable to move even a whisker from side to side, their teats visible for the piglets to feed, their heads forced onto the filthy concrete floor, their eyes glazed in a helpless, tortured despair. In one of the final cells, a tiny piglet no bigger than a human fist had just been flattened, and a fresh, thick glob of blood trickled down the side of its mouth. It was still alive, its chest heaving with the effort of life. Price watched its final gasps and quietly wept as the little thing, which had lived for no more than a day, expired in front of him.

They reached the end of the pig complex, looking at each other in disbelief from behind their semi-masked faces, their eyes unable to conceal the horror of what was before them. And then, on the far wall, they saw a heap of discoloured flesh. Dead pigs and piglets, around twenty in total, awaited disposal. A thick line was drawn across the floor where the pigs had been dragged to the wall and left to rot just a few metres from their living relatives. The stench forced its way through the men's scarves and into their bodies, whacking itself against their lungs. Both coughed, rushed to the next sliding door, and once more collapsed onto the floor of the gangway, utterly spent. The minutes passed and neither man spoke, as though no word could come close to what they had witnessed. Tom was the first to break the silence. 'Different to the open day I guess,' he said.

Price cupped his hands across his face as though to hide his despair. His eyes were sore and his lungs heavy. 'There were about fifty pigs the last time I was here and they could walk about freely. They were happy.'

'Well they're not anymore.'

Then, with what seemed like an effort of supreme will, Tom rose quickly to his feet. 'We have to go on,' he said. 'We have to get out of here.'

They walked home in silence, each man unable to articulate their tangled thoughts. Their pace was slow, as though putting one foot in front of the other was an effort in itself. Price was so deep in thought that if Tom hadn't guided them back, he would have lost his way and perhaps his fragile equilibrium too.

When they reached Tom's house, they went immediately up the stairs and into the tiny shower room where they stripped and, as though in a trance, stepped into the cubicle together to share the two precious minutes under the warm stream of purifying water. They dried themselves in silence, walked to the bedroom in silence and fell on to the bed, lying face up, neither touching nor talking. It had been more than two hours since they left the bio-factory and not one word had been uttered. Sleep came almost instantaneously to them both.

Price woke to a soft stroking of his arm. Tom was sitting on the side of the bed, holding a warm drink and when he saw Price's eyes slowly open, he placed the cup on the floor, pulled the sheets gently away and slid on top of him, kissing him first on the forehead, and gradually down the crest of his nose to his lips. It brought them back to each other and the solidity of their existence, so that when, an hour or so later, they started to talk about the bio-factory, it was with a calm, lucid intelligence. And it produced a plan.

TWELVE

T om and Price returned to the complex a week later, taking notes and images with their tablets, making diagrams of each complex and walking through every gangway to the fields. They siphoned off a few bottles of the liquid from the containers heaped up next to the machines which Price experimented with over the next couple of weeks. One was highly flammable with a noxious smell, probably some form of distilled oil to power the agricultural machines he thought, and the other, almost odourless, which he used on the wild flowers that had begun to poke out of the soft spring ground. He sprayed tiny amounts on cowslips and stitchwort, daisies, dandelions and speedwell. Within a day most had shrivelled and died.

Their final visit to the bio-factory was on the following full moon. They arrived in the late evening and went straight to the chickens. The moonlight pierced the skylights, bathing the vast space in an unbroken dusk and illuminating every move. The chickens parted frantically as Tom and Price, making sure not to slip, walked to the feed store, grabbed two sacks of grain and poured the contents into a barrow from the store cupboard. They then scattered the grain in a thick unbroken line along the corridor that led to the path, continuing until the barrow was empty and repeating the process until the grain reached the fields. The two hardly spoke and each time they returned to the complex, they shooed as many chickens as they could towards the corridor and out into the open air so by the time they'd finished only a few remained inside. It took no more than a couple of hours.

'So far so good,' Price said, 'but let's get out of here, my eyes are stinging.' He took a bottle of water from his rucksack and when they reached the gangway and closed the door behind them they took off their scarves and splashed their faces.

'That wasn't as difficult as I thought,' Tom said as he leant against the wall. 'They didn't need much encouragement to get out of here.'

'Would you?' Price replied. 'The foxes will probably have a feast, but better free and dead than shackled and alive.'

'No contest,' Tom said, 'although it'll be nicer if they're free *and* alive. He took a slug of water and passed the bottle back to Price. 'Let's go to the pigs,' he continued, 'and remember we need to stick to what we'd talked about, so do exactly as I say, it'll make things a lot less complicated.'

'You're the boss,' Price said.

'Good. Then let's go.'

Tom pulled the scarf back over his face and gestured for Price to follow and as they reached the first pen filled with about fifty pigs Tom heard Price puffing out little blasts of air as though by doing so he'd be able to control his emotions.

'Are you ready?'

'Not really, but let's get this over and done with.'

Using the metal barriers piled against one of the walls, they made a corridor from the pen leading out through the exit to the gangway. Tom slowly opened the gate, the pigs squealing frantically, and with a large rectangular wooden board drew them out of the tiny space. As soon as the first pig scurried along the makeshift corridor, the others followed, trotting tightly packed to the fields, Tom and Price following directly behind with their boards, making sure the pigs couldn't retreat.

It took them a couple of hours to clear all the main pens. Words had been compressed and resolute, Price following Tom's brief instructions to the letter. And as they sat by the entrance to the field, with their scarves loosened and breathing the unsullied air, Tom looked up at the clear sky and saw the big dipper sinking westwards.

'We've not got much time left,' he said, 'we have to get the piglets.'

They walked quickly and silently the half kilometre back to the complex, took a wheelbarrow and straw from the storehouse, and then went to the far side where five sows were weaning their young. They started with the larger ones, opening the gates gently, keeping any noise to a minimum, and ushering them out with their mother. Tom removed a crushed dead piglet and placed it in one of the empty cells. The sows could hardly stir, their legs not used to the rigours of movement, but with what seemed like a gargantuan effort of will, the separation from their young pushed them into action and they dragged themselves to their feet, keeping close to the piglets who walked hesitatingly to the exit as Tom and Price walked behind them with the wooden boards and a heaped barrowful of straw to keep them warm in the fields.

The fourth sow was strapped in, her tiny young clasped to each teat. Tom gently extracted each piglet and placed them in the barrow filled with a thick layer of fresh straw. The mother, unable to move, tried to break free from her confinement as Price, shaking, took her piglets to the field, the noise of her squealing echoing through the complex and following him along the gangway. Tom removed the straps, and the mother, unable to turn, pushed herself backwards until she raised herself from the ground like a new born foal standing for the first time. She wobbled and fell on her side, Tom using all his strength to help her back on her feet. She remained still, then started slowly walking towards the exit as though each step might be her last, but her steps quickened and by the time she passed the door into the gangway she'd begun to run, finding her piglets in the field close to Price who'd placed the straw on the ground waiting for her arrival.

'Well done old girl,' Price said, welling with tears, 'and good luck.'

The final sow had seven piglets no more than a couple of days old. She was also strapped in and squealed violently when Tom removed her young one by one and placed them into the barrow. Price wheeled them away and after five minutes Tom removed the straps. She shuddered, shaking her head from side to side, struggling to release herself from the tiny space, her flesh pushing against the bars. She then gave out a puff of air and flopped her head back onto the ground, her chest heaving pitifully up and down and her eyes set in a fearful, distressed gaze. Tom grabbed her back legs and pulled her onto the warehouse floor, but she remained on her side with no strength in her legs to pull herself up. He stroked her, whispering to her, trying to calm her down, but he knew she was too far gone.

He ran down towards the gangway shouting to Price to come back with the piglets, and when they returned, the mother hadn't moved.

'She's going to die,' Tom said. 'She won't survive the night.'

'But we can't leave her here,' Price replied.

'We have to. We have no choice.'

'But what about the piglets?'

'They won't survive Price, there's nothing we can do.'

'We can take them with us.'

'No Price, we can't. We have to leave them here.'

'No way Tom. They'll be burned alive. I can't let that happen.'

'Price, we discussed this. We knew something like this might happen, and of course they're not going to be burned alive.' He took off his rucksack and pulled out a knife he'd sharpened that day. 'We talked about what we would have to do.'

'Yes I know we did, but is there no way we can save them?'

'No Price, there isn't. And we're running out of time, so let's just get on with it.'

'Just give me one more minute.'

Price knelt down by the sow and stroked her chest, pushing his mouth to her ear. 'I'm sorry,' he whispered, 'you poor, poor thing,' tears streaming down his face. 'It'll be alright. It'll be alright.'

'Keep on stroking her Price. Keep her calm. This won't take long.'

Tom got to his knees, pulled the sow's head slightly backwards and stuck the knife into the front base of the neck, swiftly moving it across until he hit the main artery. She was so exhausted that even in the last throes of life she remained still. Price continued stroking her as blood gushed from the wound and watched as her eyes glazed and slowly closed. He could hear Tom's heavy breathing from behind the scarf that covered his mouth and nose, and saw that, just like his, it was wet with tears. He touched his shoulder but Tom moved abruptly away.

'No,' he said. 'Not now.'

Tom stood up and went to the tiny piglets who were still in the barrow. He scooped them up with the straw and placed them gently on the floor, then brought the knife across each of their throats. One by one, he picked up their lifeless bodies and placed them beside their mother, their heads touching her belly. He stood for a moment looking down at Price as he continued stroking the mother, took a deep breath and said 'Come, we have to finish this off. I'll go and check on the animals and you do the straw.'

Tom went straight to the chicken complex, filled another barrow with grain and shooed the remaining birds down the gangway to the field, scattering all the grain at its furthest edge, keeping the birds as far from the bio-factory as possible. He then ran to the adjacent fields to check on the other animals.

Price gathered as much straw as he could find and scattered it on the floor of each complex, keeping all the connecting doors open and making an unbroken line of straw that went from one end of the bio-factory to the other. Using some large empty bottles he'd put in his rucksack, he siphoned off the oil from the giant containers next to the machinery and poured it over the straw.

'It's all done,' he said to Tom when they met up again. 'And the animals?'

'They all seem fine. There are still a few chickens in the building but I've left the doors open and hopefully they'll run out when the fire comes. There's nothing more we can do.'

'This is it then.'

'Yes. This is it.'

Price hugged Tom tightly. 'You're amazing, do you know

that.'

'I'm too tired for hugs Price.' He pushed him gently away, took out the bloodstained knife from his rucksack, walked to the containers and plunged it into as many as he could, releasing streams of liquid onto the floor.

The two exhausted men walked to the side door that led directly outside and stood on its threshold. Price took another bottle from the rucksack that was already half filled with the oil, took off the scarf that had covered his face, ripped it into two, sprinkled one half with some of the liquid and stuffed it into the top of the bottle.

'Ready,' he said.

'Ready,' Tom replied. He took a box of matches from his pocket and lit the top of the scarf.

Price threw the bottle as far as he could into the middle of the warehouse. They waited for a few seconds to make sure the fire had taken hold and then ran.

THIRTEEN

T om enjoyed working on the farm. It was only temporary, until a solid plan evolved from the ruins of the old bio-factory, but when he arrived each morning in the fields, some of the pigs would welcome him like a long-lost friend nudging their snouts against his legs. And it was exhilarating seeing them alive with energy, running through the fields, sniffing, playing, eating, and the mothers, freed from their shackles, weaning their young in a natural space.

The G9, after an emergency series of meetings to discuss the ramifications of the fire, had 'requested' all C_s and D_s within a certain age group to help with the clearing up and the management of the animals out in the fields. Tom's carpentry skills were put to immediate use, building shelters first for the pigs and then for the chickens.

The town's local population arrived in large numbers each day to watch the animals in the fields and to see the charred remains of the bio-factory being painstakingly cleared and the debris building up in a massive gnarled heap of metal and black wood. Rumours of its cause swirled from the first day, people questioning the sheer numbers of chickens and pigs and the wounds some of them carried. Price was delighted to hear the animated version of events which Dan would bring back from the distributions. It created a period of calm between them, giving them something to discuss and somewhere new to take Braggle, sometimes making the hour long walk together. Land that had been seldom trod was now a popular local route. A shebeen was built along the way, serving mostly walnut wine in exchange for practically anything. Price took thimbles and carrots and ginger. And for a while, he lost his indifference around Dan, happy to indulge in wayward gossip knowing they would soon be spread and returned with extra frills and fabrications. And after a couple of weeks, the general consensus was not far from the truth. Nearly all the animals had survived, so they must have been let free – an accident, perhaps electrical, which was the account the G9 was spreading, would surely have caused more casualties. The official account was quickly thrown aside by the locals and it gave Price hope. It was a pivotal moment, and he must not, under any circumstances lose the momentum as he had done before. He watched the pigs relishing their new environment, churning the grass into a feast of mud, and imagined them doing the same on Otto's sparkling lawn with Otto screaming from the border, trussed in a tiny metal cage.

Price had seen him on the morning of the fire standing with the hundreds of others who had gathered to watch the flames bellow into the dawn sky. He was there to see the complex fold in on itself, collapsing into a contortion of red-hot dust.

It had taken him thirty minutes to run back to his house, creep in through the front door without disturbing Braggle, undress and collapse on the sofa. The next thing he knew, Dan had come thudding down the stairs with the dog close behind. 'There's a fire,' he shouted, causing Braggle to bark uncontrollably. 'Something really big has happened. Did you hear the explosion?' And despite Price's body aching with such venom that he just wanted to dissolve into sleep, he knew he had to go along with it.

A line of people scurried along the path towards the bio-factory, stopping far enough away for safety and close enough to feel the heat on their faces. Maia was there, holding her hand to her mouth, with a thick tartan shawl covering her shoulders. Price went to her with a fixed look of concern. He had to get the conversation just right.

'The animals,' he said. 'What about the animals?'

Maia placed her head against his shoulder and pulled the shawl tighter. 'Those poor creatures,' she answered. 'A few people are over there now, but I can't imagine they can get close enough. Did you hear the explosion?'

'Yes, what on earth could it have been?'

'No idea. Otto hasn't a clue how it could have happened.'

Price struck immediately. 'You've spoken to Otto?' 'I didn't know you knew him that well.'

'What a silly thing to say,' Maia replied without flinching, 'everyone knows Otto. He's standing just there.' He was a few metres away in the front line of spectators, impassive, immobile. Price walked calmly over to him and they stood shoulder to shoulder watching the complex burn. 'Those poor, poor animals,' he murmured. There was no reply.

The pig shelters were a series of simple rectangular wooden huts filled with a thick layer of straw. The chicken coops had been more complicated with a large team of workers brought in to pull it off quickly and efficiently. Locals were asked to foster as many chickens as possible whilst the work was being carried out, which they accepted with alacrity and a shared sense of duty. Price and Dan had taken ten, temporarily converting their garden shed and enjoying the extra eggs and the culinary challenges of a house overflowing with protein. Price spent more time with them, talking to them in their makeshift home with a caring gentleness and vowing they would never be maltreated again.

The coops took a couple of weeks to complete and filled two sides of one of the fields set aside for their use. Within each section were nesting boxes each big enough for three birds, and above them poles dissecting the upper reaches where they could sleep. The materials appeared without delay with a tall, gangly man overseeing the operation and Otto coming every morning. Tom watched the two in deep conversation, getting as close as possible to eavesdrop. He heard little of consequence. He saw Maia there often, waving to her with an exaggerated enthusiasm. She replied with a curt nod of her head. When Price appeared, with or without Dan, Tom had to ignore him, watching him tighten Braggle's leash to stop her bounding over. They saw each other most evenings, sharing new information whether gossip or hearsay, piecing together the course of events from the locals' perspective. It cheered them. There had been a groundswell of opposition to the defunct bio-factory and a number of people had taken to the Saturday pulpit to ask rhetorical questions with Price delighting in watching Otto squirm from his chair on the podium. He kept his counsel, biding his time, keeping suspicion away from his door, and feeling he was closing in, slowly, on his prey. He kept up with his visits to Maia, relishing in her unease when Otto was somewhere in the house.

Tom moved to the pig fields in the fourth week. The shuffle of visitors had diminished and most of his colleagues had dispersed to other duties around the farm. He now knew the gangly coordinator was Paul and that it would do their cause no harm to get to know him better. Price had been candid about his dealings with him, including those he would prefer to forget, falling short of suggesting Tom use his beguiling features to reel him in, but making it clear that anything was possible in the chase for incriminating evidence. Paul was as regular as Otto in his daily routine, arriving at the pigsties just before lunch, staying for a couple of hours before moving on to the chickens. He'd spoken to Tom a couple of times, asking him about the work, how long he thought it would take, all of it conveyed to Price the same evening, however irrelevant.

What Tom needed was a subtle ice-breaker, something to weave himself into Paul's inner space, an entry card into his thoughts and plans. 'How about some sort of accident?' Price had said, 'nothing serious of course.' Tom had laughed until he realised he wasn't joking. 'Shall I break my neck?' he'd replied sarcastically, 'or just sprain an ankle?'

'There needs to be blood,' Price said, 'make it look much worse than it is.'

Tom wasn't a squeamish sort of person and he'd seen plenty of blood in his youth as C_s had the habit of taking the rough and tumble of childhood to extremes, but Price's

146

seemingly cavalier attitude to his bodily parts irked him.

'How about I cut off a finger. That should have the desired effect,' he said. 'I can cut off my pinkie with a chisel.' He put his hand in the air and waggled his fingers. 'Who needs five when four can do the job just as well.'

The two were sitting on Tom's small sofa, Price's arm clasped generously around his lover's waist. 'There's no need to go so far,' he replied. 'Just a little chink out of it will do.'

The next morning Tom took a five-centimetre nail from his tool kit and, just after breakfast, put it in a pan of boiling water for one minute and then into his pocket. He walked to work rubbing the nail between his fingers and pressing its point against the fleshy tip of his thumb. He went first to say hello to the pigs and then on to the chicken fields where he collected his tools from the shed and placed them in a row on the work bench as though he was laying out cutlery on his kitchen table. He took a pen and made a mark on the tip of his thumb exactly where Price had told him to the night before. 'It'll be a superficial wound,' Price had said, 'but there should be lots of blood.' Tom winced. There was something in Price's tone that made him feel less than valued, as though he'd said 'that soup needs a bit more salt', and now, every time he put the nail against his thumb, it felt more like an order than an act of mutual benefit.

Paul arrived on cue just before lunch. He walked slowly around the field with his hands behind his back and talked to a couple of D_s. Tom saw him coming closer and put the nail tip onto the pen mark, keeping it in place with his index finger, his hands shaking slightly. He took the hammer, waited until Paul was a few metres away, clenched his teeth and brought the hammer down hard.

His yelp of pain was genuine. The nail slid through the flesh, breaking open the top layer of skin, blood oozing freely from the wound. Tom flicked the thumb towards his chest, scattering streaks of red across his clothes, and moved towards Paul with his right hand clenched around the wound, the blood trailing down his arm.

And then he staggered and fell, lightly, forcing Paul to hold him up and chaperone him to a bale of hay close-by. He sat down with his head flipped down into his lap, taking sharp, hard breaths. 'I'm so sorry,' he said, 'I've just banged a nail into my thumb, I'm sure it'll be ok.'

'Have you got it out?' Paul asked.

'Yes, but I think it needs to be bandaged.'

'Let me see.'

Paul gently unfolded Tom's right hand which was still clasped around the wounded thumb. 'It's not too bad, but yes, it needs to be dressed,' he said in a reassuring tone, and took a paper tissue from his pocket. 'Now wrap this tightly around it, keep your arm in the air, and I'll go and get the medical kit.'

Tom thanked him, and in the time he was away, squeezed the gash as much as he could bear, releasing a steady stream of blood which he flicked and smeared on to his top.

'I'm so sorry,' he said again when Paul returned, 'I feel such a fool. It's just that the sight of blood makes me feel a bit dizzy.'

'I wouldn't look at your shirt then,' Paul replied, 'otherwise you'll never recover,' and taking Tom's hand in his, he smeared the wound with a yellow cream that smelled of lavender, placed a dressing over it and wrapped a bandage tightly round and round. 'That should stop the bleeding,' he said, and sat on the hay bale with his arm around Tom's shoulder. 'Now then, you're going to need to change that top. Are you ok to walk home?'

Tom gave one of his smiles. 'I think so,' he replied. He stood up slowly, wobbled and fell back onto the hay bale. Paul grabbed him by the waist. 'I think you're going to need an escort back home, don't you?'

'I think you're probably right.'

Tom told everything to Price that evening who did his best not to sound jealous, although it was clear to Tom that he was – the way he rubbed his nose and made short sniffing sounds was evidence enough – and so he resolved to dilute any future details to spare any unnecessary tension; he would keep their conversations involving Paul to the important facts and add occasional bawdiness to lighten the mood.

Paul and Tom became lovers, their meetings sporadic, depending on Paul's itinerary. He was a busy man and told Tom of other work in other towns, although this town, he said, had taken up the lion's share of his tasks. Tom was a good listener, drawing him out, over time, careful not to force the conversation, homing in on information he thought could lead somewhere, his coquettish manner hiding the significance of his questions. In truth, Tom found Paul's life fascinating, and so his curiosity was real. He knew no-one who had the use of a car, who had seen numerous other towns, and who was free to travel. Paul told him how the towns were all much the same, with the same structures and facilities, the same mix of people, the same restrictions, the same ideas and frustrations, the same sense of unity and togetherness, the same hierarchies.

'So there's an Otto in every town?' Tom asked.

Paul laughed. 'If you mean a primus inter pares, then yes, every town has its Otto.'

Tom had no idea what he meant, but carried on regardless. 'I don't mean that, no,' he said. 'It's just that, well, I've only been here a short time, and I might be wrong, I probably am, but from what I've seen and from what I've heard, he's …' Tom stopped. He didn't want to push it.

'He's what?'

'Well, he's …' Again, Tom let the sentence drop.

'He has vision Tom, real vision. He's not one for standing still. He gets things done. I've seen him at meetings. He's the driving force. That's what I like about him. That's why we click.'

'I was going to say aloof,' Tom replied.

'He's not one for small talk if that's what you mean. But he's a good listener. He's not authoritarian, he knows what he wants, but he doesn't force the issue. Look at the bio-factory, that's classic Otto. He's been to so many meetings these past few weeks, done a lot of travelling, and he's had to fend off so much criticism. They want it re-built, exactly as it was. Otto is insisting the animals stay out in the fields. He's seen how they love being out in the open.' Paul rested his hand on Tom's bare knee, and gave it a squeeze. 'And he's very impressed with their new living quarters. You've done a fine job there, Tom.'

'And so what's going to happen? Are they going to stay outside?'

'Still unsure. I hope so. But it all depends on Otto's negotiating skills. He can make all the necessary noises, but if the quorum is against him, then he'll have to let it go. You see, if there's one exception, they're worried others will want the same. Every town has a bio-factory. The complex is based on a template, they're all the same, and if one is different, well, it could set a precedent, and that's dangerous.'

'But you said Otto is being insistent, won't that make a difference?'

'We have to wait and see. But yes, if Otto has his way, then the animals stay out in the fields and fingers crossed, it could well have a roll-on affect in other towns.'

Price paced across Tom's living room. 'That's bullshit,' he repeated. 'He's playing with you Tom. He's feeding you bullshit.' He paused and re-filled his glass with some elderflower wine, put the glass to his lips and without taking a sip, put it back on the table. His mind was racing. 'Tom, have you said anything, anything, it doesn't matter how small, about the conditions in the bio-factory? Is there anything you've said that might, in any way, incriminate us?'

'No, of course not. Not that I know of.'

'Not that you know of!' Price plonked himself on the sofa next to Tom, and raising his voice, said it again. Tom stood up abruptly and waving his arms in the air said: 'This was *your* idea remember. *Yours. You* wanted me to sleep with Paul. *You.* Remember? So do not start accusing me of doing anything wrong. Which, I repeat, I have not. And if I have, which I haven't, then it's your bloody fault. Not mine!' He gave out a loud puff of exasperation.

'I never told you to sleep with him.'

'What!'

'I only said do what you think was necessary to get some information.'

'Oh? Like having a nice little chat over a cup of tea and a

few biscuits? Lure him in with my baking skills?'

'Now you're being ridiculous.'

'I'm being ridiculous? What, because I'm a C_2 you mean? Some silly little C_2 homotype who doesn't know when he's being used? You *did* tell me to sleep with him Price and so don't try and re-write history. And now it's me, yes me, that's deep in the shit. And so what's going to happen to me now? Have you thought of that? Or is that of no consequence?'

'You have to stop seeing Paul.'

'What!'

'You have to tell him it's over.'

The comment stopped Tom in his tracks. He remained perfectly still with his mouth wide open as though he'd just swallowed a frog. He then picked up the nearest thing to him, which happened to be a small potted plant, and threw it at Price. It hit the wall scattering soil onto his head and shoulders, the geranium flopping on to the sofa.

'You really have no idea what it's like for people like me have you Price. You sit there with all your privilege and your arrogance with absolutely no idea of how the real world works. You think I can just click my fingers and tell Paul to go away and he'll say 'oh, what a shame, well, it was nice whilst it lasted, see you around'.
I do what I'm told Price. That's what C_{2s} do.'

Price was brushing off the soil from his hair and heard little of what Tom had just said. 'There was no need to throw that at me,' he said indignantly. 'You're overreacting.'

Tom stamped his feet on the floor in exasperation. 'I'm going to bed Price. And I want you to leave. And come to think of it, I don't want you to come back.' He left the room, thundered upstairs and slammed his bedroom door shut.

'That's fine with me,' Price shouted up at him. He grabbed the limp geranium and threw it at the door. He looked for Braggle, realised he hadn't brought her with him, then walked out of the house slamming the door behind him.

He remained at home for a week, making Dan's life more unbearable than usual. Dan had become accustomed to his absences, appreciated the breathing space, and now, suddenly, Price was refusing even to take Braggle for a walk.

He assumed he'd had a tiff with a lover of some sort, but was damned if he was going to ask or try to soothe Price's battered ego, again. He cooked, avoiding carrots (though he was sorely tempted to add an ounce or two), avoided leading questions, averted recriminations, did everything to prevent pricking Price's fragile disposition. If Price grumped or gruffed or smacked a cup on the kitchen table or remained resolutely silent during dinner, without a thank you or any mention of the food in front of him, Dan ignored it. He ensured the food was basic, no frills or piquant sauces, no artistry with presentation. The vegetable garden remained untouched. The herb garden was used sparingly. At the distribution, he accepted what was on offer, leaving his bartering skills for happier times. One evening, when Price was looking pale, his hands shaking slightly and beads of sweat forming on his brow, he said nothing. When Price vomited in one of the garden pots, he said nothing, rinsing it out when Price was safely back in his study.

Price spent most of his time there, locked away, reading Theo's journal over and over, looking for clues, anything that might incriminate Otto further. His loathing of Otto had transformed into a malign hatred, a loathing so profound it threatened his own stability. He could feel its physicality, the way it grabbed him in the throat and the stomach, wrenched at his insides, stripping him of his equanimity. He found himself banging items on to surfaces; cups on tables with a thud, toothbrush into container with a clank, doors shut with a smack. He wanted to shout indiscriminately, scream uncontrollably, bang his fists on the dining table, thump anything inanimate. His sense of colossal ineptitude deepened.

The coding system in Theo's journal gave him some respite; its subtle intelligence enveloping him, allowing him into the workings of Theo's mind and to feel closer to the dead man. He missed him terribly. Reading his words, in his own handwriting, gave him strength, a longing to be as good, as honest, as reliable as his friend, something he knew he could never be. He repeated, to the exact measurement (thereabouts), some of his experiments. He'd hidden the dried plants with the journal in his study, a hiding place ingenious in its simplicity, and which he knew no-one could possibly find. He started, as Theo did, by taking tiny doses of the least threatening plants, noting their effect and making comparisons to Theo's detailed analysis. He increased doses, tried other plants, some leaving him shaking and sweating, nothing too serious, and then abruptly gave up after a rather unpleasant vomiting episode involving an empty garden pot.

Then after a week, the day after his embarrassment with the pot, and when the late Spring heat was beating down on the parched soil, he hastily ate his breakfast and said he'd take Braggle out.

'Finally,' Dan replied, and left it at that.

Braggle needed no directing. She followed the road and path directly to Tom's house, rushing to the front door and pawing at the door sill. Price knocked, with the faint hope that Tom had excused himself from his duties at the farm. He waited for the door to open, for Tom to embrace him, and for the silence to be lifted. But he wasn't there. Price sat on the doorstep with Braggle licking his chin, yearning for Tom's welcoming smile, absentmindedly picking at the creeping wood sorrel at his feet and nibbling at the leaves. He then stood up abruptly, brushed his thighs with his hands and set off for the edge of town.

The oak tree in front of the house was unveiling its fresh coat of spring leaves, and as Price passed, he grabbed a branch, pulled it down to shoulder height, ripped off a couple of the leaves and crushed them between his fingers as he marched to the back of the house and stood in the middle of the lawn where he and Theo had stood a few months before. The grass was rigidly thick and lush, and once he found the line that ran around the replacement turf, he edged his middle finger around the sides, lifting it up and tearing it away. He held the limp, heavy square of turf aloft and looked up at the house. No-one was peering out. He strode to the back door and banged as hard as he could. Braggle barked. Still no-one came. He went to the pond, took a large stone from its bank, disturbing a couple of frogs, walked purposefully back and threw the stone through the glass. 'That's for Theo,' he shouted as Braggle barked frantically, pacing along the patio that ran along the back of the house with its sculpted box shrubs in pots standing like a little army along its length. Price pushed over one of the pots, pulled out a shrub and threw it into the house. More glass shattered onto the kitchen floor. 'And that's for every one of those animals you deprived of any sort of existence, you lump of human shit.' He went back to the pond, took another stone, smaller this time, walked to the side of the house where the car was parked and dragged it back and forth along the bonnet, then along its length. He stopped for a while to admire his work, then continued with the zeal of an artist starting a new canvas, finally dropping the stone and falling against the side of the car port.

Price's rage diminished in the frenzy of his offensive, and he could feel a steady release of pent-up anger with each slash of stone against metal, but as he squatted against the wall, he felt a ferocious emptiness. There was no salutary charge of adrenalin, just the plainness of his heart beating rapidly in his chest and the sense that he was, once again, reacting to events rather than steering them; his lack of endurance had failed him again, pushing him to the ground when he had to hold himself upright. He drew Braggle closer to his chest, roughly gliding his hands across the hair under her ears. She tilted her head upwards with that loving, unconditional response which had so often served him well, melting despairs, steadying his frailties; yet this time, as she levelled her eyes with his, they seemed to penetrate with a quizzical, uneasy stare. Price looked away, unable to gain comfort from her soft fur. He let out a terse scream, stood up, picked up the stone and started banging at the car door again and again until he was out of breath. Then he gripped the handle and tried to rip it from the door. It opened. For a moment, he stood back in disbelief, and then jumped in excitedly. He sat on the red leather seat and stared at the instruments and numbers laid out in a row in front of him. He pushed the button marked 'start', the engine coming to life with a deep, luxurious groan. He laughed and called Braggle to jump in next to him. 'We're going for a ride,' he said.

He pressed impatiently on a few other buttons as he sometimes did with the holovision remote when it stuck at the most untimely of moments, but nothing happened. He pushed down on a pedal; nothing except a gentle throbbing of the engine. He pushed on another pedal and felt the car rev and shudder. Something was stopping it from moving. He pressed another button. The car roared forwards, smashing through the front of the carport, its roof caving in and thudding on to the top of the car. The glass in the windscreen shattered, showering them with nuggets of blunt glass. Braggle leapt to the backseat barking wildly whilst Price sat stock still, his eyes fixed on the splintered strips of wood just beyond the windscreen, his mouth slightly open. He began to flick the glass from his body as though he'd been covered in a light dust, his bemused chuckles gaining momentum until they erupted into uncontrollable laughter, making Braggle bark even louder and drown out the erratic throb of the engine.

The walk back was brisk and uneventful; Price had adjusted his clothing and hair and hopped every few steps like an excitable child, tilting his head to the sky and flaring his nostrils to absorb the warm, dry air. Campions and dead nettles littered the verge, enveloped with the buzz of fledgling life. The weekly garbage truck glided silently by and he waved to the driver. He nodded to everyone who passed, doffing an imaginary hat to two women who were each holding a racket, and who, he assumed, were on their way to the arena next to the square.

He turned into the path leading to his house with an impish smile etched on his face and he grazed his hand along the hedgerow, thinking of Tom and how, that evening, he would go to him, get down on his knees and apologise for his inexcusable behaviour.

Dan was in the vegetable garden digging out clumps of grass which threatened the young leeks. Braggle bounded over and licked at his face. Price wasn't far behind, almost bouncing across the terrace with a smile. Dan stood up, took off his gardening gloves, and smiled back.

'You're looking chirpy,' he said. 'Any particular reason?'

'Let's just say it's been eventful.'

'Care to tell me about it?'

'Not really,' and Price turned to go back to the house.

Dan felt the rejection like a slap to the face. He threw his gloves to the ground and to quell his exasperation picked up the spade and thrust it as hard as he could into the earth.

'Someone came to see you half an hour ago,' he said.

Price turned quickly.

'Who?'

'I don't really feel like telling you.'

'Don't be ridiculous Dan. Who was it?'

'I don't feel like talking at the moment, maybe later.'

'Dan, this isn't funny. Who was it?'

'Oh, it is funny Price. Funny how you can't take a bit of your own medicine. Not nice is it.'

Price came closer. Dan picked up the spade and stuck it in the ground in front of him with his hands clenched around the handle. They stared at each other for a few moments, Price inching forward.

'Tell me,' he said flatly. And with a few seconds pause added 'please.'

'That's a word I haven't heard for a long time, at least not from you.'

'You're right. I'm sorry. Now please tell me who was here.'

Dan released his grip on the handle and bent down to pick up the gloves. 'Please makes all the difference,' he said as he stood slowly back up. 'It was that lanky guy we've seen at the farm a couple of times, the one you said you spilt all that gravy over at the summer festival.'

'Paul?'

'You know his name then?'

'Maia told me a bit about him.'

'How does Maia know him?'

'Dan, is that important? Why on earth was he here?'

'He's quite a charmer actually,' Dan replied, 'says he'd like to talk to you about the future of the farm. Says he's heard you're interested in animal husbandry. I told him I think he's got the wrong person, but he seemed quite sure it's you. Is that true?'

Price smiled faintly, telling Dan he'd made a few enquiries at the farm about becoming more involved with the pigs - something to keep him occupied, and that it was great he'd heard back so quickly.

'I'll go there now,' he said.

Tom answered the door with an expressionless face. His eyes seemed vacant. He looked pale; his hair limp and unkempt.

Price couldn't help himself. 'You look terrible,' he said.

'You're not looking so great yourself.'

'I've missed you.'

No reply.

'I was going to the farm, and this is on the way so ...'

'Second time lucky then.'

'Were you here earlier?'

'Yes.'

'Why didn't you answer?'

Tom leant against the door frame as though to steady himself. 'I have a visitor,' and as he said it, Paul appeared behind him, put his hand on his shoulder and invited Price inside. His tone was friendly and insistent, and Price knew better than to refuse. The three walked silently to the back of the house, with its little kitchen off to one side and the round dining table dominating the space.

'Make some tea for our guest,' Paul said, and Tom went immediately to the kitchen to boil some water. 'You must be thirsty Price, you've had an exhausting morning I hear. Please, do sit down.'

Price remained standing, putting both hands on the back of one of the chairs. His mind was racing, determining how to react, so many things to calculate at once. 'You've made yourself at home I see,' was all he could say, his mouth so dry that he had to swallow mid-sentence.

'It's cosy here. And of course, Tom is a very fine host.'

Price ignored the bait, and walked over to Tom. 'Are you

ok?' he asked. Again, there was no reply.

'He's not too happy with you. You've got him into all sorts of problems. You've been a little selfish haven't you Price, just thinking about yourself, whilst poor little Tom here has had to deal with the fallout all on his own. And I must say, whilst you've been hiding away, there has been quite a lot of that, quite a lot indeed. Tom and I have been having some long chats, amongst other things. And he's been very co-operative.'

Price moved closer to Tom and saw his body stiffen as he brought his mouth to his ear, feeling him wince as his breath caressed his skin. 'I'm sorry,' he whispered.

Tom brushed him away and with a shaking hand filled the teapot with boiling water, spilling some over the side. Paul came into the kitchen. 'Leave him alone,' he said, 'he doesn't want you near him.'

Price shoved him back with both hands, pushing him against the cupboard. The china rattled inside. Paul grabbed Price's arm, pulled it around his back, forcing him to turn, and pushed him against the same cupboard, squashing the side of his face against the wood. He picked up the pot and held it above his head, tilting it slightly, releasing a short trickle of water on to his neck. Price yelped. 'I'd be perfectly still if I were you,' Paul said calmly, 'for your own safety.'

Price remained still, with the smell of freshly polished wood streaming up his nose. He could hear Paul's breath against the side of his face – the regularity of the inhale, exhale, its penetrating coarseness, the sexuality of its intimidation – and felt disgust at himself, that he had created this moment. In a stifled voice, he asked him to release his arm. Paul did it gradually, with each loosening of his grip a gesture of his dominance.

'Time to talk,' Paul said.

That night, Price lay in his garden on the soft patch of grass hidden by a myriad of flowers which over the course of the week had surged upwards with the unrelenting force of the natural world, and as the late spring light evaporated and the darkness wrapped itself around him, he watched the colours fade from the petals, leaving silhouettes of little fragments of beauty which every now and then brushed against his face as the breeze ebbed and flowed. Looking up at the heavens and the canopy of a million stars, he felt its weight pushing him into the ground, its brilliance too complicated and powerful to question. Its majesty, which in the course of his life had given him immeasurable pleasure, was now lost to him. He felt there was nothing left but to succumb to its force and accept his insignificance. It was perhaps a relief too. There was no more need to pretend; to be something he was not. He would never disturb the universe, never alter trajectories or bend them to his will. He might be an irritation, an itch, but it could never spread beyond the boundaries of his little world, and thinking otherwise would be, as Paul had said, pushing against the forces of inevitability.

The three of them had talked candidly with a surprising calm. Paul had been blunt and threatening, listing their transgressions including Price's 'mishap' in Otto's garden that morning. And the warning was clear – stop now and survive, or continue and be swallowed into the abyss. It was wrapped as leniency in a suffocating package of restrictions. They would have time to think it over, discuss it between themselves, and if they chose for the common good, then they would avoid tribunals and certain ignominy with all the consequences that entailed. The G9 knew everything and that in turn had been forwarded to the highest levels within the Reformation. The collective decision had been unanimous – that in the spirit of forgiveness, one of the founding principles of the new order, those responsible should be allowed a second chance.

Neither Tom nor Price saw Paul out of the house. They heard a soft click as he closed the door, and watched him walk slowly out the front gate, glancing back briefly before heading away. His final words were still hanging in the air, both men submerged in their meaning and unable to speak. Paul had kissed Tom, softly brushing his hand through his hair, telling him he wouldn't be seeing him again and that Tom was, with immediate effect, dismissed from his work on the farm. 'It's been a special time,' he said. And that was it.

Tom was dumbstruck. The past week, he had been in a state of constant nervous exhaustion; Paul had all but taken over his life with demands, threats, embraces and inconsistencies, and now, apparently, it had stopped, permanently. As Paul disappeared from view, he remained looking out of the window, making sure he wasn't coming back, then sunk down on to the sofa and wept with relief. Price sat next to him and touched his arm, but it was swept away. 'Do not touch me,' Tom said sharply, and repeated it as Price remained by his side. The two sat together without words, weighed down by what had just passed, digesting Paul's offer silently, both knowing there was no option. Tom was the first to speak, and he said it with the firmness of conviction. 'You have to leave me alone,' he said, 'I can't go on with this anymore. You have to leave me in peace.'

Their conversation was as calm as it had been with Paul, and when Price left the house, he closed the door as softly as his predecessor.

Tom had chosen for safety, and Price had concurred. And as he lay in the dark on the grass, his whole life seemed empty and futile. He could hear the distant croaking of frogs, their grunts sounding like a reproach, and allowed the insects to scamper across his face and the dew to dampen his clothes. He thought of how he had let Tom slip away, and Paul's ability to dominate a room with words that, in hindsight, seemed hackneyed and formulaic. Price was certain their leniency was a sign that they were edgy; that what he knew had the potential for considerable fall-out, but he had promised Tom to keep his mouth shut and to observe the restrictions. It was for Tom's sake, not for his. But oblivion seemed eminently preferable to a life-time of hypocrisy. Knowledge was the opposite of empowerment he thought; it made one miserable, frail, inert, stripping away the comfort of ignorance and replacing it with the agony of paralysis. Why had he been spared and Theo thrown to the wolves? Had Maia intervened? Had she used her influence to dilute Otto's intentions? He needed to know before he was silenced altogether.

FOURTEEN

The next morning Price ate breakfast in silence, watching Dan spread his new batch of elderflower jam methodically on to his toast, giving the remnants to Braggle who waited with her head nestled between his legs. He had little appetite, managing the dollop of yoghurt that had been ladled into his bowl and a cup of heavily brewed tea which Dan had allowed to rest in the pot until it had turned a deep red brown and stained the inside, leaving him the task, every morning, of cleaning it with the metal swab he'd made for the purpose. Price left the house at ten taking Braggle with him, telling Dan he was going to Maia's which, for once, was true.

Ten was the optimum time to catch her with Otto, although he'd never seen him, just felt his presence, and as soon as she opened the door he knew he was in the house. Her smile was fixed, her welcome genuinely artificial, her movements contrived.

'Oh, hello Price. You just caught me in the middle of cleaning.'

'Cleaning? Again? Have you got nothing else to do with your time Maia?'

'You know I like everything in its place.'

'Really? I thought you liked a bit of disorder every now and then?'

'What on earth is that meant to mean?' she asked irritatedly.

'Oh nothing, it's just that all that order makes for a very

dull life don't you think. Wouldn't it be nice to shake it all up a bit sometimes? Or should we all go off to the woods and hide away like owls in the daytime?'

Price took off Braggle's lead and walked passed Maia and into the living room. He dropped the lead on the floor and went directly to the kitchen. Maia followed him in and watched in disbelief as he filled the kettle with water and put it on the stove.

'Have you been drinking?' she asked.

'No, have you?'

'Price, it's ten o'clock in the morning. Of course I haven't.'

'Ditto. Although come to think of it, I did have a cup of tea half an hour ago if that's what you mean. And the walk's left my mouth very dry, so another would be very welcome, thank you, the kettle's on. And while you're at it, some water for Braggle wouldn't go amiss, she's been panting all the way here. And what about one of those fabulous honey and walnut biscuits?'

'I don't have any biscuits in the house Price.'

'What, not even any crumbs?'

'Price, you're acting very strangely. What's the matter?'

'Nothing Maia. Absolutely nothing. But *you* seem a little edgy. So let's sit down, have a nice cup of tea and you can tell me all about it.'

'Price, it's a lovely idea, but I really have to get on, I'm taking Electra out for a ride in half an hour.'

'Another ride Maia? You need to be a bit careful, too much riding and it'll give you bow legs.'

 Price infused his talk with sarcasm, his comments were snide and his observations hinted at something deeper. It made Maia profoundly uncomfortable. For the past few weeks, her heart sank every time he knocked on the door. She'd given subtle hints, shortening conversations, avoiding drinks, never making reciprocal visits, but it had no impact, as though Price was made of impervious stone that deflected the self-evidence of a dying friendship. He also had an uncanny habit of showing up whenever Otto was around, and she was fed up of hiding him in the bedroom. And besides, he was a constant reminder of Theo, and that was the last thing she wanted. Price brought his name up at any opportunity which seemed to her grossly insensitive.

'This is the one Theo used to bring to the fields,' Price said as he took two cups from the cupboard and placed them on the dining table. 'He used to fill it almost to the brim with mint water and drink it all in one go.' He went back to the cupboard and took out a tea pot. I haven't seen that before. Is it pre-Change?'

He wandered back into the living room, picking up objects, placing them under Braggle's nose for a sniff, poking at things, being deliberately obtuse. Maia called him back into the kitchen and placed the cup of tea on the table. 'Now please Price, sit down and stop nosing through my possessions.'

'I'm sorry Maia,' he said, 'but you know how curious I am, and you have so many lovely new things. By the way, Tom and I aren't seeing any more of each other. Pity. I liked him a lot. What about you? Are you seeing anyone? It's been a few months since Theo died. Heard anything about a new partner? Anything on the horizon? It takes time I know. You must get them to hurry up, you must be tearing your hair out being here all alone.'

Maia banged her cup on the table, spilling some tea. 'For God sake Price, will you please shut up.'

Braggle barked. Maia snapped at her too. 'Stop it,' she said harshly.

The awkwardness lasted a few seconds before Price walked into the living room, cup in hand, poured his tea on to the sofa, and in a high voice, imitating Maia's as best he could, shouted, in tandem with Braggle's barking: 'Otto, Otto, help me,' followed by 'heeeeelp.'

He heard a roar from the bedroom, someone running down the stairs and charge into the room.

'Hello Otto,' Price said in the same high tone, and then blew him a kiss. 'Come to save the damsel in distress? Now would that be me or darling Maia here?'

'Arsehole,' Otto replied.

'The great man speaks,' Price said, 'and with such eloquence. All from below the waist, as always.'

Braggle barked hysterically, running back and forth between the two men. Otto kicked her away and she scampered into the corner. Price didn't react. He'd been rehearsing a steely composure on the way to the house, and what he would say, and was determined to keep his head and the upper hand. He clapped his hands slowly.

'You've always had a way with animals, haven't you Otto. Such a caring, sensitive creature.'

'Didn't you get the message yesterday?' Otto replied.

'What, that bit about being hanged, drawn and quartered if I didn't collapse to the floor with my legs dangling in the air so you could tickle me on the belly?'

Maia intervened. 'This is ridiculous,' she said. 'Let's stop this right now.'

Price looked sharply at her and grunted. 'You're right,' he said, 'it is ridiculous, so let's sit down and talk about how ridiculous it all is, because, I can assure you Maia, with a bit of luck, after today I will not be troubling you again.' He walked directly to the table and sat down, calling Braggle over, calming her by stroking under her ears. Maia and Otto walked together to the table.

'How did you know he was here,' she asked.

Again, Price grunted. He ignored the question and started immediately with what he'd rehearsed in his head the night before.

'My dear Maia, do you really think I've been coming here since Theo's death to comfort you? That really *is* ridiculous. Do you think it's any coincidence that Otto has had to hide so many times in, where is it? The bedroom? The bathroom? I've known what's been going on since Theo died. Remember him? That sweet, gentle man you swept aside for …. him.' Price lifted his hand to stop them interrupting. 'No,' he said firmly, 'I'm speaking.' He placed both hands flat down on the table and continued. 'I saw Theo the day he died. It was no accident Maia, so please, don't insult me by saying otherwise. Theo kept a diary, a very detailed one. And I have it. I know about the tribunal. I know how you both humiliated him, crushed him, pushed him to his death. You think you have a lot on me Otto? Well, ditto. And I have evidence to back it all up. Documented evidence. Photos of animals in desperate conditions. Did you know about that Maia? Did you know about the conditions in the bio-factory? You must have heard the rumours. Well, they're all true. And all that evidence is stored neatly away somewhere very, very safe, to be brought out and distributed if need be. You think you're the master of this town Otto Cladders, strutting around, doing what you want, threatening me with your henchman, ruling this town like it's your own personal fiefdom. I can't wait to see it all come crashing down around you, and it will, oh it will.' He lifted one hand again, with his index finger pointing directly at him. 'I would personally love nothing more than to bring you down myself, and I truly think I have the power to do it, and I think you know that, which is why there's no tribunal, no retribution, but for Tom's sake, I'm letting it go. I don't care about me and I certainly don't care about either of you, but he doesn't deserve to be caught up in all this, so I'm letting it go. But don't think you've cowed me into submission because you haven't.' He dropped his clammy hands into his lap and straightened his back. 'I'm finished,' he said.

Otto and Maia listened impassively and after what seemed an interminable pause, Otto stood up. He was about to speak when Maia interjected. 'No,' she said, 'I'm speaking first. It's nonsense about Theo of course, utter nonsense. You're suggesting I deliberately killed him?' She threw her head back and guffawed. It was so theatrical that Price knew he'd hit a nerve. 'And Otto and I seeing each other? Oh Price, we're all entitled to a bit of fun aren't we? A bit of harmless fun.'

Price bit his tongue, keeping his promise to himself to keep his cool.

'And you're behind the fire? Really? I don't believe you Price, and I don't believe Otto would treat animals like that.' She said it with such conviction that Price began to think she really didn't know. Had Otto kept it all from her?

'But Price, you practically destroyed his car. Why on earth would you do that? It makes no sense.'

'I was in the house,' Otto interjected. 'I saw it all.'

'Then why didn't you stop me,' Price asked.

'Because Els was there too, terrified.'

'You could have hidden her in the bedroom or the bathroom,' Price replied sarcastically.

'I did,' Otto said.

Maia continued. 'And it was me who asked Otto not to take it any further. It's nothing to do with being afraid of any hold you might have on him. That's ridiculous. I asked him to let it go. And he has. You're my friend Price.' Her voice vibrated, cracking faintly.

'That's bollocks,' Price replied matter-of-factly, much to Maia's astonishment. She had the firm belief that her exterior was resolutely compact and could hide, under every circumstance, the true identity of her thoughts and feelings. It had served her well all her life, including those moments at the Academy when the truth would have involved unwanted soul searching leading to unwelcome repercussions. Her response was to dig deeper into her well-tuned theatrical resources. She put her hand to her chest, and gave out a little yelp of disbelief, as though she were a cat whose tail had been trodden on. Price mimicked the sound, doubling Maia's uneasy distress.

'I can't believe you're acting like this,' she said, 'I want you to leave.'

'Not quite yet,' Price replied, with a resolve Maia had never witnessed before. She looked at Otto who was leaning against the stove with a look on his face which, at that moment, could have been interpreted in a number of ways. Price saw it as unadulterated arrogance, whilst Maia saw a smirk directed pointedly at her inability to take control of the situation in hand. It's a look she had seen a number of times before, to which, until now, she had brushed aside as a rather endearing quirk which added to his sexual attraction, but as she wrestled with several new and potentially highly distressing realities, his look suddenly transformed into something she instantly disliked. She gave him a withering sneer, turned back to Price and since she was not one to allow others to gain the upper hand, left the room. As she walked past Price, he grabbed her lightly by the arm. 'You know I always liked you Maia,' he said, 'but what has happened to you? With him of all people. Think about it, Maia. Think long and hard about what you've become.' She flicked his arm away, and walked out of the room.

Otto came back to the table and sat sideways on, with one arm resting over the back of the chair. Price adjusted his position to mimic his adversary. 'So, tell me,' he asked, 'how is it possible that the lowest form of human existence has risen to the highest position in this town? It apparently requires humility, empathy and above all intelligence, three things which are distinctly lacking from your portfolio.'

Otto remained inscrutable. 'And how is it that a miserable low-life like you can go through life without any understanding whatsoever of how the world spins on its axis? It seems to me that you're about as forward-thinking as one of those chickens you so heroically rescued not so long ago.'

'Tell me Otto, have you always been an arrogant, unapologetic moron?'

'And have you always been so blinkered that you can't tell right from wrong?'

'*I* can't tell right from wrong? Are you living in some kind of parallel universe?'

'I'm living in the real world Price. And I'm doing my best to make it better.'

'With poisons, threats and abuse? Oh, and let's not forget just a little bit of total disregard for that thing they call the constitution which, the last time I looked, went into quite a lot of detail about protecting the environment, which, to my knowledge, correct me if I'm wrong, means plants and animals. We share it with them Otto, we don't control it.'

Otto swivelled around in his chair and faced Price, leaning forward so their heads were a few centimetres apart. 'Don't be so naïve,' he said, 'we have always controlled it, and we always will. The environment bends to our needs, it flows in our direction. Has it ever occurred to you that we're in a constant state of flux, adapting things to suit changing times, changing situations. We can't stand still Price. If we did, we will not survive.'

'We've been doing pretty well for more than a century,'

Price replied.

Otto scoffed and sat back in his chair with his arms folded. 'How often have your vegetables been ruined by marauding rabbits? A few deer deciding your garden is more interesting than the wood? Ever had problems with larvae eating away at your cabbages? How about birds ravaging your berries? Now multiply that on a grand scale Price. Has it ever occurred to you that we have to feed people? That we have to keep one step ahead of the geese and the rabbits and the deer and the weeds, let's not forget the weeds … you know, those tenacious little flowers that have a habit of growing in all the wrong places. You think we can just sit back and let them spread, let them do what they want? If you think that, then you're even more stupid than I thought you were.'

Price shook his head in disbelief. 'We learn to live in harmony Otto, that's what The Reformation was all about, and it still is. Birds have as much right to eat a blackcurrant as I have. And weeds, a word I've only ever read in the archives by the way, have the right to grow wherever they want. You know very well that the constitution states we can control them by hand, to protect crops and gardens, but even then, only as a last resort. Spraying fields with poison is just nonsensical. But let's say, for argument's sake, we do need to control certain things, that's no excuse for the way you've been treating animals. You seem to get some sort of kick out of it. It's abuse of the most immoral kind imaginable and I'm glad I stopped it. And if I ever see anything like it again, even get a whisper that you're moving towards it again, then, as I've already said, I won't hesitate to bring you down.'

Otto laughed out loud. Maia, who had been listening at the door, winced. Braggle, who had been lying in the corner, rushed up to him, bending her front legs, her back arched, barking at his ankles. Otto kicked her. She squealed and ran back to the corner. Price stood up, pushing his chair forcefully back so that it fell to the floor. 'Once again you show your true colours,' he said.

'You know nothing about me Price,' Otto replied, still sitting, 'so please, don't act as though you do. Do you really think I'm doing this all alone? Where do you think my orders come from? Do you really think Paul is my henchman, taking orders from me? The man who travels from town to town on behalf of the authorities, overseeing what we're all doing, and believe me Price, we're *all* doing it. So do you really think you're going to bring me down?' He laughed again. 'Who are you going to tell? Really Price, who are you going to tell?'

'I don't believe you Otto. I don't believe one word of it. Maybe you're not alone, maybe there are some other pathetic, deluded little tyrants scattered around here and there, but there's no way this comes from the top, no way. If that's the case, why are you letting me go? I'll tell you why, because you're scared of what I can do. You're scared of the knowledge I have.'

'Poor little Price. Destroyer of factories, wrecker of cars, upholder of justice. The man who is threatening, somehow, to go all the way to the very heart of the state, wherever that may be, to let them know what they already know. Good luck with that.'

Otto stood up as though to conclude their conversation. 'And you know Price, you should go a little easier on Maia. She's a little nicer than you give her credit for. If it wasn't for her, you'd be on your way right now, far, far away, enjoying the lowly status that you so richly deserve.'

'Just like Theo,' Price replied, 'if he wasn't dead, of course.' He huffed, called Braggle and left, watching Maia slink into the side room as he opened the living room door. He went over to her, said he hoped she'd eavesdropped on it all, and gave her a withering look. She said nothing in return, but there was a sad, frightened look in her eyes, which gave him hope that she'd finally come to her senses.

FIFTEEN

I n the last month of his life, Price found ways to circumvent his inadequacies and extreme sense of impotence by enjoying more than ever the home-made wines. He found that drinking a glass or two, followed by ingesting some of Theo's dried leaves gave him the incentive to continue the day. He re-read Theo's notes for more details on those plants he felt had the potential to lift his spirits. It took him a couple of weeks to create a mix he was happy with, the salvia adding that extra little spurt of intensity he looked forward to every morning. By the beginning of June, his routine had been fixed, and his addiction firmly rooted. His behaviour changed accordingly, swinging randomly from the ebullient Price of old to the unpredictable oddities of a man unable to hide his wretchedness. He had given his word to Tom that he would remain silent and leave him alone which, at times, caused him such mental anguish that even his new-found reliance on his 'little pick-me-up' couldn't dampen his sorrow. Some days he sat at his piano staring down at the keyboard playing an A minor scale over and over, increasing its volume until it felt like a series of punches to his head, and then he'd curl onto the floor with his arms around his head and rock backwards and forwards with the same scale pounding his brain.

It made him unbearable to live with. Dan had tolerated his eccentricities for many years, accepting them, giving them space, at times enjoying the energy that circulated in the room during his more manic moments. He understood them and their particular circular rhythm, making it easier to grasp their appearance and take the necessary steps to counteract them, which generally meant staying out of his way and allowing them to take their course. It was Price at his exercise, and nothing more. But for more than a year now, his behaviour had been of a different kind. He had been abrasive and unkind and had hurt Dan so many times with his thoughtlessness and selfishness that it had created a wedge between them which seemed unbridgeable. There were moments of tenderness, but such rarities soon dissolved into the ether. The last few weeks however, had been in a different league altogether. Price had become so abrasive that Dan became uneasy in his presence, preferring to avoid him rather than being at the brunt of an inevitable tirade. It was his unpredictability that bruised Dan's sensitivities the most, making him so nervous when they were together that his headaches increased proportionally and his sleeplessness with it. Everything he said seemed to elicit a sarcastic response or, even worse for Dan's nerves, nothing at all. It was like living with ten different men, each with their own distinctive character, none of any particular charm.

The Saturday gathering was a case in point. Price hadn't attended one for months, describing it as 'a burlesque attended by sheep for the edification of wolves'. Dan assumed it was his way of ridiculing the town's rituals for no apparent reason other than sheer contempt for tradition and continuity. He understood that twenty years of the same thing over and over sometimes felt oppressive, and one longed, occasionally, for a little disturbance in the repetition, but it was what it was, and that's just the way it was. To undermine it all with a childish disrespect felt nothing more than vanity. So, on the second Saturday in June he was astonished when Price announced he was coming to the Townhouse. Dan's initial reaction, which he kept to himself, was disappointment; for the last few months he'd gone there alone to chat freely and slough away the tension of home. It had been, like the distributions, a place he could be himself, talk without side-swipes or jibes. He knew he wasn't riveting company, but he was a good listener and he could tell people liked him; he absorbed their information with an undisguised sincerity rather than swiftly replacing their stories with ones of his own.

This Saturday, Price had been monosyllabic at breakfast only to perk up an hour or so later. The contrast itself was unnerving, made all the more remarkable by his insistence that he attend the Saturday gathering. They walked briskly to the Townhouse, with Braggle by their side, Price chattering excitedly about everything and nothing as though his head had been prised open and his thoughts released in a random order.

The Townhouse was jostling with a mass of people and animals, the ambient noise so dominant that conversations took place with heads almost touching. Most of the G9 were on the stage chatting politely amongst themselves, occasionally reacting to those below as protocol dictated. And Dan stayed close to Price. He'd notice how Price's face had hardened as soon as they'd arrived and how he'd ignored everyone who attempted conversation. 'Lighten up', he had whispered in his ear. It had the opposite effect. Price sneered, saying something unintelligible under his breath, and to Dan's horror, followed it with a series of short, loud claps which thread through the general hubbub, causing a sudden drop in its intensity bar the yapping of a few dogs and the squawk of a cockatoo. Price made his way to the pulpit, muttering to himself, occasionally waving his arms in the air, and as he placed his foot on the first stair Dan grabbed his shirt to hold him back. 'No,' he said sharply, 'you are not going to embarrass me.' Price stopped, looked back at his partner, then at the staring crowd, and then to the stage. He saw Otto and Gilda glaring at him, came down from the pulpit and gave a low, sweeping bow in their direction. Dan held his arm and pulling lightly, directed him out of the Townhouse and into the open air.

'What was all that about?' Dan asked, exasperated.

Price got down on his knees and gently held Braggle's paw. 'How do you do,' he said, giving her a firm handshake, 'very nice to make your acquaintance, and if I may say so, you are a very fine dog, a very fine dog indeed.'

Braggle licked his face, making him laugh. He stood up, leaned against the porch, and without looking at Dan said: 'My darling Dan, there are things in this world that are above us all, things we cannot hope to understand or even wish to contemplate. Let's just accept that and get on with our lives as best we can. So please, no questions, because you won't get any answers.' With that, he took Braggle by the lead and walked on, leaving Dan at the entrance to the Townhouse more perplexed than ever.

Price went directly to the main square and watched the preparations for the Solstice celebrations begin to take shape. The central platform had already been installed and a couple of women were busy pulling the flagpole into place. Seeing it strengthened Price's resolve. He knelt down by Braggle and gently pulled her head to his. 'We're going to see an old friend,' he said, 'I know you've been missing him as much as I have.'

The walk to Tom's house took twice as long as it should. There were moments when Price stopped abruptly as if he'd suddenly been glued to the spot, and then, after a few minutes, he'd start off again whispering to himself over and over 'it'll be ok'. When he reached the corner of Tom's street, he sat on the kerb and watched a pair of squabbling blackbirds flit between the hedges. Braggle nudged him with her nose as though urging him to take the final few steps. He could feel the sweat on his neck trickle down his back and his insides being pulled in two. Then he stood up and started to walk away from the house. Braggle pulled on the lead in the opposite direction. 'No Braggle, I can't,' Price said. 'I promised I'd leave him alone.' He tugged harder on the lead. Braggle refused to budge. 'No Braggle, I'm sorry. I just can't,' he repeated. He sat down on the kerb again, and when she finally came towards him, he pulled her closer, buried his head in her fur and started to sob. When he finally looked up, Tom was standing a few metres away.

'She doesn't seem to want to go' Tom said.

Price released the lead and Braggle rushed towards him,

springing against his chest. Tom fell to the floor laughing and the two cuddled and played, Price watching with a huge smile and a feeling he hadn't had for many months, as though the sadness which permeated deep into his body, and which directed every waking moment, had, in those few minutes, evaporated into the warm, clammy air.

Tom stood up and dusted himself off. 'I was just on my way out,' he said, 'and there you were in the middle of a tug of war. Are you ok?'

'I'm sorry Tom, but I just couldn't stay away,' Price replied. 'I tried, but I just can't.'

Tom made the few steps towards Price, took hold of both his hands and kissed him on the side of the face. 'You're sweaty,' he said. 'You'd better come to the house and get those clothes off.'

They spent the rest of the day lying side by side on Tom's bed catching up on the past few weeks. Tom had heard nothing more from Paul, as he'd been promised, and had stopped working on the farm. And he'd had a surprise visit from Otto asking him to raise the flag at the Solstice ceremony for a second year running. Yes, it was unprecedented Otto had said, but he had performed it with such dexterity the previous year that the G9 had voted unanimously for him to do it again, and besides, his ox-eye daisy outfit was such a success, not to mention a great deal of time and effort to produce, that it would be a shame for it to be confined to just the one outing. Tom had agreed, noting in Otto's tone more of a subtle command than an offer to dwell on and refuse. He suspected there must be something behind it which seemed all the more probable when they realized Otto's visit had been the same day as the confrontation with Price at Maia's house.

'I'll make sure nothing bad ever happens to you again Tom,' Price told him.

Tom laughed. 'And how exactly are you going to do that?' he replied, 'hide me away under your shirt and whisk me away to some far, far non-existent place where A_s and C_s can live happily ever after?'

'I mean it Tom. Why shouldn't we be allowed to be together. I just can't believe that no-one has ever had the chance to dissolve a partnership and ask for a new one to be sanctioned.'

'And between different orders?'

Price pulled Tom towards him and put his hand through his hair. 'Yes,' he said, 'even between different orders. As far as I'm concerned, there's no difference between us and it's only the thinking that makes it so.'

Tom laughed again. 'We'll see. But I'm not holding my breath. And first, we have to get through the Solstice.'

Price saw Tom every day, taking Braggle with him. Their time together was intense, and they talked incessantly about how they could, somehow, make it official. Price searched the archives for any precedent and found nothing. He knew it was probably ridiculous, but his logic seemed to dissolve in his happiness. If Otto and Paul could bend the constitution to their will, then why couldn't they? Could he use his knowledge of their transgressions as leverage to get a special dispensation for himself and Tom?

Price relished those two weeks. He still took his daily wine and herb supplements, feeling their presence in his mind and body, allowing them to complement and intensify his emotions, which, for those few days, were of a kind only the happiest of people could possess, finding their peak when he was with Tom, only to noticeably fade with Dan, who saw a change in his partner but was not privy to the benefits.

And they planned how to celebrate their first anniversary: they would re-enact their meeting, watching the sunrise, standing next to each other, pretending they were strangers, touching, whispering, feeling the gush of excitement filling their bodies, the thrill of what was to come. It was their way of erasing the horrors, and starting afresh, as though by re-creating the beginning, they would have a second chance of getting it right, avoiding the mistakes, the miscalculations, and above all, the vanities of their self-absorption. It was purification; a salve to bring hope and deliverance. They talked about it endlessly, anticipating its therapeutic effect for them both, absorbed so much in the mental preparation that they conveniently side-stepped the impediments.

It was Maia who burst their bubble.

On the morning of Solstice eve, ten minutes after Price had himself arrived intoxicated with impatience for what was to come, Maia knocked on Tom's door. The knock was timid, and when the door was opened and Tom ushered her inside, she took a deep breath and walked in. She looked pale and nervous. 'Hello,' she said to Price. There was no reply. Tom asked her to sit down, offered her something to drink which she refused, only to change her mind with his insistence that he bring her something.

'Careful with the boiling water,' Price said, 'we don't want to spill any.' From Maia's expression, he could see she had no idea what he was alluding to and so he left it. 'This is a surprise,' he continued, 'and not an altogether pleasant one.'

'Nor for me,' came the reply. 'As you can imagine, it's not easy for me to be here and to speak to you after our last encounter. You were very rude, and if I may say so, wrong, about me anyway.' She looked down into her lap as she said it, as though by not looking directly at them, she was able to diminish the distress of being there. It was very un-Maia like, and Price took full advantage of her discomfort.

'Please Maia,' he said, 'just don't. I don't want to hear it. You've lied to me, betrayed me, played with me, and nothing you say will make me change my opinion of you.'

'Maybe you should look in the mirror,' she said sharply, her anxiety evaporating with every word he spoke. 'Please Price, just shut up, for once, and listen to me. I'm not here to say sorry, or to plead for your forgiveness, I have no desire to, or any need for it.' She stood up, regaining her composure, her back straight, her voice strong. 'I'm here to warn you.' She held up her hand to stop any response, just as Price had done to her a few weeks before. 'Tom, you must not raise the flag tomorrow. Pretend you are ill, do whatever you must do, but do not go to the ceremony tomorrow. Keep low for a few days, don't even go out of the house. I cannot say anymore, you will appreciate that this is dangerous for me too.' She looked at Tom. 'Promise me that you won't attend,' she said.

'What's going to happen then Maia? Price interjected. 'Is that delightful man you call your lover, that piece of slime blasting his way through all the norms and joys of life, is he going to put that rope around Tom's neck and hoist it up into the air, declaring treachery and villainy of the worst kind?'

'Don't be ridiculous Price,' she said bluntly.

'Well, don't worry, we've already decided what we're going to do if he tries anything. He'll know they'll be a backlash so we're pretty sure we can deal with it.'

'Are you being serious? Do you really think you have that sort of power over him? Don't be so deluded Price. You have absolutely no idea what you're dealing with.'

'And you do I suppose.'

'As a matter of fact, yes. I do.'

'Why are you with him Maia?' He is a truly awful specimen of a human being.'

Maia raised her chin. 'He's been good to me,' she replied firmly, 'and at least I haven't debased myself by going with a lower order.'

'Time's up,' Price responded, pointing to the door. 'Please leave. And don't come back.'

'With pleasure,' she said and without another word, marched to the door, opened it with a firm grip and strode out, slamming the door behind her.

'Unbelievable,' Price said, plonking himself down onto the sofa. 'What do you make of that?'

The reply took him totally by surprise. 'Yes,' Tom said calmly, 'it was truly unbelievable.' He sat next to Price and continued. 'It's unbelievable that that woman, who clearly thinks little of me and my lowly status, and for that I dislike her intensely, came here, under what must have been very difficult circumstances and warned us, well, me actually, that something quite bad might happen to me tomorrow if I turn up to the ceremony. To me Price. Not to you. She was warning me. She directed everything to me. And guess what happens, I don't get the chance to answer because you think you have the right, perhaps even the authority to answer for me.'

Price touched his thigh to placate him, only to have his

hand swept aside. Tom raised his voice. 'Here we go again Price. The same old thing. You're trying to own me, dictate what I can and cannot do. It's all about you again isn't it. It always is. You're so self-absorbed that you can't see what's in front of your nose. Do you really care about me? Or is it just the way I make *you* feel?'

He stood up again and started pacing around the room, abstractedly picking up objects and placing them down again with a thump. 'And this Solstice is cancelled. As from now, I'm sick and have taken to my bed, and I'm going to be sick for a few more days to come. No visitors, especially you. You're impossible Price, and I don't want to live like this. I need someone in my life who I can rely on. And it doesn't look as if it's you.'

He sat down again and took Price's limp hand. 'I'm sorry,' he said, 'I know it'll break you, but you've already broken me. It's just not possible anymore.'

Price left the house quietly, calling Braggle without putting on her lead and without looking at Tom. As he walked along the street, his legs became heavier and each short stride was like walking through treacle. By the time he reached the corner, he couldn't walk any further, as though the effort of putting one foot in front of the other was beyond him. There were no tears, just an overwhelming emptiness. He sat down in the same spot on the kerb as he had a couple of weeks before and picked at the groundsel on its edge, crushing the tiny yellow heads between his fingers. 'It's over,' he said to himself.

He spent the rest of the day doing what they'd planned before Maia's intervention, recreating the previous year's movements as best he could, returning home in the late afternoon for a nap and a perfunctory chat with Dan who had, as always, been wondering what had happened, but had, as always, fallen short of worrying, suspecting that Price would come rolling in whenever he pleased, with a curt hello and nothing more.

That evening, they went their separate ways, Dan returning home at sunset, Price staying up the whole night, waiting for the sun to rise. He sat quietly on the embankment, away from the crowd, sometimes lying flat to watch the firmament of stars staring back at him, perhaps sleeping, dreaming, fantasizing, but mostly staring blankly, devoid of any emotion, waiting for the inevitable, and when he saw the first gentle rim of light appear, he stood up, closed his eyes, and started twitching his hand, imagining Tom's first touch and the slight tickle in his palm, followed by the whisper in his ear, tears wetting his face. What was meant to be an affirmation of their love, a re-invention of his lacklustre existence, had become the exact opposite: the completeness of his misery and the realization that it would never change. He walked very slowly home, and just like the year before, fell asleep on the sofa.

He heard nothing of Dan or Braggle that morning, awaking at midday to an empty house. He ate nothing except a pinch of his dried plants and a swig of brandy wine. He then sat at his desk and wrote a note to Tom, apologizing, as ever, and describing, in detail, his movements of the previous day and his abject misery. From his wardrobe, he picked a bright green pair of trousers and a tight green top, found some card in the study, cut out a flower shape which he coloured to look like an ox-eye daisy and fixed it with wire so he could wrap it around his head. On a piece of cardboard that he'd ripped from an old box, he wrote *Time for Pruning* in thick red letters and threaded it with some thin rope. He put it all on quickly and without looking in the mirror, left the house, walked swiftly to Tom's, posted the note in the letterbox, and then went directly on to the celebrations in the main square, ignoring the stares and the nods of recognition. He saw Dan from a distance, not bothering to go to him, and waited for the toast to the Ox-Eye daisy to begin.

Otto stood at the front of the platform with a tired looking elderly man and a young, bemused-looking woman, clearly a quick replacement to raise the flag. The bell was rung at five o'clock or thereabouts, and as the old man read the toast and the woman raised the flag, Price walked to the platform, climbed the stairs, and stood in the middle of stage, turning slowly with the placard raised above his head. The toast, which was normally read as the crowd stood in silence, was given to an increasing buzz of disbelief. The man stopped half way, turning to see what was happening behind him, and in the process lost his concentration and his lines. The woman, who had swept the flag half way up the pole with ease, lost her momentum and let go of the rope causing the flag to wilt and fall to the base of the pole. A whoop of laughter came from the crowd making her freeze in terror before she ran off the stage. The old man sat in his chair, wiping the sweat from his brow with a stoical look, as though resigned to the farce unfolding around him. Price calmly walked back off the stage, giving an unforgiving smile to Otto who had dared not interrupt the ceremony, the crowd parting as he continued his walk out of the square and all the way home.

Later that evening, Dan told Price what had happened in his wake: how the ceremony was restarted, and how the participants performed their tasks reluctantly after being persuaded to return to the stage. It had been an embarrassment for all concerned and a Solstice everyone would prefer to forget, even though it was clearly one that would always be remembered.

'Why did you do it,' Dan asked.

'Because I felt like it.'

'That's not an answer Price.'

'Yes it is.'

'It's not. But as per usual, you're not going to tell me are you.'

'Your excelling yourself this evening Dan. Your powers of deduction know no bounds.'

Dan was leaning against Price's study door with his arms folded, looking down at Price who was lying on the floor still wearing his green outfit; the placard and the ox-eye daisy both torn up and scattered on the floor around him.

'People are saying you've lost your mind,' Dan said.

'Let them think what they want,' Price replied, 'perhaps I have.'

'I'm beginning to think you have too.'

'Then there's no hope is there.'

'Maybe not,' Dan replied. He calmly closed the door and walked away.

Price spent most of the next few weeks in his study. He did little except think about Tom and Theo and play the same Beethoven sonata over and over on his piano. Occasionally, he would slam his hands down flat on the keyboard, other times he'd play the second movement so slowly that he would come to a complete stop. He began to associate certain motifs with each man, feeling their presence so strongly he could sense them standing next to him and their breath caressing his neck. He went on long walks, still feeling them by his side, sometimes talking to them, sometimes shouting. He passed the farm where there was no sign of a new bio-factory springing up from the ruins of the old. The pigs still looked content and the chickens at ease. 'That's my work', Price said to himself, 'that's because of me'. It was the one positive feeling he had.

He also wrote a diary, containing all his thoughts and beliefs, with some sort of reasoning behind his actions. They were rambling sentences, with rants and outbursts of incoherence interspersed with a delicate philosophical intensity which, when Price read them back, surprised him with its precision and honesty.

He was uncompromisingly mean to Dan. He knew it, but couldn't stop his actions. It was as though he blamed him for all his heart-ache and all the sorrows and all the ills of his life and those of the town they shared. He had become so aggressively perplexing that all Dan could do was keep his distance and hold his tongue. He still cooked for him, cleaned, bartered, with no appreciation, no compliment, no interaction. Their meals together were moments of tense concealed hatred, Dan waiting for a response to his efforts, Price unable to communicate in an acceptable fashion. Mealtimes became a bubble of such un-mitigating unpleasantness that they both preferred to avoid it altogether, but both knew they had to persevere in the hope it would eventually improve.

SIXTEEN

On the Tuesday, Dan went early to the distribution. It was carrot day, with the majority of the vegetables on offer the one vegetable Price loathed. Dan would take a few for himself and be there early enough to choose from the small selection of other vegetables before they were grabbed by others. He'd make carrots with honey and lemon for himself and something simple for Price, depending on what he could find. He gave his tab to Oswald at the entrance who scanned it and told him how much he could take.

Dan saw Maia immediately. She was sitting on a bench under the shade of a tree to protect her from the fierce heat that had already taken hold. 'Can I join you,' he asked. Her response was distracted but not unkind, and she shuffled to one side to allow him to sit. 'We haven't seen each other for quite a while,' Dan said.

'No we haven't,' she replied quietly.

Their conversation was mannered and polite. They spoke first of simple things, avoiding the embarrassment of the Solstice, but Price's name was eventually and inevitably mentioned.

'How is he?' Maia asked guardedly.

'A nightmare,' Dan replied. 'He's changed beyond all recognition these past few months, and he's getting worse. You must have seen it. He's probably talked far more to you than to me.'

Maia had no idea how much Dan knew about the past few

months and chose to play it safe. 'What do you mean?' she said.

'He must have told you things. You've been spending so much time together.'

'Not really Dan. I've not really seen very much of him since Theo died. Just the occasional visit, that's all.'

'But he's spent days at a time with you, no? Nights too.'

'One of Price's little yarns I'm afraid.'

'But he told me he'd been staying with you because you asked him to. That you didn't want to be on your own in the house.'

Maia smirked. 'I'm happy being on my own actually Dan. There's not a lot I want to share with anyone at the moment. And to be honest, the way Price's been behaving, I prefer to keep my distance.'

Dan's hands gripped the lip of the bench. His neck tightened, his heart beat faster, his jugular swelled and pushed against his skin. 'Are you being serious Maia? You're saying that Price hasn't seen much of you these past few months.'

'Why would I lie Dan?'

'Sorry Maia, that sounds as though I don't believe you. I just need to be sure that's all.'

Maia had been looking down at the ground for most of their chat, but now she looked directly at him. 'I have not seen Price for quite some time Dan, I can assure you.'

As he walked home, the deceit expanded in his mind. He'd suspected a dalliance or two, perhaps an infatuation, that was nothing out of the ordinary and nothing to get worked up about, but if he'd been spending all his time with someone else, nights too, then that was a different matter; it became lies and artifice, and by the time he arrived home and placed the carrots and the leeks on the kitchen table, he was smouldering with resentment and ready for a confrontation.

Price wasn't home. He had walked to the lake and was watching the naked bathers swimming. The ground was hard and parched and he sat by a wedge of wild flowers. A butterfly landed briefly on his hand, flew to a creeping thistle by his side, then back to his hand where it remained.

Its wings were jagged and torn, veins protruding from the margin, the thin white line that would normally skirt the edge, was ripped away, its vibrant colouring faded so completely that the orange and brown had become bleached and translucent. Price brought it so close to his face he could see its bulbous eyes and its tongue coiled tight. He blew at it and it flew away instantly into the bush of wild flowers, catching itself in a cobweb where it bobbed and fluttered, unable to escape. A spider, its body as big as the butterfly's, scampered to its prey and began twisting it around and around, enveloping it in a cocoon of gossamer thread. Price watched as the butterfly, its wings clasped tight, tried to break loose, flinching and twitching, and then stopping, unable or unwilling to continue the fight, exhausted and ready to die.

Price took his diary from his bag and wrote it down. He then took off his clothes and walked slowly into the lake, and when the water reached up to his neck, he took a deep breath, bent his legs and submerged his head, staying under until his chest became tight and hard. He then slowly began to straighten his legs, pushing himself gradually up, feeling the line of water clinging to his face and the morning heat slap against his skin.

He waded back, his eyes glazed from the water. As he came closer to the shoreline, Paul came into focus, sitting naked, watching him emerge. Price ignored him, walking past without acknowledgement. Paul stood up and followed him.

'I have something I want to tell you,' he said.

'Leave me alone.'

'All in good time Price. Now sit down and listen to what I have to say.' Price ignored it, and started to dress without drying himself off.

'You're in a hurry,' Paul said.

'Wouldn't you be.'

'Maybe, but probably not.'

'No, I'm sure, you make a habit of sticking around.'

'Not for much longer Price. You won't see me in these parts again. I'm not needed anymore.'

'Good riddance,' Price replied as he pulled his t-shirt over his head.

'Don't you want to know why?'

'No.'

'That's a shame because I'm going to tell you anyway. You've won Price. The farm stays as it is. No change is coming. The resources just aren't there to replace it. Lots of happy animals.'

Price, still naked from the waist down, stopped dressing and looked directly at Paul. 'Why should I believe anything you say,' he said.

Paul touched him on the shoulder. 'No reason at all. I guess you'll just have to wait and see.'

Later that morning Price arrived home, and despite Dan's protestations, went straight to his study and locked the door. He could hear Dan's shouts of frustration and chose to ignore them. He took out his diary, sat at his desk and wrote down what happened at the lake. He then tore out an empty page and wrote as follows:

Dear Tom, here are a couple of weeks of my thoughts, feelings and movements … everything in fact since we last saw each other. You've probably heard what happened at the Solstice, for which I regret nothing. I hope you locked yourself away and are safe. Of course you are. You can look after yourself. But who knows what awaits us. I think we both know we should always be on our guard. The last part of this little rambling mess of words, which I have called a diary for want of a better explanation, will, I think, interest you the most, and is the reason I have decided to give you this to read. I was at the lake this morning. Paul was there. He told me, and I quote, that 'we have won'! He says there are no resources to build a new complex. So the farm stays. I'm not sure how to take it. Of course, it's good if it's true, which it probably is, but if the reasoning is just because of logistics and not because of the plain fact that IT IS WRONG, then we have clearly not won. I would like to think that, at some future date, when the dust has settled between us, that we can do something about it … together. You will also see that, to my astonishment, bemusement, etc. etc. …. I had sex with Paul in the wood behind the lake. At the

*moment, I feel rather excitedly confused about it. I won't pretend
that I didn't enjoy it. Perhaps it brought me closer to you (one
step removed and all that), perhaps, despite the fact that I loathe
the man, he is still, somehow …. irresistible! Or perhaps, which
is more likely, I just needed some 'release'. No doubt I will start
to feel very differently later today when it's really sunk in what
I've done … again … and I will hate myself, despise myself, beat
myself up, blah blah blah, same old story, but for now, I don't
know, I feel … relieved. Anyway, have a read. I hope it'll make
you understand me a little better. Don't worry, this isn't a plea
for you to contact me, help me, be with me, but it is my way of
still being with you and of sharing myself with you. So don't be
surprised if there are further instalments!*

*For now, be careful … and happy.
Price (and Braggle!)*

He folded the note, placed it in the front of the diary,
walked to Tom's house and pushed it through his letterbox.

Dan was waiting for him when he returned, his arms
stretched out across Price's study door. It was bad timing.
Price's mood had shifted. The lightness had given way to the
dark intransigence of self-loathing. He moved as close as he
could to Dan, their noses almost touching. 'Get out of my
way,' he said. Dan stood his ground for a few seconds then
moved aside. Price pushed past him and slammed the door.
Dan leant against the wall to steady himself, feeling his legs
almost give way with the weight of his distress. He let out
a sharp cry of frustration which Price must have heard, and
went into the garden to collect himself, brushing against a
clump of lavender. A handful of butterflies scattered into
the air. A large white fluttered in front of his face which, in
his confusion, he swatted instinctively away. The butterfly
collapsed to the ground, its wings spread flat. Dan gently
picked it up and placed it back on the flower head, but it
fell into the foliage, twitching its legs, unable to summon
the power to fly away. He started to sob. He knew it was
silly and that the tension clogged up inside him was making
him more emotional, and he knew his blaming Price for the

butterfly's demise was illogical, but somehow his thoughts liquefied into a single feeling: that if the butterfly didn't survive, he was going to cook carrots for dinner and nothing else.

He went back into the house and for an hour played scales on his violin before returning to the same spot. The butterfly hadn't moved. He went to the kitchen, took out all the carrots, peeled them slowly and methodically as though they were as delicate as the butterfly, slicing them lengthways to create a mound of perfectly symmetrical vegetables. After placing them in a large copper pan he went back to his study, thinking how he was going to cook them and how he was going to present them to Price. It had to be a surprise and it had to send a clear message that he would no longer tolerate his partner's irrational and selfish behaviour. He would explain, in detail, and with a clarity of purpose, his own feelings. It would be the moment he fought back.

At 6pm, he descended the stairs, passing Price's room, knocking gently on his door to say that dinner would be ready in half an hour. There was no response. In the kitchen, he added some oil to the pan and turned on the heat to maximum. As the oil began to sizzle he turned the carrots in the pan to prevent them from burning and as they started to brown added some cumin seeds. After a couple of minutes, he added two large dollops of clover honey and gently folded it into the contents of the pan and watched as the carrots deepened and glistened with an amber glow. He squeezed in some lemon juice, added some salt and pepper, put on the lid and set the timer for ten minutes. He then lay the table, using the best dishes and cutlery, and poured some pear cider into two long stemmed glasses. He lit a candle even though the flame could hardly be seen in the summer light, and waited for the timer to ping.

It was a simple meal, but one of his favourites, and he would explain to Price, once he'd served it onto his plate, why he had deliberately cooked something he claimed to hate. He would be rational, polite and insistent. It would be the prelude to a long anticipated, and much needed discussion on their relationship and how it could be salvaged; after all, what else could they do?

He knocked on Price's door with the glass in his hand.

'Price, dinner's almost ready. I have a glass of cider for you.'

No response. He knocked again.

'Go away.'

'Price, please, I've made dinner and I'd like to talk to you. We need to talk.'

The door opened suddenly, startling Dan and almost causing him to spill the drink. Price grabbed the glass and drank it in one, and without saying a word walked to the dinner table and sat down with his back to the kitchen. Dan followed and sat opposite him.

'We have to talk,' he said again.

Price looked down at his empty plate. His face was red and blotchy, his hair unkempt.

'Not now,' he replied. 'I'm really not in the mood.'

'I don't care what sort of mood you're in. I want to talk.'

He filled Price's glass with more of the cider which he again drank in one.

'I'm going to talk and whether you respond is up to you,' Dan continued. 'In fact, it might be better if you just listen.'

And then the timer pinged. Dan went to the stove, turned off the heat, opened the lid and gave the carrots a stir. He prodded a carrot with a fork and it fell apart. They were overcooked, giving off a sweet pungent aroma reminiscent of Academy dinners. He poured the mixture into a white ceramic bowl, sprinkled some chopped parsley on top, covered it with a lid, and brought it to the table.

'Before I show you what we're about to eat I want to explain why I've cooked it.'

'I already know what it is,' Price replied. 'I do have a nose. It's carrots, probably with honey and lemon.' He was still looking down at his empty plate.

'I want you to try them. Just this once. I want you to put one to your mouth and however difficult it might be for you, I want you to eat one. Why? Because I need you to. Because I'm asking you to.'

He leant over and touched Price on the arm who continued to stare resolutely down at his plate.

Dan continued. 'Can't we sweep away all this unfriendliness and start all over again? Can't we actually be nice to each other? I've never cooked carrots for you, ever, not once, because I know you don't like them. I've always cooked what I know you like.'

He squeezed Price's arm.

'Aren't you even going to look at me? I'm asking you, just this once, to eat a carrot and that gesture will be, as far as I'm concerned, an act of friendship and a sign of our mutual respect.'

Price pulled his arm away, lifted the lid of the bowl and waved his hand over the food with a short jerking movement, wafting the smell in his direction. He looked up at Dan and smirked.

'No,' he said firmly. And with a swift, violent movement swept the bowl from the table. It careered in a curved trajectory across the room and smashed against the opposite wall. Braggle, who always sat on the floor beside them, whimpered and left.

'No,' Price said again. 'I will not.'

Dan stayed rigidly still and listened in disbelief as his act of reconciliation was swatted aside as though it was a fantasy; a whim of so little worth that it could be laughed at, spat upon, ridiculed.

'And I will not be clearing that crap up either,' Price continued. 'It's your fucking mess. You deal with it.'

Dan stood up and almost in a trance went to the kitchen, picked up the empty copper pan, walked behind Price and smashed it hard against the side of his head. Price seemed to absorb the impact and for a few seconds remained still. He then brought his hand flat to his ear and ran his bloodied palm down his cheek, bringing his fingers slowly along his chin and up onto his lips. With his eyes closed, he gently caressed his lower lip with his index and middle finger, his tongue protruding slightly. Opening his eyes, he staggered out of his chair, letting out a series of little snorts as he moved around the room.

'Not like this,' he said faintly.'

He looked up at the ceiling, rolling his head in a circular

motion. 'Not like this,' he said again, and then lurched towards the table and fell, catching his head against its edge. It bobbed up slightly and then slammed hard onto the floor.

SEVENTEEN

D an stood at the door, Braggle whimpering at his side, as Tom walked down the path and out of view. They'd hugged silently and unashamedly a few minutes before, both acutely aware of the volte-face that had taken place in the week they were together.

Tom had looked after Dan with all the care of a partner, cooking and cleaning and washing the bedridden invalid with a gentleness that he knew he didn't deserve. He could now walk unaided, still limping, with his upper body at a forty-five degree angle to his lower half which looked as though it had broken off and glued back on by a child; a deformity that would right itself over the course of the coming weeks as his back muscles relaxed and the pain subsided altogether.

Dan had talked like never before and it had been a revelation – not only to be party, finally, to everything that had been kept from him, but also to talk freely to someone who wanted to listen. It was as though by chatting openly about his life and the vicissitudes of the previous year, he was able to make sense of it and create a logic that had been sorely missing, and it soothed his over-arching feeling of being forever on the outside looking in. His recuperation had been more than physical. An inner strength had taken shape, born from the shame of his actions and the relief of no longer feeling like an outsider.

They had eaten a breakfast of berries and yoghurt which Dan had prepared, insisting Tom sit down and be waited on for once. He'd made the tea far too strong and the freshly picked raspberries had been handled a little too roughly. Their conversation had the listless discomfort of goodbyes and Dan had the overwhelming feeling that Tom had put something to rest; that by revealing all he knew, he could now push it aside and start afresh. The night before, they had once again read the letter Price had written to Tom on the day he died together with extracts from his diary, the two of them crying helplessly.

They'd also found Price's hiding place where he'd stashed Theo's diary and all the incriminating evidence about the bio-factory. Two days before, as Dan was beginning to move a little more freely, they'd gone into Price's study where he'd said he'd hidden it all, and where nothing had been touched since his death. For a while both stood in silence. Dan then went over to the piano, its lid still open, and slowly traced a finger along a few bars of the sheet music resting against the stand, and he thought how, in those final days, he'd stand outside the closed door of the room listening to Price's playing, deciphering his mood from its tempo and how, sometimes, it would be so beautiful and played with such a lightness of touch, that he would put his ear to the door and listen to a whole movement, unable to fathom how a man, who could be so vile to him, could play with such tenderness and warmth.

He closed the lid of the piano and turned to face Tom. 'So it's all in here somewhere, tucked away on the bottom of the top of something. I wish Price could have just written exactly where it was.'

'That wasn't really his style was it,' Tom replied.

The two sat on the sofa and once again talked about the man they'd both shared their lives with, trying once more to untangle his many sides. Price's diary had been the light that led them through his final months, a microscope on his actions and thoughts; their own versions of his last few weeks brought into a sharper, clearer focus. They knew that Price had been to Maia's and confronted her and Otto. They knew he'd told them about Theo's diary and other incriminating evidence. They knew he'd been eating Theo's dried plants. They also knew that none of it might even be in the house anymore, that whoever broke in during Dan's tribunal, might have found it already, as they were now convinced that's what they'd been looking for.

'I don't think it was Maia though,' Dan said. 'She told me she'd followed me from the tribunal and so she couldn't be in two places at once.'

'What Maia says and what Maia does aren't always the same thing,' Tom replied.

'It sounds so weird to hear that Tom.'

'Maybe, but it's true.'

'She did go to warn you though, about the Solstice celebrations.'

'Yes, that's also true. Maybe there's a softer side to her somewhere.'

'And Price did write that he thought she was beginning to see Otto for who he really was.'

'Let's hope so,' Tom said. He stood up and walked around the room. 'Let's try and find it. If it's so well hidden I doubt they did.' He got on his knees and looked under the sofa. 'It's on the bottom of the top of something which must mean it's hidden underneath something.'

'Sorry you have to do most of the work Tom.'

'I'm used to it,' he replied smiling.

For the next hour, he was on all fours looking under the desk, the cupboard, the swivel chair, and a couple of small tables; he felt for loose floorboards and panels, anything that could possibly hide Theo's diary. Dan looked in all the drawers, feeling for any secret compartments, frustrated at the restrictions imposed on him by his temporary disability, and as the pain in his back became too much, lay gingerly on the sofa, watching Tom shuffling across the floor from one piece of furniture to the next. He closed his eyes, his thoughts returning to Price's piano playing, the notes reverberating in his head, and then, as though compelled by some unknown force, he slowly got back up, went directly to the piano, lifted the top lid, and there it was, tucked into a thin wooden shelf attached along the length of its underside. 'The bottom of the top,' he said smiling. He slid his hand in the gap and pulled out the handcrafted notebook with a mottled green cover, together with a collection of handwritten notes and drawings and photos relating to the bio-factory, and a large envelope filled with dried leaves and flowers.

The two spent the afternoon going through it all, adding extra layers to what they already knew, and were so exhausted by the end of the day that Tom slept on the sofa instead of returning home.

But now, two days later, it was time to say goodbye. They would see each other again, that was for sure, perhaps even regularly, but without spelling it out, Tom had made it clear he would be shaking free from the upheavals of the past year. He'd heard nothing more from Otto, hoping he would be left alone to fit into the workaday fabric of town life with a new life partner.

Dan felt the exact opposite, and as Tom disappeared down the path and around the corner, he went straight to his study and made a list, with the promise to himself that he would tick each item off one by one, and be ready to add to it when the need arose. What he had to do first was re-acquaint himself with the topography of the town, visit all the places that had come up in conversation, seeing them with clear, unblemished eyes.

For three days, he walked with Braggle through the town along the roads and paths, absorbing the shapes and contours of buildings, the silences that morphed effortlessly into sounds. On the first afternoon, he walked to the communal pits on the edge of the town and knelt next to the soil that had been freshly disturbed. He scooped some of it into his hand, rubbing it into his palm, then slowly released it, the stream forming a mound which he scooped up again, repeating the process over and over, each time saying sorry. As he stood up, the pain in his back seemed to dig freshly into him and he remembered nothing of his walk home.

His sleep was fitful, his top wet with sweat, but when he woke, later than planned, he sprang out of bed, pushing the jabs of pain aside. After breakfast in the garden watching the butterflies scurrying amongst the flowers, he walked directly to the farm and watched the animals in the vast fields that surrounded the burnt-out carcass of the bio-factory. He sat on one of the gates and a large black-and-white pig nudged its snout against his feet. Dan scratched her head and she rolled on her side. He jumped down and started rubbing her belly. The pig squealed with delight, her eyes closed and mouth open. In the coming weeks, Dan returned as often as he could, apples in his pocket, and he never ate pig meat again.

That same day, he went to the lake, stripped naked, threw his clothes hurriedly to the ground, and waded into the water up to his chest. He then sprang into the air and plunged downwards, submerging his whole body. And with all his strength, surged up again with his arms splayed, splashing with the exuberance of a child. He walked slowly to the shore, the water clinging to his nakedness, put on his shoes and walked into the woods, following a path which strayed haphazardly between the undergrowth. He passed a few men and women, and saw, now and then, a cluster of bodies through the trees.

Each day, with the exception of Tuesdays (he could no longer stomach carrots), he showed himself at the distribution, giving his tablet to Oswald and collecting his provisions. He spoke to those he knew, nodding politely to others. He saw Maia occasionally from a distance and managed to avoid her every time.

He spent hours in the archives studiously researching in Price and Theo's footsteps, familiarizing himself with things he'd long forgotten, sometimes banging his fists on the table as he read tales of the desecration of land and sea.

He walked to Otto's house, saw the giant oak and the manicured lawn, not caring whether he was seen, and from there took the long walk to the furthest edge of the town, across fields baked hard from the heat, to the copse where Price had seen the hunting.

On the first Saturday, he arose early and put on the linen trousers and shirt he first wore twenty years before at his homecoming. The trousers were a little loose around the waist, but all in all, he was happy with how he looked. He combed Braggle's ears and brushed her back and tail, which she accepted, as always, with a begrudging compliance, and when they left the house, he closed the door with a defiant slam and walked purposefully to the Townhouse. They arrived early; a scattering of people chatting quietly, a couple of dogs sniffing around the edges. Three of the G9 were on the dais, sitting in their allotted chairs, making conversation with their hands clasped between their thighs, waiting with the studied impatience of privilege. Dan strode up to them to say hello, something he'd never done before, and then sat in the first pew and beckoned Braggle to sit on the chair next to him. He remained quietly in his seat and watched as each chair on the dais filled, the adrenaline pumping through his body as he bided his time, waiting for the Townhouse to fill and for Otto to appear. A small woman with cropped hair went to the pulpit and said something about the quality of the vegetables at the distributions. She was roundly ignored. Another woman, younger, who rose to speak every Saturday, talked animatedly about the smell from the communal dump, raising her voice to command attention, but few took much notice. As she left the rostrum Dan stood and began slowly and rhythmically to clap, just as Price had done a few months before, continuing as he walked up the eight stairs and stood under the arch of the pulpit looking down on the crowd. At first, no-one took much notice, but the clapping became stronger, and its echo more forceful, propelling its way through the chatter until only the whispering hum of expectation remained.

'I finally have your attention,' Dan said loudly. 'And I suggest you keep listening because you'll find what I have to say very interesting as it involves every one of you.'

There was now silence. Dan breathed in deeply, holding tight to the sides of the rostrum.

'Most of you will know me of course, at least by sight. Yes, I'm the one who killed his partner a few weeks ago, brutally, with a copper pan against the side of his head, something I regret with every fibre of my being. Price wasn't easy, as many of you will testify, but it should be him standing here now and not me.'

He looked at Otto who was staring directly at him and saw

a hint of unease flick across his face.

'I love this town. I've been here for more than twenty years and guess I've sort of taken it for granted. I've spent the last few days exploring it anew, every corner of it. And it's made me realise how lucky we all are to have what we have.'

He paused, mainly to compose himself, but it had the effect of heightening the tension. 'As many of you will also probably know, I was not punished for my actions. I kill someone and nothing happens. Isn't that strange? And how many of you remember Theo Fanter? He was killed last December by his partner. She wasn't punished either. Well, downgraded to an A_4, but that's like being denied chicken for a month.' A collective chuckle rippled through the Townhouse.

'You might say to yourself, that's ok, it's better to be lenient, let's give everyone the benefit of the doubt. And there's something to be said for that, and of course, I've benefited from it. But what if that's not the reason I was let off. And that's not the reason Maia Gertler was let off. What if I said to you that we were let off because there was extreme relief among certain influential people that Price Hamilton and Theo Fanter were no longer free to sniff around. Because that's the truth. They knew too much you see. They knew, and had evidence, that bad things are taking place in this town. Change is happening under our very noses and most of us let the odour waft around us and we do nothing.'

He paused again, taking another deep breath.

'It was Price who burnt down the bio-factory,' he said calmly.

The room exploded into a flurry of excitement. Dan took off his shoe and smacked it hard against the lectern. Silence once more enveloped the room.

'He burnt it down because he'd seen what was really happening in there. Cruelty you wouldn't believe. I'll leave it to your imagination to picture the scenes he witnessed first-hand, but double it, and then double it again. And then you'll come close. I could also tell you about hunting and the use of poisons on our land. All taking place here. In our town. And all sanctioned by whom? I'll also leave that to your imagination.'

He stretched his arm high above his head, brandishing the shoe for all to see, and then threw it towards the dais. Otto stood up, pushing his chair hard behind him so it collapsed to the floor with a thud. Words formed in his mouth, and for a moment it looked like he would respond, but he hesitated and called for all the doors to be opened. 'Bring in some air,' he shouted and walked off the podium followed closely by the rest of the G9.

The crowd filtered quickly out into the open. Those who knew Dan waited for him to descend from the pulpit and surrounded him, bombarding him with questions. 'All in good time,' he said, and grabbed Braggle before leaving the building and a whirl of bewildered townsfolk. He was still shaking when he reached home, but he felt elated, wandering around the house in a daze, thumping his hand against walls and doors, splashing his head with cold water to calm him down, and thinking, hoping, that Price would finally have something positive to say about him. He sat in the middle of the garden surrounded by the lavish smell of late summer flowers, picking distractedly at the daisies and dead nettles with Braggle cupped between his legs, feeling alive with the possibilities of his own existence. He had abandoned the comfort of ignorance and embraced the thrill of conviction. He knew there would be consequences, but he knew, absolutely, that he would be ready. And most importantly, he was no longer afraid.

The letter came the next day, a Sunday, so Dan knew it was important. He opened it up with a swift thrust of a knife and read the following:

To Daniel Marks,
It has come to our attention that you are in possession of a small wind-up clock. As you know, this is a non-negotiable item with serious consequences. Your presence has been requested at an emergency meeting of the G9 this coming Wednesday at 1100 hours.
Do not bring your dog.

The Highest Authority of The Reformation.

Dan laughed out loud, screwed the letter into a tight ball and threw it in the bin. He spent the rest of the day writing as many pamphlets as he could, which read:

I, Dan Marks, have been summoned to appear before a tribunal this coming Wednesday at 1100 hours. My offence – the alleged ownership of a small wind-up clock. It has come as no surprise, and should surprise no-one who was present at the Townhouse on Saturday.
I kill my partner Price Hamilton and there are no repercussions.
Theo Fanter assaults (slightly) a member of the G9 and is downgraded from A_3 to C_3 and told to leave the town!!
I own (allegedly) a small clock … and what?
In the past year, there have been serious infringements against the very principles of The Reformation. Unspeakable cruelty to animals. The use of poisons on our land. Both of which Theo Fanter and my partner had discovered.
Our collective values and way of life are in danger.
If you are a concerned citizen please show your support at the Townhouse on Wednesday. I will be there from 10.30 am.
Please pass on this information to your neighbours.
Thank you.
Dan Marks

He spent the next day delivering the little pamphlets which he folded neatly in two and, as there were only a limited number, used his intuition to decide which houses received one, using the types of butterflies and flowers he saw in the garden as a rough guideline. Braggle went too and dragged him, after a battle of wills, to Tom's. Dan knocked on the door. No answer. He looked through the windows and saw no-one. The pictures had been removed from the walls. There were no used cups or plates on the kitchen sideboard. And the door was locked. An old woman with long, greasy hair came out of the neighbouring house and stood next to him, looking into the room.

'I'll be next,' she said. 'Seventy-five in a few months.'

'Is he gone?' Dan asked.

'Yesterday afternoon,' she replied. 'A small van came. I saw a few boxes.'

'Did you see Tom?'

'Oh yes, he waved to me. Seemed ok. Wasn't smiling though.' She folded her arms tight across her chest. 'Pity, he helped me a lot in my garden. It's only small but he was a Godsend. My partner died last year you see and it's all a bit too much for me now.' She spoke quietly, her voice resigned to the indignity of her age. 'Sweet boy,' she said, and walked slowly back to her own little house and shut the door behind her.

Dan walked directly to Maia's house on the other side of town, passing her horse in the stable and a tangle of brambles which threaded along the hedge and looped threateningly over his head. Maia was in the garden sitting rigidly in a chair, a glass of water by her side. She saw Dan and Braggle immediately, but stayed in her chair, making no effort to greet them, and as they approached she took a sip from the glass, not bothering to look at them.

'Tom's gone,' Dan said directly. 'Where? Where has he gone Maia?'

'How dare you mention my name in the Townhouse,' she replied.

Dan snorted, standing a few metres from her with his hands behind his back. 'I can do what I like Maia and you're lucky I didn't say a lot more. I know everything. Now tell me, where is Tom?'

Maia kept her gaze on the sycamores that lined the edge of the garden and took another sip of water. 'I have absolutely no idea where Tom is,' she said sharply. She looked up at Dan. 'And if you know everything, then you'll know my relationship with Otto is over.' She stood up, throwing the remaining water in her glass onto the ground. 'So it's him you should be asking and not me.' She took a few steps closer to Dan. Braggle started to bark. 'Shut up,' she barked back. Braggle lowered her head and lay under the garden table. 'And if you really know everything, you'll know I've been trying to help you, but that seems to have evaded your rather limited, self-centred little brain.'

Dan snorted again, louder this time. 'You! Help me! Tell me Maia, is telling Otto about the clock helping me? My brain might be limited as you so beautifully put it, but it's not so vacuous that I can't see exactly what you were doing when you came to me the night before my tribunal, trying to find out what I knew. And you'd have left feeling mighty relieved of course. Because I knew nothing.'

He moved closer. 'And then going straight to Otto who was probably waiting for you right here, the two of you laughing out loud at my ignorance. 'Oh, and he has a sweet little wind-up clock which he left on the kitchen table.' Am I right Maia? Is that what happened?'

'I have no idea what you're talking about, but if you come any closer I will smash this glass over your head.'

'And I thought I was pathetic,' Dan replied.

Maia threw the glass to the ground and walked to the garden table. She banged her fist onto the metal surface and let out a long, despairing wail.

'Oh Dan,' she said, 'you really have no idea have you. Can't you just stand back and think, just for a moment?' She scraped a chair along the ground and sat down, her back straight. 'I ended it with Otto before Price died, once I knew what was going on with the poisons and the bio-factory, and a lot more Dan, a lot, lot more. I came to you because I wanted to make sure that you had been kept in the dark, not to protect me but to protect you. I know what Otto's capable of and if you made the G9 aware of what you know, then it's bye bye Dan. But that's all nothing now isn't it. You've blurted it all out haven't you. And I can assure you, there will be consequences.'

'I don't care about the consequences Maia, not anymore.'

'Good, because you know what to expect then.'

'I don't care,' Dan repeated. 'And if you were trying to protect me then why, the very next day, did you give me the poison? That's not exactly protecting me is it.' And without waiting for an answer he handed her a pamphlet. 'I'm not going down without a fight,' he said.

Maia read the pamphlet and released it from her hand. The

paper fell and shuffled along the ground, catching in a clump of verbena. Dan picked it up and folded it in two.

'Dan, I didn't tell Otto about any clock, I swear. I didn't see a clock. Yes, Otto knew I was going to you before the tribunal, don't think I can get away from him that easily. And I know they raided your house the next day, but they weren't looking for a clock, they were looking for all the evidence Price said he had.'

'And they found nothing.'

'Apparently not.'

'Apart from the clock.' Dan pulled up a chair and sat next to her. He now remembered he'd brought it down to the kitchen the morning after Maia's visit and so she couldn't have seen it. She wasn't lying. And he'd taken it back upstairs when he came back from the tribunal, not for one minute thinking it could be used against him. 'I'm not surprised they didn't find anything else,' he continued, 'it was very well hidden.'

'So you've found it all then?'

Dan smirked and avoided answering directly. 'Did you know that Price and Theo had both written diaries?'

Maia clasped her hands tightly together. 'No, I didn't know that,' she replied, her eyes beginning to water. 'I know Theo knew about me and Otto almost from the beginning, even though I thought I'd kept it all a secret. Ridiculous of course, but that's what infatuation does to you, makes you totally blind to the totally obvious. And Price did tell me that Theo had written something, but I didn't know whether he was telling the truth. But there is one?'

'Yes, there is one, and I've read all of it.'

Maia didn't respond immediately. She looked down at her hands, rubbing her thumbs agitatedly together. Without looking up she asked: 'And when was it written?'

'The last few months of his life, up to the last day.'

Again, she took her time to reply. 'Do you think I could have it?'

'You won't like what's in it.'

'I'm sure I won't,' Maia said, 'but I'd like to read it all the same.'

'Maybe,' Dan replied, 'let's see how things go.'

'Don't you think I have a right to read it? It involves me after all.'

'That's true Maia, there's a lot about you in it, but some might argue that you've abdicated any sort of rights where Theo is concerned, don't you think?'

Dan could see that Maia was trying to keep calm, holding herself in. 'Couldn't I say the same about you and Price,' she said.

'You could,' Dan replied quickly, 'but you'd be wrong. I didn't plan to kill Price.'

'And I've told you before, I didn't plan to kill Theo.'

'That's not quite what Theo seemed to think.'

Maia immediately stood up, the chair falling backwards. Braggle gave a sharp bark and moved next to Dan.

'That's a lie,' Maia exclaimed, 'there's no way Theo thought that. That's just not true.'

'Then perhaps I really ought to let you read it Maia, then you'll see for yourself exactly what he was thinking.'

Maia kept her composure. 'I would very much like to read it,' she said, 'so if I can come and collect it, I would be most grateful.'

'Maybe,' Dan replied. He beckoned for Maia to sit down again, which she did hesitantly, picking the chair from the ground and sitting so straight that Dan could see she could explode at any moment. 'And whilst we're talking about poison,' he continued, 'why did you give me that vial in the market place? And in front of everyone.'

'This has become something of an inquisition hasn't it Dan.'

'Perhaps Maia, but to throw your words back at you, don't you think I have a right to know, after all, it does involve me.'

Maia gave a hint of a smile. 'You've changed Dan.' She seemed to loosen up slightly, her back not so straight, her shoulders less stiff. 'It was foolish to do it in public, I realise that now,' she said, 'but it was my way of getting you started, releasing you from the dark. The tribunal was over and I thought it was time.'

'You could have just told me directly, and in private.'

'Yes,' she replied. 'I should have. But I didn't. Maybe I felt that doing it in public was some form of protection. Silly I know, but I wasn't thinking straight. I haven't been thinking straight for quite some time.' She picked up her glass from the ground and asked him if he wanted anything to drink. 'I need something a little stronger,' she said, and walked briskly to the kitchen.

She returned with two small glasses of homemade blackberry gin. 'I'm sorry for giving it to you in the market place. It was wrong of me, but at least it made you get your top off. That was a first.'

Dan chuckled softly. 'That's true,' he said. 'and I have to admit, I quite enjoyed it.' He took a sip from the glass. 'But then you lied to me the next day when I came here and asked what was going on.'

'Yes, I did. I'm sorry. I guess I'd become so used to doing things in secret that it became something of a habit. And as I said, perhaps it was my way of protecting myself.'

'By lying?'

Maia stiffened once more. 'We're all liars Dan. Pretending that everything is oh so lovely and cosy and fine. This little town with all its flowers and bees and butterflies. Do you really think that's the norm? That there are thousands of other towns just like this one, wrapped in their own little cotton wool cocoons? Perfect little worlds where everyone lives happily side by side?'

'So you know otherwise do you Maia?'

'Yes, as a matter of fact I do.'

'Have you seen it for yourself?'

'Of course I haven't,' Maia replied indignantly.

'So you've just heard it all second hand. From Otto I guess.'

'Yes,' she answered defiantly.

'And Paul?'

'Yes, from that creep too.'

'And you didn't stop to think that perhaps they were also lying? Little seeds of doubt, so that you'd think what they were doing wasn't anything unusual? Putting you off the scent? The lady might know too much, no?'

Maia walked to the verbena and plucked a flower head, rubbing it heavily between her fingers before dropping it and plucking another.

'I can't imagine he'd do that to me,' she said.

'But you did end the relationship didn't you. That must have been for a reason.'

She squeezed a couple more verbenas and took another sip of her drink. 'I hate him,' she hissed. 'He has ruined my life.' The words seemed to suck the life out of her and she sat down again with a heaviness that had eluded her for most of her life. 'I ended it when he told me what he was going to do to Tom and Price at the Solstice ceremony. Nasty, spiteful, vindictive. You know I went to warn Tom.'

'Yes, he told me.'

'Price was so unpleasant. That was the last time I saw him.' She went to the kitchen, opened a drawer and took out two letters. Returning outside, she passed the first one to Dan. 'He wrote this,' she said.

Maia, I don't know how you can live with yourself. We have been friends for so long. We've experienced so much together. We've laughed, drank, gossiped. God, we even had sex once didn't we, I mean ME with a WOMAN. When I think of that moment all those years ago, it makes me want to peel off my skin and throw it in the garbage. Not because it was a woman, because it was you. I'm an arsehole too of course. So perhaps we deserve each other. Two idiots destined to fall into a pit of our own making. But at least I haven't sided with the devil, a man who believes he IS this town, who OWNS this town. Tell me Maia, does he own you too? Have you sunk that low? Those paintings and furniture, all little gifts of endearment? You came to warn Tom this morning about the Solstice. Was that another of Otto's little pranks, with you playing the willing supplicant? Well, it's created a wedge between Tom and me which is never going to be bridged. I blame you for that. Our friendship was already torn into shreds but now, after yesterday, if I see you again, I might not be held responsible for my actions. You and Otto have morphed into one malign being. So if you do see me, by accident, I would advise you to keep OUT OF MY WAY. We will not speak to each other again. And tell your man to rot in hell. Price

It was scrawled hurriedly in red ink, a scurry of almost unintelligible handwriting, curving down from right to left. It took Dan a while to read and when he handed it back all he could think of was that this was all happening under his nose and he knew nothing. If Price had confided in him, opened up just slightly, then maybe it could have been avoided. Why hadn't he said anything?

Maia then handed Dan the second letter. 'This arrived this morning,' she said.

To Maia Gertler
We are delighted to inform you that a perfect match has finally been found for you. The homecoming will take place on October 1st.

Name: Reynaldo Graves
Age: 45
Rank: B$_2$

Type HW45B22136 into your system to view the hologram.
We are confident you will be one hundred per cent satisfied with this match.
More information will be forthcoming in the following weeks.

The Highest Authority of The Reformation

Dan handed the letter back. 'B$_2$?' he said. 'Did you have any interviews?'

'Nothing,' Maia replied. 'It's a stitch-up of course. All Otto's doing.'

'And how do you feel about it?'

Maia gave him a withering look. 'Do I really need to answer that,' she said. 'And it'll be your turn on Wednesday.'

'Not if I can help it,' Dan said. 'I'm not frightened of him, or any of them. I'll be ready.'

Maia said nothing, but Dan could see she was unconvinced.

He stood up. 'You really don't know what's happened to Tom?'

'No idea,' Maia replied immediately. 'Probably re-housed and now waiting for a new homecoming, far from here no doubt. Maybe it's better for him anyway. Maybe he even chose it.'

'I doubt that,' Dan replied, 'He would have come to see me first.' He held out his hand. 'Goodbye Maia. I can't imagine we'll be seeing much of each other in the future.'

'Then that would be a shame.'

'Really? After everything that's happened?'

'Maybe we might need each other after everything that's happened.'

She held out her hand. Dan held out his. The hand shake was short and firm.

'Maybe I'll see you on Wednesday,' she said.

'Maybe,' Dan replied, and as he began to walk away, he turned back to her. 'By the way Maia, how did you get hold of that poison?'

'There's loads of it in Otto's shed,' she said. 'Lots of different kinds. Pesticides, herbicides, fungicides, even stuff for killing worms and snails. I'd love to push it all down his throat.'

EIGHTEEN

T he Wednesday morning Dan rose especially early. He'd slept well and awoke at six feeling refreshed and ready for whatever the day might bring. He had been buoyed at the distribution the previous day when numerous people, even those he didn't know, questioned him about his pamphlet and wished him luck. No-one said expressly that they'd come to support him at the Townhouse, but he had the impression that word had got swiftly around and people felt his stand was an important one that deserved backing. Oswald seemed piqued though, grabbing Dan's tablet with a little more force than was necessary and rummaging through his bag of green veg more thoroughly than normal when he left. Dan smiled, waiting politely for its return, muttering under his breath 'drop dead'. He'd never really like Oswald, his bullish behaviour had always felt contrived with its hint of intimidation simmering under the surface, the few words he uttered chosen carefully to give lustre to his position. And besides, he had never, not once, given Braggle any attention, even when she was wagging her tail with all the ferocity of an overactive fly swat. It was as though she didn't exist, and that had always irritated Dan. And for a few weeks now there was an added intimidation to his gruffness. At first, it had the desired effect, making Dan feel ill at ease, as though he was being mentally frisked at the entrance, but now he couldn't care less and looked at Oswald with disdain. He closed his bag after the inspection and said 'just vegetables Oswald, no poison, not even a clock.' And as he left, he couldn't help himself: 'Maybe see you tomorrow Oswald, 10.30 outside the Townhouse.' And off he went.

It made him chuckle even thinking about it, which he did often during the rest of the day, and now, sitting at the garden table eating some toast with homemade blackcurrant jam, he could see Oswald's look as he walked away. It reminded him of a frog that had just been caught by a heron and was waiting helplessly to be swallowed whole. He'd already showered and shaved and was wearing his gardening clothes, smeared with the green and brown stains of hard toil. It would be one of the many statements, verbal and visual, he'd be making at the Townhouse in a few hours. He'd gone over his speech he was planning to the assembled crowd and his words to the G9 he had honed to perfection, making sure his points were concise and precise, and with the power to punch an irreversible hole through Otto's scheming. He knew from what Theo had written that Otto would do his best to avoid any confrontation and would probably attempt to shorten the proceedings, but he was ready for it; he knew the rules and would make sure they were adhered to. He would keep calm no matter what.

Dan's life had been a haze of anxiety, a nervous disposition which he'd learnt to subdue by keeping close to home. His forays away from the house were minimal, preferring solitary pursuits such as playing the violin to the many sports and clubs which gave the town its social cohesion. He'd tried in the first few years to join in but it was no good, his character didn't suit it, and so he learned to live vicariously through Price's exploits and more rounded personality. He had often questioned in his own mind the validity of their union; how could they possibly have been a 'perfect match'? What fault in the system had brought them together? But he now realized there was invariably one in the shade, the other grabbing the full light of day; it had to be so. Of course, it had all gone horribly wrong and the pain of it cut through him every day, but how much of Price's dominance had affected his own behaviour, preventing him from exploring his own boundaries? He was now alone, free from the shackles of compromise, with the space to finally acquire his true equilibrium.

He spread some more jam on his bread and then stretched his arm to its full length, still holding the knife in his hand. There was no shaking. It was as though a new Dan had risen from the catastrophe of Price's death, the two morphing into one stronger being. A couple of worker wasps rimmed the jam jar and glided harmlessly around his head. Dan scraped some jam from the knife on to the table, giving them the sweet fix they craved, and walked back to the kitchen with his breakfast things. Braggle followed, a little unsure, her routine hampered by the early rise and a shorter walk than normal, and when Dan put on his best shoes, she twirled around the floor with a display of such intensity and longing that Dan couldn't help but take her with him.

They walked the same route as he did the previous tribunal a few months earlier, skirting the town in a latent curve which almost imperceptibly led them to the Townhouse. The hedgerows had lost their sheen, the summer heat sapping them of their strength, the campions and crane-bills long since wilted away.

They arrived at the entrance at around 10.15 and Dan sat on the wooden bench tapping one foot on the hard grass with the other leg clasped under the bench. He could see people walking along the thoroughfare fifty metres away and a few looked briefly across to him, some gave a quick smile, one person waved, he waved back. No-one turned up towards him. A gnawing unease began to grip his body. He stared at the fingernails of his outstretched hands and the words and sentences he had so meticulously crafted refused to come to life in his head. He sank further down into the bench, his shoulders hunched, each minute that passed feeling like a solid, viscous mass enveloping him and his surroundings. He lifted Braggle onto his lap, holding her tight in his arms. 'I don't need words after all,' he whispered into her ear and then kissed her neck softly. 'What would I do without you?' he said.

With five minutes to go the giant oak doors of the Townhouse opened. Oswald poked his head around the corner. 'Come in,' he said in his usual efficient manner.

'So you did make it,' Dan replied sarcastically.

'Are you coming in or not?'

'Give me a few more minutes.'

Oswald didn't answer and walked back in, his footsteps clacking on the hard floor. Dan stared down at his own feet and the black shoes he'd deliberately chosen, the same ones as the first tribunal, knowing how each stride would snap and chime through the space; he'd meant it as a statement of intent, a defiant rebuke which would help define his confidence. Now, he wanted to pull them off and throw them into the pond that lay along the side of the building. He looked at his clothes; the sagging knees of his gardening trousers, his top smeared with dried soil, and felt ridiculous.

'Are you ok?'

Dan looked up. Maia was standing a few metres away.

'It's not quite what I'd expected,' he replied faintly. 'You're the first, and by the looks of it, the last.'

Maia knelt down beside him, took his chin in her hand and lifted it up, forcing him to look directly at her.

'This was inevitable Dan. No-one was going to come. People are nervous. They'd support you if they could, I'm sure they would.' She went over to Braggle and stroked her tenderly along her back. 'I'm sorry,' she said, 'I've been mean to you and I apologise.'

It made Dan smile. 'Thank you,' he said, 'that means a lot.'

Maia took his hand, forcing him up. 'Let's go in,' she said confidently, 'they'll be dealing with the two of us now.'

So they walked defiantly together into the Townhouse, tapping their soles heavily on the floor, taking their time to reach the stage where the full complement of the G9 sat, each with their hands in their lap, looking like a row of ancient stone boulders, Otto in the middle with Gilda Rosen on his left. At one end was Oswald, at the other, with his head down, sat Tom wearing his ox-eye daisy suit.

Dan tightened Braggle's lead to stop her tearing across to him.

'Don't let anything distract you,' Maia whispered as they came closer.

Otto stood up. 'This is a tribunal for Daniel Marks and no-one else,' he said firmly. 'The dog and the woman must leave now.'

'That woman is called Maia Gertler, as you well know,' Dan replied sharply, 'and she stays. There's nothing in the rules that states she can't. And nothing about dogs either despite what you wrote in the letter.' He turned and collected another chair from the middle of the hall for Maia. The two sat side by side with Braggle in between, her attempts to reach Tom unsuccessful. 'And what the rules do state, very clearly, is that a tribunal quorum is restricted to members of the G9 and no-one else. So I must insist that the men sitting at each end must leave, otherwise this tribunal has no validity.'

'I know of no such rule. The men stay.'

'Maia and Braggle are going no-where either then. That's the deal.'

'You are in no position to negotiate.'

Maia intervened. She stood up and in a loud, authoritative voice said: 'Oh cut the crap Otto, and just get on with it.'

For a few seconds silence erupted in the room as the other G9 members waited for Otto to respond, not daring to speak themselves. He looked at the ceiling, the windows, across to Tom who was still sitting with his head down staring at the floor, his hair ruffled as though he'd only just risen from his bed, and finally directly at Maia. 'Very well,' he said, 'let's get on with it.'

'Good,' she replied firmly. 'Dan and I both know the rules and so please, don't attempt to circumvent them. We know our rights, and the rules are clear that anyone facing a tribunal is allowed to bring a 'friend' who can give them support and advice, as well as an opening speech, which is what I intend to do now.' She raised her hand, palm out, to stop any intervention, and walked methodically back and forth along the length of the G9, her heels striking the floor. She gave a little nod to each member in turn, and with the exception of Gilda Rosen and Otto, received one in return. Then she started the speech she'd been practicing for two days.

'It wasn't so long ago I was here in front of a few of you after the death of my partner Theo Fanter. I killed him, not deliberately I have to say, with dried poisonous plants I'd wrapped in a spring roll, and you reduced my rank by one grade. Lucky me. Dan here killed his partner too. You had the collective wisdom to let him go with no penalty whatsoever. Theo however inflicts a few scratches on one of your members and he is totally humiliated. Dan is here now because he was found to be in possession of a small wind-up clock. One measly little clock which happens to be on the red list for some archaic, ludicrous, arbitrary reason. And what are your plans? No doubt you have already spoken behind closed doors, with Otto holding sway, explaining why the penalty should be an extreme one. Sorry, I will re-phrase that; *telling* you it should be an extreme one. Otto has decided, and every one of you rolls over on your backs whilst he tickles you on your stomachs. And why do you allow him to preside over you like some feudal lord from half a millennia ago? Let me tell you why. And of course, I can because, as you all very well know, I have intimate first-hand experience of Mr Otto Cladders, something I regret more than any of you could imagine. What Otto wants, he gets. And he's willing to do anything to make sure of it. This is a man who thinks it's his birth right to control this town, just like his father, and his father's father. He's never been a whole-hearted supporter of The Reformation, quite the opposite, he sees it as a massive hindrance to his own desire for change. Change that he truly believes is for our ultimate benefit, but actually is just a massive backward step which will undo everything The Reformation stands for.

But why am I telling you this? Because every one of you sitting up there on that platform, well, apart from poor Tom of course, knows all of that anyway. You know all about the bio-factory, the poisons, the hunting, and yet not one of you does anything about it. Is it because you agree with the policy? That, I just can't believe? How can you condone the abhorrent treatment of other animals and the use of poisons to destroy the land? So it must be something else. Are you scared? Surely not. There are eight of you and just one of him.

You do have collective power you know. The whole *is* greater than the sum of its parts, or have you forgotten that? So what is holding you back? Has he blinded you with gifts as he did with me? Probably. But that's not enough to just give in to everything. My guess is that he's made you believe things that just aren't true. Has he told you that his policy comes from a higher authority? That it's not *his* policy, he's just the messenger. Tell me, how many of you go to those meetings with him? Any of you? No? Have any of you heard directly from the horse's mouth so to speak?

And what's to happen to Dan? Have you already decided his punishment? Of course you have. And you know it's not about the clock, everyone's got something on the red list hidden away somewhere, whether it's a watch or a crucifix or a piece of Pre-Change memorabilia. No-one cares about that anymore. Dan's here today because he knows too much, and too much dissent is a little too, shall we say, challenging. But it's out there already. People in this town are talking. This is something you can't push back into its hiding place.

So I hope, at the very least, I've pricked your conscience. It's certainly time to examine your conscience. Perhaps it will make human beings out of you all. And I hope, soon, that your loyalty won't be to Otto Cladders but to the wellbeing of the people in this town. And that you recognize, once and for all, that time is up.'

When she finished speaking, she walked along the length of the stage one more time and stopped in front of Otto. The two stared implacably at each other. No words were said. No emotion crossed their faces. She turned abruptly and sat down next to Dan, placing her hand on his thigh. He took it in his own hand and squeezed. 'Thank you,' he said, 'that was amazing.'

Maia glowed with a sense of accomplishment. It had gone better than expected. There were no interruptions, for which she'd also prepared, and she could see most of the G9 fidgeting in their chairs, hands clasped, thumbs rubbing uncomfortably together, Gilda Rosen looking the most uncomfortable of all. Maia knew she'd touched a collective nerve; she could feel its intensity vibrating through the

Townhouse, and felt her shame slip away and disappear into the fundaments of the building. When Otto stood to respond, she kept her head raised and her hand on Dan's thigh, listening to his unbending voice, which sounded cold and uncompromising. She flinched when he claimed every word she'd uttered was a fabrication; an embittered release of pent-up frustration; the outpouring of a revengeful ex-lover. None of the G9 responded.

And then he changed tack.

'One thing you're right about,' he continued, 'is the clock. The red list has its merits, but it's been known for some time, perhaps a generation, that we've moved on from those early days when these things were essential to the orderliness of The Change. The ownership of a clock is inconsequential.'

Dan interrupted. 'Then why in the letter summoning me here was it described as a non-negotiable item with serious consequences?'

'It shows the G9 is sensitive to public opinion and open to change when necessary and with the shift in public sentiment.'

Dan scoffed. 'How refreshingly candid of you,' he said. 'Your broad-mindedness is a thing of rare beauty.'

Otto ignored the jibe and continued. 'Since that letter was written, there has been a significant development, and it is that which the G9 has discussed in an emergency session and which we will be considering at this tribunal.'

'You can't just change the goalposts,' Maia said.

'I think you'll find we can.'

'Get on with it then,' Dan replied, and bringing his head closer to Maia whispered 'this is where Tom comes in, it must be.'

And he was right. Otto took a letter from his coat pocket stating it was a declaration from Tom Othwell who was sitting on his far left. He read it aloud.

I, Tom Othwell, declare that on the night of March 2nd of this year, together with Dan Marks, we unlawfully entered the bio-factory of this town, released all the animals and set fire to the building, destroying it in its entirety. I deeply regret this action

but was pressured into it by Mr. Marks with whom I was having a long-term relationship, also under duress. He has threatened me with serious consequences if I reveal our actions, but I have been racked with guilt over my reprehensible behaviour and now feel compelled to finally tell the truth, despite his threats against me. I can also reveal that it was Mr. Marks who destroyed the car used by Otto Cladders and which was the property of The Highest Authority of the Reformation.
Tom Othwell

Dan clapped slowly, joined by Maia, the rising echo clawing at the walls. Braggle barked and ran frantically from one end of the Townhouse to the other, trailing her lead along the floor before she stopped in front of Tom, jumped onto the stage and pawed at his suit. Dan walked slowly towards them, grabbed the lead and before pulling her away said, 'I'm so sorry you have to go through this Tom. It's ok, I know what's happening. I know you had no choice.'

Tom lifted his head. His eyes bloodshot. His face withered with tiredness. 'I'm sorry too,' he replied softly.

Dan took his hand. 'Don't worry, everything will be fine.'

'I hope so.'

'Are you ok?'

But before he could answer, Otto intervened. 'We must continue,' he said. 'We haven't got all day.'

Dan gave the dog to Maia, walked to the middle of the stage, directly in front of Otto, who was sitting with his legs crossed and his hands lost in the pockets of his tweed jacket. Dan shoved his hands into the dirty side openings of his gardening trousers pushing them a little further down his legs.

'According to the rules, which we're all deeply committed to,' he said sarcastically, 'the defendant, which apparently is me, gets to say something at this point. But you know what. I'm not going to. What's the point? You all know this is ludicrous. So why should I waste my time and energy. You've already made up your mind. Well, been told how to make up your mind, and I'm not going to wait to hear it. Just send me a letter like you did to Theo. No doubt with the same judgement. And I'll rip it to pieces.' With an imaginary letter in his hands, he folded it three times, and in a series of rapid downward strokes ripped it apart, before throwing his arms into the air and watching the pieces fall slowly to the floor, like feathers torn from a pillow.

'And this is just the beginning,' he added.

Otto Cladders began to smile. 'Oh yes,' he said, 'we're all very, very scared. Now why don't you do what you said you were going to do - and go. You will receive the judgment in due course.'

'You may smile and smile Otto Cladders, but you're still a villain.'

'And you're stuck in a time warp,' he replied. 'We all learned the classics Dan, so don't try that A_3 bullshit with me.'

Dan walked back to Maia and picked up Braggle's lead from the floor. 'Time to go,' he said. He went back to Tom, held his hand again and squeezed it firmly. 'Everything will be fine,' he said, 'I'll make sure it is.'

He waited for a letter, convinced it would arrive the next day. It never came. Nor the next day, or the day after that. On the Saturday, he walked to the Townhouse. A cluster of people assembled at the entrance. A simple message posted on the door read: *Closed for essential repairs until further notice.* It was unprecedented. The Townhouse had never been closed before. A middle-aged man, whom Dan had known as one of the stalwarts of the Saturday gatherings, was banging on the locked door. No-one came to open it.

'They're frightened,' Dan said. 'They think there could be trouble.' The others nodded. Word had quickly spread about his tribunal, and there were rumours that sources within the G9 had been talking, breaking the code of silence which every member swore to uphold.

'It's beginning to crack,' he said, 'It's one of the guiding principles of the Reformation that they remain quiet. And if some of them aren't, then we know that it's serious.'

In the days following, Dan became embroiled in the general hubbub surrounding the closure. He made sure to go to every distribution, pushing himself to the forefront, listening, watching, gauging the mood of an increasingly agitated crowd. On the Thursday, he clapped his hands as loudly as he could, as he'd done in the Townhouse a couple of weeks before, people quickly gathering around him. 'You all know by now what's been happening,' he said, 'and you would have all heard the rumours that some G9 members are breaking their silence, which is extraordinary in itself.' He took out a piece of paper from his pocket. 'Listen to this,' he said, 'it's page three of the G9 rulebook which I looked up in the archives and I've written some of it down. Here's what it says, and I quote: *G9 membership is not bestowed lightly, and adhering to a strict policy of silence in matters of town policy allows for the free and smooth running of every town, and without which would undermine the trust and responsibility of such an important post. G9 membership is bestowed on those thought worthy advocates of such judicious policy and any breach of this trust will be seen as a serious failure of duty'.'* Dan waved the paper in the air. 'A serious failure of duty,' he repeated, pausing theatrically between every word. 'So for any of them to break that pledge shows how bad things have become doesn't it? Well, it's time for answers no? It's time for them to speak to *us,* let *us* know what's really happening in this town. Don't we deserve some explanation?'

The crowd roared its approval. Dan smiled with all the confidence of a man on the ascendant.

'And with the harvest celebrations coming up, they're all going to be on stage right here in this market place, but how can we take them seriously if they've lost our trust, if it's all falling apart behind the scenes? The G9 has always kept a discreet distance, that's the convention, the assumption that they don't need to waste their time on the small things and that the big things look after themselves, but that's no longer the case is it, we know that now, we know that if we leave it to them, bad things happen. So how can they possibly sit on that stage and expect everything to carry on as usual? It can't and it won't.'

He left the distribution feeling elated, his bag filled with extra fruit and vegetables which the stall holders insisted he take, and as he walked past the main gate, Oswald waiting to check his bag and tablet, he strode straight on and Oswald didn't dare stop him.

NINETEEN

Otto Cladders's routine had been severely disrupted and he was not happy. The last few days he had not slept well and his inner clock had not been its usual self. The first thing he knew of the morning was the sound of Els flushing the toilet. It had been an irritation the first time, but this was the fourth morning in a row, and as he was filled with an unfathomable dislike for anything which disturbed his own rigid universe, being woken to the sound of someone else's ablutions was akin to having his head smashed against a wall.

Being angry with himself wasn't an option, so he created an escape route by blaming his partner for everything. It wasn't so difficult. She had been his battering muse since he had chosen her from a hundred other hopefuls more than twenty years before. There was something wonderfully subservient in her eyes which had attracted him, the way she held her head slightly down and her eyes with it. Her genetic profile was promising too – a solid B_2 which was probably a good few rankings under him. There was an assumption, neither queried nor legitimized, that he was a high A; his whole childhood had been woven around it and his short period at the Academy suggested he was destined for the top drawer of administrative life, like his father and his father's father. His own father, it has to be said, had made a bit of a hash of things and had to be replaced on the town's G9, spending the rest of his life tending the garden, with great success, and making sure Otto was groomed for something special. And it had paid dividends; Otto's star had risen quickly, and amongst all those boys and girls who came from the Old Families, he was seen to be one of the best. It helped that his frequent visits back home were a constant re-affirmation of his gifts, his parents showering him with waves of love and generous helpings of confidence enhancing praise. His looks were adequately appealing. His side profile was exceptional, with a fine nose and jawline, but there was a slight disappointment when observed full on, as though the sum of his parts failed to justify the hype of his individual features. Perhaps it was the eyes, which seemed a trifle too close together and never seemed to look directly at you.

When Els came to live in the family house, one of Otto's first tasks had been to take her by the hand and lead her to the oak tree. He asked her to admire its imposing size, telling her it had been planted generations before when his family were the region's biggest landowners whose wealth exceeded all imagination. 'This tree gives me strength', he told her, 'and it should do the same for you too'. In the years thereafter she heeded his advice, leaning against its vastness, attempting to draw strength from its wisdom. But it failed to give her the answers she craved, and she came to see it more as a looming dominance than a soothing oracle, a constant reminder of her inadequacies, not least her inability to provide an heir. She had been given the ultimate gift of The Reformation, to have her own child, and despite all the positive clinical signs, she had failed. Otto didn't tell her directly of his profound disappointment, he didn't need to, his attitude towards her was enough, forcing her into herself so that her inherent shyness overwhelmed her more outgoing traits. She was rarely seen at the distributions and never at the Townhouse, choosing to have their food delivered with the minimum of fuss, although it was Otto who sorted out the more extravagant supply of meat. She tried to soothe him with the finest cooking, learnt from the finest books, avoiding recipes with ingredients she knew he didn't like (he hated anything resembling a gourd) and making sure the meat was amply seasoned but not overpowered by an accompanying sauce. It was seldom that her efforts failed to please, and she ensured a semblance of pleasantries by showing a keen interest in the machinations of his day, although his activities, when he patronised her with the details, made her dislike him the more. However, she knew not to contradict and when to appease, and when to shut up altogether.

But the past few days had been more than challenging. She could only surmise the latest developments, piecing together moods and the sporadic ill-tempered sentences from Otto and the way locals treated her on the few occasions she did leave the house. It was clear (and often embarrassing) that information was being withheld, whether to spare her blushes or to avoid potential repercussions. Gossip was rife, but one still had to be circumspect about whom one gossiped about, and the honourable Otto Cladders was out of bounds, especially when the gossip had a hardened foundation. So Els's ignorance was magnified by the nature of her relationship with her partner. She was on the inside and the outside at the same time, and yet so far removed from both that she may as well not exist at all. Even the cleaner, never one to allow domestic work to get in the way of a good story, became hyper-diligent around the house, with no time for a cup of tea and a homemade biscuit, and when Els tried, in a roundabout way, to elicit even a crumb of information, he doubled down on his work as though his life depended on it.

It wasn't something that fell without warning. There had been hints over the preceding months which had pushed Els into an unwelcome self-reflection. Her instinct was to shake it off as she would a persistent cough, but as each event grew in magnitude, it became impossible to let it go. The two men who defaced the lawn seemed to be the beginning of it all. She would have found it faintly amusing if it wasn't such an integral part of Otto's well-being. She'd found his obsessive desire to control things to be more of a flaw than an attribute, and had watched with an increasing silent disdain as it hardened and expanded, with the lawn a symbol of his stark beliefs. So when one of the men lifted the turf above his head, Els had to resist the temptation to join him, pretending instead to see nothing and pushing it to the far reaches of her consciousness. She could have settled with the familiarity of denial if it wasn't followed by other incidents which she could not just swat aside as an unwelcome guest, however much she tried. The destruction of the bio-factory twisted the sense of foreboding deeper into her, making her so nervous as she watched Otto's tirades that she began to dread even the evening meals. The cleaner was her only life-line into the town's machinations although she was well aware of his avoidance of any direct reference to Otto.

And Otto's absences, often days at a time, were directly proportional to the gravity of the situation. She knew only what he chose to tell her, which was little at the best of times. And as these were the worst of times, his ability to share his troubles declined even further.

It was the smashing of the windows which pushed it all into another league altogether. It was a personal violation; an infringement on her right to avoid confrontation which she had honed over many years and which had stirred her ability to go on with life. And she blamed Otto entirely. His actions had reached home, her home, and had affected her directly, punching through her wall of self-induced ignorance. She could no longer tip-toe through her life, at least, if she felt it worthy of living. Her conclusion was to avoid any direct conflict with a man she could not fathom, but in its place she must listen, observe and be open to all possibilities.

It had given her the space to breathe in the most trying of circumstances, including this past week, which was beyond anything she had experienced. She knew something was seriously amiss when one morning Otto failed to rise at seven. Once was surprising; four days in a row was deeply disturbing, magnified by his relentless bad temper which even her cooking couldn't ameliorate. The first morning, when she rose at her usual time, went to the toilet and then downstairs to the kitchen for breakfast, she became so flustered he wasn't there, that when their paths finally crossed on the stairs, she held on to the bannister and failed to acknowledge him as he thundered by. The second day was a carbon copy of the first. On the third day, she pressed her ear to her bedroom door to make sure he was awake, waiting another half an hour before descending herself. And today she did exactly the same, biding her time, going to the toilet when she knew he was already downstairs, then quietly entering the kitchen as though nothing was wrong. Morning communication was muted at the best of times, relating mostly to sleep patterns and the freshness of the milk, and as she was now loathed to mention anything about sleep, she concentrated on his drink, only to be rebuffed with an accusation that she had, for the fourth day running, woken him by flushing the toilet. She remained silent, bursting inside with resentment at his blatant lie, concentrating on her toasted bread which she had just smeared with more homemade greengage jam than she was accustomed to. She put the toast to her mouth, took a sharp crunch and a sliver of jam slid on to the floor.

Otto watched as the jam slid gently off the side of her toast, and saw it fall, as if in slow motion, onto the part of the marble tiled floor covered with an antique sisal rug. With exaggerated moves, he took a handful of kitchen paper, picked up the blob of jam and threw it into the bin, leaving a greenish, brownish stain on the rug. He wet a cloth and rubbed it on the stain, all the while saying nothing as Els stood in the same spot just a few inches from the sticky commotion, refusing to budge an inch as Otto puffed his way through his personal little crisis. This was his great grandfather's sisal rug, after all, and had survived a century of upheaval unscathed. He would not allow a blob of greengage jam to come between him and his immaculate ancestral lineage.

Els couldn't help herself. She took one look at her half-eaten piece of toast and, jammy side down, pressed it onto the crown of Otto's head, giving it a little horizontal shove so that the jam and toast became one and merged into his hair.

Otto and Els had been together more than twenty years. It had been an unhappy time for both, with the feeling that a moment would come when the built-up frustrations would burst open. Miraculously, despite provocations which would dent the stoicism of the most sedate of people, nothing of any consequence materialized, based on their ability to internalize their feelings and deflect whatever was flung at them. But there comes a moment when a crack grows so wide that the resentment flows out like an erupting volcano, spurting words and accusations which had been locked inside for far too long. The greengage jam was Otto and Els's moment.

Otto sprang up like an old-fashioned jack in the box, instinctively flaying his arms as though swatting away a swarm of wasps. He caught Els's jaw, an accident but nonetheless one he did not regret, and clutched his head as though she'd ground glass into his scalp. He wasn't one for expletives, preferring more rounded sentences which became the dignity of his station, but this time one syllable words burst from his mouth as befits a dormant volcano which has had enough of pent-up inactivity. Els responded in kind, adding lustre to her performance by grabbing her glass of milk and throwing it in his face. It did the trick of stopping Otto in his tracks. He paused, wiped the liquid slowly away, dragging both hands down from brow to chin, and flicking the milk in her direction. He then formed his first complete sentences.

'You have made my life a misery,' he said. 'I wished you'd died long ago from the pox and been thrust into the communal pit without ceremony. And I can tell you now, you will not be buried in the family vaults. I decided that long ago. I will not allow your body to defile my ancestors. They deserve to be left in peace without your dull, pathetic, and if I may say so, very plain corpse, filling the air with a very common decay.'

He said it in a subdued tone with his arms by his side as though he was officiating an actual burial and as though they were sentences he'd formulated long ago and was waiting to give them breath, so when he had finished, the look on his face was of someone finally putting something to rest. Els made no reply. She waited until he had finished, went methodically to the cupboard, took out the pot of jam, opened a drawer, took out a large spoon, opened the pot, thrust the spoon in, scooping a fistful of jam, and then flicked it onto the rug. She then stomped on the droppings and gave a little swish of her body and feet to ensure the stain was as large and as messy as possible. 'I don't need words,' she said. 'Actions speak far louder.' And she walked out of the room, up the stairs, and into her bedroom, where for the first time ever, she turned the key.

Els sat on the bed and refused to cry. Otto's words were so horrible, so full of venom, that the shock outweighed any necessity to break down. She held out her arm, watching her hand tremble, and felt the rumble of shakes wafting through her body. She took deep breaths, closing her eyes with each inhale, and as she puffed out the air with added force, her thoughts clarified into a simple, rational equation. And she knew she would act on it. 'Actions speak louder than words,' she repeated aloud.

Otto left the house within the hour without a goodbye. It was a Friday so he took the car and Els watched from the window as he revved a little harder than usual and drove a little faster along the driveway, past the oak tree and out through the front gates, the tyres throwing up pieces of gravel in their wake. He would be gone all day, possibly the following day too and so Els knew she had time to herself, and as she was bent on not preparing any dinner, her day would not be determined by meat and vegetables.

She took a deliciously long, hot shower. She wanted to look good today. Fresh and alert. She put on a pale-yellow silk top and her favourite black trousers which Otto had given her, saying they'd come from far away and were based on a famous pre-Change design. And they made her feel special, the sort of trousers which accentuated the good bits and toned down the less appealing aspects of her lower half, and if she was going to visit Maia, she needed to look her best.

She had known about Maia almost from the beginning. She'd spent two decades observing Otto and had learned to define his moods and behaviour with an expert eye. And the difference between an affair and a brief encounter was clear, not that she minded either, although she preferred the former as it meant he was out of the house more than usual.

A few months into the Maia affair, as that was what she now considered it, she had followed him over the period of weeks, not out of any sense of betrayal but from a curiosity born out of necessity, as she needed to understand his movements in order to gauge his moods. Knowing was far more palatable than lacking the building blocks to decipher the vicissitudes of her philandering partner. It cost far less energy.

She had a hunch Otto's relationship with Maia had ended around the Solstice celebrations when he began spending more time at home and was more capricious than ever, although the disastrous Solstice ceremony may have had something to do with it too. She'd watched it first hand in a state of bewildered excitement, suppressing a desire to clap as the flag wilted half way up the pole and the Ode to the Ox-Eye Daisy was plucked mid-sentence. She'd never seen Otto look so emasculated and humiliated, and it thrilled her. But everything was conjecture, feeling and nuance. She never felt fully in charge of events. She foraged for details and meaning rather than shaping them from any direct source. It irritated her. Made her feel even smaller. Even more irrelevant. And that was about to change.

'Hello Maia,' she said calmly.

Maia was sitting in her garden with her eyes closed, her gardening gloves lying on the small round table next to her together with a large cup of mint tea which Els could smell as she approached.

She opened her eyes slowly and looked across with little enthusiasm, thinking it was yet another person come to disturb her morning and ask her opinion on the unfolding events, but on seeing Els she rose quickly from her chair, the metal scraping against the stone floor. 'Els,' she said in an octave higher than her usual tone.

'Indeed,' she replied. 'I didn't think you'd recognize me.' And when no reply came, she calmly walked to the spare chair, sat down clasping her hands in her lap and added: 'Don't worry, I'm not here to make a scene, I don't care about what's been going on between you and Otto, I just need some answers.'

It was an ambush of impeccable fortitude. Els's natural

timidity seemed to dissolve as soon as she said it. She felt strong and more than Maia's equal, taking control from the outset, quashing any chances of deceit or sabotage.

Maia sat down with a thud as though the air had been sucked out of her.

'Maia, I need to make myself very clear from the beginning,' Els said. 'Yes, I've known for a long time, but I know none of the details. And that's why I'm here. I just want the plain truth. And I want to know what's been happening these past few days. I want to know everything.'

It took Maia a while to find her balance. She had been expertly wrong-footed and she wasn't used to it. Her instinct was to skirt around the truth, finding ways to circumvent her actions and by doing so convincing herself that it was with the best of intentions, sparing others any unnecessary hurt; protecting herself from criticism was merely a bonus. For the first few minutes, with Els staring at her, she climbed into her usual pattern of deflection, explaining that it was never a relationship, just an enjoyable distraction and anyway, it had been over for a long time, it meant nothing to either party. But she said it without conviction and a simple nudge from Els was all that was needed to make her change tack.

'Maia, please. I'm here for the truth. It's not so difficult is it? And don't worry, I'm not going to make a scene, I'm not going to scream or throw something at you. I'm way, way beyond that now. So please, start again, from the beginning.'

And to both woman's surprise and relief, the next few hours sped by as they revealed everything they knew, releasing a shared sense of betrayal and a bond which grew with every revelation. Otto became utterly real and exposed. His life and behaviour stripped bare in forensic detail. Two sides joined, melding their experiences, halving their anguish and doubling their strength. Before Els said goodbye, Maia invited her back the following day. 'And I'd like to bring Dan and Petra too,' she said.

Els accepted without hesitation.

Maia no longer felt wretched or even guilty for her behaviour, as dwelling on her faults was time-consuming and energy draining and would detract from the fights to come. The mornings gave her sustenance for the rest of the day when she would meet up with Dan and a few others and go into the centre spreading information and gauging opinion. Petra Fortune had been a godsend, breaking away from the G9 and holding long, detailed discussions with a new unofficial group which included Dan and Maia. She told them everything she had been privy to, but was the first to admit she was unable to offer anything of the inner machinations of how it all *really* worked because only Otto left the town and returned with information he said came directly from the highest authority. So, her counsel was second hand and perhaps not to be completely relied upon. It came as a shock to Maia to recognize this fact and when she used those same words in her first meeting with the new group to describe what she knew, she stopped mid-sentence, as though the gravity and incompetence of what she was saying had sunk in for the first time.

Petra said she'd never met anyone from the exalted ranks of the Highest Authority of the Reformation and thought no-one else had either, except Otto. So he was the binding oracle who, she said almost apologetically, was not overbearing in his manner towards her or the other members, just a link between the inner and outer layers of control who shared his instructions in a quiet, no fuss, direct and professional manner. His notes were detailed, his affectation left for public occasions. Petra liked him and trusted him and looked up to him, and until recently had no reason to think otherwise. Her first misgivings came when she felt she was being by-passed for expedience. There had been four tribunals over the previous year dealing with serious issues and each one had not adhered to the rule-book, Otto manipulating their course so blatantly that she felt undermined and manipulated. Once or twice was bearable, but four in a row seemed heavy-handed and oppressive. It rippled through the G9, gradually eroding respect until it was no longer possible to ignore.

And she knew one thing for sure. 'Otto would do whatever it took to regain control,' she said, 'and he won't move to the sidelines without a fight.'

Otto's life was unravelling quickly and his composure with it. He had always been in control; had never known a moment of uncertainty. He was predestined to lead, to inspire, to uphold the values of his station, to have an instinct for what was right and wrong, all for the good of the Reformation and the well-being of its people. He was a natural leader who wasn't afraid of confronting change and new ideas when they were so palpably needed. With Paul at his side, offering guidance and support, he felt invincible. As his mother and father had always told him, it's in the stars that you will leave your mark, become the guiding force for a better world in which the principle and the practical merge; you have destiny engraved in your DNA.

But Otto's humiliation was now complete. The glass-domed amphitheatre of the Highest Authority of the Reformation, with centuries of history embedded in its stone, had absorbed the roar of disapproval and Paul had thrown him to the wolves; the man who had encouraged him to take chances, to experiment, to lead from the front, had disowned him publicly. Otto should have seen it coming. For the past week, Paul had been out of reach, not responding to calls or texts, and so the way he denounced him in front of hundreds of his compatriots should have been no surprise. But it was. Otto was so utterly disemboweled that his response to the accusations lacked either clarity or conviction. After all, he was the one who had pushed for change (with Paul as his guide), insisted on its necessity, taking experiments to a new level, and then pushed on regardless when the necessary quorum fell just short. He'd show them who was right, who had the boldness to tackle the real issues which few were prepared to face head-on. He had it all planned, including basking in the success and watching his star rise as naturally as Orion's belt each winter night. But now the bio-factory had been destroyed, his attempts to smother any threat had backfired, he'd been made to look a fool at the Solstice celebrations, his G9 had collapsed, its members failing to support him, and now the one man who had truly believed in him had stood in front of some of the most important people in the land and described him as a liability, someone whose vanity had curdled his reason, a man who had jeopardized decades of stability and balance. The Reformation must not be undermined, must resist fools and upstarts, must be coherent in its policy and take the constitution's original text as a living gospel, with a few nips and tucks to keep up with changing times.

Otto sat in his usual spot in the second tier looking up at the clouds as they thundered over the dome, listening to one rebuke after another, waiting for the vote that would strip him of power forthwith. The walls, floor and ceiling, and even the cushions on which they sat, were covered with tiny Ox-Eye daisy motifs and engraved over and over with the Five Great Dictums. 'Know thy Place' etched itself into Otto's brain and for the first time in his life, he felt it was pointed directly at him.

A disembodied voice came over the main speakers calling for the vote: *Should Otto Cladders be held in contempt?* The delegates pressed their buttons. Within seconds the giant stage screen went red. Motion not carried. The dome erupted. 'Scandalous,' someone shouted from the third tier, followed by a chorus of others. A shoe was thrown towards the screen. Then another. Otto kept his gaze on the skies above, not daring to look down. The woman sitting next to him squeezed his thigh. 'Who'd have thought it,' she said, 'you're a lucky man Otto Cladders, someone out there obviously likes you.' Then a tall woman wearing a tight yellow suit appeared on the far side of the stage and as she walked slowly to the podium the shouts subsided and stopped altogether as she took the microphone and began to speak.

'Shame on you,' she said. 'The majority has clearly stated that Otto Cladders should keep his position, and as we are a democracy we will abide by that vote. And that's final. So stop this nonsense. It will not be tolerated. Yes, Otto has been foolish, but no doubt he will learn from his mistakes and come out of it a better person. Who here hasn't made mistakes? Who here hasn't always abided by our guiding principles? The Reformation is a feeling, living organism and has always been so. It's why it is so effective, and it's why everyone cherishes its existence. The Reformation is forgiving. It is gentle. It is alive. And it must not be undermined by dissent. So please, go home, this meeting is over.' And with that, she walked briskly off the stage and disappeared behind a slit in a giant red velvet curtain which someone had slid open so she could breeze through without stopping.

Her interception worked. The delegates dispersed quietly, Otto staying in his chair abiding by the message that had popped on to the personal screen in front of him. *Come to the main office behind the entrance hall in fifteen minutes.*

The four-hour drive home went quickly. Otto's head was buzzing with relief and excitement. He had been reprieved beyond all expectations and it was clear what he must do to rehabilitate himself. He must start re-building his reputation without delay, and with the full support of the Highest Authority. He opened the windows, feeling the early autumn warmth caress his arms, and turned the music to its highest level, tapping his fingers against the steering wheel with a cheerfulness he hadn't felt for a long time. He would contact the names on the list he'd been given first thing the next morning and arrange a meeting with the new G9 before the Harvest celebrations. A few of the names he didn't know, but at least Gilda Rosen was there, she'd been a stalwart and the only one of the old G9 who had stood by him; it would not be forgotten. He would draw a line under a chequered past year and start with a renewed vigour knowing there were higher beings watching each move and giving him their blessing. He must show benevolence and a degree of humility. A new Otto would rise from the tangled mess of his town's shenanigans. Ok, the bio-factory was history, at least in his town; other towns would be found to take its place, and the plant and insect 'demotivators' (as they'd been so quaintly re-named) would be scaled back temporarily, to begin with a fresh burst of enthusiasm when the timing was right. Otto's head was full of delicious hyperbole which caused him to stop half way to catch his breath. He stood in a shallow lay-by under a myriad of oaks saying over and over to himself 'I know my place.'

He reached home just before ten and sat beneath his oak tree breathing in his town's cleansing air. A wasp buzzed around his foot and was stamped on without ceremony. He looked up at Els's window and saw her looking out from behind the curtains. He waved. She did not. He went inside and called her name as he looked in the fridge for his evening meal which she would always leave wrapped in foil if he'd been away for the day. There was nothing. It didn't surprise him. He knew how spiteful she could be. Yes, he'd been a trifle overbearing at breakfast, and she was prone to be over sensitive to his little moods, but in the spirit of forgiveness he would make amends and apologise even though it certainly wasn't all his doing. He made himself a cheese sandwich with a green tomato pickle, poured himself a glass of dry white wine he kept for special occasions and which very few had the privilege of drinking, called Els's name again just in case she would make an appearance, and sat in the living room with a view across the back lawn. With the remote, he switched on the outside lights releasing a swathe of luminescent green. A hedgehog scurried away into the bushes. The lawn, like the grand old oak, was Otto's strength and guidance. He loved its clean, strong lines and its ability to withstand the vagaries of the weather and the myriad of wild flowers which, given the opportunity, would wreak havoc. The herbicide (he must remember to call it a demotivator) had worked its magic for many years and perhaps next year he would try the front of the house too, although he rather liked the white and red dead nettles that languished around the oak tree each spring, so maybe he'd defer any spraying until they'd wilted away.

He stood up with the glass of wine in his hand and slid open the glass doors leading on to the terrace. A few dried leaves spread themselves across the lawn. He walked out and felt the lush bounce of the grass against his soles. It needs a slight trim he thought. He continued walking, thinking of weeds and wine, looking up at the surrounding trees towering above him, only noticing the hole when he was almost upon it, a hole wide enough and deep enough to stick his head in and in exactly the same spot as the previous damage. Otto got down on his knees, placed the wine glass gently onto the grass and grabbed some earth from the hole with one hand. It was soft and damp. He squeezed it between his cupped palms, making a tight ball, then stood up, kicked the wine glass and threw the ball as far as he could. 'Daniel Marks,' he said out loud. 'Only Daniel Marks would have done this.'

The next morning he woke at seven or thereabouts, and sprang out of bed with the energy of a ten year old. He slung open the curtains and focused (it took him a while) on the hole in the lawn fifty metres from the house. A contempt had replaced his anger, and he would channel it for good; for a better future. His dreams had been filled with bright lights and positive vibes although most of the content was blurred except for the floating above a crowd like a skylark, or was it a hawk? Whatever it was, it made him feel good and centred and sharp. This was definitely the beginning of something new.

His morning routine clicked back into place as though it had never deserted him. Bathroom, kitchen, milk, bread. Els appeared at eight. 'Good morning,' he said cheerfully, 'sleep well?' The response was disappointing but not unexpected and Otto carried on regardless, ignoring her monosyllabic reply. 'I'm sorry about yesterday,' he continued. 'You know I didn't mean any of it. And by the way, you didn't see anyone on the lawn did you?'

'Why?'

'Someone's dug a hole in the lawn.'

'Oh. Again?'

'It's a deep hole this time. And I know who it is.'

'Oh? Are you going to tell me who?'

'Not quite yet. You'll find out in good time.'

Els poured herself some milk and put her bread in the toaster. Otto was being irritatingly upbeat and it unnerved her.

'How did it go yesterday?'

'Very, very well,' Otto replied. 'Much better than expected actually.'

'In what way?'

'In every way.'

'Oh?'

And to her surprise Otto told her about the forum and his reprieve and that there'd be a new G9, forgetting that he hadn't told her it had disbanded in the first place. He'd be busy sorting all that out today without delay. 'Speed is of the essence,' he said, 'and I have to make sure it's all done before the Harvest celebrations, so you won't be seeing much of me, but I'll be here for dinner.'

Els didn't tell him that there wouldn't be any dinner. Or that he'd not be seeing much of her either.

TWENTY

Otto had already received messages from some of the new G9 and without exception they were full of enthusiasm and more than ready to take the helm. Gilda Rosen had also been in contact. She sounded a little subdued and irritated Otto with her luke-warm eagerness to be part of it. She didn't say it directly, it was more in the questions she asked. *Is it wise? Isn't it too hasty? What will the others say?* This was no time for doubt or indecisiveness, he said, this is a time for action, to show who's the boss. *But shouldn't we let the dust settle, just for a few more weeks?* No, was Otto's short reply, absolutely not.

Otto contacted the remaining three names on the list, and all agreed to participate. He felt they also weren't bubbling with the zeal he would expect. Their responses were a little tardy and less than obsequious, and he made a note of it in his new notebook, which he'd titled 'The New G9. A New Beginning.'

A meeting was arranged for the next day in the Townhouse, at 10. They must bring their own lunch, Otto had said, and something to drink (no alcohol) as it would last well into the afternoon. Dress smart. Remember, you are representatives of this town with responsibility, position and dignity, and you've been carefully chosen to reflect this. Don't let me down.

He put on his tweed jacket, brushing down the sleeves with an old clothes brush from his grandfather, called out to Els that he was leaving, not realizing she'd already left the house, and walked out the side entrance next to the car port. It was his habit to go first to the car and stroke the bonnet with the tips of his fingers as though it was a living creature needing the soothing caress of its owner. The upholstery was a deep burgundy red and real leather with his initials embroidered on the side arms (he'd asked for that especially). Damaging his car was like punching him in the stomach and so, as he walked towards it and saw the long, solid scratch flowing the length of the car, he let out a whelp of pain. Daniel, he thought immediately. But he kept his composure; he was going to pay him a visit anyway and this time the repercussions were going to bite, he'd make sure of that.

Otto had never been to Dan's before and felt a sting of resentment as he walked the long pathway to the house passing a swathe of blackberry bushes with berries the size of walnuts. He put one in his mouth, and another, then another, and methodically wiped his stained fingers and mouth using his cotton handkerchief with an ox-eye daisy motif in one corner. He walked to the end of the path, made a left turn and was glad to see the house was rather plain, if not slightly larger than he would have liked. The cedar wood which clad the front wall was green with age and the porch so overrun with dandelions Otto's instinct was to run home and grab a bottle of demotivator (yes, the word was beginning to sink in). He rang the bell. And again. And when no-one answered after a third attempt, he walked to the back of the house. The lawn, if it could be called that, was covered in daisies and red clover and other wild flowers he couldn't name and didn't want to. Thistles clung to the edge with wisps of seed peeling away from their tops. It had the look of one of his anxiety dreams. Another reason to get him out of this town he thought, and I'll personally oversee the procedure for the next occupants. He peered through the back door into the kitchen and saw a row of copper pots on a shelf above the stove. Otto grabbed a small rock from the garden and smashed it through one of the glass panes, opened the door, took the largest pot, filled it half-full with dandelions he'd ripped from the lawn and placed it back on the shelf, walking away with a whirl of pleasure filling his body.

It was a fifteen-minute walk to Maia's, a house he knew intimately and which gave him a pang of anxiety when he approached. He wanted to hate her, despise her, to truss her up in a package and send it to God knows where. She had betrayed him and humiliated him and, all things considered, he should have no qualms in revelling in her downfall. And yet the letter he sent informing her of her new life partner made him feel wretched. He could still quash it of course. He'd have to see how contrite she was first. If they could go back to how it was, then there was a chance. Her companionship had meant a lot to him after all and he missed that. He needed it.

It's one thing to cling on to threads of hope, quite another to clutch at straws which have long since blown beyond reach. It took just thirty more minutes for Otto to be confronted with the reality, and it was far worse than he could ever have imagined. He knocked at the door using his special code; two hard knocks, a pause, then three quick knocks. It took a while for Maia to answer as she spent a hectic minute or so debating with the five others in the house whether to let him in. It was Els who insisted he should. So she hid in the study with Dan, Petra and two others, biding their time for their cue.

Maia opened the door with a smile and a 'what are you doing here'? The answer was polite with a hint of contrition. She guided him directly to the living room, offered him a drink of anything he fancied, and after a few minutes began to relax. She flirted and danced around his suggestions, hoping Els could hear everything he said. She listened to his accusations, his hurt, his feelings, allowing the charade for half an hour (the amount of time she told the others she'd take) until the moment Otto tried to touch the back of her waist to bring her closer. Maia felt the blood rush to her head with that sense of falling she'd always had when he came so close, then with a gentle push she asked him to sit down on the sofa.

'I have a little surprise for you,' she said. She walked calmly to the door and called the others. Dan came in first with Braggle by his side, followed by Petra. Otto remained silent with his hands clasped tight between his thighs as they each took a kitchen chair and sat opposite him whilst Braggle barked and snarled, Dan holding her back with the leash.

'It's time for *your* tribunal and all dogs are welcome,' Dan said, 'but we need a quorum, not that that's ever stopped you of course. Let me introduce you to Bernard Volt and Frances Cornell. Do they ring any bells?'

Otto said nothing as they came into the room, recognising the names instantly as two new members of the new G9.

'And the pièce de resistance …' Dan stretched out his arm, withholding the temptation to say *ta-da*. And Els walked in.

Bernard Volt was a tall, strong man who spent every afternoon in the town gym, which was just as well because his bulk was needed as Otto stood up abruptly and raced over to his partner in such a fury that if he'd been holding his glass of homemade lemonade he would have smashed it into her face. He got as far as Bernard's impressive chest and was unceremoniously bundled back on to the sofa. All Otto could do was grab the cushion and throw it in Els's direction, letting out a primal scream of such agonizing force that Braggle whimpered and pushed her head under Dan's chair.

'Now you know what it feels like,' Dan said.

It took Otto five minutes to calm down. He shouted so many obscenities and cursed so rhythmically that all but Els started to laugh. She couldn't watch his meltdown. It was too tragic. Too pathetic. Too comical. And far too personal. She walked to the kitchen, poured a large glass of water and drank it in one go, leaning against the sink to steady herself. Maia came over, held her hand and stroked her hair. 'I'm so sorry,' she said. 'And don't worry, you can stay with me.'

The two women remained in the kitchen for the remainder of Otto's ordeal. Neither could bare to make eye contact with a man they knew so intimately and who was now being humiliated. Petra did most of the talking, telling him his behaviour had been unacceptable, no-one trusted him anymore, his authority had evaporated, the G9 old and new would no longer accept him as their leader, his time was up, there was no point protesting.

There was no malice in her words. She didn't raise her

voice. Her accusations were made plainly and with an unassuming authority Otto had never had. Bernard and Frances told him they could not work under him and would not be attending the meeting the following day, and would do everything they could to make sure it didn't go ahead. Dan spoke last and was less constrained; 'Price, Theo and Tom deserve retribution and justice,' he said, 'and I will make sure they get it if it's the last breath I take.'

'It will be,' Otto replied.

It was not a tribunal. It had been an impromptu chance to pull the rug from under Otto a few days earlier than planned and they were pleased with how they'd worked as a team. Petra concluded by describing a new era in the town's history with the founders of The Reformation as a guiding principle, as it should always be, and what had happened in their town must never happen again. She was well aware it sounded a little grandiose in front of six others and a dog, but she was starting to enjoy the attention and surely there would be grander occasions. 'We cannot be cruel, and we cannot be ignorant,' she said, 'then we are no better than our forefathers.' And with that Otto was free to go.

'But before he does,' Maia said, as she came in from the kitchen, 'can you take his phone from him and lock him in the bathroom, we need to go and get some of Els's possessions.

Els took Maia and Dan back to the house. She was subdued and emotional and asked them to leave her as she walked into each room, touching surfaces and taking deep breaths. She had only ever felt secondary to these surroundings, surplus to its fabulous history, and had contributed little to its make-up, but this had been her home for more than twenty years and she felt the weight of her own history embedded in the walls with its imposing portraits and dark corridors. She walked into Otto's bedroom, which they had once shared, and glided her hand across the bed sheets which had been meticulously folded back, the creases smoothed out, the two feather pillows plumped up. The room was tidy and clean, nothing out of place. And to her amazement, a photo of them stood on his desk. She remembered it being taken, shortly after they got together, both smiling under the oak tree, Otto's arm around her waist, pulling her towards him. She picked it up and brought it closer to her face. She saw how her arms were clenched to her sides and her shoulders slightly raised, and if she looked more closely, how her smile was slightly off, as though someone had told her what to do. She remembered it clearly, that feeling of not being herself, of being someone else's property, and she had never shaken it off. She placed the photo face down on the desk and walked to her own bedroom. She sat on her unmade bed and closed her eyes, taking in the enormity of what she had done.

Maia took Dan to the barn where Otto had shown her his stash of poisons and where she siphoned off a couple of vials a few months before. 'Let's torch the place,' Dan said. 'Let's do here what Tom and Price did to the bio-factory.'

When they met up with Els back in the house, her response was immediate and definitive. 'Absolutely not', she said. 'Do you want to see that house and that wonderful old oak tree go up in flames? No. That is not justice. That is callous and thoughtless.'

There was something cold in her manner. The last few days had worn her down and as she crammed as many of her clothes into as many bags as she could find, she felt empty, as though her whole life had been wasted, leaving only an emotional exhaustion which she would never be able to dislodge. She had already made a hole in the lawn and defaced the car, that was enough for now. She needed to stand back from it all and wait. And when the time was right, she would do what was necessary.

They returned to Maia's, each carrying two full bags. Their walk back had been subdued. Els said nothing and went directly to her new room where she remained until Otto had left. She heard them open the bathroom door and Otto's calm voice say something about 'not hearing the last of this', which she found laughably trite. Is that the best he could do? It was like saying the sun will rise each morning. 'He knows he's losing', she thought. 'They're the words of failure'.

Otto spent the rest of the day thinking otherwise. He contacted the G9 members (minus two) to tell them what had happened, or at least his version of it. He left out the bit about being locked in the bathroom, it was too humiliating to be spread, and the bit about the dog barking incessantly in front of the door, making him want to rip it from its hinges and smash it over her head. He had been so flustered by the noise that when he was finally released after what seemed an eternity, all he could say was some silly comment which he regretted as soon as it came out of his mouth. Where was the dignity, the gravitas? He felt like a child who'd been cornered and bullied and then gone crying to the principal. So he knew better than to be entirely truthful; that was the sign of a good leader after all.

He put Els's limited possessions into a couple of medium-sized boxes into the barn, wondering how she could have been so deceitful. He'd given her everything she could have wanted, and more. It was nonsensical, as though she'd been bewitched. Maia and Dan must have turned her with incorrigible lies. Another reason to bring them down. He'd never been one to hate, his life had been above any need for it, and yet when he thought of Maia it was of such monumental betrayal that his wish to purge himself of her existence became an immovable force, and as he was clearing Els's things it was Maia's face he saw in front of him and not his partner's.

The next morning two G9 meetings took place. One in Petra's house, the other in the Townhouse. And as the first one was without incident and proceeded as expected, with all those present (including three from the original G9) expressing a willingness to work together to become, at some indeterminate date, the legitimate G9, it is better to skip directly to the other meeting which didn't go quite so well.

Otto arrived half an hour early bringing Oswald along for assurance. He could always rely on Oswald, and had done so since he could remember. Oswald was strong, steadfast, and above all stupid, with loyalty guaranteed. It was Oswald who told him to keep going during periods of doubt and Oswald who kept him informed of developments on the ground. Oswald was his eyes and ears, his connection to the real world. So having him in tow on such an important day in his life was like bringing along his safety net. They entered through the back door and sat in the old vestry which smelled of old clothes, bringing each other up to date on developments. Oswald spoke of the discontent at the distributions, people hanging around longer than normal, in larger groups than normal, leaflets being exchanged, an unpleasant, disquieting feeling in the air, and Otto talked of betrayal. Oswald shook his head in disbelief as though he was listening to the fall of Kings. It must not be so, he said.

Otto had spent the previous evening replenishing the legitimate G9, bringing it back to its full complement. He'd contacted higher authorities, explaining an edited version of what had happened and was told not to worry, they'd find the right people for the job. Gilda Rosen was the first to arrive, giving Otto a cursory hug and a less than enthusiastic greeting. She was nervous. The right words eluded her, her customary ease of spirit giving way to guarded reticence. By trying her best to seem normal, she amplified her discomfort, and after five minutes excused herself to go to the toilet, locking herself in until she heard other voices. When she re-appeared, the room had swelled to a further four new members, all dressed smartly and all looking as nervous as her.

'We'll wait for the other three,' Otto said, 'and then we'll start,' but after some fifteen minutes, with no sign of anyone else, he asked them to take their flasks and sandwiches and to follow him to the conference hall; they must wait no longer.

'You all know who I am of course,' Otto began, 'and you all recognize the importance of your new role with me at its helm. I cannot emphasize enough how much I value your support, your guidance, your knowledge, and your full co-operation.' He hid his apprehension behind an imperious tone, but could hear an arrogance in his voice which he wanted to avoid. He needed to draw them effortlessly into his inner circle with a natural leadership. It was a delicate balance which needed the right words at this crucial juncture. He must not mess it up and he must not appear overbearing. So as he spoke, two competing thoughts battled inside his head and it made him falter.

'I love this town,' he said, 'this town is me, it's in my blood, as it was in my father's and my grandfather's. I have lead this town for many years with the zeal of someone who was born to lead, leading you all with the passion of a leader and leading from the front, that's what leaders do and that's ...'

He stopped mid-sentence. How many times had he said leader? He must not say it again. What's another word for leader?

'...and that's what ruling is all about ....'

Again he stopped. Did he just say ruling?

'I didn't mean ruling of course, I meant commanding, well, more directing. I'm the captain and you're the captain's mates.'

He paused, looking around the room. Everyone had their head down. No-one looked directly at him, not even Gilda. Was that someone sniggering? Smirking? He looked over to Oswald who was sitting in the corner of the room by the door. Even he had his head down. Otto banged his hand on the table. It was harder than he wanted it to be.

'Do I not deserve a bit of respect? Have I not served this town well? Have I not been a good leader?'

From the open door Paul's voice came hurtling through the space in reply. 'Everyone plays their role,' he said as he walked in. He said hello to Oswald telling him to stay seated, and walked across to the table. 'I've come as a direct request from the Highest Authority,' he said as he put his hand on Otto's shoulder, gently forcing him to sit down.

Otto could feel his knees weaken and his voice crack. He coughed and said nothing. Paul remained standing, directly behind his old friend.

'There's been a change of plan,' Paul said. 'You will have noticed that this G9 is in fact a G6, and that's because we couldn't find anyone else who wanted to be involved. Now as you know, this is a privileged position and for anyone to refuse it can mean only one thing, that there's been a breakdown of trust and leadership.' He emphasized each syllable of leadership as though they were three individual words, and each one was like banging Otto further into the floor. Otto remained still, his eyes beginning to water.

'We've been patient,' Paul continued, 'observing from a polite distance, not immune to the discontent beginning to take hold in this town, hoping that things will calm down and that a new G9 would restore confidence and respect. It now seems clear to us that with all the good will in the world, this town is far from calm and is unlikely to repair itself without some drastic measures. It is unprecedented for a G9 to disband. As you know, membership is for life, giving the continuity all communities crave and deserve. So what has happened?'

He spoke for fifteen minutes detailing the troubles that had befallen the town. He didn't mention Otto's name but it was clear to everyone that it was Otto who was being crushed. Paul was wielding the executioner's sword in an expert demolition of his former friend. And his final words were final:

'This G6 is disbanded forthwith and you will be contacted in due course to let you know your new role in any new set-up. You may well be aware that there is another so-called G9 that's meeting at this very moment. It is the Highest Authority's wish that these two competing councils will join, with a new …. ,' Paul paused for effect, ….'leader.' He again put his hand on Otto's shoulder, more in conquest than in comfort, and those watching would have seen Otto flinch. He brushed the hand away, stood up and the two men stared at each other, their noses almost touching. Oswald walked cautiously over, whispering into Otto's ear 'let's go.'

For a moment Otto did nothing, refusing to give way to Paul's spite. He then looked across to the others sitting around the table and saw Gilda Rosen with her arms folded and her head tilted with a look of such contempt that he let out an uncontrollable plaintive cry which he knew instantly was the sound of defeat. He turned, walked slowly to the exit, with Oswald following, and went straight home.

TWENTY-ONE

T he rain hadn't stopped. For more than a week, the crops in the fields had been battered and crushed, strewn across the ground like seaweed along the shoreline. The ground, which had grown a hard shell over the piercing summer months had become a slather of mud, churned by the C_s and D_s as they attempted to salvage the harvest. The G12, which had been formed a few weeks before, had gone into emergency session to decide on a plan. The forecast was bleak, another week at least of strong winds and debilitating rain, and so the decision was made to start the harvest regardless to minimize the damage, and keep to the festival on the full moon as was the custom. The lower orders in the town were called into action to cut the crops and divert the rising waters which threatened to engulf the lower lying eastern edge. They were helped by a smattering of B_s and the encouragement from the A_s who had been asked to provide the food and drinks and a hearty dose of camaraderie. The town's symbiotic tendencies fell swiftly into place, each person knowing their role and performing it with a collective sense of purpose.

It was all performed with an enthusiasm spurred on by an open and inspiring leadership. The G12, made up of four old members and eight new, including Maia, and with Petra as its spokesperson, and certainly not its leader or primus inter pares or anything which smacked of the old order in the town, had been transparent from the start.

Anyone could attend the weekly meetings to listen in on the discussion, privy to the machinations of its representatives (as the members now called themselves). The more delicate discourse was conducted privately, avoiding the scrutiny of its constituents. It was recognized by all G12 members, with extra input from the old members such as Gilda Rosen who were able to impart invaluable lessons, that there was a limit to how open they could be, and that its ultimate success depended on its ability to avoid, as much as possible, close inspection.

Gilda had been straight-forward in the first meeting (behind closed doors), describing leadership as a delicate balance of light and shade in which the perils of each must be deconstructed before deciding on a particular course. It was also Gilda's attempt to stress her incomparable experience. She didn't mention the word seniority, but everyone recognized her intentions, especially Maia who found it difficult to share the same room, let alone sit and listen respectfully to someone she despised. She had done all she could to ensure Gilda was not selected for the G12, and Gilda had done the same to her, but the Highest Authority, in its desire to bring harmony from discord, had plumped for the experience of the old and the energy of the new, taking the unprecedented decision to expand the membership, an experiment it would watch closely and perhaps duplicate if the signs were good. It actively promoted a just and impartial G12 without a defined leader, with Petra as its public voice, and the G12 was eager to impress and to show its worth.

The first Saturday was a triumph as the Townhouse re-opened after more than a month, with Petra and her colleagues mingling with the public, stroking dogs and cockatoos, effortlessly chatting, being normal, showing interest in everyone and everything. Word quickly spread through the town of an inclusive, caring G12 which was a listening ear and a sympathetic voice. Petra went to the distributions, bartered, did all the things normal people did. She had the people's touch, the common touch; the personable characteristics, finely honed, of a leader. The new car was a necessary evil to allow her to drive the four hours to the glass-domed amphitheatre, and was carefully stored away in her garden. She'd only used it once, the previous week, and played down the exhilaration of leaving the town, the sound system playing any music of her choice, and an unknown landscape gliding by as the navigation system guided her effortlessly to her destination despite the heavy rain impeding her view. The first week, Paul had driven her, using the journey to feed her the essential ingredients of the forum, preparing her for her role, dampening any shock as she witnessed the opulence of The Reformation at fingertip distance. Petra had heard a few details from Otto over the years, but it was clear as she entered the dome that he'd been over-indulgent in underplaying the simplicity of the weekly meetings. Paul took her to her seat on the second tier, to a chorus of cheers and clapping, and later introduced her to those she needed to know. It was a rare occasion for everyone, and Petra revelled in its importance. The return journey disappeared in a delicious haze of post-adrenaline euphoria as she re-enacted the day in her head, repeating it over and over to make it more real, more indisputable. 'You must be careful what you say to the others,' Paul said. 'Your position involves discretion. Jealousy and knowledge are a potent force, which you must be wary of. It was Otto's downfall.'

Paul mentioned nothing of his brief encounter with Otto the day before where he'd gone to his house more out of curiosity than any need for closure. He knew that Otto hadn't been seen for a couple of weeks and that Oswald had been taking him food from the distribution, and that Els, who had been staying at Maia's, was asking for special dispensation to invoke a permanent separation.

He found Otto sitting under the giant oak protected from the rain by the huge cloak of the tree's canopy. 'I have come to apologise,' he said as he sat next to his old colleague and friend, raising his voice above the hammering of the rain against the leaves. Otto made no reply.

'You look awful, by the way,' Paul continued, 'shall we go inside?'

'No.'

'Can I get you anything?'

'That is the most ridiculous thing you have ever said.'

'At least it got a response.'

'I would like you to go.'

'You know that's not going to happen Otto. Not yet anyway.'

Paul leant against the trunk of the oak and reached up to grab a leaf, plucking it loose, releasing a wash of rain water on to his head.

'I'm sorry what happened Otto, but it was either going to be a triumph or a disaster. Unfortunately, it was the latter. And you were always going to be the fall guy, it's your patch after all.'

'But you pushed me from the beginning Paul. *They* pushed me from the beginning.'

'Pushed is a strong word Otto. You wanted this. You wanted the glory of success.'

'Someone had to do it.'

'But you wanted it to be you.'

Otto turned his head and looked at Paul who was now sitting next to him on the bulging trunk of the oak. 'I wanted it because you convinced me, *they* convinced me of its importance. How could I refuse?'

'That's not quite true is it Otto. It was you who started it all. It was you who came to us first, so let's not try to distort history shall we. But it was important Otto. It *is* important. All of it. The experiments. The hunting. The poisons. Nature's out of control and with the population being slowly increased we have to do something.'

'I did. And this is the thanks I get.'

'You failed Otto.'

'You betrayed me Paul. You stood under the dome in front of everyone and condemned me, humiliated me.'

'That was all theatre Otto. I had to. We have to keep up appearances, you know that. And besides, you were given a second chance, and you blew it. Let's face it Otto, if you'd been less up your own arse, it may all have worked out differently.'

'I thought you'd come to apologise.'

'I'm sorry that it failed Otto. I'm sorry for you that it failed. But it did, and you have to take the consequences.'

'And you? Do you take any consequences?'

'I do what I'm told Otto, just like everyone else.'

'And you expect me to believe that?'

'What you believe is no longer relevant. And I'm afraid it's something you just have to accept. Your father made a hash of things, and so have you. Perhaps it's in the blood.'

At the mention of his father, Otto stood up abruptly and took a sweeping, heavy kick to Paul's leg. Paul grabbed his foot and twisted it so that Otto fell back against the oak, smacking his head against the trunk and rolling on to the sodden floor. Paul lifted himself up, unleashing his full, impressive length, towering over Otto as overwhelmingly as the oak towered over him.

'It's time for me to go,' he said without expression. 'I'll be back in the town every now and again to keep an eye on the place. Maybe we'll bump into each other. I'm sorry that it didn't work out Otto, I really am. But pull yourself together. What I'm seeing in front of me is a little pathetic and there's nothing more worthless than someone feeling sorry for himself.'

Paul walked briskly towards his car, the rain penetrating his clothes, and feeling genuinely sorry for his old colleague. He had been brutal, perhaps unnecessarily so, and it was painful to see Otto spread-eagled on the grass, unshaven and unkempt as though he'd give up altogether. He reached the car, opened the door and before he got in, heard Otto's voice through the rain.

'There is something you can do for me,' he shouted. 'I want Els back.'

Dan hadn't felt this good for years. He swam naked in the lake when the weather permitted and occasionally drifted into the woods. It wasn't much, just some light touching with a man who looked uncannily like Price. It was only later, back in his garden, that he made the connection and took it as a sign of his increasing mental rehabilitation that it hadn't sent him into a swirl of self-hatred. The week before, he'd eaten carrots (with chickpeas and mint) without each mouthful reminding him of his dead partner. A large photo of Price stood on his desk encased in a dark wooden frame given to him at the Thursday distribution by a man who refused his chipped ceramic vase in exchange; it was the least he could do, he had said.

Dan had the feeling of being the unofficial mascot for the resurgence of well-being in the town, sensing the good-will swirling around him at the distributions and the Townhouse gatherings. He'd refused a position on the G12, there were others who were more suited to leadership he said, and he'd prefer to watch it all from a courteous distance, he wasn't the type to push and persuade and interfere. But he had asked the G12 (after all – it wouldn't exist without him) to make a special request for Tom to come and live with him. Do it at the same time as seeking special dispensation for Els he had said. Maia told him she'd do her best; it was inconceivable either would be denied she had said, as her own request to annul her second 'homecoming' had been approved within days. Petra had been a little more reticent saying, as far as she knew, both were unprecedented, but considering the extraordinary recent events where so many precedents had been swept to one side, of course it was worth a try. Dan took it as a yes and prepared the house in anticipation of the new arrival, although he had no idea where Tom was or how he felt. Braggle twisted like a spinning top each time his name was mentioned, sometimes dragging Dan to Tom's little house, scratching at the door and refusing to leave. Dan knocked on the door of the old lady who lived next door and peered through the window when there was no reply. It was also empty. She's reached seventy-five, he thought.

His relationship with Maia had the subdued rationality of a friendship born from necessity. It could never be squeezed into something it never was and both recognized its limitations. It was a solidarity between comrades rather than a genuine closeness, and neither could bring themselves to divulge their deepest thoughts to the other. Their dinners together seemed more like meetings than casual downtime and they were both more relaxed when others were present. But they both understood its importance, the history that had entwined them and the violence which bound them. It was a friendship forged from the blood of their partners which neither wanted to forget nor discourage. Maia kept Dan up to date with those aspects of G12 affairs deemed not too sensitive, and she clung happily to her new status, basking in the dignity of her station, feeling alive and fully formed in a role she felt she was born to play. She was one of the bright lights in the G12; outspoken, confrontational (especially with Gilda Rosen), alert to new ideas, a burst of freshness it sorely needed. Her style cut into the collective seniority of three of the original members who bristled with a silent resentment, the harmony of their public face belying the private tensions. Petra Fortune rose above the petty jealousies, binding the group with a singular ability to combine a listening ear with a commanding presence. She had come out of the shadows of the G9 to become the dominant force in the G12.

And she came into her own as the rain pounded the town and threatened the harvest. She convened an emergency meeting at the Townhouse which was made open to the public, and rallied those present with the imperative of bringing in the crops. The next day the work had started, each man and woman clicking seamlessly into place to perform their tasks. The C_s and D_s in the fields, the B_s in support and the A_s doing what they saw fit under the circumstances. Dan excelled, baking continuously for three days, supplying pastries and pasties and salads and dips, the regulations for the food distributions relaxed to allow people to take whatever they wanted. Dan filled a whole bag with carrots, chopping them thinly and cooking them in lemon and honey with a sprinkling of cumin seeds, taking his stash to the temporary marquees which had sprung up along the fields, staying to pour drinks and give moral encouragement to the workers as they came in wet and exhausted, and a little discouraged when they avoided his carrot salad and delved heartily into the potatoes, leeks and pastas.

On the fourth day, Dan sat in the corner watching the

workers come and go, admiring wet cotton shirts cling to chests as taut as stone. The wind had calmed, the giant tents no longer shook threateningly, and the rain had settled to a continuous rumble against the canvas, replacing the roar which had drowned out conversation the whole morning. It was hot and humid. He sat crossed legged in the shadows of the marquee and looked down at his spindly white legs protruding from his shorts. He felt like the runt from a litter. It was time to re-build his physical image to parallel his new emotional state. He would start as soon as the weather improved. For the moment though, he would take pleasure in the build of others and the steady stream of C_s and D_s who seemed to work with neither fuss nor conceit.

At three in the afternoon, or thereabouts, the marquee had emptied to a smattering of people. Dan kept his eye on the canvas flap which acted as the entrance, Braggle laying by his side, eyes closed, having lost all interest in the comings and goings. She wanted to go home, away from the teasing aroma of roasted chicken and pork belly, occasionally nudging Dan's leg with her nose, eventually flopping to the ground in capitulation as her efforts were brusquely pushed aside.

And then she felt her leash tighten and Dan's legs stiffen against the chair legs. She bounced up, alert and ready, her nose in the air, sniffing sharply. A man in a tweed jacket and green leather boots put his umbrella into the communal stand, walked to the buffet table and started poking at the dishes. Braggle gave out a low, prolonged growl, her teeth clenched, her tail straight and stiff. Dan pulled her back as she lunged forward. The man took a plate and spooned on a morsel of carrot salad and a scrap of pulled pork, walking to the further end of the tent, ten metres from Dan. He took one mouthful then walked to the bin and scraped the food away, theatrically dropping the plate and fork in with it. He moved towards Dan who was drawing Braggle's leash shorter and tighter, her front legs forced off the ground. She barked the moment the man spoke, his words dissolving into the noise. He came closer, his hands in his trouser pockets, a smirk on his face, calmly watching Dan struggle with the leash.

'That's a dangerous dog you have there,' Otto said.

'Not as dangerous as you,' Peter quickly replied.

Otto shook his head with a contemptuous slowness as though he'd been told a crude joke. He scratched his nose and rubbed his right eye, pulling the palm of his hand across and down his face, squeezing the loose skin around his throat with his fingertips as he looked up at the roof of the tent. He took a long breath and then exhaled with an ostentatious smack of his lips, bringing his eyes back to Dan's and smirking once more before turning around and walking unhurriedly away.

He returned every day at around the same time, despite the rain. The floor, which had been covered with cardboard and sheeting, had become a squidgy layer of sludge and the soles of his boots were clogged with mud, the green leather covered in a membrane of sludge. Dan went too, keeping to his chair in the corner with Braggle on her leash, refusing to be bludgeoned by Otto's presence. Otto ate the food and poured his own blackberry cordial. The two men did not speak further.

The harvest continued for a week, and so did the rain. The fields became a thick, sticky mess. The workers came into the tent exhausted from trudging through its depths. They were tired and subdued. The final day passed without ceremony, everyone too drained to celebrate. Otto helped dismantle the marquees, patting tired bodies on backs to show support and thanks. He turned up at the Saturday gathering at the Townhouse, and spoke about the gallant efforts from the pulpit. He went to public meetings of the G12, sitting in the front row, listening intently. When the decision was confirmed to go ahead with the harvest festival the following week to coincide with the full moon, he spoke against it, saying the workers needed more time to rest. Was it fair to expect them to prepare everything for the celebrations so soon after their gallant efforts in the fields. He used *gallant* and *heroic* a lot. The G12 ignored him, although Gilda Rosen went to him afterwards and thanked him for his contribution. Otto held her hand tightly, drew her closer to him and told her it was his duty to speak up for those less privileged. Gilda pulled her hand sharply away. 'Well, that would be a first,' she said, half in jest. 'And if I might give you a word of advice Otto, it's time to move on. Your time is past.' She said it impassively and without malice. They were old friends and she had not revelled in his downfall. But her ambition outweighed her loyalty. 'And Otto, we've heard that Els's request has been rejected and she has to go back to you. Is that wise?'

'I love her,' he replied, 'and besides, she's already back where she belongs.' And walked away.

Maia had not expected it. Petra had shown her the official letter laying out the reasons for the refusal. It had always been fanciful Petra told her. What did you expect? And asking for Tom's return? It's a pipe dream, she said. We have to be thankful for what we have, how much they've given us already.

Maia had told Els the day before. Els shrugged as though she was not surprised and, without replying, went to her room to pack. She filled one bag, saying she would return each day to collect the rest. She walked to her home, looked up at the old oak which had bronzed in the time she'd been away, saw Otto waiting at the doorway, politely said hello and went directly in, her wet shoes leaving a muddy trail on the terracotta floor. She took them off before she climbed the stairs, went first to the bathroom to wash her face and put her toiletries into the cabinet, then to her room where she placed her bedclothes carefully on the pillow, refolded the other clothes and placed them gently into the drawers. Otto could hear her footsteps from below and waited until they'd stopped before calling her down for dinner.

'I've cooked,' he said.

At the table, Els said little, eating her food in tiny portions, refusing the wine and dessert.

'I forgive you,' Otto told her.

'Thank you,' she said.

'Please leave your door open tonight.'

'Of course,' she replied.

When she returned to Maia's to collect more clothes, she kept her arms to her side as Maia embraced her, and spoke only to answer questions. Her replies were brief. She went to her room as though in slow motion. Maia followed and watched as she methodically tidied her possessions into the remaining bags.

'You don't have to go Els. We can defy the order. Stay here. Stay with me. We'll all look after you,' she said.

'No,' Els replied. 'I'm going back. I'll get used to it.'

She didn't once look directly at Rosa, preferring to look down the whole time, but at the door, as she was about to leave, she touched Maia's arm and said 'you really don't need to worry anymore. I know exactly what I have to do.'

The G12 met every morning in the lead up to the Harvest celebrations, the final hour open to the public. Otto came each day, sitting in the front row in his tweed jacket, his legs apart and his hands resting on his thighs with his elbows slightly bent as though ready to spring up at any moment. The decision was made, because of the rain and mud, to hold the festival in and around the town square. There was to be no use of the fields for the harvest concerts, and no huts were to be erected where townsfolk could eat and sleep in the lead up to the harvest moon. It was the first time in living memory it had been forbidden. Otto rose to lambast the decision, turning to the crowd behind him to vent his frustration, complaining of a disregard for the traditions which had bound the town for a century. Petra thanked him for his concern, but we are not miracle workers, she said, we cannot turn the mud into solid ground, perhaps we can do something later in the year. Her manner was soft and calm and the public softened to her will. Otto sat down, his heart thumping against his chest, his dislike of Petra growing by the day.

Maia watched Otto's performance with the pragmatic guardedness her new position compelled her to uphold. She was emotionless and still, listening to all that was said with a deepening hatred of a man she once craved. She avoided his line of sight, staring at the vaulted ceiling with its embedded stars, waiting for the show to be over. Her excitement at being part of the new order had begun to wane as the limitations of her position began to sink in. Els's plight had hit her hard and her own role in her new friend's misery weighed her down, her guilt pounding in her head as though she was being shaken by an invisible phantom. On the third day, as the meeting ended, she could bare it no more, and went directly to Otto.

'How could you do that to Els?' she said.

Otto turned as though she wasn't there and walked towards the door. She followed and pulling on his jacket sleeve said 'please Otto, let her go.'

He slapped her hand away and turning abruptly, grabbed the collar of her shirt, pulling her close. 'You are a hypocrite and a liar Maia Gertler. And never, ever touch me again.'

Dan spent the lead-up to the celebrations helping with the harvest decorations. He baked mooncakes and wove corn-mothers from the sheaves of the last day of the harvest, thinking of Tom and the reasons for the rejection of his request. He'd asked if he could write to him to have confirmation of his status and health. He'd had no reply. Let be, Petra had said. Her unwillingness to intervene disappointed him, although he kept his thoughts to himself and his resentment hidden at being so simply by-passed. He remained home, away from the elements, and truth be told, away from Otto. Their encounters in the marquee had distressed him, and almost of week of it had left him drained, but on the fifth day of self-isolation the clouds began to disperse and the sun nudged through for the first time in more than two weeks. Dan put on his waterproof canvas jacket, just in case, and walked with Braggle to the town square to watch the final preparations for the festival. The stage had been built and the centerpiece was taking shape as people brought their floral decorations and wove them around the scaffolding. Fruit and vegetables were scattered around the dais and more would certainly follow until the stage gradually transformed into a voluptuous splash of colour. Dan spoke to Bernard who was overseeing the arrangements, waved to some of the workers, thrilled to see them wave back, and out of the corner of his eye could see

Otto watching his every move. He'd been aware of him from the moment he entered the square, a shadow on the sidelines in his trademark tweed jacket.

'Has he been here all morning?' he asked Bernard.

'About the same time as you,' he replied.

Dan walked to Tom's house. The door was open, the walls whitewashed, the floors polished, and two women in overalls sat on a crate in the corner drinking tea from flasks. They answered his questions with a boredom edging towards rudeness, and pushed Braggle away as she brushed against their legs. Dan had never been in the house before, and in its bleak emptiness felt the drama of the previous year fold into the space around him. He touched the wall, slipping his fingers across its chalky smoothness, capturing images he'd only heard from others. This was where Price came to life. Dan closed his eyes and saw him coming towards him in his blue linen shirt and battered old denim cap. He felt Price embrace him, hold him, touch him, as though time had shrunk into its loveliest form capturing moments of the purest joy, more real than they ever really were. For weeks now he'd clung to those moments, pushing the decline away from his gaze, resurrecting his partner from the calamity of their final years together. And through the prism of reflected memory came the release Dan so desperately needed, pushing his guilt, in all its complexity, further away.

He opened his eyes and saw the two women staring at him. He apologized. I have memories here, he told them. I'll go now.

Then suddenly they both stood up, tea spilling on their laps. Braggle barked and growled. Dan tightened her leash. He turned to see Otto in the doorway, his arm leaning against the door frame.

'No need to rise just for me,' Otto said to the two women, 'but if you don't mind taking your drinks outside for a while.'

They did what he said, Otto patting them on the back as they went past, Braggle's growling echoing in the empty space.

'How about locking her in the toilet for a few minutes,' he said. 'It's not so bad.'

'Absolutely not,' Dan replied. 'She stays close to me.'

'Then is there any chance of getting her to shut up?'

'Only if you leave.'

'Then we'll just have to shout.'

'Why are you following me?'

'It's a free country.'

'Hardly.'

'So you're finally seeing the light.'

'The dark, you mean.'

Otto came a little closer. Braggle bore her teeth. Dan held her tight.

'You're right,' Otto said, 'I am following you, but more from curiosity than intention. Why should I not be curious about the life of the man who thrust a knife into mine. I am human after all. I do bleed. And my blood cannot so easily be washed away.'

He put a finger to his mouth to stop Dan from talking.

'Daniel, do you know what has happened to Tom?' And without waiting for an answer said, 'I'll tell you, I'm no longer in any position to keep secrets after all.'

He walked to the side of the room and leant against the wall.

'He's gone to a camp for re-education. He'll never come back, not here. There are no more homecomings for people like Tom. He had his opportunities and he blew it. You'll never hear from him again. It would have happened to Theo too if Maia hadn't killed him. She didn't want him to go to the camp. That's the reason she killed him. She knew he wouldn't have survived it. And she was probably right.'

Again Otto put a finger to his mouth.

'And they all know about it, the G9, sorry, G12. At least Petra does, and Maia and Gilda. Maybe not the others. It's very sensitive after all. And do you know what happens to the dispossessed? Do you know what'll happen to you when you get to seventy-five?'

Otto smiled, something he rarely did. 'I'll leave that to your imagination.'

'It's all nonsense,' Maia told him later that day. 'He's trying to get into your head. Ignore it. He's good at playing little games like that. It's his way of thinking he's still in control.'

'Are there camps Maia?'

'I have no idea Dan. I really don't. And I think Petra would tell us if she knew. She wouldn't hold anything like that back. There is an oath she has to take, a pledge, that much we do know, and it's clear she keeps a few things to herself, and it's frustrating Dan, it really is, but camps? She wouldn't hold that sort of information from us. Petra has integrity. You know how she is.'

'Have you asked her about things?'

'Of course I have Dan, and it's like banging your head against a solid surface. I've given up trying.'

'Do you think Tom's in a camp?'

Maia put down her glass of white wine, one of her G12 perks, and rolled her legs on to the sofa. 'I've heard nothing about anything like that Dan, honestly. Or what happens to the dis-possessed. Otto never, ever talked about it, I promise. As far as I know they're re-housed in a community for people of their own age and very well looked after. You've seen the pictures for yourself. Why should it be different to that? What benefit is there from lying'"

'That's a stupid question Maia, and you know it. But I'd hate to think that Tom is unhappy, in pain, being ill-treated.'

'Even if he is in a camp, it doesn't mean he's not being well looked after.'

'So he is in a camp.'

'Oh Dan, stop this. It'll just torment you. Tom has gone and he's not coming back. I tried, I really did, but it's no use. Let it go. Cling on to the good things.'

'You realise that without Tom there would have been no change in this town. Doesn't he deserve to be happy.'

'Of course he does Dan, and maybe he is. Maybe he is.'

Dan spent the next morning in the town archives. He typed in 'camps' and found old footage of emaciated figures, hollowed features, people pressed against wired fencing, faces paralyzed with the impotence of their fate, shoes piled high like old compost, leather bags jumbled into heaps of ridicule and malice. It's nothing he didn't already know. The horrors of Pre-Change were drummed into every Academy student, its brutality ingrained into the collective conscience as much as the crimes against nature.

He found volumes of photos of the dis-possessed under its official name *The Seventh Age* and saw people laughing, playing, reading, healing, sewing, cooking, all in the warm embrace of the massive complexes built specifically to house the over seventy-fives. *Living with dignity* was its slogan.

But 'use your imagination' had slipped into Dan's mind and he couldn't shake it off. He left the archives in a state of anxious confusion. Otto had implanted something in his head and it grew bigger as the day progressed. Back home he lay on the sofa staring at the ceiling with Braggle tucked between his legs, his thoughts a tangle of concentrated uncertainty. Were these photos real? Were people really laughing or being told to laugh? Was there a cold, undeniable fact lurking under that warm embrace? He neither ate nor drunk, the improbable becoming unpleasantly palpable. He went to bed without cleaning his teeth, slumped naked under the sheet, Braggle stretched against him, and dreamt of Price and Tom and Theo with an intensity which had eluded him since they had all disappeared from his life.

TWENTY-THREE

D an went early to the town square. He placed one corn mother, tied with a red ribbon, on to the main table with all the others, and put a couple of yellowing courgettes around the dais, which had become almost submerged in vegetables and fruit. Two women, both wearing threads of chamomile and knapweed in their hair, were decorating the lectern with sunflowers and singing a crude variation on the harvest anthem.

Corn and wheat may beat the sheet
In coarseness and discomfort
But making hay
In harvest play
Is full of pricks and hardship
So the beat of the wheat and the cry of the corn
Are the sounds of a perfect September
When the rain makes you wet and the sun makes you dry
And the day is a play to remember.

They giggled, holding hands, one putting a sunflower in the cleavage of the other, giving her a gentle kiss on the side of her temple. It was an exchange of such sweet friendship that Dan watched mesmerized by its purity. He sat on the edge of the stage, closed his eyes, and brought his fingers lightly across his forehead and down the side of his face. He then wetted the tips in his mouth and traced a circle around his lips, pressing so softly that it felt like the touch from another. When he opened his eyes one of the women was kneeling down beside him offering the sunflower. 'It will bring you luck,' she said.

'Thank you,' Dan replied, 'I think I'm going to need it.'

He walked back to the house, collected Braggle and folding the stem of the sunflower in two, placed it in his jacket pocket. Together they wound their way through the town, going first to the bio-factory fields where the pigs and chickens still thrived in the open air, walking past the vast wooden shelters built for the winter period. From there he went to the Townhouse, tracing the tower in the distance and watching it grow larger, until it loomed over him like a sentry guard. He sat on the bench and looked down at his muddied shoes, the same ones he wore to his tribunals, and taking the sunflower from his pocket, he plucked one petal at a time. *Do it, don't do it, do it, don't do it ....* until he reached the last petal. 'Do it,' he whispered, and he let the remains of the sunflower fall to the ground.

They walked to the lake, passing the fields which were convulsed into a mass of dark, cloying mud. He sat on the sandy bank and felt the wetness seep into his pants. And as he stared hypnotically at the water, he started to undress. Shoes and socks first, then his jacket and shirt, and finally his trousers and pants, both darkened where he'd been sitting on the wet sand. He stood up, raised his arms in the air and letting out a peal of shouts, ran into the water, stopping only when its force was stronger than his own. He turned and called Braggle to join him but she remained on the bank, barking and uncertain of what to do, watching as Dan twirled and twirled and then disappeared under the water.

Els was insistent. She would not go to the festival with Otto. Large crowds had never been her thing, he knew that, and so she was not about to change just because, for the first time she could remember, he wanted her by his side. She hunched her shoulders as he came closer, unable to hide her contempt and recoiling with such obvious revulsion that Otto winced. She'd become more withdrawn as the week progressed, cloaked in the shadows of the house like a mouse hiding from a cat, listening for the sounds which could bring her into the light, and when she emerged, drifting from room to room like a ghost, unable to break through the wreckage of her misery. She became almost speechless in his presence, forming sentences in her head but unable to give them breath. And now, the morning of the festival, as a flood of no's emerged from her mouth, and as Otto left the house, slamming the front door behind him, she knew she could take it no more.

Otto had never slammed the door. But he just couldn't help himself. Els's selfishness had left him no option. The door had to be slammed. And he slammed it with the fervour of the wronged. He walked to the barn, grabbed a large tennis bag from a hook by the entrance, went to the metal cabinet on the far side and took out the shotgun Paul had left there for his hunting expeditions. Otto had been to some of them, watching as Paul and his underlings obliterated the local populations of rabbits, hare, deer, geese, foxes. He'd never taken part, showing his approval only by his presence, but Paul had convinced him they were the best methods, and Otto had always been one for following the most rational and astute advice with the added benefit of taking meat home for the dinner table. Paul had shown him how to use the gun, loading cartridges, holding it snuggly in the shoulder to reduce the kick effect, taking him far from the town to practice his techniques. So it gave Otto a sense of well-being as he put the gun into the tennis bag knowing he'd be able to find his target.

He walked to Maia's house, standing on the pathway in full view just like he'd been doing over the past week. Maia had seen him a few times, gone out to remonstrate and received a stony silence. She told the G12, and Petra had been to see him to get him to stop, but it was of no use, Otto went anyway as though it was as natural as a salmon returning to its spawning ground.

This time Maia came out holding a glass of water.

'I thought you might be thirsty,' she said sarcastically. 'Been playing tennis? I guess you have to keep yourself busy somehow, now you're not involved in any of the official celebrations. They're saying this one's going to be one of the best ever.'

'I think it's certainly going to be one to remember,' came the reply.

Maia placed the glass on the grass next to him and returned to the house, slamming the door behind her and turning the key. She was shaking, as she had each time she confronted him. She sat in front of the mirror in her bedroom and saw only lines and blemishes, as though the old Maia had evaporated in the space of a year, revealing a new layer she hardly recognized. She dusted some powder onto her face, added a dash of rouge to her lips and some kohl to her eyes, and put on the orange-and-brown suit she'd had especially made for the day's festivities. She'd been told to get there early and assemble in the side marquee attached to the main stage, so that, in a flush of staged grandeur, as someone struck the bell, the G12 would walk out one by one and be officially introduced to the crowd. She was to be the last to come out and she wanted to make the most of it. Petra had also chosen her (much to Gilda Rosen's disdain) as the guardian of the vegetables (Gilda had been given the not so prestigious fruit duties), and as such, it was her task to bless the heap of gourds and roots before they were taken away, chopped and cooked, and served as a vast communal soup later in the day. Maia felt she had been moving towards this moment her whole life but as she looked out of the window and saw Otto still standing there with his tennis gear, she knew it might not be so straight forward.

Els put a waterproof rug on the grass directly under the oak tree and lay there looking up at the browning leaves which whispered to her in the breeze. She knew exactly what they were saying and she nodded her head in agreement. She closed her eyes and the intensity of the whispering became a rage, until she shouted at them to stop. She should have known better. It had never given her the comfort she craved. The vast back lawn with its jarring neatness was just the same. She walked from one end to the other, stopping in the middle and stomping on the soggy mess of soil and grass which Otto had been trying his best to rectify. Back in the house, she walked from room to room, thumping walls, picking up objects and slamming them back down, increasing her pace and her movements until she suddenly stopped, fell to the ground and let out a wail of unutterable hopelessness. She knelt on the floor with her head between her knees moaning with such intensity that it rocked her rhythmically back and forth. Then all went quiet. For ten, fifteen minutes, she was perfectly still, her arms clenched around her head so tightly it was as though she'd turned to stone. And as she slowly unwound, with her eyes closed, she stood to her full height and stretched her arms above her head with her fingers locked together and her palms facing the ceiling. She took deep breaths to steady herself, brought her arms slowly down to her sides, opened her eyes and said simply and without expression, '*Yes*'.

Maia looked in the full-length mirror, flung the chiffon scarf, with its intricate leaf motif, over her left shoulder, put on her favourite heeled shoes and took one more look out of the window. Otto had gone, the water had not been touched. She unlocked the door, walked to the pathway, picked up the glass and went back inside. The shaking had started again and she leant against the kitchen sink to steady herself. It unnerved her; the way it buried itself into her composure, pushing her off balance, shrinking the impact of such an important day. She slammed her hand down onto the counter. '*No, no, no*,' she said aloud, and stood up straight, lifted her chin, stomped her heels on the floor, and left the house.

It was the first time anyone could remember that the celebrations were anywhere other than in the wheat fields on the edge of the town. The two hectares of the open countryside had been squeezed into the concrete orbit of the main square, where the traditional spread of picnic rugs had been replaced by hay bales, and the gentle meanderings of a sun-drenched crowd by a hubbub of laughter and shouting. People stood shoulder to shoulder, making the most of the improvised setting. There was a general relief that the harvest was in and the flooding on the east of the town had been contained, and a consensus that the new G12 (although it still sounded strange to everyone to call it that) had done an exceptional job given the circumstances. The festival backdrop might be cramped but there was a sense that the town had spread its collective wings; that they may be bound in a quiet little corner of the empire but the horizons were wide and fresh.

And this year, the brass band seemed to play with an added enthusiasm and the vegetables seemed brighter and more succulent than ever. Maia walked onto the stage and inspected the decorations which engulfed her with colour and spectacle. She picked up a courgette, then a red potato, then an aubergine, and finally, after prodding and squeezing and sniffing, settled on a pumpkin which sparkled with a deep red-orange and which, as far as Maia was concerned, was calling out to be the centre of the harvest ritual. She picked it up, held it in her palm and brought it to eye level. 'You shall be my guide,' she said, 'and there's no way you're going into the soup.' She placed it next to the lectern and walked backstage where the rest of the G12 were gathering. Petra had given them their instructions, which wasn't much beyond sitting in the right place and standing when necessary; it was essential to get it absolutely right, she said, first impressions count and we have to show that we might be new and we might have fresh ideas, but we're a continuation of the proud traditions of this town and we can be relied upon to do the right thing. So when your name is called, walk straight to your seat, don't wave, don't smile, don't show your excitement, just show the gravitas of your position, and that involves not doing very much.

Maia half listened. She could hear the music and the build-up of voices, and she could see the way Gilda Rosen, with her pursed lips, was swaying almost imperceptibly back and forth on the balls of her feet. If looks could kill, Maia thought, then half the G12 would already be convulsing on the floor, taking their last breaths. Gilda had chosen a bunch of large, slightly rotting grapes as the honorary fruit and it was clear to everyone that it was a deliberate show of defiance for the way she'd been side-lined. 'A fine choice,' Maia had said directly to her, 'it suits you.'

The cooling water of the lake had done the trick. Dan felt revived. Braggle had come to join him, and they swam side by side from one end to the other, the dog puffing and panting as she pawed her way through the water. And as they reached the shoreline Dan rushed out, hastily put on his clothes and felt the clawing wetness cling to his trousers and shirt. He plucked some red clover from the grass bank and walked as fast as he could to the communal pit. The incessant rain had mashed itself into the pit's top layer, its weight pushing the soil deeper and giving it a dark, shimmering hue. Dan grabbed a handful and pushed it into his forehead and cheeks, feeling it slither against his wet skin. He then knelt on the edge and made a little hole where he delicately placed the clover. He had planned to say something, but as he formed the words in his mouth they collapsed into his throat. Price and Theo were there, a few metres away, rotting and useless, and all he wanted to do was to scrape away at the earth, down and down, gather them in his arms, and wail an apology of such force that the birds would fall from the sky.

Otto chatted briefly with Oswald who stood at the entrance to the square, although in what capacity no-one quite knew, and walked directly towards the stage, the crowd opening up as though he was gently blowing them out of the way. The front had been decorated with a myriad corn-dollies. Otto plucked one from its fixing and put it in his pocket. A keepsake for Els, he thought. He walked through the crowd, responding with a polite nod of the head to those who acknowledged him before setting his tennis bag on a bench at the far end of the square under the shelter of a beech tree. And like the day before, he stood on the bench, giving him a clear view across to the stage above the heads of the burgeoning crowd. He watched the chairs being placed in a gentle semi-circle behind the dais, and saw Petra walk briskly around the stage, poking and adjusting, before she hopped onto the dais and sat on a large high-backed chair, not unlike a throne, to the right of the lectern. Otto jumped off the bench, sat down and opened the tennis bag. He stroked the barrel of the gun and slid the chamber back. From his pocket he took two shells and placed them in the chamber.

At three o'clock or thereabouts, a woman wearing a vast straw headdress not unlike a stalk's nest, struck the small bronze bell. The crowd went still and surged forward towards the stage leaving Otto a lone figure at the back of the square. Petra stood and walked to the lectern, and with her arms held wide as though embracing the entire crowd, she gave her welcoming speech.

Peter was running. He mustn't miss the beginning of the ceremony. He'd spent too long next to Price and Theo squeezing the earth in his hands, taking bullet sized pieces and placing them in his mouth, feeling the grit in his throat. And before leaving, he'd lifted his head skywards, his arms outstretched, and watched a few swallows darting and swirling. 'Fly away,' he said, 'get away from here.' He took one last handful of the soil, mashed it into his hands and on to his face, and then started to run.

He could hear the buzz of the crowd as he got closer to the main square. Just a few more minutes and he'd be there. He was sweating and wet, and as he wiped the drips from his eyes, he smeared the mud further across his face.

And then a bell. And silence. It was about to begin. He must run faster. *Come on Braggle, come.*

Maia stood in the wings, her mind on the pumpkin. She had to get it exactly right. *This pumpkin gives us life and we are thankful for its bounty*, was playing in her head, *and we are thankful for all the fruits of this harvest, may it sustain us through the winter and comfort us and protect us.* She looked out at the crowd, recognizing many of the faces, some wearing flowers in their hair, others the traditional wheat crown. And there, right at the back, standing on a bench, detached from the rest of the crowd, was Otto. Of course he'd be here, she thought, why wouldn't he be. And yet.

A thunderous applause. Petra was working the crowd. She was good at it. This was something different, something fresh, something alive with possibility. Words full of optimism, sharing, trust, openness, truth. The crowd prickled with excitement. And at the back, standing on a bench, and with no-one around him, Otto listened with the rising hate of the fallen. He clenched his jaw, inflated his nostrils, and felt every word as a personal betrayal. And then that applause, that collective pummelling, the ungrateful conceit of the masses. It was too much to bear.

Petra called the first name.

Frances Cornell.

Frances walked on to the stage. The crowd applauded. Her partner, standing at the front, whooped with delight. She did what Petra had asked, keeping her excitement at bay, going directly to her chair and sitting down, placing her hands on her thighs, her back straight.

Bernard Volt.

Bernard glided on to the stage with all the dignity of his new station, walking directly to his chair and taking his place next to his colleague and good friend. And as the rest of the G12 was called, Maia waited with growing unease. Otto was still standing on the bench and now he had something in his hand. What was it? She couldn't see it clearly. It wasn't a tennis racket. It was longer and thinner. Was it some sort of walking stick, but it was too broad, too unwieldy.

And now someone who needs no introduction. Gilda Rosen.

Gilda walked on to the stage, stopped half way and waved to the crowd. She stood there for ten seconds, absorbing an applause that was far less enthusiastic than she thought she deserved, saying to herself behind gritted teeth and a fabricated smile, *you ungrateful mass of nothing,* before walking past the line of seated colleagues and taking her seat.

And finally, Maia Gertler.

Maia didn't move. She stood, stock still, fixed to the wings of the stage, unable to put one foot in front of the other.

Maia Gertler.

Maia looked towards Petra and shook her head. Petra beckoned her.

Nothing.

Petra descended the dais, walked quickly over to the wing and placed her hand gently on to Maia's shoulder. *Come on,* she said, *it'll be fine,* and holding her hand, pulled her tenderly out and into the bosom of the stage.

Otto lifted the gun and rested the butt stock flush against his shoulder, gripping the forearm tight with his left hand.

Maia took her seat and closed her eyes, unaware of the thunderous applause that had welcomed her on to the stage.

I'd like now for Gilda to come forward to make the blessing to the fruit.

Gilda walked to the dais and took the bunch of grapes from the top of the harvest pile where she'd placed them an hour before. She gave Maia's pumpkin a gentle nudge and it rolled off the heap and across the stage floor.

Otto brought the stock up to his cheek and looked through the sight.

Gilda raised the grapes above her head.

These grapes give us life and we are thankful for their bounty.

She then plucked one and put it in her mouth. The crowd gasped. Was she eating the harvest fruit? She plucked another, and again, in it went.

We are thankful for all the fruits of this harvest. May it sustain us through the winter and comfort us and protect us.

Otto brought his finger to the trigger.

The crowd buzzed harder. Gilda spoke louder.

May the wealth of the land and the beauty of all life give us .....

A shout pierced through her speech. A man and a dog were running through the crowd and hurtling towards the stage.

Stop, the man shouted, *stop.* The dog barked and barked.

Dan, his face and clothes covered in mud, jumped on to the podium and ran to the dais. He grabbed the microphone from Gilda's hand and shoved her away. He was breathless. *I have to speak,* he panted, *I must say something. There are camps.*

With a sweep of her arm, Gilda smashed the grapes into the side of his face. Dan fell to the floor. The microphone thudded and clanged and rolled along the stage. Maia, who was sitting the closest, rushed towards them. Gilda, months of pent-up frustration suddenly bursting into life, violently shoved her away bringing her adversaries long-held contempt raging to the surface. Maia grabbed the grapes from Gilda's hand and whacked them against her head. Gilda, her hair filled with pips and juice, grabbed Maia's scarf and pulled her to the ground. The two women rolled along the stage and into the heap of fruit and vegetables. Tomatoes squelched, bell peppers popped, kiwis splattered. And as they furled around each other, limbs entwined, clothes sodden with a multi-coloured pulp, and with Bernard Volt trying desperately to part them, Dan, still breathless, picked up the microphone and between deep convulsing breaths tried to speak.

I know this looks ridiculous but ...

Petra grabbed the microphone. *No,* she said, *you cannot do this. Not here.* He tried to grab it back, and when that failed, to shout towards the crowd, but there was no power in his lungs and the din wiped-out every word. He looked across to Maia and Gilda who had been parted by a melee of their G12 colleagues, then down to Braggle who was jumping against the front of the stage, barking herself raw, and the absurdity of what he was doing smacked into his consciousness. He sat on the edge of the stage with his head slumped, a thousand thoughts swirling through his mind. He closed his eyes and saw Price and Tom and Theo staring blankly at him with their arms raised, their heads shaking in tandem; a pulsating barking growing louder and louder, thumping into his head. He opened his eyes. A thousand faces stared at him. He jumped off the stage, grabbed Braggle's lead and walked briskly away, a path opening up before them as a bewildered multitude let them pass unhindered.

Maia stood facing the crowd, her scarf stuck to the side of her face, Gilda spitting words in her ear, Bernard Volt pulling her back. She peeled the scarf away, brushed off some of the tomato pips from her shirt and looked across to the back of the square. Otto had gone.

TWENTY-FOUR

D an headed towards the edge of the town. A numbness had taken hold of his body as though he'd been anaesthetized by what had just happened. His mind was empty. He walked along the old railway track and took the easterly path out into the fields, the spire of the Townhouse falling gradually away. The ground was sodden and slimy. He took off his shoes and socks and threw them into the hedge. Braggle raced after them, stuck her head carefully into the hawthorn and pulled out a shoe with her mouth. Dan continued. The lane became narrower and the hedge thicker until they reached a field churned with mud, the remnants of the path folding its way towards a copse. Dan took off his trousers and shirt, folded them neatly and placed them on the top of the hedge. Braggle nudged his ankles with her nose, but he brushed her aside and went on. His steps became ankle deep squelches and his movements slowed as he grappled with the thickening mud. He then stopped abruptly as though he'd hit a wall, knelt down, and curving his back with his face to the sky and his arms outstretched, let out a searing cry. Price's name cut through the air. Braggle pushed herself against him, slowly circling him, licking the tears on his face. Dan pulled her towards him and embraced her, holding her head against his, rubbing his face against her matted black coat. He closed his eyes and hummed a simple tune in her ear. She remained perfectly still. And when he finished, he kissed the top of her head and smiled. *What would I do without you,* he said.

'You'll just have to get used to it,' came a voice behind him.

Dan grabbed Braggle's leash and twisted himself around in the mud. Braggle growled and barked, and pulled as hard as she could. Otto stood five metres away with the shotgun pointing towards them.

'Shut her up,' he said.

Dan embraced her and stroked her back and chin, calming her until the barking stopped.

'Well done,' Otto said sarcastically.

Dan remained crouched, shushing Braggle as she bore her teeth and snarled each time Otto spoke.

'Look at you Daniel, what a fool you've made of yourself. This was going to be for Maia, but I guess I'll just have to make do with you. Always second best, eh.'

Otto moved closer, his finger on the trigger.

'One bullet for you and one for her.'

Dan slowly raised himself up. 'Let her go Otto,' he said calmly, 'she's harmless.'

'Absolutely not.'

'Why?'

'Because she's yours.'

'She's not mine Otto. I don't own her.'

'Yes you do Daniel, without you she won't survive.'

'Of course she will.'

'What will she do? Roam the streets at night? Live off scraps?'

'Like you do, you mean.'

'Oh Daniel, to think I almost thanked you for killing Price, for getting that vermin out of the way, but you're just as pathetic, just as ridiculous.'

Dan pulled Braggle's leash tighter.

'Maybe I am Otto. But it was me who brought you down. Remember that.'

'But I'm on the rise again Daniel and you won't be able to stop me a second time.'

'On the rise? You?' Dan snorted.

'Yes, me Daniel. And you're sinking further into the mud, exactly where you belong.'

Braggle was pulling, pulling on the leash. Snarling. Dan

tightened it further.

'Let the dog go,' Dan said again.

'No.'

Dan pulled Braggle's head towards him. 'I love you,' he whispered, and with one quick jerk of his hand, let go of the leash. Braggle plunged towards Otto, sinking her teeth into his leg as Dan lunged forward and smashed his head into his stomach. The gun fired into the air. The two men rolled over, grappling and sliding like eels out of water, Braggle turning round and round next to them, barking, barking, sinking further into the viscous mass.

Dan grabbed Otto around the neck but his arm slid down across his shoulders and on to his chest. Otto grabbed his arm and tried to bend it behind his back, but again it slid away as they rolled and squelched and merged into the mud.

Their bodies became heavier, thudding, slopping, sliding against each other.

For a moment, exhausted, the energy sucked out of them, they stopped. Dan slowly pulled himself to his knees and wiped the mud from his eyes. Unfocused, he stretched out his arm to feel for Braggle. She was still there. By his side. Breathing. Alive.

Then a massive force collided into the side of his head, splitting open his temple and cracking his skull. He fell face down into the mud.

Otto raised himself up, the gun in his hand, and prodded Dan's side. He didn't move. Otto kicked him. He still didn't move.

He put his foot onto the back of his head and slowly pushed.

Dan's nostrils and mouth filled with mud and trickled down into his lungs. His limbs didn't thrash, his body didn't convulse.

His breathing slowed.

The light around him grew brighter and brighter. And as

he looked down and watched his death unfold, he saw Otto holding the barrel of the gun, wiping his blood from the stock. Braggle was next to him, a mass of clotted, muddy fur, pawing at his chest, willing him to move.

She was alive. She was going to live.

So calmly and without fear he followed the incandescent light, and as he got closer, he stretched out an arm to touch it and heard a soothing voice not unlike Price's saying, *come, it's time.*

TWENTY-FIVE

O tto wasn't sure he'd made the right decision. There was one last bullet and as he wiped away the blood from the stock of the gun which had pounded into the side of Dan's head, he looked at the dog pawing at the body and his instinct had been to shoot it dead. His leg was throbbing and he could hardly stand, and yet when he lifted the gun and aimed the barrel to within a few centimetres of the dog's head, she looked at him briefly and then continued dabbing her paw against Dan's shoulder, whimpering pitifully. It sounded like the purest of sorrows and reminded him of his mother as she buried her head into the chest of his dead father. He turned the gun ten degrees and pulled the trigger. Dan's body convulsed as the bullet smashed into his pelvis, blood and flesh splattering Braggle's muddied coat. The force of the blast pushed her violently backwards. She thudded into the mud, and for a few seconds thrashed back and forth with her legs in the air as she tried to regain her balance. She then flopped to one side and with one last shove managed to right herself. She trudged over to Dan, nudged him three times, and as though a click had gone off in her head she turned suddenly, and as fast as she could made her way through the mud. Otto watched her reach the path and run out of the field and towards the town.

And now, as he stood over Dan's body, he wished he'd killed the dog too. Would it lead people back here? Would anyone see the blood on its coat? It had probably gone back to the house. He must go there later. But first he pulled off

Dan's underpants, walked to the drier part of the path and placed them with the shirt and trousers on the hedge. He then stripped naked himself, leaving his muddied clothes in a heap on the ground, went back to the body, grabbed its legs and dragged it towards the copse. It was easier than he thought. Dan wasn't a big man and he glided through the mud like a sledge through the snow. Otto pulled him into the densest part of the copse where the ground was soft, and made a shallow grave, clawing at the soil with his hands. Dan fitted snuggly in and disappeared under a heap of dried leaves. The foxes and boars and worms would do the rest.

He walked back through the mud to the path and lay on his back, looking up at the dabs of cloud and picking at the hairs on his chest. A gentle wind caressed him and the sun warmed him. A crust started to form on his skin as the mud began to dry. He liked the feel of it, as though it was someone else's, and when he brought his fingertips along his chest it felt like the touch from another. He scraped his hand across his skin and licked his palms. It tasted like rain and metal. He traced a finger down his mid-riff and across his belly, releasing a smudge of a cross which made him chuckle. Public nakedness had always appalled him, it was unbecoming a man of his station, his parents said. If his father was here now, he would have smacked him on the back of the thighs. But he wasn't. No restrictions, no rules, no constraints. Otto was naked and free, the past blasted simply away like the pull of a trigger. He was cast loose from the shapes that had guided him from the moment of his birth. He knew it, felt it, absorbed it. And there was no going back.

A simple melody came into his head and he whistled softly, tears streaking his face. He saw his mother and father sitting together under the oak tree, hand in hand, their mouths slightly open, their eyes fixed directly on him and their heads moving imperceptibly from side to side. The melody grew dimmer. His parents melted away into the afternoon air.

He turned his head to the side and watched a vole flick through the bottom of the hedge. He stretched out his arm and opened his hand. The vole disappeared into the undergrowth.

He stood slowly, unfurling himself bit by bit. His clothes, heavy with mud, were placed gently in the tennis bag with Dan's underpants which he'd used once more to clean the gun. He caressed the hedgerow with his hand, took Dan's neatly folded shirt and shook it free, making short snaps in the air, doing the same with the trousers. A tiny blue butterfly darted close to his face which he followed as it flew towards the open field and fluttered out of sight.

He stood on the edge of the field. The ashes and the elms rippled and waved. The line he'd drawn across the mud with Dan's body was already beginning to fade.

It took him more than an hour to reach home. At the house, he saw Els looking out of the top window as he walked past the oak. He waved and she gave a little wave back. It was habitual for him each day to run his fingers down one of the tree's deep fissures. Today he didn't think about it.

The front door was locked and he heard Els descend the stair and release the catch. She opened the door slowly.

'Where are your shoes?' she asked.

Otto dropped the bag and wrapped his arms around her, almost crushing her with the force of his hold. Els could smell a damp earthiness.

'Let's get those clothes off you,' she said gently.

Otto sat on the bottom stair as she carefully pulled off the trousers and folded them neatly on the floor in the corner of the hallway. She then methodically unbuttoned the shirt, saying nothing about the muddied lines which crisscrossed his chest and stomach, nothing about the strange clothes which were way too tight, nothing about him not wearing underpants or socks, nothing about the wound to his leg and the dried blood which had stained his ankle and foot.

She guided him to the upstairs shower and watched as the water bounced off his head and shoulders and spattered brown swirls onto the ceramic basin.

Otto stood under the shower longer than he had ever done before. He felt the grit in the lather as he prised apart strands of hair, and watched Els fade away behind the steaming glass door. The hot water pounded his body, sweeping away the dirt, pushing him further from the muddied field and Dan's body. By the time he turned off the tap and opened the door, the events of the day seemed blurred and confused as though they no longer belonged to him.

'I've made a chicken casserole,' Els said as she handed him a towel and watched him dry himself. 'And then I have something to show you.'

They sat opposite each other at the dinner table. Els had lit a candle and used the china with the delicate gild edge. The white wine was poured into crystal glasses which had belonged to Otto's great-grandmother and which she'd taken from the back of the huge cabinet in the side room.

'Tell me about her?' Els asked.

It was nothing she hadn't already heard. Generations of his family had been etched into the contours of her brain. She watched Otto's mouth opening and closing, listening to sounds, not words, feeling the beat of her heart like the seconds on a clock counting down to zero. And when he finally clinked his knife and fork against the plate and pushed them to the side, she was ready. She looked into the flame of the candle, tracing the deep blue around its lower edge and the fierce white yellow of the tip, and recognized it as the last material object she would ever be fully conscious of.

'Come,' she said, 'I still have something to show you.

Otto followed her out into the garden. His hair was still damp and he could feel the air cooling the crown of his head.

'Where are we going?' he asked.

Els said nothing. She walked to the barn at the side of the house and in the twilight beckoned Otto to follow. He stepped into the darkness of the huge space and heard Els close the door behind them and lock it. A pungent, acrid smell smacked into his lungs. He started coughing, and as he put his hand to his mouth, he heard the scrape of a match and saw Els's face light up against the flame. She was smiling. He looked down and saw a glistening film of liquid lapping against his shoes.

'Goodbye,' Els said, and with the slightest of yelps, which sounded like the squeak of a mouse, she let go of the match.

TWENTY-SIX

Maia pulled sharply on Braggle's lead. The dog just wasn't listening. The first few weeks were understandable, and she'd given her some leeway, after all, she'd had to get used to so much change; a new home and a new owner, but Maia had had enough of being pulled in directions she didn't want to go and as much as she'd tried to avoid Dan's house, and Tom's, the dog seemed to find that extra surge of energy to drag her there anyway.

The rain hadn't helped her mood either. It had been a relentless autumn of wet and damp and in these first winter days, a northern wind had wrapped itself around the town with such venom that a sharp mist had swirled into every crevice forcing the temperatures unusually low.

But dogs need walking, especially this one. Braggle spent most of the day pawing at the door, ready to bound out at the first opportunity, and if Maia wasn't careful, she would. She'd wasted many an hour going to Dan's house, apologizing to the new residents, and then, somehow, getting the dog back home. The first few times it brought her to tears: who could not be moved by the pull of an animal to its natural home, and Maia would hug her and they would share their loss, but three months of it was enough, it was time to move on.

She pulled sharply on the lead, knelt down and brought Braggle's head to hers. *No more of this*, she said, and to sweeten the pill gave her a quick tickle under the ears. Braggle lifted her head skywards and closed her eyes, and when the affection had stopped, carried on regardless.

Maia pulled again. *No, no, no. This has to stop.*

For a couple of months, she'd called her *Mable.* She just couldn't bring herself to use Braggle; it was too raw, too painful, too much a reminder of things she'd prefer to forget. Mable seemed like an honest, legitimate compromise, but the dog ignored it so blatantly that she came to believe it was a deliberate act of defiance, and so in the past few days, with a slight admiration for her stubbornness, she'd started saying Braggle again and had noticed a slight improvement in her behaviour.

Maia had found her on Dan's doorstep the day after the harvest festival, dishevelled and listless, and had taken her home, bathed her, nurtured her, waiting for any news of Dan. She feared the worst, how else could she explain the water turning red as she washed the dog's matted coat, and how Dan's underpants, spattered with blood and mud, were found in Otto's tennis bag with the shot gun? It had all been hushed up of course, the gun, the clothing, the tennis bag. She'd been kept informed of the details (as a G12 member) with a strict edict for it not to go any further – the explosion at Otto's home was an accident, Dan was missing not dead. But he was out there in the mud somewhere and the only person who knew exactly where had been blown to pieces.

She'd wished she'd been spared some of the more gruesome details. She couldn't get out of her head the image of a charred arm, complete with hand and three fingers, hanging between the branches of the oak tree. The same fingers that had caressed her, manipulated her, known every curve of her body. She'd walked to the house the morning after the explosion as the body parts were being removed, including a foot nestling inside a shoe which had been found in the middle of the lawn, a lawn so scarred with burns and pits that they were already talking about digging the whole thing up.

The extent of the damage had shocked her. The oak had lost a couple of its vast side branches and looked so deformed and overwhelmed by its new form that Maia had the feeling it wouldn't survive the humiliation. And there was also talk of the house being knocked down altogether. They'd be discussing it at the next G12 meeting, although how long she would stay a member was debatable; she'd never quite recovered from the embarrassment of the harvest festival, and Gilda Rosen, who had somehow managed to cling on to her position, was being more obstreperous than ever. Perhaps she would resign in the coming weeks. She first wanted to invite Petra over for dinner to gauge her reaction, and of course, if she implored her to stay, insisted she was an essential member of the team, one without equal, then perhaps she might re-think her plans.

Before that though, she had to control this dog.

'Come on Braggle, this way,' she said, and she pulled her homewards.

the end

afterword

I started writing this book after moving to a small village in the Netherlands following thirty-five years living in cities (London and Amsterdam). I grew up in the Devon countryside and felt I was returning to my roots where I could again be in nature's full embrace. The reality was very different. Not only the intensive farming surrounding me, which has been well documented, but also the manner in which many people use and treat their own outdoor spaces. And I thought - what if I flip it on its head and create a society where the natural world takes precedence and it's an anomaly to see and think otherwise; where it's unthinkable to use poisons or to hunt animals; where wildlife is treated with respect; where people understand the fragility of their environment and behave accordingly. Everything in fact, in which, in my experience, the majority of people have little interest in, despite all the evidence suggesting that we need, more than ever, to counteract the devastating consequences of our species' impact on this extraordinary planet.

Chris Chambers   August 2022

acknowledgements

Many thanks to Rodney Bolt and Anik See for reading through earlier versions and making important suggestions.

And to Willem Dekens, without whom it would not have been possible. You helped make writing this book an enjoyable and relatively pain free experience.

And to Betty. Of course.

about the author

Christopher Chambers was born in Plymouth, England in 1965 and has a degree in Biology from King's College London. He has worked as a journalist for thirty years, starting his career at the BBC, first as a reporter at BBC Radio Devon and then as a feature reporter for BBC Radio Four's Woman's Hour. He moved to the Netherlands in 1998 to become a documentary maker for the Dutch World Service where he won numerous international awards for his work. He became the producer of the human right's programme 'The State We're In' and the editor of the environmental programme 'Earth Beat'.

He now teaches feature writing and journalism at Groningen university.

Printed in Great Britain
by Amazon

28932291R00172